HEATHER GRAHAM

DARK
RITES

mira

mira

ISBN-13: 978-0-7783-1992-4

Recycling programs for this product may not exist in your area.

Dark Rites

For questions and comments about the quality of this book, please contact us at CustomerService@Harlequin.com.

www.Harlequin.com

Printed in U.S.A.

Also by HEATHER GRAHAM

* * * * *

Look for Heather Graham's next novel
WICKED DEEDS
available soon from MIRA Books.

In memory of two men from Massachusetts.

My uncle George Law.
An amazing in-law I would have been proud to have
as a blood relative, as close and giving and supportive
as any family could be. Kind, generous, wonderful.
A true hero in his strength and kindness.

And my dear friend Dennis Cummins.
Musician, bandmate, Lizzie Borden house protector,
Biography Channel Andrew to my Abby and Chynna Skye's
Lizzie, amazing friend who quietly made every occasion
together one that made me smile.

I loved them both, and it is true—
the world is a poorer place now that they are gone.

CAST OF CHARACTERS

Victoria (Vickie) Preston—historian and author

Griffin Pryce—special agent with the FBI's Krewe of Hunters

Jackson Crow—field director, Krewe of Hunters

Craig "Rocky" Rockwell—special agent with
the FBI's Krewe of Hunters

Devin Lyle—children's author and Krewe agent

Dylan Ballantine—ghost of a seventeen-year-old boy
who haunts Vickie

Darlene Dutton—ghost of a nineteen-year-old girl

Roxanne Greeley—Vickie's best friend

Alex Maple—history professor and Vickie's friend

Milton Hanson—professor

Ron and Cathy Dearborn—local musicians

Isaac Sherman—man whose wife went missing

Law Enforcement

David Barnes—detective with Boston PD

Jim Tracy—sketch artist

Wendell Harper—Massachusetts State Police

Robert Merton—detective from Bristol, Rhode Island

Cole Magruder—detective from Fall River, Massachusetts

Charlie Oakley—retired detective in
Fall River, Massachusetts

DARK

RITES

Prologue

Alex Maple wasn't sure, as he first became aware of *himself*, if he was alive or dead.

He was miserable; he knew that.

Alive—he had to be alive to hurt in so many places.

He hadn't opened his eyes. Slowly, he tried to do so. At first, he thought about the Undertakers—the duo of kidnapping killers who had recently terrorized Boston. He was probably buried—deep in the earth, in a hole, in a Dumpster, in newly poured roadwork…

No. When he opened his eyes, there was light.

Too much light, maybe. Looking around, he realized that he wasn't buried. The harsh light of a naked bulb filled the room where he lay.

He tried to move; he sat up. He saw that he was on a gurney. The walls had once been painted that awful sickly green color that graced most of the country's hospitals. Paint was peeling; dust and dirt covered the floors; spiderwebs were visible around the hanging lightbulb. There were several other gurneys in the large room—four or five of them. Scattered throughout and by the gurneys were tables, some made out of wood, some that appeared to be newer, made of stainless steel.

There were tools on those tables. Knives, clamps, more—instruments that resembled those used by doctors years and years ago, some not so different now. He narrowed his eyes to study the one set.

From the 1800s, so it seemed: bullet extractor, amputation knife, saw, cervical dilator, lithotome, scarficator and trephine, among others he couldn't quite see.

Surgical instruments—the trephine for creating gouges in the skull.

And the strange shadowy color on some of the tables...

Dried blood.

He quickly turned to look at another table. Instruments for lobotomy, he thought—the controversial procedure invented by a Portuguese neurologist in the 1940s, known to create as many side effects as the initial mental problem, almost stripping the soul from a man.

He tried to rise from the gurney.

It was only then that he realized that he was shackled to it. One huge chain on his left ankle. Another on his right arm.

His heart raced; he couldn't breathe. It seemed that his vision blurred before him and the world started to go black.

What the hell? What in God's name had happened to him? Kidnapped, taken, was he going to be killed? Worse—tortured and killed.

The fear was nearly overwhelming!

He fought the sensation. Hard! He didn't have any kind of training for this type of thing; he hadn't even been a Boy Scout. But he was bright, and he wanted to survive.

He was—not all that useful in such a situation!—a historian. He had to make do.

Okay, that meant that, at the least, he was pretty darned sure he knew where he was. The Mariana Institute for the Mentally Unfit, opened circa 1840, closed down when the Commonwealth of Massachusetts had approved the disincorporation of several valley towns in order to create the Quabbin, a reservoir of water for Boston, in the 1930s. The Mariana Institute remained on high ground, ground that was deeply forested, now inhabited and visited only by the wildlife that proliferated the area—bobcats, black bears, moose, red foxes, eagles, deer, weasels, coyotes and more.

It was supposed that it existed no more.

But Alex was in it!

According to official records, it—like so many other buildings—had been razed circa 1936.

But clearly it hadn't been, and he only knew that it was still here because of an obscure reference he had recently found in a book of incredibly boring records. Reading between the lines, he realized that they'd run late with the demolition—a complaint by the man in charge chalked it up to the fact that the doctors had been trying to find new placements for the remaining patients. And no more crews had been sent out after the date that it had been recorded as demolished.

The area was called "the accidental wilderness," because no one had realized what a reserve they would create when they flooded the towns.

He'd been so excited about what he'd discovered.

He hadn't been able to wait to…tell Vickie!

The terrible thought filtered in: *no one knew it was here. No one would know* he *was here!*

Of course, people hiked along trails that weren't that far away. There was a visitor center, there were wildlife refuges…

None of them near the site of the abandoned mental institute—which had just been left there as the Commonwealth of Massachusetts dealt with matters far more serious than a derelict building that most people wanted to pretend had never existed. It wasn't anywhere near any kind of an actual large city, with no real roads left to reach it. The wretched place—known for death and mayhem—was not even up for grabs to the many entrepreneurs who loved to create Halloween horror houses or museums out of such old institutes. Massachusetts had a solid grip on the area.

How the hell had he even gotten here?

He couldn't remember. He had just woken up and…

Found himself shackled to a table.

Think! he commanded himself. He was supposed to have a brilliant mind. He was one of the youngest professors of history at one of the finest institutes of learning in the United States. That was, of course, why he could figure out where he was.

None of this helped in the least in explaining how he had gotten chained up in a supposedly nonexistent mental hospital!

Remember! Remember where he had been, what he had been doing.

For a moment, his past eluded him. So he went back to the beginning: he'd been born in Auburn, Massachusetts. He'd grown up on State Street. He'd always been a nerd, but thank God, it was okay; time and society—and *The Big Bang Theory*—had made nerds acceptable. He was a hair over six foot three, but his weight was a mere hundred and eighty-five—no matter what he ate! One of the biggest, toughest football players in the school had been his best friend. He hadn't been stuffed into school lockers or had his head shoved into the toilet. He'd been treated like some kind of guru, really.

And after high school, Harvard.

Graduation. He'd dated Allie Trent; they'd been a good pair. But Allie had died, way too young, way too smart and lovely, to have been lost so sadly to the horrors of disease. That had been a few years back now. He'd gone on a dating website and had a few okay experiences, but nothing that had touched his heart. He indulged in a moment of regret, missing Allie again. His excursions with the opposite sex since had barely awakened his libido.

Maybe he needed a wilder libido. Not something to worry about *now*! *Focus*.

So…

He worked at the college, he came home and he researched historical events and whatever else grabbed his fancy; he loved coffee shops and acoustic music and…

Then he remembered. Three weeks ago, he'd been savagely attacked right in front of his apartment. Struck so violently on the head he'd spent days in the hospital. He'd never known what had hit him. Although he'd been somewhat involved in the Undertaker case, but that situation had been solved. His friend Vickie Preston and FBI Special Agent Griffin Pryce had come to see him in the hospital; they—and the police—were still looking for the attacker or attackers, but they'd discovered nothing so far. But there had been a note left on his battered body.

Hell's afire and Satan rules, the witches, they were real. The time has come, the rites to read, the flesh, 'twas born to heal. Yes, Satan is coming!

The cops, he knew, had chalked it all up to some gang or even cult, acting out. Especially since he wasn't the only one attacked; a young woman on Beacon Hill had been struck and left with the same note, as had an older man—one who had barely survived!—in Brookline.

Boston had never been crime-free—not even during the days of the very harsh Puritan laws that had first ruled the Massachusetts Bay Colony.

So far—in this rash of knock-'em-out-and-leave-'em-with-a-Satanic-warning attacks—no one had died. The police did what they could, but maybe they were busier with other murders than they were with the head-knockings by a would-be Crowley-esque cult.

Vickie and her agent friend would be on it, though. He was certain!

Alex had been left hurt but alive. And once he'd healed a bit, he'd looked up the rhyme that had been left on his chest. It wasn't even original. It had first been used in the 1600s by a man named Ezekiel Martin, the bitter leader of a shunned Puritan group, and then again in the 1800s by a gang of thugs in Fall River; it had been used there again in the 1970s. But there were no known serious Satanic cults holding forth in Massachusetts now—not the kind who drew any attention.

The cops had watched over him for a couple of weeks. In fact, he'd become pretty friendly with the cop assigned to watch him most days. But nothing else had happened. Nothing had been found. He'd gone about his daily routine.

And the city budget hadn't allowed for police protection for him.

Then there were other victims of other crimes. And life went on.

He'd accepted an invitation to a special art showing; he'd seen the newest superhero movie—he'd gone about life. He even went to see the duo playing at the coffee shop.

That was it!

The coffee shop by Faneuil Hall! He'd gone to sip a cappuccino and listen to a great musical set, a brother and sister with a pair of guitars, lead and bass. A pair of lovely out-of-time hippies, he thought, doing a delightful session of folk music.

Professor Hanson had called him about the paper he would soon be publishing on relationships between the founding fathers. Milton Hanson was a friend— one who was helping him make his position at Harvard permanent. Since Alex had been attacked in the street, with centuries-old Satanic cult words written in bloodred marker on his chest, Professor Hanson had also been trying to help him with research in that direction. But that had little to do with the night...

There had been the music. He loved music!

Then there had been the girl.

The girl! The waitress, who had waited on him even when he hadn't really needed to be waited on. She'd been great.

He tried to remember what she had looked like. About five-six, a brunette—a bubbly brunette. She worked for the coffee shop, or so he thought. He'd gotten a chair before his drink had been ready. He hadn't stood at the end of the counter waiting. The girl had brought him his cappuccino. She'd been so cheerful and nice.

He remembered listening until it was late, until even that beloved and heavily trafficked area of Boston had gone quiet. He'd stayed to the last song. He'd been thrilled because—right in the middle of it all— the pretty young singer had come to him and thanked him for being such a great audience member.

He'd stood; he'd gone out to the street...

And then the world had gone dark, and only images had swum before him, the people in line at the coffee shop, the musicians playing, the pretty singer, the bubbly waitress...

Dark had turned to black.

And he had woken up here, chained to the table.

Why?

Who the hell kidnapped a quiet and unassuming professor of history and brought him out here, far from Boston, to an abandoned mental institute in the wilderness? He wasn't worth anything; he had no fortune. He sure as hell held no state secrets; he knew nothing about anything important. There was absolutely no reason to kidnap him, bring him here.

Maybe someone who was mentally deranged themselves had done this. And they were just going to leave him chained here—leave him to slowly die without food or water, chained to the gurney, rotting away until something found him—a bobcat, a rare mountain lion or a black bear.

Or even the rodents and insects that abounded…

Stop; stop, he told himself.

He was brilliant, or so they said. He should be able to find a way out.

Screw brilliant. He wished he was a mechanic— or a superhero. Yeah, a superhero with the power to break chains.

He studied the metal around his wrist and the chains.

At least he wasn't a victim of the Undertakers. He wasn't buried alive; he had plenty of air to breathe.

He thought of Vickie Preston. They had first met at the coffee shop—she had asked for his help. He knew she'd been instrumental in catching the killers who had so recently terrorized Boston and the city's surroundings.

Nice person, beautiful woman…she'd quickly become a true friend, visiting him at the hospital, working on the history of the note—she'd even gone to a concert with him. She was supposed to have been…

Meeting him! Yes, with a friend! She would know

that he wasn't in the city—because he'd be standing her up!

He could picture her now, emerald green eyes glazed with concern. She'd worry, twirling a lock of long dark hair as she wondered why he wasn't there. She might even stand—tall and willowy—and pace.

Surely she wouldn't just think he'd suddenly become rude? Would she somehow know, and start to search for him, would she have any idea…?

She had been working with the FBI. With the agent she'd brought to see him, the one who had probed the note, who had promised that he wouldn't stop until his attacker or attackers had been found.

He suddenly realized that he was thinking intently.

Find me, Vickie, find me! Find me, find me, find me…

He decided that his IQ statistics were wrong, and that he was an idiot—really, what kind of genius could he be? Did he really think that the woman had ESP and would hop up and send out the troops?

But she saw the dead!

True or not.

He was a scholar. He believed in science but he also believed she spoke to the dead. He had kiddingly accused her of it one day when he'd come upon her and she'd appeared to be talking to herself.

Of course, everyone looked as if they were talking to themselves these days—because they were wired to their phones!

But it had been different with Vickie. The way she'd flushed, the way he'd even felt as if something was there… someone else! He'd been joking, of course, and yet…

He'd never had such a feeling. Naturally, as an academic, he was above such fantasy. And, then again, because he was an academic, he did mull over the concept of memory and self and…

There was so much about her that was extraordinary. He'd seen that when she'd worked with the FBI during the recent rash of murders in the state. He'd seen her incredible mind.

Find me, Vickie!

Maybe, just maybe, she really did talk to the dead, and if that was true, maybe, just maybe, it was possible that she had ESP, too!

He frowned, realizing there was a lump of something in the corner. He twisted around enough to rise and see what it was.

Oh, God.

A body. A human body.

And the head…

Was gone.

And there was movement upon the remains…rats running havoc!

Terror raced through him, making it feel as if his blood ran hot and cold and then hot again, as if it tore through his muscle, turned even his bones into something more wobbly than gelatin.

He fell back on the table.

Then he heard the awful creaking sound of an old door, a sound something like a squeaky scream that cried out into the night.

Someone…something…was coming in.

1

Griffin Pryce leaped over the fence that connected the houses and yards along the Hyde Park neighborhood. He'd been running hard, chasing a man in a red cape. A woman had just been attacked—the fourth victim of the thugs terrorizing the area. This time, the attacker hadn't gone unseen; a neighbor had called it in right when it had happened.

Miraculously, Griffin had been about to have dinner with friends and was being dropped off by another friend—Detective Barnes—at a restaurant on Hyde Park Avenue when they had both heard the call for help come over the police radio.

He'd reached the scene just as the attacker—down on his knees to leave the rhyme about Satan in red marker on his victim's chest—had seen him.

And run.

Griffin had taken thirty seconds to assure himself that the woman was alive; the neighbor's call to 9-1-1 meant that an ambulance and police cars were on the way. He could already hear the sirens.

And so he ran after the attacker, who was wearing a red cape.

Stupid, Griffin thought. *You want to wear a cape and attack people? Makes it harder to run and leap fences—and stands out like a...a red light!*

But the young man was fast and agile.

Griffin leaped fences, tore down alleys, ducked beneath drying sheets and leaped another fence.

At one point, he could nearly touch the young man. When he turned to glance at Griffin, his face was clearly visible. He couldn't be more than twenty, twenty-five tops. He was clean-shaven with green eyes and a clear complexion, long nose, good mouth.

Then he was gone. This time he ran into an alley that led to a seven-foot fence—no Dumpster to use to leap over it...nothing at all.

The man threw himself against the dead end.

"Stop!" Griffin demanded, pulling out his Glock and aiming at the young man. "Stop. Put your hands behind your head. Get over here, and get down on your knees."

The young man stared back at him.

"Throw down your weapon."

The man did; he tossed the club he'd used—it resembled one of the billy clubs used by British police—and shouted, "I'm not armed."

He started to open his cape.

"Stop—I'll fire," Griffin warned.

"Hey, just showing you... I'm not armed! So shoot me. Come on, shoot me."

"I'm not going to shoot you. I am going to arrest

you. Do as I say, get down on your knees, hands be-hind your head."

The man ignored Griffin. He reached for something in his cape; Griffin rushed the twenty or so feet that stood between them.

The man stuck something in his mouth. Griffin shoved him to the ground, reaching into his mouth, trying to find what he'd taken.

Too late.

Even as Griffin sought whatever it was, the man began to tremble—and to foam at the mouth.

Griffin swore, trying to support him as he began to thrash and foam. As he did so, Detective David Barnes—who had been close behind him all the way—came running down the alley.

"Ambulance, med techs! He took something," Griffin shouted.

The man stared up at Griffin with wild eyes—ter-rified eyes.

Maybe he'd never really imagined what dying might be like.

But he was defiant.

"Long live Satan!" he choked out.

Then he twitched again, and again—and went still.

Barnes hunkered down by Griffin and the young man. "He's gone. What a fool. He must have taken a suicide capsule!"

"He wanted me to shoot him," Griffin said, shak-ing his head. What a waste of life.

"Anyway, it's over. People in Boston will be safer,"

Barnes said. "You caught the guy, Griffin. Bastard killed himself. Sad as anything, but it's over at least."

"Ah, hell, Barnes, come on!" Griffin said. He liked Barnes, didn't mind working with the detective, and they had a pretty good rapport. But Barnes was way off base with this one.

"It's not over," Griffin said quietly. "Why do you think he killed himself? They've got some kind of a pact. There's a cult working here."

"Well, yeah, obviously, this kid is some kind of Satanist. But, Griffin, you were right on top of this one. And we're looking at one man. One man who smashed the skull of a young woman—and ran. This has been too hard for us because the attacks have been so random. But it's got to have been the act of one crazy man. All he had to do was find someone alone on a dark street, strike fast, leave his message and run. It just took one person, Griffin."

"Yeah, well, we don't know if it's been the same one person. I'm telling you, Barnes, we've got a real problem here. The violence isn't going to stop."

"Griffin, you're concerned because you thought you'd be heading back to Virginia by now. You chose to stay because of the attack on Alex Maple—Vickie's friend," Barnes told him.

It was true; after the Undertaker case, he'd planned on going back to Krewe headquarters in northern Virginia.

But it wasn't just that Alex had been involved.

The writing on the victims had been disturbing. His instincts told him there was more to it.

"I wish I felt like celebrating, Barnes. I'm sorry. I'm worried. I'm afraid that we have a Charles Manson, David Koresh or Jim Jones–type active here. I believe you've got someone out there who has been preaching witchcraft or paganism or—from what we've seen—the rise of Satan. If that's true, you've got a *group* of people running around assaulting random but *easy* targets—and this won't be the last attack."

"He's never stood me up—I'm worried," Vickie Preston said to her longtime friend, Roxanne Greeley, looking at her phone again as she did so.

She'd been looking forward to the evening; she had become good friends with Alex Maple. She really liked him. He was boyish and enthusiastic, smart as a whip—and it was wonderful to know someone who loved history as much as she did. Alex was a professor; Vickie wrote guidebooks, and she was known for making the history within those books readable and relatable. She'd called on Alex for help in the recent Undertaker case and they'd quickly become good friends. And Alex had a great time talking to Griffin, as well. Ever since she and Griffin had come together during the horror and solving of the recent murders in the city, Vickie couldn't imagine having friends who didn't get along with Griffin. She was very much in love with him. As far as he and Alex went, they had similar taste in music and sports—Alex might be quite the intellectual, but he loved the Patriots. While others might scoff at the home team's arrogance, in Alex's mind they deserved to be a bit arrogant.

Griffin had gone to dinner with old friends, members of his unit who were passing through Boston on their way to their home a bit north, in Salem; Vickie hadn't gone with him only because she'd already made plans with Alex this evening, and she'd invited Roxanne—she had it all set up. She already regretted the fact that she'd made previous plans. She really wanted to get to know Griffin's friends—Devin Lyle and Craig Rockwell. Craig was known as Rocky, she had learned, and he'd grown up in Peabody, Massachusetts, while Devin had grown up in Salem. Now they were a married couple, and though Devin was still a children's book author, she had also gone through the academy and become part of the Krewe of Hunters unit down in Virginia.

But Vickie had never ditched one friend for another, or ignored a promise of a dinner date with one person to go out with someone else. She had thought of switching dates with Alex. That hadn't worked, however, because she hadn't been able to reach him.

And she couldn't just not show up—Alex had been so excited. He'd made what he thought was a pretty amazing discovery about something that had to do with Massachusetts. He was enjoying lording it over her— though he said he couldn't wait to tell her about it.

Even though their friendship was pretty new, Vickie felt she knew Alex. He was often crazy busy, and still, like her, if he'd made a date, he'd be there. He didn't seem to be the kind of man who would simply forget a friend, under any circumstance. Not that unexpected things didn't happen, but he did have a cell phone, and he should have called.

Naturally, Roxanne was aware that Vickie had been entertaining ulterior motives in insisting that she come with them to dinner at the café.

They were both great people, and Vickie wanted them to get together. She *wasn't* matchmaking; if they happened to like each other, that would be great. If not, it was just a dinner with friends.

Vickie's pretense to have Roxanne join them at dinner was that she was worried; Alex had taken quite a beating when he'd gone down. Vickie had said that she was afraid that she'd be ridiculously emotional, embarrassing everyone, if they were alone.

Dumb excuse, yes. And Roxanne had finally accused her point-blank of trying to set her up.

"You are playing matchmaker," Roxanne said. "Never a good thing."

"No, not *usually* a good thing," Vickie had corrected.

But Roxanne had laughed. "Let's do it. My last affair fell apart quickly enough. Hot and heavy—and over in the two seconds we realized I love a good art show and he loves watching sports in his boxers and guzzling beer. I mean, lots of guys do that, but not twenty-four hours a day or every single second out of work! I don't seem to choose well—maybe you choosing for me will be the right thing. How could meeting this guy be anything worse than what happened before?"

Roxanne had been—for a brief time—growing

heavily involved with an old boyfriend of Vickie's, but in the rising intensity of the case just solved, she'd not only been seriously injured, but forced to rethink where she wanted to be in a relationship.

And yes, Vickie wanted to set her up with Alex.

But now, of course, the guy wasn't there.

Vickie dialed his number again. No answer.

"Maybe he knew I was coming," Roxanne said. "That could scare a guy away."

"Don't be ridiculous," Vickie said. "You're beautiful." Her friend *was* beautiful: blonde, trim, with a great smile. She just didn't have luck with men. Vickie continued. "I know he wants to see me. I've been working on all kinds of things having to do with his assault. I was tracing that rhyme that was left written on his chest—and now, the same rhyme that was left on the other victims of this attacker, as well."

"Of course you have," Roxanne murmured. She was a visual artist, filled with all kinds of insight and art appreciation, but she was nowhere near as fond of history as either Vickie or Alex.

"Bear with me," Vickie said. "That saying that was written on him—it goes back—way back. I don't believe there were really any kind of Satanists running around when the whole thing started. I found reference to a man named Ezekiel Martin, who had studied to be a Puritan minister. He was never ordained, but he practiced his own brand of religion and managed to take a slew of people with him west into the woods to form a new colony and sect—one that he ruled through preaching a different higher power—that, apparently, being Satan.

"In truth, he seemingly followed a young woman named Missy Prior, who had left of her own accord, being against the repression of the society. Anyway, Ezekiel had a thing for Missy—but she didn't have a thing for him. He managed to blame her for every ill that befell his community. He *claimed* to have found those words written in the ground near where Missy Prior lived, and that Missy was trying to conjure Satan, and that Satan came to him at night and claimed that Ezekiel would have Missy Prior. Naturally, he saw himself as Satan's representative. Satan in the flesh until Satan should appear... His personal religion afforded him lots of benefits."

"Wow—and yuck! Even way back, people were going on icky 'I'm close to God so I get to have all the sex' trips, huh?"

"I'm still trying to find more on Ezekiel Martin," Vickie said.

"Isn't Alex a history professor?"

"Exactly. He's in a guest position, or whatever they call it right now—and he loves Harvard, so he's hoping to stay on."

"And I'm sure he's researching all this himself."

"He is, but that's also why he's anxious to meet with me. Compare notes."

Their waitress came by, a pretty, gamine-faced young woman with dark brown hair.

"You still waiting for your friend?" she asked.

"We're going to give him a few more minutes," Vickie said.

"Is it that fellow you've met here before?"

Vickie looked at her with surprise, and then realized that the young woman usually wore her hair down, and that—yes, of course—she'd had her several times as a server at the coffee shop.

"Yes, I'm waiting on Alex," she said.

The girl smiled cheerfully. "He was here last night. I'm sure he'll be along."

"There—she's sure Alex will be along," Roxanne said.

"He was here last night?" Vickie asked.

"Yes, he's always in when the Dearborn duo are playing. He loves them," the waitress said. "I'll keep my eye out!" she promised as she moved on.

"Thanks," Vickie said. She'd been with Alex when he'd come to see the Dearborn brother-and-sister performers before. They were talented guitarists and played folk music, ballads and covers of Simon and Garfunkel tunes, John Denver, Carole King and more.

She'd heard that the pair were twins; if so, they were fraternal. He was blond with soft brown eyes; she had extremely dark hair and smoke-gray eyes. They were an attractive pair, and they definitely seemed to have a casual, easy way with a crowd.

"I just wish that he'd answer his phone," Vickie said.

"Vickie!"

For a moment, her heart jumped. But it wasn't Alex calling her. She looked through the milling guests in the coffee shop and saw Professor Milton Hanson, one of Alex's closest associates. He knew Vickie's father, though was more of an associate than a friend.

Actually, her dad didn't like him very much.

"Who is that? Cool-looking guy, distinguished… dignified."

He was "smarmy," according to her dad. A little too good-looking. A little too close to some of his students.

"Hello, young lady. How are you?" he asked, stopping by the table. He had an attractive woman on his arm; she offered Vickie a big smile.

"Professor Hanson," she said, introducing him to Roxanne. He, in turn, introduced his lady friend.

"I wanted to come by to check out this café," Hanson said. "Our mutual friend, Alex Maple, loves this place. But there's no music."

"Yes, Alex loves it," Vickie agreed. "But the music is on Saturday nights."

Roxanne opened her mouth; she was clearly about to say that they were waiting for Alex.

Vickie kicked her under the table. A little tiny squeak escaped her.

"Saturday night. I'll have to come then. Well, nice to see you!" Hanson said, and he moved on.

"Hey! That hurt," Roxanne said.

"Sorry."

"Why didn't you tell him we were waiting for Alex now?" Roxanne asked.

"I don't know."

"He's still here somewhere," Roxanne said. "We could find him."

"No, I just don't feel comfortable asking him about Alex."

"Okay. But Alex isn't here. So, seriously, maybe something just came up," Roxanne said. "Let's face it. Not that I blame you—I mean, you were kidnapped and nearly killed recently—but you're overly suspicious of the world. I'm overly suspicious, too, since that wasn't such a great time for me, either. And I'm your basic coward, so that adds to me doubting everything. But honestly—aren't you getting a little carried away, being so worried just because Alex didn't show up for dinner? Maybe his sister was sick, or maybe he had to rush his dog to the emergency vet or something. Things do happen."

"But someone like Alex, Roxanne, he would let me know. You know, maybe I *am* being ridiculous. I just can't believe he'd be so rude."

"I'm sorry, Vickie. I love you—you really are the best friend and most courteous human being—but maybe his emergency was just more important than you."

"I hope that's true," Vickie murmured.

Just as Roxanne spoke, Vickie's phone rang. It was Griffin.

"Hey! How's it going? I wish I could have joined you," Vickie said.

"Dinner didn't happen. Barnes was dropping me off at the restaurant when someone called in an attack down the street from where we were—we heard it on the scanner. Anyway, to make a long story short,

I gave chase, caught the guy—and he took some kind of a suicide pill," Griffin told her.

"So, he's dead?"

"Who's dead?" Roxanne demanded, looking at Vickie with alarm.

"An attacker," Vickie murmured quickly.

"That's great!" Roxanne said. "No, I mean, not the dead part. He's been caught, right? But… Griffin killed him? I mean, we shouldn't want anyone dead. Except this guy really hurt a lot of people, so—"

"He killed himself," Vickie said quickly.

"How, what, why?" Roxanne asked.

"I don't know! Let me listen," Vickie pleaded. "Griffin? The attacker is dead?"

Griffin didn't seem to have noted her absence from the conversation to whisper to Roxanne; whatever had happened that evening, it was still consuming his mind.

"Yes. Strange, he was trying for suicide by cop. I told him I wouldn't shoot him. He took a pill before I could stop him."

"But it was the man who attacked Alex, right? I mean, was it? You just said that it was an attack. It was the same kind of attack—with the same words written?"

Griffin hesitated on the other end of the phone line.

"A guy is dead. A guy who was seen leaving the same note that was found on Alex and the other two victims. I'm sure Alex will be glad to hear that. Tell him for me, and that I'll give him details in the morning. Except…"

"Except what?"

Griffin seemed to hesitate a long time.

"What is it?" Vickie persisted.

"I don't think the man who killed himself tonight is the only one in on this," Griffin said. "But hey, that's for later. Anyway, I'm at the station. Devin and Rocky are going to stay at my place tonight. I told them I seldom use it and they kind of figured that. Salem is only forty minutes away—well, forty minutes or two hours, depending on traffic! They were actually taking a little personal time to check on their homes up there, see some family and friends. I'm glad they're here, though. I can toss around what's going on with them. You can give Alex the news that we've stopped one of them, anyway."

"I can't tell Alex anything. He didn't show," Vickie said. "We're still here—we're having the café's Sunday night special and hoping that he will make it eventually."

"He didn't show? You know him better than I do, but that's not like Alex, is it?"

"No, it's not like Alex at all."

"Did you call him?"

"At least a dozen times. And I've left just as many messages," Vickie said.

Griffin was silent for a minute. "How long have you been trying to reach him?" he asked her.

"Um, let's see… I started calling him this morning, when you got the call from Devin telling you that she and Rocky were going to be heading up to Salem, and did you want to meet for dinner. So, I've called and texted all day."

"I can come and join you. Well, in a while. A woman was attacked—she's on her way to the hospital. And a man died. I've still got things to do and, you know, paperwork."

Paperwork.

She'd learned all about police paperwork during the Undertaker case.

"Roxie and I will go ahead and have dinner and then head to my place," Vickie said. "We'll wait for you there. In the meantime, I'll hope that Alex calls me with some kind of an apology!"

"Is his family near?"

"He grew up in Massachusetts, but his folks are living on an island off Georgia now—his dad started getting asthma," Vickie said. "He has a little sister, but she's studying in Europe somewhere."

"Okay." Griffin was quiet for a minute. "I just have to report to the local office, get my statement in. And Barnes has to do the same, but he can kick this over to one of the task force members. Finish eating. I'll get to you as soon as possible."

"I'll head home," she said.

"I'll see you soon."

She hung up and looked around the room again with frustration, hoping—perhaps ridiculously—that Alex might have appeared. No Alex.

She frowned, though. A young blonde woman was standing at the end of the counter bar, as if waiting for a coffee creation.

But she was staring at Vickie intently, with unusual intensity.

"Why is that woman looking at me like that?" Vickie murmured aloud.

Roxanne turned to look toward the counter, but at that moment, several young men walked by—all of them a fine size to serve as tackles for the Boston Patriots, should they choose.

"There—she was right there. Really pretty blonde. Young, long hair—white summer halter dress with a flowy white wrap…"

"I don't see her."

"She's gone. She was staring at me, weirdly."

"Maybe she got a bad shot of coffee, Vickie. Hey, not trying to be insulting or anything here, but it's not always about you, Vick!" Roxanne said lightly.

Vickie laughed. "Yeah, yeah, honestly, I know!"

"So! Back to earth here. Griffin is on his way?" Roxanne asked.

"In a roundabout way," Vickie said. "We'll just have dinner and go to my place."

"*You'll* go to your place," Roxanne said. She shivered. "I want to stay a mile away from whatever it is you have going on!"

Vickie didn't blame her friend; Roxanne had gotten a concussion when she'd been dragged into the investigation during the Undertaker case. She might have been killed.

"Oh! What I said—it sounded absolutely horrible!" Roxanne said, wide-eyed. "I mean, I'd like to think that I'm a good friend, that I'd be with you through thick and thin, but—"

"It's okay!" Vickie assured her.

"You two will want to talk. Do you think that Griffin caught the person who attacked Alex? Do you think that Alex is safe now?"

"I don't know. Griffin seems to think that there's more than one person involved."

"Oh! Then…maybe Alex isn't just rude, or forgetful, or having an emergency with his dog," Roxanne said.

"He doesn't have a dog, Roxanne, and I am getting more and more worried."

Vickie managed a smile for her friend. "It's okay. Go home. I do understand. And Griffin will be tired and we will need to talk. So, we'll finish dinner…and hope that Alex is okay. That he's just being rude—and the danger facing him is going to be from me!" Vickie said. She tried to speak lightly.

She just didn't believe that Alex was rude. He was too good a guy.

And that meant…

She tried to keep her worry at bay as they ordered and made small talk as they waited. She didn't do so very well. She picked at her food. And finally, Roxanne said, "Hey, let's go. I have to wrap up my latest painting to bring to a gallery at Copley Square tomorrow. And you're not enjoying your time with me. And I'm enjoyable. So let's just cut it short. I know you're worried."

They left the restaurant, walking together as far as they could to their apartments, and then warning each other to keep their eyes out for trouble.

Both women carried whistles and mace—something Griffin had insisted on after all the trouble during the Undertaker situation.

But Vickie reached her apartment with no one doing anything other than giving her a nod in acknowledgment as they passed—that was Boston's method of a smile, she thought. A nod!

Entering her apartment, she called Griffin's name, but she didn't believe that he'd returned yet, and he hadn't.

Her apartment, however, wasn't exactly empty.

It appeared that a young couple was seated on her sofa.

They were both just teenagers, and attractive. He had been a high school football hero, well-built, charming, quick to smile. She had been a light-haired, light-eyed beauty, incredibly sweet, tragically naive. They were really adorable—completely absorbed with one another...

And dead.

Of all things, they seemed to be watching a marathon showing of *The Walking Dead* on Netflix.

The boy was Dylan Ballantine. He'd saved Vickie's life when she'd been a teenager—and he'd haunted her ever since. A good thing, since he'd helped incredibly in the recent Undertaker situation. His family had been involved, and Dylan dearly loved his family.

The young lady...

She was newer at being a ghost.

Tragically, she'd been a victim of the Undertaker.

Vickie saw the remote on the coffee table and picked it up to turn the volume down.

"Hey," she said to the two.

"Hey, Vickie! We didn't expect you back yet!" Dylan

jumped up, looking as guilty as a teen caught petting in the back seat of an old Chevy. "We thought you'd be late, that you and Alex would go on forever and ever over all you'd dug up!" Dylan added. "We aren't really TV hogs, you know."

"It's okay. You know you're welcome to the television. I'm happy that you guys are enjoying your…"

She almost said "lives"!

"Enjoying each other, being together. Enjoying…"

"The Walking Dead?" Dylan asked, amused.

"You're ghosts, not zombies," she reminded him. Dylan did have a wicked sense of humor—he'd spent years totally enjoying tormenting her, trying to make her speak to him in public and, in short, look entirely crazy.

Years ago, Vickie had been babysitting when an escaped serial killer had targeted her. Her charge—Noah Ballantine—had been born after the death of his older brother, Dylan, who'd been struck by a drunk driver at seventeen. And when the psycho had been in the house, Dylan had materialized before Vickie, warning her to grab Noah and get the hell out.

Terrified, she had done so. At that time, Griffin Pryce had been a cop and was out on the street, and he'd been the one to bring down the man who had been about to kill her and Noah.

While she'd felt an instant connection to Griffin, she hadn't seen him again until he had returned to Boston as an FBI agent, looking into the Undertaker kidnappings and killings.

But while the ghost of Dylan Ballantine spent much

of his time in his parents' home, which wasn't far from Vickie's, he'd apparently made it his vocation *in death* to haunt Vickie, down in New York City when she had been at the university, and again here, in Massachusetts, since she had moved back. He'd actually become an amazing friend—although one who still liked to taunt her in public and make her appear to be insane when she forgot herself and responded to him.

And now, Dylan had a friend of his own—a ghost friend.

Darlene Dutton was a couple years older than Dylan, but she was equally sweet and innocent. She had been the first victim of the Undertaker murders. And while she had seen justice done, it appeared that she liked learning about the spirit-world-on-earth—and being with Dylan. So it seemed she was sticking around.

Dylan was now an experienced ghost. He was quite capable of manipulating items, like moving a can of pop a few inches or using a remote control. And he had no problem making himself seen to those with the special gift of seeing the dead. Vickie had noticed that while most of the population didn't see Dylan or Darlene, they did often stop and frown when the ghosts passed, or shiver, as if aware that they'd been brushed by someone or something that they hadn't seen.

"Alex didn't show," Vickie told them.

Dylan immediately looked perplexed. Alex couldn't see Dylan—he didn't see ghosts. But Dylan had tagged along with Vickie to a couple meetings with Alex.

He liked the nerdy historian. And he admired him.

"Alex didn't show? I think he lives for his time with

you and other friends with whom he can actually talk a lot of history. I don't mean that in a bad way, but… It's weird he flaked."

"I've told Griffin that Alex didn't show up. We'll figure out something when he gets here. By the way— since I doubt you guys watched the news at any point—Griffin stopped one of the attackers tonight. A head-smasher, just like Alex's assault. And the guy killed himself rather than be taken."

"Wow, heavy," Dylan said, very serious despite his words.

"That's extremely scary," Darlene agreed. She hopped up off the sofa. "Vickie is worried, and Griffin is headed home. Let's go, Dylan. We need to leave them with some privacy. We'll go see how Noah and your folks are doing."

"Sure, yeah, sure, we should get out of here," Dylan said. He looked worried, though. "Darlene is right. Griffin is going to be wrecked after a night like that. He'll want to talk."

"He'll want to be alone," Darlene said softly.

"That's fine," Vickie said.

"No, you're in a relationship now. Can't let it grow ho-hum," Dylan said, grinning at Vickie.

"Thank you. I'll remember that!" Vickie said.

"Dylan, really," Darlene murmured.

"It's fine. Dylan has enjoyed tormenting me for years, Darlene. And I'm sure it will all be okay."

"No, none of it sounds okay," Dylan said. "Alex is a cool guy—it won't be okay until you know that he's all right. Don't forget, we're always here when you need us."

"But you don't need us tonight," Darlene said firmly.

"Not to worry, Vick—we always come back to haunt you!" Dylan told her, trying for a light grin.

"Haunt me—and help out," she reminded him. "Remember, I'm quite accustomed to you and that we both—Griffin and I—appreciate the two of you very much."

"I just wish my parents watched *The Walking Dead*," Dylan said, shaking his head in puzzlement that anyone wouldn't want to watch the series from beginning to end. "And Noah, well, he's great, he'll put on anything we want, but…he's only nine."

"Maybe in a few years we can do a marathon viewing with Noah," Darlene said.

"That will be fun!" Dylan agreed, grinning at Darlene. But then his grin faded and he turned back to Vickie. "I will see you tomorrow. We need to know everything that went on with Griffin—and, most importantly, with Alex."

"Absolutely," Vickie said.

She watched them go. They both simply disappeared through the wall. When Dylan came to visit when she was home, he made a point of knocking. Only emergencies caused him to do anything less thoughtful or proper.

When they were gone, Vickie tried Alex's number again. No answer.

Maybe he'd lost his phone. No—he would have called her from another phone. Actually, he'd have been at a store in two seconds to get another—he had a Facebook group that talked about all kinds of history, travel, weird places and such similar things, and she was pretty sure that Alex went into withdrawal if he couldn't catch up on the latest at every possible opportunity.

She opened the app and checked Alex's Facebook page.

He hadn't been on the site in over twenty-four hours.

She called Griffin quickly then. He didn't answer at first. Frustrated, she plopped down on the sofa in her parlor.

Her phone rang right back.

Griffin.

"You all right?" he asked.

She smiled; she could tell he was trying to keep any touch of anxiety out of his voice. She knew that he'd always be concerned about her—it was part of what he did for a living, *and* by vocation. He saw too much that was bad.

"Fine. I'm home. In the apartment. I had an idea. Can you trace Alex's phone?"

"Well, there are a lot of legal ramifications," Griffin said.

"I'll report him missing—how about that?" she asked.

"You know, unless we have good reason, twenty-four hours is—"

"We have good reason! He was clunked on the head. He had a police guard for a couple of weeks after. Go figure—he disappears after that guard is taken off."

"The attacks appeared to be random," Griffin reminded her. "No community has the manpower to watch victims endlessly, especially when it appears the danger has moved on."

"I know that."

"He could be fine."

"No. I don't believe that even as a ray of hope anymore," she said.

"Okay, we'll take the angle that something is wrong. We'll get a missing-person report going, and…we'll get into his phone records," Griffin said. "I'm in a paper tangle right now as it is—I'll get Barnes to have a man from the right department get everything started for Alex. Lord, if he's just off doing…doing whatever scholars do…well, I guess that's the best-case scenario. But we'll treat him as a missing person and work on finding him with all possible resources, okay?"

"Much better. Are you coming home soon?" she asked.

"Well," he told her, his tone ironic, "I'll be a little longer now."

"Don't be too long."

"You going to make it worth my while?"

"Hmm. You bet," she told him.

"Aha."

"I can be full of surprises," she assured him before hanging up.

Restless, she headed into the kitchen, made herself a cup of tea and then settled down at her computer with the pad of scribbled notes she'd made from research sites and her own library.

Ever since seeing the scrawled quotation on Alex,

she'd been looking up Satanism and witchcraft in Massachusetts.

Most of what she could find on witchcraft had to do with the travesty of justice that had occurred during the Salem witchcraft trials of 1692. She'd recently turned in a nonfiction book for a university press that had dealt with the Puritan rule in the Massachusetts Bay Colony, with a special focus on Puritan ministers. While Cotton Mather had "saved" a few witches, by caring for them himself, he'd also been instrumental in the executions that had occurred in Salem. There had been a few other trials and executions of so-called witches in the colony, as well. It seemed so appalling now and, in her mind, so ridiculous she couldn't believe anyone had abided it—even in the devil-fearing darkness of the early days of the colony.

Of course, Salem—and surrounding areas—also had a nice population of modern-day real witches: wiccans. They were an acknowledged religion and Vickie had friends among them. They didn't cast evil spells—they lived by a threefold rule, where any evil done to another comes back on one threefold. It was a pretty good framework for not hurting people!

But there were instances of *Satanism* rather than *witchcraft* that had taken place in Massachusetts. According to the Puritan fathers, there would be little difference. In the Puritan world, witches danced naked in the moonlight, signed the devil's book and frolicked with all manner of decadence and enjoyed the pleasures of the flesh—in return for being wicked, of course.

The first accusations of witchcraft had occurred in

Springfield, Massachusetts, in 1645. Hugh and Mary Parsons had accused one another. Hugh was eventually acquitted; Mary was set to hang for the crime of killing her child—by witchcraft, or so the records implied. Between 1645 and 1663, eighty more people were accused and thirteen women and two men were put to death.

The fear of the devil had begun in Europe in the 1500s—thousands were put to death, burned at the stake or hanged, or through some other even more painful means. In comparison, what went on in the colony was pretty tame.

But even then, there were dissenters, and there were those who were ready and eager to take a faith and twist it around and give it a few new guidelines.

At the same time—circa 1665—Ezekiel Martin was growing stronger in influence among the young people swayed to his sect.

Missy Prior was a stunning young Puritan woman, an orphan who survived through selling produce from her small garden and from doing handcrafts—mending and sewing. Ezekiel Martin wooed the girl.

She turned him down. Sweetly. She talked about her youth—and mourning for her parents.

Ezekiel was hurt—deeply offended.

Since he'd never made it to being ordained—suspected of not being a learned or good man himself—his orations weren't sanctioned by the church. But according to the diary of an ordained minister of the time, Ezekiel was capable of talking the good talk; he could preach convincingly and sway people, and he had a following that terrified the others before they even began to become aware of just what kind of a danger he could be.

He lured many people away from Boston, taking them west. There, he created the village of Jehovah.

Jehovah was no longer in existence, but it had once been situated between present-day Barre, Massachusetts, and what was now the Quabbin, the massive water reservoir created in the Swift River Valley.

Missy Prior, along with some of her friends, had been ahead of Ezekiel; she'd left Boston in order to escape Ezekiel's attention, and she'd had a cottage in the woods, right in the area that Ezekiel would soon name Jehovah. It seemed that no matter how far she went, she couldn't outrun Ezekiel, a man who had become obsessed with her.

There was nowhere else to run, and Missy's friends were forced from her side as Ezekiel gained power and determination. But she still wanted nothing to do with Ezekiel.

He, in turn, woke one night screaming and shouting words of warning about Missy—and he woke the population of Jehovah and rounded them all up in front of Missy Prior's cottage.

And he'd showed them all the words that had been written in the earth.

Hell's afire and Satan rules, the witches, they are real. The time has come, the rites to read, the flesh, 'twas born to heal. Yes, Satan is coming!

According to the diary and journals from others who had lived during the time, Ezekiel then proceeded to convince a number of people that he was their salvation. They could not stop the arrival of the devil; they could only embrace him when he arrived. He would reward them, of course, if they were to come to him through his vessel on earth—Ezekiel Martin.

Missy Prior was terrified; she had turned down a madman one time too many.

She feared for her life.

She didn't die; not then. She was taken in to be "healed" by Ezekiel.

Missy Prior, however, wasn't enough for Ezekiel.

Ezekiel did what those who were both charming and evil at heart had a talent for doing—he seduced his followers into his House of Fire and Truth, a cult in which, of course, they followed a Mighty Power, pretending to still be Puritans to those around them, since those who were not Puritans in the colony at the time were killed or banished. What he was really doing, ministers and public officials became certain, was practicing out-and-out witchcraft or Satanism. He, Ezekiel, as Satan's disciple on earth, was absolute ruler with absolute power, demanding the sweet fruit of the innocent and beautiful among the maidens, bestowing those he had used and deflowered upon those of the men of his congregation, those who had earned his admiration and devotion.

Missy Prior tried to flee. She was caught. By then, of course, Ezekiel had many women. She was to meet the fate reserved for one who betrayed her master. Death.

How that death came about, Vickie could not ascertain with certainty. She tried a number of her resources. Some suggested she was burned, not as a witch, but as a heretic. Some said that she might have actually been drawn and quartered, and others suggested that her throat was slit and that her blood was passed about to imbue the rest of the congregation with strength.

But while the Massachusetts Bay Colony was, at that time, still working under the charter that allowed for Puritan rule, the Crown did have a decided interest in the county. Cromwell had died in 1658 and Charles II had been asked back to rule in England—a good majority of the population had grown weary of Cromwell's very strict ways. Charles happened to have men in the colony, soldiers under Captain Magnus Grayson. Grayson eventually got wind of Ezekiel's activities. Heading into the village, he hadn't the least problem demanding the immediate arrest of Ezekiel and his little pack of cronies. The small would-be self-governing colony was dispersed. Ezekiel found himself deserted when his men were faced with the armor and arms of the king's men, and he slit his own throat—swearing that Satan would embrace him in his fiery power, and he would live again.

Captain Grayson had found skeletons and an altar stained with blood. It was believed that one of the skeletons found belonged to poor Missy Prior.

It seemed a heartbreaking story to Vickie.

Poor Missy.

She had been relentlessly pursued by Ezekiel Martin in life.

Perhaps her only escape from him had been in death.

Jehovah had been quickly begun—and even more quickly ended.

Captain Grayson had loathed and been sickened by the entire place, and he'd had all of what had been Jehovah burned to the ground. The settlement disappeared into the landscape, and where it had been, no one now knew.

Erased from memory.

But not all memory.

Because someone was violently attacking people and leaving behind the words Ezekiel Martin had once written into the earth in order to have Missy Prior.

Vickie couldn't wait to tell Alex the depths of what she had discovered.

She looked at her phone and tried Alex's number again.

No answer...

"Alex! Where are you?" she murmured aloud.

And she wished that she wasn't alone. She wished that Griffin would come soon.

It seemed that the wind suddenly began to howl outside.

Summer was waning and fall was on the way.

And it sounded as if the earth itself was moaning...

Crying out a warning.

2

Griffin sat behind the desk in David Barnes's office, typing out the last words of his report regarding the evening. As he did so, he saw everything replay in his mind. He shook his head, damning himself. He couldn't see how he could have stopped what had happened.

The door opened and Rocky walked back in. "How's it going?"

"Almost through here," Griffin said. "I'm waiting for a callback from Dr. Loeb."

"Medical examiner? Theodore Loeb?" Rocky asked.

"You've worked with him?"

"No," Rocky said, "but I did meet him at a crime summit a few months back. Guy is brilliant and looks like a mad professor, right? Crazy white hair and thin as a sack of bones?"

"Yep. That's him," Griffin agreed. He drummed his fingers on the table. "I don't know what he can tell us about our dead man that we don't already know. He appeared to be healthy before, young and hardy looking. And now dead. Suicide capsule. What makes someone do that?"

Rocky took a seat in one of the chairs in front of the desk. "Well, usually you have to be more afraid of living than you are of dying, I imagine."

"Right. Afraid of what—or who—he had to face."

"That's a solid theory, anyway," Rocky said.

"If we look at most things that have had to do with that kind of behavior—suicidal sacrifice behavior," Griffin said, "it's usually because we're looking at those who feel disenfranchised or forgotten. If we look at history, men and women born in dirt and poverty are willing to practice terrorism when they're promised something wonderful on the horizon—a special place in heaven or Valhalla or Mount Olympus. From Japan to Germany to the Middle East, Ireland and beyond. Those who feel that they have been chosen by a higher power to strike back at their oppressors are often ready to fight and die, whether it's beneath a hail of bullets or on a suicide mission. Then again, there's the fear that if you don't carry out the suicide mission, what comes next will be even more terrible."

"You think we're looking at domestic terrorism?" Rocky sounded doubtful.

"No, no, I really don't. So far, people have just been sent to the hospital. We're not looking at anyone having been murdered—that we know about. But I believe that some kind of statement is being made, that there is something larger going on."

Detective Barnes came into his office.

"The body is at the morgue, the forensic team is

done in the streets and the techs are trying what they have to get an ID on the body. Autopsy won't be until tomorrow, so we won't really have real physical answers until then, but then you know that, and you know that we have been able to get Dr. Theodore Loeb on our case. I swear, if there is anything we can get from the body, Loeb will get it."

Barnes was, in Griffin's mind, a good cop. He was willing to put in whatever hours were needed. He had nearly a decade more experience on the force than Griffin, but had no qualms about working with him or the FBI.

Except that now he looked at Griffin, and then Rocky, and shook his head.

"Ah, hell! We couldn't just be pleased—we couldn't just be certain that we'd gotten the attacker—and that the newest craze in Boston beatings was over. No... you think it's something deeper, and that we're about to find out."

Griffin glanced at Rocky and shrugged.

Devin Lyle tapped at the door and then walked in, carrying a foam tray with four large coffee cups.

"One is for me?" Barnes asked.

"Of course," Devin assured him. She was about five-nine with a headful of long black hair. Devin had great stature, though; in her "real" life, she wrote children's books. She still had the ability to appeal regal—and very authoritative.

"Thank you, thank you!" Barnes said.

Then he rose. "I suppose I'm glad I have a few specialists from your division of the bureau here. But I'll leave you to it. I'm going to run the attacker's finger-prints, see if he's in the system." He started out, then turned back. "Oh! I've got a report written up for Alex Maple. I've pushed accepted protocol around on this, you know. But we're looking for his phone, and we're checking out his apartment. I'll let you know if I find out anything."

"Thank you, Barnes," Griffin told him.

"Yep. All right, I'm getting out of here."

"Actually, this is your office," Griffin reminded him.

"I do know that. You all take your time. If I don't find you here, I'll call when I've got something."

"Thanks."

He left them.

Devin silently handed out coffee.

"So, nothing yet?"

"Nothing but musings," Griffin told her.

"And they don't bode well," Rocky added softly.

"Wow," Vickie murmured to herself. She realized she'd been on the computer for hours.

She looked at her watch; she knew it was late, of course. Paperwork did take a long time. She had to give up working for the night, though.

Her shoulders were beginning to hurt!

She winced, rubbing the back of her neck, wishing Griffin was there to do it.

Then she remembered that she had promised she'd make it worth his while to hurry home.

A wicked little smile crossed her face. She leaped

up, heading to shower and shave her legs, now hoping that he wouldn't arrive until she was ready. After toweling dry, she touched up with some makeup.

Since he was the only other human being in the world to have her key, she figured she was safe with whatever she did. And so, wearing nothing but a towel and a pair of spiked heels, she set up a perch on the sofa with throw pillows. She brought out an ice bucket and, since she didn't have any champagne, opted for two bottles of Sam Adams beer. All the while keeping an ear out for the entry door to her complex—an old brownstone converted into four apartments.

Lastly, she arranged a plate of strawberries and chocolates and set them at the end of her little throne, right by the ice bucket. She turned most of the lights off and set just a couple lamps down low.

She took off the towel, curled her legs beneath her and posed and waited.

"Ho-hum, eh? Call this ho-hum!" she said aloud.

Then, of course, she felt a little ridiculous, naked on her sofa with high heels on. But their lives seemed to be twisted all the time by life-or-death situations, and—with Griffin's work—it always would be that way. He'd told her that agents learned to seize their personal time, love it and embrace it. It was how they all managed in their world day after day, to appreciate every life they saved—and accept when there was damage they could not stop.

She decided to turn on the television—if she just held the remote control, she could keep it low and ditch it the minute he came in.

The news was filled with the evening's reports. A recording of Detective Barnes was shown, giving out what information he could. The assailant was as yet unidentified. Yes, he had committed suicide with a pill; exactly what it contained, forensic experts would soon inform them. Did he believe there would now be a stop to the assaults? The police would be investigating all avenues, along with agents from the FBI.

He promised that new information would be forthcoming as they had it. He reminded the citizens of Boston and environs that they were a large and important city and never immune to harm; whether they had stopped the assaults or not, residents should always be vigilant.

As the news rolled to the next story, Vickie was certain that she heard someone at the building's front door.

She quickly switched off the television—Griffin didn't need to hear about the night he had experienced.

She switched into what she hoped was a truly sexy pose.

She heard the key in the lock. And the door opened.

For a split second, she froze.

And then she let out a scream.

At first, Alex Maple stared in disbelief at the man— the creature?—who came toward him. His mind was not working at all well, he determined.

Why *would* it be working well? He'd been kidnapped; he was a prisoner in a defunct loony bin!

Get it together, Alex. Survive! he told himself.

So. Figure, yes, figure—that was safe to say. The

figure coming toward him was wearing something like a KKK outfit—only it was bloodred and trimmed with strange black markings.

"Ah, Professor! You are awake—ready to join us!" the figure said.

It spoke; it moved. It appeared to be human.

Man.

Alex fought for reason and reaction—for the ability to move his mouth and form words.

"Join what? Who are you? Why am I here?" he managed to ask.

The man came closer.

"I am the high priest," the man told him. His face was more or less covered by a mask that appeared to be loosely connected to his conical red hood. Alex could see the man's eyes, though. They weren't burning red or anything—they were just dark brown.

"I am the high priest, Professor, and you will join with us."

Alex blinked. It would be laughable if it weren't for...

For the chains that held him.

For the headless body that lay crumpled in the corner, with rats destroying it.

"I'm sorry, join with you for...what?"

"The resurrection."

"The resurrection of what?"

"You, sir, are not just going to join us, you see. You are going to help us!" the high priest said.

"Help you...?"

"Well, we're going to bring Satan to earth, sir! More specifically, we're going to bring Satan to Boston. And you, Professor, are the man with the knowledge to help us do it."

He couldn't see the man's mouth, but he was sure that he smiled.

Did this dude know how ridiculous his words were?

"Yes, you are the man!"

What if I refuse?

Alex wasn't exactly an atheist. He considered himself a deist, believing in a higher power, but not in all the myth that went along with it—through any religion.

Satan wasn't real to Alex, and, therefore, he couldn't be summoned.

But...

He didn't bother to ask what happened to him if he refused. He knew.

He could see the instruments of medicine, surgery—and torture.

He could see the rat-riddled body in the corner.

"How intriguing," he said. "I assume you believe that I will somehow be able to find the proper rites and means by which to do this through historical research?"

"Oh, yes. You see, Satan has come to Massachusetts before," the high priest said. "You will bring him again."

"Great challenge!" Alex said, trying to put some enthusiasm into his words.

Find me, Vickie, find me, for the love of God. Yes, there is some kind of a God, I do believe that, Vickie, find me, find me...

The high priest spoke, apparently accepting Alex's words.

"Indeed! Yes, hail Satan! He has lived among us before. Through you, he will return. All hail! Satan shall return!" The high priest stepped forward, a key in his hand. He was going to free Alex.

Free, if he was free...

He was skinny, but he was no weakling. He could try to overpower this man...

"Hail Satan! Hail Satan!"

It was a chant. Alex looked up; there were several people there now, in the doorway to the old operating room. They were all in the red capes and masked hoods.

He could not fight...

"Come, brother!" the high priest said. "We will initiate you by letting you witness our sacrifice!"

He was going to see a sacrifice. *Please, let it be a chicken!* he thought.

It wasn't going to be a chicken.

He suddenly found prayer, prayers he had known as a kid.

Please God, he prayed silently, *don't let the sacrifice be me*.

"Vickie!"

Griffin suddenly came bursting into the room, pushing past the unknown man who had stood in the doorway when it had opened.

"Oh! Oh! Ohhhhhhhh!" Vickie cried.

She felt like an absolute idiot—no idea what to do, how to react. She was sitting on the sofa, naked and in heels, and Griffin was with Craig Rockwell, one of Griffin's closest friends—*and coworker*!

A man she had met just once!

Pillow! She grabbed a pillow and pressed it before her.

Griffin was doing his best to block her, and Rocky and Devin Lyle were backing away, excusing themselves awkwardly—and laughing, certainly.

She wanted to disappear. To sink beneath the floorboards.

Vickie could hear herself talking, garbling out something. Griffin was talking…his friends were apologizing as they moved back into the hall…and she was backing her way into the bedroom.

In the bedroom she grabbed a robe from the closet and slipped into it as fast as humanly possible. By then, Griffin had reached the room. She started in on him furiously. "Why didn't you call me, why didn't you let me know, why…"

She couldn't help it; she let him have it with a pillow.

"Hey!" he protested, catching the pillow. And she saw that he was almost smiling. His dark eyes shining in his rugged face, drawing her in and almost making her forget her embarassment.

Almost.

She got another pillow and let it fly.

"I just wasn't expecting such a greeting!"

"Oh! Your friends! Your work associates. Your professional work associates!" Vickie said, shaking her head. "Oh, my God. What must they think? Oh!"

Griffin pulled her tight against him, smoothed back her hair and looked down into her eyes. And now he was smiling. "They're thinking I'm the luckiest man in the world," he told her.

He kissed her—a tender kiss, a great kiss. She wanted to forgive him.

Her level of humiliation was just a little too high.

"They're still out there, right?"

"I think they're standing awkwardly in the hall, maybe trying to leave…"

"You can't…you can't just leave people in the hall. Or make them leave. I mean, you—get out to the parlor. Go. Try to…oh, I don't even know what you can try to do. When I can, I'll come out."

"They'll leave. They won't mind."

"No!"

"But after everything you did for me, your preparation…"

"Out!"

"Got it. I'm on it," Griffin assured her.

"I'll never be able to face them if I don't face them now!" Vickie said.

He left her, heading on out to the parlor. During the moments the bedroom door was open, Vickie could see that his Krewe friends hadn't stayed in the apartment; they were out in the hallway waiting. Or they had left altogether.

She could also see that Griffin was still smiling. She felt like crawling beneath the floorboards.

But as much as she wanted to, she knew that she couldn't hide out in her room forever.

Vickie slid into jeans and a T-shirt, and stood in front of the mirror again. Totally unsexy, she decided.

Except for the flood of color that rose to her cheeks every other second.

She hesitated, then opened the door to her room. She could hear Griffin speaking, hear a female voice, and another male voice. Griffin was in the kitchen, making coffee, it seemed.

She paused, listening.

"You think that there are a number of people, all of them assigned to randomly attack people?" Devin Lyle was saying. Vickie had met her—and Rocky—just briefly, earlier during the day. She'd instantly liked Devin. They had a lot in common. Even if they'd grown up in very different cities, they had both been born in Massachusetts, steeped in the history of the state, come and gone, seen the good and the bad—and still loved it as home.

"I get how you figure it might be a number of people, but…why? I've been thinking about it since you were so convinced that the young man who died had to be one of many," Devin finished.

"I don't know. Gut feeling. I can't help it. But from the beginning, someone has been making a statement. That poem. Attacking people without killing them… thank God they're not dead!"

"Maybe the attacks are the statement," Rocky said.

"Or the attacks might be a way to distract law enforcement from what is really going on," Griffin said.

"If you believe that, what do you think is really going on?" Rocky asked Griffin.

Vickie heard plates being set on a table. She figured

that maybe Griffin and his friends hadn't quite gotten through dinner. She hadn't had much of a meal herself.

And they weren't talking about her, didn't even seem to be thinking about her...

She had to get over herself and just step out into the room.

She managed to do so. It didn't go quite as well as she'd hoped, but then again, she had no control over the flare of heat that rose into her face.

Devin Lyle was sweet and charming and tried to pretend that she'd seen absolutely nothing when they'd come in. Rocky was just as circumspect. But then she could see that the man lowered his head and turned away, and that he was trying to keep from smiling when he looked over at Devin. But then Devin shook her head and gave Vickie a tremendous smile and said, "Hey, hi! Well, let's try to get a bit more comfortable here! We're so sorry..."

"So, so sorry!" Rocky agreed.

"On so many levels!" Devin said with a grin. "And even now, well, we have to mention the elephant in the room. Only way to clear it out. We are beyond sorry!"

"And, wow, envious," Rocky said.

"What?" Devin demanded. "Hey!"

"I'm referring to the fun of it, my love," Rocky assured her. "What a cool thing to have thought of to do for someone after a hectic night," he added.

Devin grinned and looked at Vickie. "There you go—the pressure is on!"

"So, anyway, we're all good?" Griffin asked Vickie hopefully.

"Terrific," she said, deadpan.

"That doesn't sound good," Griffin said.

"I'd leave it," Devin told him sagely. "Take whatever you can get right now!"

"Yep, just leave it for now," Rocky said. "Anyway, for the last time, please forgive us the invasion. We were going to head straight to Griffin's apartment and go to bed. Then we figured we'd talk among ourselves, see if we got anywhere, over a midnight snack. We never ate. The night became very long and convoluted."

"Because, of course, there's what happened," Devin said.

"And the fact that your friend Alex is now missing. You still haven't heard from him, right?" Rocky asked.

"No," Vickie said.

"We've made sure that we—as in the Bureau, and especially the Krewe of Hunters—are involved at every level," Griffin told her seriously.

"FBI participation? In investigating the attacks, the death of the man tonight—or with the disappearance of Alex?" Vickie asked. "As far as I know, everything that has happened has happened within the state. And we're not looking at murder here."

"We may be looking at a kidnapping," Devin said.

"Rules and protocol have changed," Griffin said. "You know, Vickie, that all kinds of boundaries and jurisdictions changed after 9/11." He turned toward the counter and she saw that he'd brewed coffee. It was late for coffee, but she doubted that it would keep any of them up.

"Here," Vickie murmured, moving forward. She

went to get mugs. Griffin opened the refrigerator and drew out sandwich makings.

"The FBI even does more on foreign soil," Devin murmured. She looked at Vickie and asked, "May I help with anything?"

Vickie laughed. "I'm not even sure what Griffin is doing."

"This is it, I'm afraid," Griffin said. "Sandwiches, chips..."

"A gourmet buffet at this point!" Rocky said. He took a plate of cheese from Vickie and told her, "Roles change, and it's often good—we're sometimes involved with cases that concern just one state or area—or the Commonwealth of Massachusetts, as it is here. It can be a really good partnership, especially when the local police want help and are ready to become part of a task force with a lot of cooperation."

Vickie poured the coffee, taking her own cup and sinking into a chair at the table. "Well, naturally, I'm delighted that you're all on this—whatever this is. You're working with Detective Barnes? And everything is going well?"

"Fine—I like Barnes," Rocky assured her. He seated Devin and then he and Griffin took chairs at the table, too—and dug in. The three were obviously hungry. "He seems to be a very good man. Comfortable and assured—and not in the least daunted by the feds. But then, you've already worked with him, right?"

"Yes, during the Undertaker thing," Vickie said.

"Doesn't hurt to have a precedent set," Rocky said. "So, do you know who the man was tonight—the man who killed himself when Griffin caught him? Was he the one who hurt Alex Maple before? And if so, why is Alex still missing?"

"I admit that no one can reach him, but are you still convinced that Alex *is* missing?" Griffin asked her. "Even Barnes helped us start a report before it'd normally be done."

"I haven't known Alex that long, but I do know him pretty well. He didn't show for dinner. I really believe that if he could, he would have found a way to have called me by now," Vickie said. "I am seriously worried."

"We have people checking the local hospitals," Devin said.

"And the morgue, of course," Rocky added.

Devin nudged him hard.

"Hey, it's all…necessary," Vickie murmured.

"I know that Barnes said he'd call us, but…" Devin said, looking at Griffin.

"I'll go ahead and call him," Griffin said.

He dialed. Vickie listened, looking at him hopefully.

"Have they found anything?"

"They're still tracing the phone. Alex is not home. His landlord opened the apartment and he wasn't there. Also, there was no sign of a struggle in his apartment," Griffin told her. "They've checked with every hospital—and the morgue. No sign of Alex."

Vickie nodded. "Thank goodness for that, anyway," she murmured.

"So far, people have been attacked in the street," Devin said. "Are we assuming that the same perps who struck Alex Maple so hard they could have killed him have now kidnapped him?"

"I know it sounds strange, but let's face it—everything to do with these attacks is strange," Vickie said. "Here's why I'm scared that what you're saying just might be what happened, Devin. There was a great deal of publicity about the attack when Alex was hurt. There was information about him on every channel, in every newspaper and on the web, as well. Alex is young and brilliant. He may know more about Massachusetts history than just about anyone else alive. What if...?"

Griffin looked up from his sandwich, considering Vickie from across the table. "What if whoever is doing this needs someone who knows the ancient lore of Massachusetts?"

"It doesn't explain the random attacks, really," Vickie said, looking at Griffin earnestly. "But from the beginning, those attacked had the same historical words written on them. So whoever is behind this is making a statement. Alex was the first victim— the press and media went wild with the story. Details about Alex were shared with just about everyone. He was happy at first—it was nice to be recognized as one of the youngest professors. Of course, he hoped the publicity would help his attacker be caught. This is just a theory—what if Alex's attack was random at first. The attacks were random, or carried out on vulnerable people when help didn't seem to be near. But after this person or these people learned about Alex, they wanted him."

Griffin, Rocky and Devin were silent, looking at her.

"Yes, it's a stretch. But hey, the attacker or the cult or the group is saying that Satan will come back. That implies that he's been here, and we all know that the devil and Massachusetts have quite a history. We have the very sad truth of the worst witch trials in the New World, for instance. But there's more because of the very harsh situation of the times—brutal winters and repressive societies and, of course, constant fear of Indian attacks. The darkness in the forests—all those things made it easy for impressionable minds to believe in Satan. The human creature hasn't changed so very much. People have always wanted power. They've always coveted what others have."

Again, silence greeted her words. Then Devin smiled. "I like her, Griffin. I really like her."

"We know a little bit about that witchcraft thing," Rocky said ruefully. "And very sick minds." He looked at Griffin. "She really might have something."

"But where does it all lead?" Vickie wondered. "Where do you start?"

"Well, the good thing is—we are part of the Krewe of Hunters," Griffin said. "Adam Harrison and Jackson Crow call the shots, but they're the kind of guys who just don't believe in micromanagement." He smiled at Vickie. "When we need help, we can call the office. When we don't, we go where our intuitions take us. We start with what we know, and we investigate from there. And sometimes, what we know about the past— in this case, the witch trials—can lead us into answers for what is happening now."

"Here's the good—God help us, the trials are remembered for their inhumanity! We look back at them now and shudder at the concept that anyone was condemned on spectral evidence. And the thing is, I don't think we're looking back at Salem."

"The good old founding Puritan fathers might not have seen a difference, but today, there is a tremendous difference. We're not looking at any modern form of witchcraft—or the midwives and other healers who might have been persecuted as witches. We're really looking at Satanism," Vickie reminded him. "'Hell's afire and Satan rules, the witches, they were real. The time has come, the rites to read, the flesh, 'twas born to heal. Yes, Satan is coming!'"

"But you told me that rhyme is not even original," Griffin said. "Right?" He glanced at Devin and Rocky. "Alex and Vickie had been researching the words left on the victims. They date way back."

"From 1665," Vickie said. And she went on to explain what they had discovered about Ezekiel Martin, his obsession with Missy Prior—and his early invention of cult wherein he was able to "marry" any woman he chose, share them with his closest male followers and wield strict control over his little colony of "Jehovah."

"I have heard of Jehovah," Rocky said, "and we even learned about Ezekiel Martin. Of course, Devin grew up in Salem and I'm from Peabody. That history was just a brief side note for us, though. When you grow up anywhere near Salem, you kind of live and breathe the Salem witch trials. And due to the case occurring when we met, we've been pretty heavily steeped in it all, too."

"We all knew there were other instances of supposed witchcraft and that there were other executions in Massachusetts—and even the other colonies," Devin said. "I believe that the Salem witch trials just grew in such hysteria, volume and ridiculousness that they dwarfed everything else we learned. And, of course, for the Puritans anything suggesting witchcraft had to do with the devil, so it wouldn't have been like today. Wiccans these days have a recognized religion in which they honor the earth. But in the 1600s, the only concept of witches was one which included Satan." She shrugged. "Even if, when you look at the pagan religions from which the Wiccan derived, the tribes practicing the religions wouldn't have even heard of Satan."

"To be fair, in Boston, you pretty much had to rub the faces of the powers that be in the fact that you were a Quaker or other religious dissenter to be executed," Vickie said. "You were usually banished. And, from what I've read, I believe that Ezekiel Martin was furious that he wasn't permitted to become a minister and given a congregation. We know that when people are disenfranchised, miserable and can't find their place in society, they are most vulnerable to join a cult. There must have been people back then who were equally susceptible, especially if he was a charismatic speaker."

"That quotation," Griffin said. He shook his head. "Whoever is pulling the strings here knows all about Ezekiel."

"And whoever it is has Alex," Vickie said. She

looked at them one by one, ending with Griffin. "I just have this strong feeling that he's been kidnapped. They want to use him, use what he knows about history, about old cults, about ancient religions, about Massachusetts," she added.

"About Jehovah?" Devin asked.

"He definitely knows about Jehovah—he is a veritable encyclopedia on the state," Griffin said.

"So, should we head for Jehovah to look for Alex?" Vickie asked.

Griffin looked back at her thoughtfully. "You know that, officially, at the moment, the powers that be believe that a single person was responsible for the attacks and leaving the message, and that one person committed suicide tonight."

"I don't believe it and you don't believe it," Vickie told him.

"Jehovah doesn't exist anymore," Griffin said.

"But we can find out where it was!" Vickie argued.

Griffin's phone rang and he excused himself but didn't move away to answer it. He looked at them and nodded.

Yes, the call had to do with the case.

He listened, gave brief answers and then hung up.

"Our young attacker-turned-suicide from tonight has been identified. He was Darryl Hillford of Framingham, twenty-five."

"What a waste of life!" Rocky said.

"Sad," Vickie agreed softly.

"Tragic," Devin agreed.

"Except, of course, that he was willing to hurt other people. Possibly kill," Rocky said flatly.

"Barnes did some checking on the guy, and I think we are looking at a 'type' that is easily maneuvered," Griffin said. "He dropped out of college—too much debt, too many drugs and a few arrests. His past didn't look so great. Alcoholic father, mother not in the picture. They're doing a toxicology screen, of course, and we'll know everything that was in his system tonight." He paused for a minute, casting his head thoughtfully to the side. "I don't think they will find that he was on drugs. He was doing what lots of people do…trying to find some kind of meaning for himself in the jumble of the world. He strayed onto a bad path. His last known address was a fraternity house, but he hasn't lived there in over three years."

"Well, then, he was living somewhere. If we can find out where…" Vickie murmured.

"Maybe we'll find Alex!" Griffin said.

Alex was provided with an outfit to go over his jeans and T-shirt; it was a red cloak, conical hat and attached scarf-type mask, just like that worn by the man who'd called himself a high priest.

While other people were with him, none of them identified themselves—even by a fake name.

Not one of them seemed to even notice the headless corpse in the corner!

He tried to still his shaking hands. He didn't know what the others thought, but he was pretty sure that the so-called "high priest" had left the rotting corpse there with calculated intention.

And now...

They led him out of the surgery room.

They didn't speak much. There were four of them with him, two about his height, two a little shorter. He wasn't even sure if they were men or women, young or old.

They brought him to a little cubicle. It had a heavy wooden door with a little panel that opened in so that he could be seen from outside. He was pretty sure that, once upon a time, such a space had held dangerous patients, the criminally insane.

Or perhaps those made dangerously insane by the crude treatment of the disabled in years gone by. Actually, he'd seen a few places where things hadn't changed so much.

The small room had a cot. With a blanket. And a bedpan. That was it.

The blanket gave him hope.

He wasn't going to die. The high priest seemed to want him. He had to play this right.

And pray that he wasn't going to be asked to stick a knife into a living sacrifice!

He wasn't shut up in the locked room for long. They came for him again—the four red-clad figures. They chanted as they led him out beneath the moonlight. Once, there had been something of a courtyard—a place where patients might have precious moments in the sun.

When there was sun, of course. It was, after all,

Massachusetts. His mom used to joke that everyone should come for summer in Massachusetts—it happened every July 27.

He almost laughed aloud; he was so terrified, and grasping at strange, old memories.

He wondered if he was supposed to chant. He didn't know *what* they were chanting, so he probably couldn't chant with them.

Others joined.

He saw that an old tiled garden table had been stripped and set with inverted crucifixes. There was a large empty space on the table…

Room for the sacrifice!

Maybe there was no sacrifice. Maybe…

There would be a sacrifice. There was a large knife on the tiled surface. Its clean blade glinted in the dim light.

The chanting continued. They began to form a circle—twelve, all in all, including him. And then, as the chanting increased, another figure stepped into the center. He raised his arms, and he began to speak. At first, it was some other language—what, Alex just couldn't be sure.

And then his words were in English.

"Do what thou wilt! For the day is coming, the day that is his! He will embrace his followers, those who bring him to flesh, to the pleasures of the flesh. For those who bring him to blood…oh, yes, the sweetness of the blood!"

As he spoke, a tall blonde woman was led into the

group. She seemed to come willingly, but she walked as if she was in a trance.

She wore white where the others wore red.

Alex began to tremble.

Sacrifice...this beautiful young woman!

The high priest raised his hands. He reached down for the knife on the altar. He lifted it high.

Alex's knees were giving; he was going to fall. They were going to sacrifice the young woman!

But the high priest continued to talk. "The time comes for the ultimate, as we prepare this world for he who is coming—he who will touch you all, and give you life and freedom. We prepare, we come closer and closer!"

Someone stepped forward, touching the young woman by the shoulders. The white gown fell to her feet.

No! He had to protest; Alex had to do something, had to stop this...

Alex heard a noise. A horrible bleating, a protest.

He turned.

It was a goat.

And as Alex watched, the poor creature was trussed up by a pair of the figures and stretched, screaming and terrified, over the altar.

And the knife went down on the creature's belly and then its throat.

Blood sprayed across the table and down onto the cobblestones. The bleating stopped.

"All hail Satan!"

The cry went up. The gushing blood was caught in a chalice. The cup was passed around.

It was brought before the girl; she was marked in blood over her breasts—what the markings meant, Alex didn't know.

But she was alive!

The chalice was passed again. It came to him.

He was supposed to drink.

He did.

It was amazing what terror and the will to survive could do for a man.

He didn't vomit until he was back in his little cell.

He fell on his little cot, shivering and sick.

"Vickie, please, please, find me!" he said softly. "Please, please!"

He thought he might cry; he felt he should, but didn't. He was too bewildered, too weary, after the night.

He just lay there. He tried to assure himself that help would come.

"One thing for sure, Vickie, if I make it out of here alive. This fellow is going to be a vegetarian! Maybe I'll even be vegan!"

His cell had no windows, but he thought that it was late in the night when he finally slept.

He might be an agnostic, but he drifted off whispering the Lord's Prayer.

And he couldn't forget the woman, the beautiful, blonde woman standing there, obviously drugged, smeared in the blood as if…

As if she was being prepared for a time when it was *her* blood that would be spilled.

3

"Oh, no, no—I think that the mood has been quite killed for the night," Vickie told Griffin.

"All right, I imagine that was a bit uncomfortable."

"*Un*comfortable? *Un*derstatement!"

"But so cool!" Griffin told her. "And it wasn't like the postman walked in or anything—"

"It was worse! Those are your friends."

"Who thought you were incredibly cool, beautiful, sexy, sensual…"

Vickie couldn't help but burst into laughter; Griffin was trying so hard.

Rocky and Devin were gone; they had headed to Griffin's apartment, where they'd stay for what was left of the night. But they'd all determined their course of action.

Rocky and Devin were on a week's leave from work, heading up for a visit to the Salem area, which they did at least once every year. But it wasn't necessary that they hurry. Jackson Crow, Krewe field director, had told Griffin to take whatever time he needed weeks ago, when Alex Maple had first been attacked.

They had time to devote to this. So they'd start looking for Alex as a team. They'd find as many people involved in Alex's life as they could. And they'd keep looking into the saying that had been written on Alex's chest.

And then finally, after making all their plans, for what remained of that night, Vickie and Griffin were alone together at last.

"Glorious, gorgeous, naked flesh and spiked heels," Griffin said huskily, sliding his hands beneath the oversize T-shirt she'd chosen for bed. "Beyond sexy, beyond sensual."

There was nothing like the feel of his hands on that naked flesh for her, Vickie knew.

"Forgive me!" he murmured.

His kiss, hot and deliciously wet, all along her naked flesh. T-shirt gone, panties shed, his mouth, his touch on the length of her...

"You're forgiven," she told him.

He rolled with her, straddling over her, looking down deeply into her eyes.

"Prove it!" he challenged.

And so, her lips on his then-naked flesh, she did.

It was very late when they finally slept.

Vickie assumed that she'd sleep well.

She didn't.

She dreamed that she heard her name being called. There was a plea to the sound; it was desperate cry for help.

She got up in the middle of the night. It was very dark at first—there was just the bed with Griffin lying on the light patch of the white sheets, the darkness stretching before her.

She found her robe and slipped into it, seeing a vague form of light in front of her.

She was walking through a forest trail. The trees were rich and deep and beautiful. She could smell the lushness of the earth.

"Vickie...please..."

The sound was closer. She kept moving.

She could hear a rush of water. She was coming to something...a stream or a river.

She hurried through the trees, and she came to a clearing.

The water was to her left; it was a big river, or a lake. Little mountain-peak-like islands seemed to rise from it.

"Vickie..."

She looked straight ahead.

There was a terrible scream; the misty light increased.

In front of her there was an inverted cross and, from it, a woman had been hanged upside down.

For a horrible moment, it seemed as if she looked at Vickie. As if she was pleading for help.

But that was impossible. The world around her was red. The ground pooled with red. Her hair fell in crimson streams.

Her throat had been slit.

And the red everywhere was the blood that ran from her throat. Ran...

And then gushed. And it filled the path and the

river and began to climb, obscuring even the mountains, and Vickie turned and ran back, tried to run away from the blood.

"Vickie!"

It was Alex's voice. Alex was behind her, calling for help.

"Vickie!"

She woke up in Griffin's arms. He was holding her, cradling her, soothing her.

"It's all right…it's all right."

"Griffin…"

"You were dreaming. A nightmare."

"It was Alex, Griffin. I mean…is it possible? He was calling to me. I could hear him, I could hear him in my mind just as clearly as if…as if he was here."

Griffin pulled her closer, smoothing back her hair.

"We're going to find him, Vickie. We're going to find him."

"Do you think that he could be calling to me?" she asked.

He eased her back down with him. "From what I've seen in life—and death—just about anything is possible," he told her softly.

She would never sleep again, she thought.

But, in his arms, she did.

When she awoke in the morning, she found a note on her pillow; he had showered and headed out to get started on the task of researching Alex's last known whereabouts. She smiled, got up and stepped into the shower.

She was startled to see dirt in the water around her feet.

She lifted a foot…

There was dirt on it! Rich, dark dirt!

As if she had walked down a forest path.

Suddenly, it seemed as if the water off her body ran red…

Bloodred.

She gasped.

But the dirt faded into the bloodred color of the water…

And the blood faded away, as well, and she was just standing in the shower.

Seeing things and losing her mind.

By nine the next morning, Griffin was waiting at the office of Professor Milton Hanson.

Hanson was a trim man who appeared to be in his midfifties or early sixties. He had iron-gray hair and kept fit; he was about five foot ten and leanly muscled—a handsome academic with nicely angled features and clear gray eyes. He must have readily claimed the attention of his classroom, Griffin thought. His voice was rich and powerful and his manner commanding.

"I've actually been trying to reach Alex myself," Hanson said after Griffin had shared why he was there. "Yesterday was Sunday, so I didn't expect him in school, but I was calling him about work we were doing." Hanson frowned thoughtfully. "Alex is an exceptional researcher. Never stops—he can always find another reference or another book. He's great with the Internet and has no problems finding out what obscure library might hold a source he wants to investigate. I wasn't worried, but… I'll call his assistant now."

He did so. Griffin waited.

Hanson sighed and hung up the phone. "Alex hasn't shown up to work. He had an early class this morning, but he didn't make it."

"Do you know where he might have gone?" Alex asked.

"No. Or yes—as in anywhere they might have made some kind of fantastic new historical find. Except— no. Alex is extremely responsible. He doesn't just take off and go places."

"That's what I've heard," Griffin said. He lifted his hands in question. "Friends? Enemies? Is there anything you can tell me?"

"He's friends with everyone," Hanson told him. "He has no enemies—not that I know about. I'm sure some professors or academics out there are jealous. He's just naturally brilliant, his theories always test out when the research is all done… Oh, no. You think that something has happened to him?" Hanson frowned, then his brows shot up. "But you're him! You're that federal agent who brought down the attacker last night. Some kind of crazy man who killed himself rather than be caught. But when Alex was attacked, it was random, right?"

"Yes, we caught a man last night who had attacked a woman. He died," Griffin said. It was all over the news. He decided not to explain. "A friend of mine is a close friend of Alex's. He was supposed to meet her last night. Now he hasn't shown up for class."

"My God! He could be lying dead in his apartment!" Hanson said.

"He isn't lying dead in his apartment. It's been checked."

"Already? But—"

"He has friends who care," Griffin said, not telling the man that the "friends" he was referring to were himself, Vickie and Detective Barnes.

"Oh, well, that's a relief!" Hanson said. "Good. I mean, good that he's not dead. I'm so sorry that none of us seems to know where he is!"

Griffin rose, presenting one of his cards to Hanson. "If you see him or hear from him or think of anything that might help us, please call."

"Of course."

"What about other friends here, in the department?" Griffin asked.

"Well, he came here as a guest professor, you know. I believe that he's about to become full-time, but that's up to many people, really—after all, this is truly one of the finest teaching institutions in the world."

"Yes," Griffin agreed, lowering his head to hide a slight smile. It wasn't that he disagreed; it was Hanson's absolute assurance in his words.

"You might speak with Lacy Callahan. She is a professor of history, as well, specializing in ancient myths and all form of religions, especially as pertaining to the human psyche. They are friends, and they love to argue. In our world, that makes for good friends," Hanson said.

"Great. Thank you. Where do I find her?"

"It's summer session, so I'd say that she'll be in the courtyard in about fifteen minutes. She always takes a tea break after first class in the summer—she loves the sun. Students know they can find her there," Hanson said.

Griffin left Hanson's office and headed out to the street.

The sun was out; the day was perfect. It was Monday morning, and Boston was alive with activity.

There was a crime rate in Boston—no way out of it. But he loved his city.

Yes, it had once been a bastion of ungodly religious intolerance, but from that harsh and cruel base, some of the greatest minds in the history of the country had risen to the Age of Enlightenment and then the birth of a new kind of freedom and a brave, new country.

He'd also been with the FBI long enough to know that while men and women could rise to the greatest of accomplishments, compassion, intelligence and more, there were those who could twist anything into something dark.

And he could *feel* it.

It seemed all the more reinforced by Vickie's nightmare last night. It wasn't just a dream.

He didn't know how it worked. He didn't know if it was the *gut* thing that men and women in law enforcement all seemed to develop, or maybe it was something more.

And perhaps that something more defined the members of the Krewe—whatever gift or sense it was that allowed them to speak with the dead.

However it worked, he knew: *the attacks weren't over.* They were just a tease of something more sinister. And somehow, Alex's disappearance was part of it.

Devin arrived at Vickie's apartment as she was still dressing and gulping down a cup of coffee.

Griffin had headed off to speak with Professor Hanson; Rocky was going to speak with the police who had been on guard duty over Alex following his attack.

She and Devin were off to follow in Alex's last footsteps.

Since they were headed to the café by Faneuil Hall, she wasn't sure why she was drinking coffee, except that, of course, it was part of her general morning ritual.

"Coffee?" she asked Devin.

"I can wait," Devin told her. "I already made some at Griffin's place. But we're going to go talk to the waitress who knew Alex and mentioned him last night, right? That means I can get a coffee there. Except we don't know the waitress's name, and it's really unlikely that she works nights and mornings."

"I'm hoping that the manager who is on duty now will at least know who she is—and possibly call her for us. If not… Devin, Griffin told me that you still write your series of children's books featuring Auntie Mina, but that you went through the academy, joined the FBI and became Krewe of Hunters, too. You can throw some weight around, right?" Vickie asked.

Devin laughed. "I can show my badge. And yes, most of the time, people become cooperative. We're only trying to reach one of their employees for help. I doubt we'll need to throw any weight around."

"Let's hope not!"

They opted to walk to the café; it was far easier to go the distance than it was to try to find parking any closer to their destination.

"So, I haven't met your *haunting* residents yet," Devin said lightly.

Vickie glanced at her uneasily. Knowing—and conversing with!—others who saw and spoke to the dead was still a new situation for her.

"Dylan—and now Darlene," Vickie murmured.

Devin flashed her a warm smile. "For me, it's my auntie Mina. I love her dearly—I loved her when she was alive, and…now, too! She's great. I use her as my main character in my children's books. Sometimes we find her hitching a ride to head down to Virginia with us, and sometimes she chooses to stay in the cottage on the outskirts of Salem."

"Devin, I understand about the Krewe—and the rest of the world, really. There are actually many people out there with a sixth sense, the ability to talk to the dead, find spirits, see ghosts. But last night I had a nightmare. It was horrible. I was looking for Alex because he was calling me. I wasn't in the city—I was out in the woods somewhere. And there was water. A river or a lake. I could hear Alex crying out to me, but when I came to a clearing, I saw an inverted cross with a woman hanging from it. Her throat had been slit— and the river and the lake were blood. It was terrible. But the freakiest part is that this morning, when I got into the shower, I thought that the water started to run red—like blood. And there was dirt on my feet. Real dirt, as if I had walked through a forest. Then...it was all gone, just like that."

"What did Griffin say?" Devin asked her.

"That I'd had a nightmare. But—"

"You think Alex is really calling out to you."

"Yes. Griffin didn't deny that there are all kinds of possibilities out there. I mean, if we can see the dead, maybe we can hear the living? I've heard of twins who each react when something has happened to only one, or cases of a mother knowing when a son or daughter in the military has been injured on foreign soil."

"So, if the dream means anything, we're not going to find Alex anywhere in the city. But in the dream, the person dead on the cross was a woman, right? Definitely not Alex?"

"Definitely not Alex."

"Let's see what we find out today."

"I keep thinking about the words written on the victims' chests," Vickie said. "And that they date back to one of the first men we might consider a fanatic— twisting religion to what he wanted it to be. Ezekiel Martin. And Jehovah."

"Maybe Jehovah is where we need to be, then," Devin said.

They'd reached the coffee shop. Devin opened the door and Vickie entered first. Naturally, there was a line at the register and she headed for it.

"Busy time of morning," Devin said.

"Yep. I'm usually here later in the afternoon," Vickie told her.

They reached the register and the young woman taking orders. Vickie opened her mouth and the young woman said, "Medium latte, extra shot of espresso?"

Vickie laughed. "Yes, thank you. That would be terrific."

"And you, miss?" the cashier asked Devin. "Are you together? Same check?"

"Coffee with a little cream," Devin said. "And yes, we're together. We're actually looking for someone." She nodded at Vickie to go ahead.

"A waitress who works here later—night shift, I believe. She's very pretty and has dark hair. She's about five feet six inches. Nice, polite, very efficient," Vickie said.

"Audrey Benson," the girl behind the cash register said. "I'm afraid she doesn't come on until about two in the afternoon. She works the late shift."

"It's really important that we speak with her. We don't want you doing anything that wouldn't be right, but if you could call her…?" Vickie suggested.

"It's a little busy!" the girl whispered to her.

"Is there a manager on?" Devin asked.

"You're looking at her. And I am really sorry, but—"

Devin reached into her shoulder bag and produced her badge.

"It's really important," she said.

"Can you give me ten minutes and let us catch up with the rush? Then I'll be right with you."

"Of course," Vickie and Devin said in unison.

They headed to the end of the bar and waited for their drinks.

A young man brought their coffees to the end of the counter. "Hey," he said to Vickie. "I know you ordered at the counter, but you look as if you'd like to sit. Please, right over there. My table, and I don't mind. We see you here all the time."

"Thanks," Vickie said. "Sure. And…really? I'm here that often?"

He laughed. "Yep—you and your friend. Alex. Well, Professor Maple to me!"

"You know Alex?"

"I have a class with him."

Vickie studied the man speaking to her. He was, she thought, in his midtwenties, maybe even as young as twenty-one or twenty-two. He was lean and about six feet even with close-cropped black hair and warm brown eyes.

"Political science major—working my way through school," he told them. He offered them his hand. "My name is Manny," he told them.

Vickie introduced herself and then Devin, adding, "Devin is actually Special Agent Lyle. She's with the FBI. We're looking for Alex."

"Oh?" Manny asked. "Well. He missed a class this morning. I know because a friend of mind dropped by about an hour ago to say that he was cutting class because there wasn't a class. But I didn't know that Professor Maple was *missing*. He was in here Saturday night."

"You were working Saturday night?" Vickie asked him. "You work days and nights?"

Manny nodded. "I work whatever shift I can each week. I have some scholarship money, but college—especially this college!—isn't cheap."

"Good for you. And us," Devin murmured, glancing at Vickie. "So, did you see Alex do anything out of the ordinary on Saturday night? I realize that's probably not an easy question—hard to tell what is usual or ordinary for someone else!—but it does sound as if you somewhat know Alex."

"Saturday was a big night. We had the music duo, the Dearborn sister and brother, Cathy and Ron."

"A lot of people came to see the show? To stay?" Devin asked.

"Yes."

"Did Alex speak with anyone? Did he come in with anyone? Did anyone seem to be bothering him? Did he…did he look okay?" Vickie pursued anxiously.

"Come to think of it, he was a little off. Friendly as ever—the professor is a great guy!—but he started to seem a little out of it. As if we were serving booze instead of coffee," Manny told them.

Vickie glanced at Devin anxiously.

Could that mean something? she asked with her look.

Devin gave her a barely perceptible shrug. *Maybe.*

"Did you see him when he left?" Devin asked.

"No," Manny said. "I was running around like crazy, and I wasn't Alex's server on Saturday night. Audrey had his table—Audrey Benson."

"So we heard. We're just waiting on the manager to help us get in contact with her," Vickie said. "You don't happen to have her number or a way to reach her, do you?"

To her surprise, he smiled. "Sure. And she's a good kid. She'll be happy to help you."

He pulled out his phone and dialed, smiling at them, happy to be of assistance.

But after a moment, he began to frown as he listened to a recorded voice on the phone.

"Um, well, I thought I could help you," he said. "Her number is no longer in service at the moment. I think it was some kind of a prepaid cell phone. Odd. Though, not so odd. Lots of college kids can't afford the plans where you pay the big guys on a plan every month."

"Do you know where she lives?" Devin asked.

"I'm afraid not. She said that she was somewhere near the aquarium, though. She hasn't worked here that long. We just exchanged phone numbers in case we had to cover for one another somewhere along the line. I like her—she's always very cheerful," he told them earnestly.

The cashier/manager walked over to them, sighing as she smoothed her hands down over her apron. "What is going on? How can I help you? I'm Susan. Acting manager now, but I suppose I should call our overall manager. I mean, we really want to help, but I don't know anything about privacy laws and all that."

"Manny here just tried Audrey on the number that he has for her. Perhaps you could just call her and ask her if she minds talking to us. This is an official missing-person case," Devin said pleasantly, but with an impressive authority Vickie definitely admired.

"Oh, yes! Of course!" Susan said.

She waved a hand in the air. "Thank you, Manny," she said, as if she'd realized that, at the moment, she was the queen of the situation and he'd been a retainer to handle things in her wake. Manny grinned good-naturedly and turned to start wiping down a table.

Susan continued to a little office in the back. She indicated that Vickie and Devin should follow her. She walked around behind a desk and opened a computer, punched in a few keys and found a phone number. The office had a landline and she used it to call Audrey Benson.

But her expression was much as Manny's had been; she had evidently called the same number that Manny had in his phone, and received the same response.

"Well, the phone is disconnected," she murmured.

"Do you have an address for her?" Vickie asked.

"I don't know if I should—" Susan began.

"We're not after Audrey! We're trying to find a missing person who may be in danger. We're just looking for some help," Devin said. "Please."

"I'm desperately trying to help a friend!" Vickie said.

"All right, all right," Susan murmured, looking at the computer. She rattled off an address.

Vickie and Devin looked at each other, frowning.

"Say again, please?" Devin said.

Susan rattled off the address again, then paused, frowning. "Hmm. That can't be right."

"Nope. Not unless she's living in the Atlantic Ocean," Vickie murmured.

"Someone just transposed a figure wrong, or something," Susan said.

"Right. Good job checking out your employees," Devin said.

"Hey! We check, we do everything right."

"You have a social security number for her?" Devin asked.

"Hey! Now, I think you have to give me a warrant or something like that for a social security number," Susan said. "If you want more than that, you'll have to wait until eleven o'clock. Our general manager comes in then. And he's the one who hired Audrey!"

"But you do have a social security number for her, right?" Vickie asked. "I mean, seriously? Anyone who has visited Boston would probably know that was a sham address. Anyone who knows that we're on the east coast would know—"

Devin jabbed her in the ribs. Vickie fell silent. She knew that she was getting more and more worried by the minute.

The waitress seemed suspicious now. Could she have drugged Alex, giving him something that made him either pass out or become out of it and pliable?

"You do have a social security number for her, right?"

"Of course!" Susan snapped. "If you'll excuse me, I have to get back to work! We are a busy place, if you haven't noticed."

"We will get a warrant," Devin said.

"Just come back when she's due into work," Susan said.

"I think you probably need to get someone to cover her shift," Vickie said. "I think last night might have been her last night on the job."

Devin grabbed Vickie's hand, pulling her out of the office and out onto the sidewalk by Faneuil Hall.

"You can't beat her up—not legal and won't get us anywhere!" Devin said.

"I wasn't going to beat her up. I just… I just had to let her know that…she's…she's dangerously careless and stupid!"

"We'll get a warrant," Devin said. "Not to worry, we'll get a warrant."

"Well, you can, but you don't need to," the two of them suddenly heard.

Vickie whirled around.

Dylan Ballantine was there, hand in hand with Darlene.

They were as real as the sidewalk to Vickie, and Devin, too, she imagined.

Others walked by them as if they were air.

"Hi," Devin said. "You must be Dylan—and Darlene."

"She's one of them. She sees us clearly," Darlene said, delighted.

"Yes, and…hi! Dylan Ballantine, and my friend Darlene Dutton," he said, glad to meet Devin.

"Lovely. I'm Devin Lyle. I thought I'd meet you two soon enough, but a true pleasure," Devin said. "So, why don't we need a warrant?"

"Because I slipped into the office. And I memorized the number for you," Dylan said.

"He's so good!" Darlene said adoringly.

Devin glanced at Vickie and grinned. Then she drew out a notepad. "Okay, Mr. Dylan Ballantine. Let's have it!"

It took Griffin a few minutes to realize that Professor Lacy Callahan was sitting in a wheelchair.

When he came upon her, she was under a massive oak, a shawl draped over her shoulders and her head bent over a sketchpad as she thoughtfully drew. She was an extremely attractive older woman—perhaps fifty or so—with delicate features and almost platinum-blond hair that shimmered around her, casting her in a gentle glow of beauty as if she were a mythical goddess.

"Professor Callahan?" he asked softly.

She looked up, just a bit startled, and then she studied him, head to toe.

Then she nodded gravely. "And you're Special Agent Griffin Pryce," she said.

"Yes."

"I watch the news."

He wasn't sure what to say to that. There was a stone garden box near her and he took a seat on the edge.

She smiled suddenly. "You are quite a topic of conversation. Some people believe that you scared a man into suicide. Some just think you're incredibly macho."

"Professor, I didn't scare a man I'd never seen before into carrying cyanide capsules, that's for sure."

"Well, good point. Still, you've given us a great deal to speculate over."

"I actually try to stay out of the public eye—without being secretive. It's a tough wire to walk."

"I imagine it is. Which fascinates me. And, of course, makes me wonder why you're here, speaking with me. Nope. Don't tell me. There's only one mystery in my life right now. My friend Alex Maple didn't arrive for class this morning. He never misses. He wants a permanent position more than you can begin to imagine. Not only that, he loves teaching. I called him—I can't reach him. And let's see—Alex was the first person attacked by the man who died last night."

"Maybe," Griffin said.

"Maybe? You mean, an innocent man committed suicide rather than be questioned?"

"I didn't say he was innocent. I just don't know if he was guilty of all the attacks."

"Hmm."

"And Alex is missing. So, can you help me?" he asked her.

She was thoughtful, looking out across the yard.

Groups of students moved about here and there, walking through the courtyard or lounging in the sun. Griffin could overhear some of the chatter. Young men and women talked about different subjects, many of them animatedly.

"I wish I could help you. I love Alex—such a great guy. He gets so excited about any kind of knowledge." She turned and looked at Griffin, and he thought again that she was just so incredibly beautiful; she should have been floating above the ground, rather than tethered to a wheelchair. "I do worry that something is very, very wrong. He doesn't miss class. He has family, but they're not in the area right now, and he wouldn't just disappear to go for a visit, anyway. He loves art shows and good music venues. He's not a drinker. He loves coffeehouses, although he will go to a neighborhood bar for some good music. He's a great friend. He…" She hesitated and shrugged. "He has always treated me with the utmost respect. I don't know where to tell you to look. He has his apartment—he has his spots around the city. Here, a coffee shop by Faneuil Hall, an Italian restaurant just across the highway. If he were going to be away from Boston, I think he would have told me. It would be something that he had planned. I'm… I'm very afraid for him!" she finished.

Griffin stood. He reached into his pocket and produced one of his cards again.

Every once in a while, people actually thought of something that they hadn't said—and they did call him.

He hesitated, thinking about Vickie's dream of the night before.

"Does Alex ever go…to the country. Is there anywhere he loves where there are forest paths, anything like that?"

"Alex?" she asked. "Not on purpose! Roughing it to Alex would be a roadside motel instead of a Hyatt or Hilton."

"Thanks," he said. He started to walk away.

"'Hell's afire and Satan rules, the witches, they were real. The time has come, the rites to read, the flesh, 'twas born to heal. Yes, Satan is coming!'"

He turned back around. Lacy Callahan had just repeated the quote word for word.

She looked at him. "There was a place called Jehovah, once upon a time." She shrugged. "There was also an incident—besides the Lizzie Borden case—out in Fall River. Those words were taken from the distant past once before."

"You think that Alex has been taken somewhere else. By cultists."

"It's what you think, too, isn't it?"

"Yes," he said softly. "Yes, it is. Professor, thank you again."

Griffin hurried on. His phone was ringing. He glanced at the caller ID.

Vickie.

He could almost feel her anxiety, as if it was part of his special ring for her.

He answered the phone.

"There's a real witch out there, Griffin!" she announced over the line. "Seriously—I think she drugged him and then she kidnapped him. And she doesn't even seem to be real."

"What?" he asked.

"Audrey Benson. She doesn't even really exist. Devin had the social security number she was using called in to headquarters—Audrey Benson with that number died in 1958! And her address—she'd have to been living a hundred feet deep in a shipwreck or something. Griffin, I think that Devin and I found out a very scary truth. There's no question anymore. Alex has definitely been kidnapped."

4

Kidnapped...

Vickie's words kept repeating in Griffin's mind as he looked over records.

Missing: Carly Sanderson, twenty-three, college student from Barre, Massachusetts...

Missing: Natasha Jacoby, twenty, day care worker, New Haven, Connecticut...

Missing: Lawrence "Larry" Meyers, twenty-six, construction worker, Ware, Massachusetts...

Missing: Taylor Genera, twenty-five, hostess, Fall River...

The list went on, and it was long.

Griffin had done a search that encompassed the last several years. There were at least twenty-three cases of young people gone missing in the general area—who had never been found. They included not just those who hailed from New England, but those who had been visiting Massachusetts or a neighboring state when they had vanished.

He drummed his fingers on his desk. Cult activity

wasn't usually so hidden. Mainly, of course, because it was hard to hide a community that might include dozens of people. There was usually some kind of compound, and a charismatic leader who drew in lots of followers. There was nothing like that on the FBI's radar lately. These people who were listed had been reported as missing to the police. They all seemed to have vanished.

Darryl Hillford had not been reported as missing.

Maybe no one had cared enough to report him—and maybe that was why he had clung to a leader or philosophy that demanded self-sacrifice should he be caught.

Why? What a waste, what a waste of human life! *And he hadn't been able to stop it!*

Griffin was in a spare office at the Bureau offices at 1 Central Plaza. Barnes and Rocky were due to meet him here.

Vickie was still with Devin; they were also on their way in. Vickie was going to describe the pretty brunette waitress who had been using a social security number stolen from a dead woman to a forensic artist.

There was a tap on the door; Rocky stuck his head in.

"Anything?" Griffin asked.

Rocky walked in and took a seat in a chair in front of the desk.

"Okay, I didn't get much from the officer who'd been Alex's protection detail. Our friend Mr. Maple went to work, went home, made it very easy for the cops. He liked Alex very much. He was smart, friendly—and always bringing coffee out to him when they were watching his place. His main entertainment was going to the café by Faneuil Hall."

"Vickie and Devin are headed here from the café, to get a sketch made of a waitress who was working there under a false identity. She's disappeared, it seems."

"Alex is gone…this waitress is gone. A man died last night." Rocky lifted his hands. "And someone is spouting Satanism."

"I've been pulling up state records," Griffin said. "Finding all kinds of young people who are missing. I feel like we have a bunch of puzzle pieces and I can't figure out how they go together. We have Alex missing. We have the attacks. We have a young man who committed suicide rather than be arrested. It's crazy—he wouldn't have been up for murder. The victims didn't die."

"No, they didn't die," Rocky murmured. "And you think that the attacks were just a cry for attention by someone out there?"

"Or a way to divert attention," Griffin said. "That's why I'd really love to start looking into some of these disappearances. Check with authorities in Barre, Ware and other places. Maybe some of the missing persons have joined a cult—and some have been victims of a cult." He hesitated. "Last night, Vickie had a terrible nightmare. She heard her name being called, and she walked through a forest and found…"

"Alex?"

"No, a woman hanging upside down on an inverted cross, her throat slit. There was water nearby, and the water was running red with blood."

"Has she had dreams like this before? You know, Griffin, that a lot of us have had vivid dreams that seem to be messages from somewhere else," Rocky said. "When I was a kid, I thought I heard a friend calling me. I followed the voice. There was a reason I was being called. In my case, I had to grow up, join the Bureau, come back to Salem and meet Devin to find out why and bring it all to rights. I say that whatever Vickie saw could be our best clue at the moment."

"I agree," Griffin murmured. "I'm not sure where to start out. Follow up on missing-persons cases, I'm thinking. Maybe we should head to Fall River. That's where a Satanic cult used the saying in the 1800s—and again in the late 1970s. We could start there."

"You said that in Vickie's dream, the water ran red. So we're also looking for water," Rocky said.

"We have water just about everywhere from the Atlantic to the Quabbin and through a zillion rivers and lakes in between."

"True."

"Yes," Griffin said. "But I think you're right. We trace it on back to the source."

"You have to be careful," Devin warned Vickie. "You're becoming…a little crazed."

"I know," Vickie murmured. "I heard myself when I was talking to Griffin. It's just that my dream was so bizarre, and then, finding out that the waitress, Audrey Benson, doesn't even really exist… I'm so frightened for Alex, Devin."

"I understand. We tend to have personal involvements with what is going on around us, but it makes the concept of control really important," Devin told her, smiling. "You only realized that he was missing last night. Griffin only ran down that poor fool, Darryl Hillford, last night."

"It only takes a matter of seconds to kill someone," Vickie said softly.

"Okay, true."

"And the attacks and Alex's disappearance are absolutely related, I'm sure of it," Vickie said. "He was the first one attacked. And we know that he never made it home from the coffee shop the night before."

"And we know that he's brilliant, right? So, we have to presume that they're after him for something that he either knows or can figure out for them. He's alive, Vickie."

"So why was there so much blood in my dream?" Vickie murmured.

Devin was quiet for a minute. "I don't know. It could mean…someone else is dead. Let's face it," she said flatly, "with what's going on, I think we're all afraid that someone somewhere has been practicing blood sacrifices."

"Isn't that usually a young blonde virgin?"

"Who said it hasn't been a young blonde virgin?" Devin asked her dryly. "Though, of course, young blonde *virgins*—or those of either sex with any color hair—aren't so easy to come by these days. Then again, maybe human sacrifices have come along with the times."

"And for it to matter at all, you need to believe that

your sacrifice means something and that there is a devil. Hell, in my mind, anyway, tends to be on earth. Dante Alighieri pretty much invented hell as we envision it, and while *we* know there is something...something beyond, I don't particularly believe that anyone brought Satan back in the 1600s, the 1800s or the 1970s!" Vickie told her.

They were lingering outside the coffee shop while Devin made calls. A search for a local address for Cathy and Ron Dearborn had not gone well at the departmental level, even after they'd searched their way to the registered business name that the duo went under, which was just "Dearborn."

And Vickie didn't know why, but she was determined to talk to the sister-and-brother act. They were just performers.

But Alex had loved them.

And he just might have said something to them.

Vickie tried to catch the eye of the server, Manny, through the café window. He saw her right away and hurried out to them. "Hey, what's up? I heard about Audrey. Wild, huh?"

"We can't find an address for the Dearborn sister and brother. Can you help us?" Vickie asked him.

"Actually, I can," he said. "I helped them haul a speaker over here from their place a few times. It's easy walking distance from here."

He showed them the best way to get there.

And he wouldn't let them leave without coffee.

They thanked him, and soon they were headed along Tremont Street, on their way to the residence/hotel where Alex's beloved duo were staying, according to Manny.

"We try to talk to these guys," Devin said, "and then we'll head in to speak with the forensic artist and get an image of Audrey Benson going."

They reached the address they'd been given just in time to see a dark-haired woman carrying a big box out to a minivan that had been pulled illegally into a small laneway.

"Cathy Dearborn?" Devin asked Vickie.

"Yep, that's her," Vickie said.

"Miss Dearborn!" Devin called.

The young woman stopped and turned, smiling as she looked at them curiously.

"Yes? Can I help you? We've got a few dates out in Worcester County, so I'm not sure we're available if you're looking for a booking," she said.

They reached where she was standing, ready to hike the suitcase into the back of the minivan.

"Hi, I'm Vickie Preston. And this is Devin Lyle."

"Vickie, hi. I've seen you around—nice to meet you. Devin, nice to meet you, too. How can I help you?" she asked. "Our calendar is online, if you'd like to check it out."

"Actually, we're here to find out if you happen to know anything about a friend who has disappeared. Alex Maple."

The girl's face scrunched up for a minute. "Alex… yes! One of the best audience members we've had— ever, anywhere! Great guy. I saw him at the coffee shop by Faneuil Hall the last time we played there—night before last actually."

"Have you seen him since? Did he say anything to you about leaving town?" Vickie asked.

"No, he told me he loved it when we did Fleetwood Mac music. That's about the extent of our conversation that night," Cathy said. "We have talked about other things. He is amazing. I'm from Athol, and I don't begin to know any of the things he knows about my area of the state. Is he okay?"

"I hope so," Vickie said quietly.

"Did you see him leave with anyone? Talk to anyone—meet up with anyone just outside of the shop?" Devin asked.

"No. I'm so sorry. I can't help you."

"What about your brother?" Vickie asked.

"Why don't we talk to him? He's on his way out, too. We're heading west today. We were here for a few months so we just did a short-term condo rental. We're thinking about expanding—we've got a meeting with a wicked good drummer tonight. Anyway, come on in—oh. Here's Ronnie. Men, you know. Whether you're related to them or dating them, they just don't seem to get the concept of time," Cathy said, indicating her brother, who was now coming out the front door, dragging along a large suitcase.

"Hey! I heard that. And women are notoriously slow!" he protested.

He really was good-looking, Vickie thought. Light-haired, with very unique eyes. He had a good smile, too, both slightly apologetic and slightly mischievous.

"Ron," Cathy said, "this is…"

She grimaced, clearly having already forgotten their names.

"Victoria Preston and Devin Lyle," Vickie said. "We have a friend who is missing. You have come to know him or, at the least, you've seen him often. Alex Maple."

"Alex, sure! I love Alex. I wish he came bottled. We'd be rich and famous. Have I seen you with Alex?" he asked Vickie.

She nodded. "Alex is missing."

"We just saw him the night before last," Ron said.

"That's the last time anyone has seen him," Vickie said.

"Is that really missing? Maybe he popped out of town. Maybe…hey, he seems to be on the straight and narrow, but you never know. Maybe the guy is just out on a bender or something."

"We're looking into all possibilities," Devin said. "We were hoping he might have said something to you or your sister. Or that you might have seen him with someone."

"I'm so sorry. I know he was there. He was supportive and enthusiastic, as always. But I didn't see where he went, or if he met up with anyone." He turned and shoved his bag into the minivan. "Sure wish we could help you. But…"

Devin produced one of her cards. "If you think of anything, if you see him, if you can help us in any way, call me, please," Devin said.

Ron Dearborn looked at the card, and then at Devin.

"FBI?" he said. "The FBI is looking for Alex—when he's only been missing a day or so?"

"Alex was attacked and left for dead," Vickie reminded him.

"But they caught that guy last night!" Ron said. "Offed him—or he offed himself."

"It's an ongoing investigation," Devin said.

"Wow," Ron Dearborn said.

Cathy caught his arm. "We've got to get going. If there's anything at all we think of, we'll call."

"Sure. Of course," Ron said. He glanced from Devin to Vickie. "I guess you have friends in high places. Friends besides Alex."

He looked intently at Vickie. "You're like him, right? You're one of those historians. A teacher?"

"No. A writer."

"But smart, like Alex, right?"

"I love history."

"We really have to go!" Cathy said.

"And so do we," Devin said. "Thank you for your time."

Ron turned to his sister. "Is that everything?" he asked her.

Vickie and Devin turned away, heading back toward Tremont.

"Well? Anything?" Devin asked Vickie.

"No. I guess they're just a pair of pleasant entertainers. They both know Alex, and like him."

"It's true that under most circumstances people wouldn't even be worried yet."

"I know," Vickie said. "But I also know that something is very wrong." She let out a sigh. "Do you think that they're for real?" she asked. "Maybe they have different names, too. Maybe it was a massive conspiracy at the coffee shop. Or not a massive conspiracy—a small conspiracy. And the Dearborn brother and sis are in on it with Audrey Benson—who isn't really Audrey Benson."

She was sure that Devin had to think that her ideas were both paranoid and pretty far-fetched.

"There's so much we don't know," Devin said. "I called an Uber—he'll get us right up ahead on Tremont Street," she added.

They were heading into a bright and beautiful afternoon and the street was busy. All manner of people were about—couples wandering, groups chatting and some hurrying along as if they'd stayed out too late for lunch. She clutched Devin's arm and pulled her to the side when a troop of tourists—all holding hands!—came through, something like a herd of creatures not about to be stopped.

"Saved!" Devin said, laughing. Then she sobered. "Here's the question. Does this guy—or woman!—really believe it's possible to raise the devil? Or is it just some kind of ruse to gather followers together for some other end?"

"What other end?" Vickie asked.

"You never know," Devin said.

They turned the corner. As they did, a young redheaded woman, a handbag over her shoulder and a cup from a local coffee vendor in her hands, came rushing up to them.

"Vickie? Victoria Preston?" she asked. The woman's eyes seemed a bit unfocused and wild.

Vickie frowned. "Why?"

"Who are you?" Devin asked the young woman. "And why are you asking?"

The woman didn't answer. She suddenly hurled the contents of her cup at Vickie. Thick, warm liquid covered her front. The redhead turned and tore down the street, thrusting aside the busy walkers and disappearing into the crowd.

"What the hell?" Devin demanded.

The liquid was deep red.

Blood.

Luckily, it had missed Vickie's eyes.

"You all right?" Devin demanded.

"Yes! I'm fine."

"I'm going after her," Devin said, already running.

"Well, what the hell, so am I!"

"Hey," Barnes said, joining Griffin and Rocky. He walked in and perched on the desk and seemed to read something from their faces.

"So, we didn't just stop it all last night, huh? You know this because…?"

"Right off the bat?" Griffin asked. "Well, Alex Maple disappeared…along with a waitress, a young woman who apparently lived in the Atlantic Ocean and was very corporeal despite the fact she died in 1958."

"Ah, come on," Barnes said uneasily, "we're not talking ghosts here."

"I said corporeal—no ghosts, just a stolen identity,"

Griffin said. He was never sure what Barnes did and didn't know about the Krewe of Hunters, or what he suspected. He tended to be a man who was willing to take whatever help he could get to solve a case, but that didn't mean he'd be open-minded about their skills.

Information about Griffin's unit was certainly out there in the news, if you knew where to look. They weren't officially the Krewe of Hunters; it was a moniker they received because Adam Harrison had brought the first Krewe members—including Jackson Crow and Angela Hawkins—together on a baffling case in New Orleans.

They were considered an elite unit, and when they went out, it was usually on "special" assignment.

Griffin continued. "Vickie and Devin sleuthed out that information. I got just about nothing from the college professors I spoke with." He decided it wasn't a good time to dwell on their inability to get answers.

"I don't get it—how did they get this information so quickly?" Barnes asked. "And how do we know this waitress is missing? Just a few hours missing? People have similar names. Numbers can be transposed in the wrong order."

"Barnes, she served Alex Maple on Saturday night. She also served Vickie and her friend Roxanne Greeley last night. She was only working at the shop a few weeks and she gave them a social security number that belonged to someone who died years ago."

"That is suspicious," Barnes agreed grudgingly. "But as you said, this woman served Vickie and her friend last night. So, she didn't disappear when Alex disappeared, right?"

"I don't believe anyone is seeing the full picture, Barnes," Griffin said.

"And you know that he's right about this thing going deep," Rocky added quietly.

Barnes sighed fully. "We could still be off. I mean, it's possible. Alex Maple is an adult. He doesn't really owe anyone an explanation of his whereabouts."

"He is an adult who was attacked, who had been under protection—and who received a lot of media attention after the attack," Griffin said.

"Come on, Detective!" Rocky said. "There's obviously something going on here."

Barnes protested. "Hey. I rushed things for you guys on the city level. We went into the guy's home—and he's definitely not there. But there's still the possibility that he's just gone. *You* come on—he's one of those nerds—crazy academic types. He's lost his phone—misplaced it. He's just off."

"You don't even believe that," Griffin said.

"Everyone wants Darryl Hillford to have been guilty of carrying out all of the assaults. The people of Boston want to walk the streets safely—they want the Satanist attacker to have been stopped," Barnes said impatiently.

"That's natural. You know what? I watched a guy—*in his twenties*—take a suicide pill rather than surrender to me. You don't think I want it to be over? Hell, we were headed back to Virginia before the attacks started, Barnes."

"I know, I know!" Barnes said, wincing. "I just…

dammit! I want it to be over. I don't like any of this. It's frightening. It's creepy. *'Satan rules'*…" Barnes shivered. "I'm a Boston cop. I've seen about everything. But I really don't like this. Thing is, I go way back in this city, but the whole history thing—I don't know what people like Vickie and Alex Maple know. I was never a historian, a professor or a writer. But you guys specialize in that kind of thing, right, Agent Rockwell? You've dealt with people who twist religion all around before, right?"

"Yes," Rocky said quietly. "I've dealt with it before."

"And this does extend beyond the city, I think," Griffin said. "But it involves the city. Barnes, we do still need your help."

"Vickie and Devin are coming in soon. Vickie is going to work with a sketch artist. I need you to support us—I need the BPD as well as the FBI to get the pictures out there."

Barnes nodded. "I can work the city," he said. "And you can do what you feel you need to do."

"We'll be heading to check out the past in Fall River first," Griffin said. "I'm going to be trying to find information from the 1800s and the 1970s, when the Ezekiel Martin quotation was used by other criminals."

"You can drive out and be back in a day," Barnes told him. "And what about Jehovah?"

"If we don't have answers by the time we're done in Fall River, we'll start investigating the areas that are farther west in the state," Griffin said.

"So you're leaving me with the city," Barnes said.

Griffin laughed softly. "Detective! If I weren't completely aware of how competent you are, I might have fallen for that line."

"Still, wish you'd be here."

"You have other FBI support, and the Boston police are some of the finest in the country," Griffin said.

"Yeah, well, now I have to worry about you out in the suburbs," Barnes told them. "May not be civilized!"

"Half of 'those guys' out in the suburbs work in the city. The others are probably too smart to do so."

Barnes chuckled softly. "Once you head farther west? Used to be farming and manufacturing. Barre was huge on providing gunpowder for the Union during the Civil War. Learned that in a trivia game. Not that I think it will help you much now."

"Probably not, but knowledge never hurts," Griffin told him.

"Well, here's something that will help you. I have a friend with the state police who lives out there in Barre. He's friends with the local cops. Good guy—I'm sending his number, and I'll text him so he expects your call. His name is Wendell Harper. He may be of help, at some point in this investigation."

"That's great!" Griffin said. "Thanks."

"I can still hope that all this…that all this is nothing. I can still hope that you took down the Satanist Smasher yesterday," Barnes said.

"Satanist Smasher?" Rocky repeated.

"So dubbed by the press," Barnes told them gravely.

"You'd have thought they could do better."

"Hey. Sadly, you can run out of good names for serial offenders."

* * *

It might have been a great deal easier for Vickie and Devin if they hadn't been on Tremont Street.

The area was filled with pedestrian traffic—schoolchildren in groups, tour companies leading their clients, men and women here and there, together, solo, in pairs. Some leaped out of the way when they saw the women running toward them, and everyone turned to stare at Vickie.

Devin was ahead of Vickie at first, but Vickie managed to catch up.

She was the first to zig and then zag when her attacker turned onto Essex, and then onto the Boston Common. The young redheaded woman ran hard, and it was all that Vickie could do to keep up with her.

The redhead hooked sideways and went streaking into the Central Burying Ground, leaping over old slate stones, tree roots and anything that seemed to be an obstruction.

It was ridiculous! The girl must have been a college sprinter—certainly on a running team of some kind somewhere!

Vickie got a glance at Devin, who was racing hard herself. Devin had made it through the rigors of training at the FBI Academy and even she was having trouble keeping up!

And then, miraculously, while attempting one of her gazelle leaps over a crooked headstone, the redhead went down.

Vickie managed to sidestep the stone.

The redhead saw her. She reached into her pocket.

"No!" Vickie cried, gasping for breath as she surged the final distance and threw herself down on the young woman. "No!"

All she could picture was what had happened with Griffin.

How he'd caught the young man...

How he'd died in front of Griffin.

Vickie caught the girl's arm; she now had something in her hand she was trying to get to her mouth.

"No, no, what is the matter with you! That is insane!" Vickie cried as she held the girl's arm back.

By then, Devin—panting and gasping for breath, as well—fell to her knees on the ground beside Vickie.

"Stop her!" Vickie cried.

Devin quickly saw the situation.

The redhead, however, was strong, and had wrestled her hand close enough to her mouth.

She dropped the pill in.

"No!" Devin cried.

"Her cheeks!" Vickie cried.

Devin caught the girl's jaw, forcing her mouth open. Much of a tiny pill remained on the redhead's tongue; Vickie plucked it off, wondering how much of it had dissolved already. The fight had gone out of the girl.

Suddenly, she began to buck and twist, going into convulsions.

Devin was already on the phone, calling for an ambulance.

"Keep her from hurting herself!" she told Vickie.

Vickie did her best, throwing her weight back on the young woman, trying to stop her flailing limbs, trying to keep her airway clear, trying to keep her from biting her tongue. Devin put down her phone and held the girl's head. Long minutes passed.

As the med techs raced through the tombstones to reach them, the girl went motionless. Her skin was red, and she was so still.

"Here, here, let me help you!" one of the EMTs said to Vickie.

Vickie stared at him blankly, and then pointed.

"It's her… I think it was cyanide."

"You're covered in blood!" the EMT said.

"No, no, it's just something thrown at me. I'm fine," she said quickly.

Vickie backed away, still on her knees, just staring at the redhead, watching as the emergency personnel went into rescue mode and listening as Devin explained what had happened—describing the pill, how quickly they had gotten it and how the redhead had reacted.

"Vickie!" Devin said.

Vickie looked up.

"The bit of pill…you still have it?"

"Yes! Yes!"

It was in her hand. She passed it over and someone took it, using a glove and quickly sealing it into a bag. Someone else rushed over, working some kind of cleaner or antibiotic over her hands. They did the same to Devin, who barely seemed to notice.

"What…what…?" she asked.

"Cyanide, some form of cyanide, but…she's alive right now. We'll get her stomach pumped, and we'll start going with a Cyanokit," the med tech told them.

"Hopefully you got most of it. What the hell happened? Why would she do such a thing? You're FBI, right?"

Devin had introduced herself as such when they had arrived.

"I'm FBI, yes."

Vickie realized that the man was staring at her. She remembered that she was covered in whatever red substance the redhead had thrown at her.

Was it blood? She didn't know. Paint? Whatever it was—was it worth this young woman's death?

She cleared her throat. "Can she live?" she asked.

"She can. It depends," he said. His coworkers already had the girl on a stretcher; an IV had been inserted in her arm.

She was quiet, though. And as still as death.

There were police on-site; Devin kept her credentials out, giving the same explanation of events over and over again.

Vickie's phone rang. She glanced at the caller ID. It was Griffin, of course.

She winced.

They'd never made it into the offices.

It was all a mess.

She found herself wishing that she'd never chased the redhead.

She wished desperately that she'd let it go.

There was just no reason that this young woman should die—just because she'd thrown something red, something that might or might not be blood, at Vickie.

She managed to answer her phone as Devin continued speaking with the police and the med techs headed out of the cemetery. The size of the crowd of onlookers continued to grow.

"Griffin?" she said.

"I was getting worried—you're not here yet."

"I think you need to come get me," she said.

"Where? What happened?"

She tried to sound just like Devin, calm, concise and yet relating important detail. "A woman on the street attacked me. She—"

"What?"

"She threw a cupful of red stuff at me. I'm not even sure what it is yet. We chased her. Oh, God, Griffin! She did what the man did! She took a pill. We got it out of her mouth, Devin and I. But the med techs took her, and they're heading to the hospital. Devin is talking to the cops. Griffin, why? In God's name, why would they do something so stupid, so horrible? It's so sad. Griffin, if I hadn't chased her. If *we* hadn't chased her…"

"What's the red stuff?"

"I don't know. We just started chasing her—"

"Is your skin burning? Does it hurt? God, Vickie! It could have some form of acid in it, whatever it is. Are first responders there?"

"EMTs. Yes, and cops, and—"

"Get yourself to the hospital," Griffin told her.

"I'm fine. I'll be right here," she said, knowing that Griffin was close, and just how quickly he could move, even in Boston, when he chose.

"No, no waiting! Get to a hospital now," he told her. "I'm hanging up—you get going. I'll meet you at the hospital."

And he did hang up.

Vickie realized that the redheaded woman was gone, hurried away from the cemetery in an ambulance.

And now, the remaining EMTs and the cops were staring at her.

"I'm fine!" she said. "Really."

"We have to get you to the hospital, too. Get some samples of whatever that is—and get it off you," an EMT said.

"Let's go," Devin told her.

"But…it isn't any kind of acid. I'd know by now!" Vickie assured Devin and the others.

"I don't think it is any kind of an acid," Devin said.

"No," an EMT agreed.

"What?"

"Can't you smell it?" Devin asked.

"Smell it?" she murmured, frowning. And then she could.

She hadn't before, because of the adrenaline running through her. Because of her focus and determination to catch the young woman.

But now she could smell the substance. Metallic and earthy.

And she could feel it soaking her clothing. Heavy and sticky.

And she knew what it was.

Blood.

And she was so very afraid…

That it was human.

5

Vickie knew that she was never going to feel clean enough—no matter what kind of a thermo-shower she was able to take at the hospital, no matter what kind of special anti-everything chemicals existed in the soap she was given.

The sticky red substance was blood.

And it was human.

On the one hand, what happened had provided authorities with an important lead.

There was a possibility that the forensic department might just find a match for that blood.

She had still been drenched in blood.

A very good thing was that the blood had been quickly tested, and by the time she'd gone through her cleansing ritual, she was relieved to learn that it was unlikely that she'd been exposed to any diseases of the blood, such as HIV, hepatitis C, malaria or other. There were still tests being done, and testing took time, but it looked as if she had been covered in the blood of a nicely healthy person.

Griffin had met them at the hospital; he'd spent his time switching between the different areas—the "containment" sector with Vickie, and to the emergency and then the intensive care unit to look over the young woman who had attacked her.

It had been stressful and frightening to Vickie, cleaning off the blood and wondering what might be in it.

Yet, all the while, she couldn't help but worry and wonder about the redheaded woman. If she had just left her alone…

Vickie was finally clean—fully sanitized, really—and dressed and ready to leave. Devin had gone to her apartment for fresh clothing for her.

Griffin came toward her; they might have been standing in a hospital hallway, but he took her tightly in his arms and held her for a minute. She clung to him, and then she eased away.

"How is the redhead?" she asked.

"She's hanging in. She's fallen into a coma. I don't pretend to know a great deal about the effects of cyanide poisoning, but the fact that she's not dead—that you got enough of the poison out that she didn't die instantly—bodes well for her. You and Devin did amazing work."

Vickie shook her head. "It was instinct, I think. Maybe not in a good way. She threw something at me—I wanted to catch her. And, of course, I felt that I had to keep up with Devin."

He smiled at that. "You two have a lot in common. She writes fun children's books and you write for adults."

"Not so fun, huh?" Vickie asked.

He laughed. "No, just more serious. Anyway, let's head to ICU, and then, well, you have to be exhausted."

"No police artists at night?" Vickie asked.

"You're up to it?"

"Up to it? There was nothing wrong with me. I had a lot of baths. I'm good to go."

"All right. Barnes is up in ICU. He'll make arrangements."

They headed to the ICU section. The redhead was behind glass, but they could join Rocky, Barnes and Devin, who were looking through the window.

The girl's color was better; she wasn't the wild, rash-riddled red she had been. She lay perfectly still, an IV in her arm, a machine at her side making a rhythmic sound, as if, with every droning pulse, it helped her breathe.

Barnes turned to look at Vickie. He was a good man; he'd become a friend, and it had meant a lot to her when he'd told her that he admired the way she had managed herself during the Undertaker case.

He shook his head. "Can't stay out of it, huh?" he asked her.

"Hey. I was minding my own business," she said.

"Actually, you were out questioning a pair of guitar-playing siblings regarding Alex's disappearance," Barnes reminded her.

"Well, according to Special Agent Lyle, this young woman approached the two of you and asked if you were Victoria Preston."

Vickie nodded. Barnes looked at Griffin. "You two should have gotten down to Virginia," he said gruffly.

"Detective," Vickie said, touching his arm. "Griffin

is an agent—he'd be called out on something no matter what."

"Very strange people might not, however, be asking for you by name," Barnes said.

And that, of course, was true.

"Vickie still wants to work with the police artist," Griffin said.

"There's a young man already here," Barnes said. He cleared his throat. "We've taken some pictures of this young lady, but since we don't know when…or if… she'll recover, we've had an artist portray her for the newspapers and the media. Hopefully, we'll be able to find out who she is." He shook his head with wonder. "It's pretty amazing that you and Special Agent Lyle were able to save her. Anyway, the artist is downstairs in one of the waiting rooms."

Vickie nodded, but she kept staring at the girl on the bed.

"Hey, we're going to keep someone guarding her, but the group of us watching her is not going to change her condition," Griffin said firmly. "Come on. Let's see the artist."

He set a hand on her shoulder and led her out of the ICU and down to the waiting room. It was empty. Griffin saw the coffee machine and prepared cups for the two of them. Vickie sat nervously and waited for him, accepting the cup of coffee as he joined her.

"It's been such a strange day!" she told him. "I can't begin to understand. Sure, Devin and I went after her, but…she hadn't done anything that would have sent her away for her whole life or anything. Why would she want to die? Or, more to the point, how could she be so willing to give it all up—to thrust that pill into her mouth? I just don't get it. I can't help but wonder what good we're doing, if trying to catch these people is causing them to commit suicide."

"First off," Griffin said, "we can't control what other people might choose to do. But it's my job to stop people who might harm others. I'm sorry as hell that I couldn't prevent Darryl Hillford putting a pill in his mouth, but I can't be sorry that I went after him."

"But...suicide!"

He sighed. "Most of us can't begin to understand something so...sad. But we are human, and humans believe all kinds of things. And we are frail. Maybe there were threats, maybe promises of grand rewards. Then there's brainwashing—the effects are real. We haven't even scratched the surface here. But we can hope that this girl lives. If she'd just thrown blood at you, run away and escaped, we might have had to wonder if it was a separate occurrence—you know, maybe an extreme critic who really hated your books."

He offered her a dry smile.

She punched him in the shoulder.

"Seriously, because of you and Devin catching her, we know that this young woman is part of the cult, whatever it may be. If she wakes up, she'll be our best lead. We may also discover something through the blood that she threw on you." He paused. "That was a lot of blood," he said quietly.

"So much that the person who supplied it is...dead?"

"I don't really know. But—"

"Agent Pryce? Ms. Preston?"

Griffin stood and Vickie leaped up.

The officer entering the room was about six feet even with brown hair, brown eyes and an easy manner.

"I'm Officer Jim Tracy." He shook hands with both of them before indicating that they should take their seats again.

"So, let's get right to it. Face shape?" he asked Vickie.

She began to describe the waitress who had used the name Audrey Benson. She was in the middle of doing so, remembering details—such as the little freckle on the young woman's upper lip—when Roxanne Greeley suddenly came to the waiting room.

She paused dramatically at the doorway, looking in. Then she saw Vickie.

"Vickie! Oh, thank God, you're all right!"

She ran in and hugged Vickie. Then she looked at Griffin, shook her head and hugged Vickie again. "Thank God! Thank God! I can't believe you were in danger again. Of course, I mean, I suppose it's your doing. Kind of like Oscar Wilde, you know. 'To lose one parent may be regarded as misfortune…to lose both seems like carelessness.' Oh, wait, I'm sorry, your parents are just fine. And I'm hoping they stay alive and healthy and all. I mean…you! Throwing yourself into danger all the time. Maybe you shouldn't, maybe you're inviting these things…wow. Sorry. I'll stop. I'm just glad you're okay. Oh, and oh!"

Roxanne finally noticed the police officer who had risen behind Griffin.

"It's okay, Roxanne," Vickie told her.

"Seriously, it's good to worry about friends," Jim Tracy said, offering Roxanne a hand.

"I'm glad you're here. Officer Tracy is doing a sketch of the waitress we had at the coffee shop the other night," Vickie said.

"Oh. Nice. Good," Roxanne said. Then she looked at Vickie again. "Why?"

"She's disappeared, too. And she was using a fake name."

"Oh…okay."

Jim Tracy showed her the sketch he'd begun.

"You're very good," Roxanne told him. "Don't you think that her face was a little thinner?" she asked Vickie.

"Yeah, maybe," Vickie agreed.

"Take a chair, please," Griffin said. Vickie glanced at him with a quick smile. He quickly rearranged chairs so that Vickie was on one side of the artist, Roxanne on the other. He stood a distance off, quietly waiting.

"Now you tell me what you remember, what you think might have been a bit different," Officer Tracy said.

"Just the bit thinner," Roxanne said. "Maybe her bangs were thicker… The rest…may I?" Roxanne asked. "Vickie does have a great eye. But I'm an artist. I'm actually making a living with my watercolors and oil paintings," she added.

"That's great!" Officer Tracy said. He flipped pages and offered Roxanne a clean sheet.

Roxanne began to sketch. In a minute, they could clearly see the face of the woman who had disappeared.

"That's her," Vickie murmured.

"Great image," Officer Tracy said.

"But your sketch is just as true to her," Roxanne said. "It's just easier because I really saw her."

"I'll take these back to the precinct, scan them and do some mash-ups and we'll have a pretty perfect image," Officer Tracy assured them. "By tomorrow morning, we'll have the lady in the bed upstairs on the news, and this disappearing, SSN-stealing waitress out there, as well."

He stood. "I'm done here. If you need anything or if you think of anything else, please call."

"Thank you," Griffin said, shaking Tracy's hand. Roxanne and Vickie thanked him, as well. As he left the waiting room, Griffin said, "I'm just going to check on our young woman in ICU. Then we'll call it quits for the night."

"We're just going to…leave?" Vickie asked.

"She's in a coma. Nothing much we can do unless she awakens," Griffin said. "Don't worry, between all the agencies, we'll have someone watching her around the clock."

"Around the clock. They watched Alex around the clock. And then they didn't. And now he's gone," she said.

Griffin hesitated, glancing at Roxanne. He moved closer to Vickie and said softly, "Don't go thinking that was Alex's blood you were wearing. You dreamed about a woman with her throat slit on an inverted cross—not a man. Not Alex."

"Let's get you guys home right away. I'll be back."

Griffin left. Roxanne glared at Vickie. "You should be really glad your folks are in England, being spared the worry! This has been all over the television. Reporters and cameras get places so fast!"

"But they couldn't have gotten today on camera!"

"Not the first part. They got you—covered in what looked like blood—being led to an ambulance. I guess one of the EMTs or cops did some talking. The reporter said that you were covered in red stuff, but he said that witnesses reported that it wasn't your blood, and they also knew that the girl had taken some kind of a capsule or pill that you and Agent Devin Lyle had gotten from her. Naturally, they're referring back to your involvement in the Undertaker case. At least there's been no mention of Alex's name so far," Roxanne told her.

"Great, just great," Vickie said.

"What was it that she threw on you? Was it actually blood? It was? Oh, God. You don't think—"

"Griffin keeps assuring me that it isn't Alex's blood," Vickie said quickly. "He's convinced that they want Alex for his mind, want him to help them find something that has been lost for decades, or something like that."

"So where are they keeping him? And where are these people coming from? That guy who killed himself because Griffin caught him attacking a woman— and now this girl! Taking a pill because she was caught throwing blood on you. Where did all the blood come from? Vickie, I'm just worried!"

"Don't be, please. I've got Griffin—"

"Thank God for that!"

"And he has close coworkers here and we're working with Detective Barnes and his department. It's all good."

Roxanne smiled. "I guess you were actually kicking ass today!"

Vickie winced. The girl swallowing a pill didn't seem much like kicking ass.

"She tripped over a tombstone."

"Because you were moving like greased lightning!" Griffin reappeared at the door.

"Come on, we'll see you home," he said, beckoning to Roxanne.

"To my door, and then you two go away. Shoo. Keep your deadly shenanigans away from me!" Roxanne said. "Sorry, kidding. No, I'm not. I'm scared again, Vickie."

"Don't be scared. Just be careful. Be extra careful. You know the ropes now, right? Well-lit places with lots of people, no super-late-night excursions," Vickie began.

"No candy from strangers. Yeah, I know the drill. I'll be cautious," Roxanne said. "And I'll keep in touch. Hey, have your talked to your mom? If she and your dad get wind of the stuff happening here with you involved, you're in for it," she warned.

"I'll write them an email tonight," Vickie promised.

"Let's get going," Griffin said.

The three of them left the hospital.

Griffin thought that he tended to be aware of the world around him—it was part and parcel of his training. Tonight, it seemed ever more important.

He understood why David Barnes had wanted to believe that it was all over. There was no way for an average citizen to prepare for a spontaneous attack when just walking down the street. And it was impossible to ask the population of Boston to just hole up in a house or apartment and never go out.

Constant fear was debilitating. It wore on the mind and the nerves and therefore, eventually, the whole of the body. Random attacks set the entire city on edge.

But now Barnes knew. Now they all knew, for a fact, that it wasn't over. And it was all connected. Alex had been attacked first, then others. Alex had disappeared. This girl had called Vickie by name, and most importantly, she'd attempted suicide in the same manner as the young man the other night.

They reached Roxanne's place, and Griffin warned Vickie to keep the car doors locked as he walked Roxanne up to her apartment, even though Vickie was in his sight line at all times. She smiled at his overprotectiveness.

With Roxanne safely in, he returned to the car and pulled out onto the road, heading the short distance from Roxanne's to Vickie's.

Vickie was thoughtful as they drove. "She was a redhead."

"Yes, definitely, a redhead. Why?"

"No reason, I guess. I just…"

"What?"

"Going back to Sunday night, when Roxanne and I were in the coffee shop looking for Alex, I thought that I saw a blonde woman—really pretty, just staring at me."

"Ah, well, maybe she admired you," Griffin said, trying to speak lightly. "I love looking at you. Let me try to get a little poetic. Eyes like emeralds, hair like a raven's wing…you're pretty beautiful yourself, you know." His left hand on the wheel, he reached out briefly with his right, drawing his knuckles down her cheek.

She caught his hand and turned to him, smiling. "Thanks. I was just thinking… I can't begin to understand or make sense of what is going on. We keep trying to come up with explanations. A guy dies the other night by his own hand, the girl today tried to die and may still die, and…"

"And?"

"I dreamed of someone dying or dead, Griffin. I thought that it was Alex calling to me, and this is absurd, yes, but I do think he's trying to reach me somehow. But Alex wasn't hurt in the dream. It was definitely a woman. I keep trying to remember details, but the cross was upside down, she was all bound to it upside down and everything was covered with blood." She shuddered suddenly. "Like I was today!"

He squeezed her hand. "You're pretty good at this, you know. Okay, so you may have been foolish and rash, as well, chasing after the woman who threw the blood at you."

"Devin went after her."

"Devin went through the academy. She's armed."

"Yeah, well, there's that. But I was pretty sure the redhead wasn't armed with more than that cup. It's just so sad, Griffin. And so confusing!"

He agreed.

When they walked into the apartment, she turned in his arms immediately. It had been a ridiculously long day, an emotional day, and he was glad that she was turning to him—rather than away. And yet she seemed keyed up and distracted.

She suddenly stepped away from him, murmuring, "I've got to take a shower."

"You were just sanitized!" he told her.

"That's the point. I need to feel like I'm not a large swab of disinfectant soap," she told him.

She turned and headed toward the bedroom.

He followed more slowly, taking off his jacket and sliding his Glock and its holster onto the bedside table. He sat on the bed and wondered if he should just walk in and join her, or give her a moment.

He smiled, thinking about the incredibly erotic way she had intended to greet him the night before.

The water was still running.

Why not? Griffin thought. He looked around the room. Maybe he simply needed a few props.

Vickie was startled to hear music playing.

After the long day—food and coffee just snatched up here and there on the run, the last hours at the hospital—she'd been zoning out under the shower when the music jolted her back to reality.

She frowned. The water was falling around her, steam rising, and she was holding a little round ball of her favorite rose soap in her hands.

Griffin had not come into the shower.

She had really at least half expected him to do so.

She rinsed quickly, stepped out, grabbed a towel and headed out of her bath and into the bedroom.

And there, of course, he was.

Returning the favor.

He looked like a million bucks, she thought, lying across the foot of the bed on an elbow, a rose in his hand, wearing nothing but a white collar and tie, and a fedora.

Rod Stewart was singing away on the radio, and as she stood there, laughing, Griffin stood and tossed off the fedora and drew her to him, pulling away her towel and dipping her low in his arms. "Laugh at me, will you?" he demanded.

She stroked his face, curled her fingers around his neck and kissed him long and hard. "Laugh at you," she said huskily. "That was fantastic. Wonderful. I really would like to see just how far it could go—the music, the tie is a nice touch…and you, well, the display of the body, the muscles…wow. Just one thing missing."

"What's that?"

She laughed softly. "Some friends at an open door!"

"You're heartless, wench. Will I never be forgiven?"

"These muscles really are great," she told him. "If you let me up a little, I can try to show my forgiveness?"

He eased her up. He lifted her and she jumped up, winding her legs around his waist. She loved the strong hot feel of his naked flesh against hers, and loved even more that he had thought to amuse her, tease her, arouse her…

Take the day away and make magic of the night.

He fell backward on the bed, bringing her down

on top of him. She found his mouth first, and then moved against him, bathing his bronzed flesh with erotic sweeps of her lips and tongue. It lasted only so long before he reached for her, tossing her underneath him and rolling with her, returning each kiss, each feathery tease and aggressive touch.

They made love.

Sighing, her head on his chest, Vickie slept deliciously. He was the greatest nectar ever for her, body and soul, and he could exhaust her, as well, and let her sleep...

So peacefully at first.

And then the dream came again.

She heard her name being called. She wasn't certain—she just *couldn't* be certain—but she thought that it might be Alex's voice.

She rose and found her robe and slipped into it. She started down the path that seemed to be forming in front of her.

She paused, and looked back.

She could see Griffin, splayed out on the bed, his body a glorious bronze against the opaque white of the sheets. She wanted to go back to him, crawl into his arms, or at the least wake him and make him come with her.

"Vickie, Vickie, Vickie...please!"

She turned. The note of anguish in the voice calling to her was so very deep.

And, so, she walked the path again.

She could hear running water, see a deeply forested region before her. Pine needles lay upon the path where she walked. She could smell the very richness of the earth.

The voice kept calling to her.

She stepped out of the path and into a clearing.

And there it was—the inverted cross. There was something else there—a table, a large tiled concrete table. People were gathered in the clearing. They were chanting lowly.

"Vickie, Vickie, Vickie, please!"

Chanting and swaying.

She heard a scream. The cross wasn't empty. The woman was upon it, upside down. Her throat was slit, and blood…

Blood was rushing, along the trail, into the water beyond the clearing, and it was becoming a tidal wave.

She turned to run. She screamed and screamed and screamed…

She awoke; Griffin was there, holding her, shaking her lightly, trying to get her to focus on him.

She stared up at him.

He stared back at her with his incredible dark eyes, empathy heavy within them.

"The nightmare again?" he asked her softly.

She nodded.

"I'm so sorry!" he said. "They are—such dreams—common with *us*. People who speak with the dead. But, Vickie, though I know how bad they are, I also know just how important it can be to remember them. Someone is trying to reach you. Maybe it's Alex, maybe it's someone else or maybe there's more than one person." He smiled gently, holding her even closer. "None of us has answers. Really. You'd think that we—who speak with the souls or remnants of our humanity, ghosts, what have you—would have more answers. We just don't. Maybe we're not meant to."

She cupped his face with her hand. "You're... I really do love you," she murmured. "You're so...special."

He winced, laughed and kissed her fingers. "Special. Great."

"I didn't mean...oh! Never mind. You are kind of *special* in a fedora!"

They both jumped when there was a knock at her door.

"What the hell?"

"Someone must have left the front door to the building open again—hate to say it, even after the Undertaker thing, none of my neighbors ever remember to lock the outer door," Vickie said, jumping up.

"Seven-thirty," Griffin muttered, looking at the clock on her nightstand. He stood and slipped into a T-shirt and shorts and headed out. Vickie found her robe and did the same.

Griffin reached the door first and looked through the peephole. He opened the door right away, just as Vickie came up behind him.

Rocky and Devin were there.

"What's happened?" Griffin asked them. He didn't mention the hour.

And he wouldn't, Vickie thought. He knew that if they were there, it was for a reason.

"Barnes called you and then me," Rocky said. "They—"

He broke off, staring at Griffin, and frowning.

"What's on your neck?" he asked Griffin.

"What? Ah!" Griffin reached up and grabbed at the white collar he'd donned for his pose the night before.

Vickie hadn't thought it was possible for someone so tanned to blush so fiercely.

"Oh," Rocky said.

"Ohhhh!" Devin said, and laughed.

"Hey!" Griffin protested.

"Don't tease, it's all great," Devin said. She punched Rocky in the arm. "No judgment. Go for it, you guys! Anyway, we're not here to ruin your sex lives."

"Well, you're not doing a bad job!" Griffin said.

"You didn't ruin anything. We just woke up," Vickie said. She couldn't help giggling, and then they were all really laughing, and it felt good—their lives could be far too filled with tension. Yes, it was good, even if a little embarrassing.

"Do we know who the young lady is in the hospital? Our redheaded Jane Doe?" Griffin asked.

"No," Rocky said, "but they've found a match for the blood that was thrown on Vickie."

"A match? Already? You mean, they have more than O positive…a real *match* to someone?" Griffin asked.

Rocky nodded. "Helena Matthews, twenty-five. She was reported missing six weeks ago. The police took a DNA sample from her toothbrush during their initial search for her. She left work in Bristol, Rhode Island, to meet up with friends for an annual dinner in Fall River."

"She never came home," Devin finished quietly.

6

"All right, there might have been several relevant events in the past," Griffin said, reading from the file in his hand.

Rocky was driving the Bureau-issued SUV; Griffin was in the back with Vickie, his computer on his lap and a pile of printed files on top of them. Since Rocky and Devin had arrived at Vickie's door, they'd been in a flurry of activity: packing a few things since they'd stay overnight, and making arrangements.

Griffin had spent more than an hour all told on the phone, first with David Barnes, and then with Jackson Crow and Adam Harrison down in Virginia. Barnes was going to see that Boston was flooded with a likeness of the woman who had claimed to be Audrey Benson, along with a recent picture of Helena Matthews, garnered from her missing-person file.

She was—*or had been*, Griffin reluctantly thought—beautiful. Her face was serene, heart-shaped and lovely. She'd had warm amber eyes and long honey-blond hair. In her picture, she was smiling.

Agents in the Virginia office would be doing record searches, seeking anything they could find, and, of course, clearing paths for Griffin and the others with other law enforcement agencies.

"First off," Griffin continued, "Fall River was once alive and prosperous with textile mills. When the mills began to go down, it was just a quiet town. Then, of course, you had the 'trial of the century,' that being the trial of Lizzie Borden in 1893, as in 'Lizzie Borden took an ax and gave her mother forty whacks. When she saw what she had done, she gave her father forty-one.' Except, of course, she was acquitted, and to this day, historians and scholars argue over whether she did or didn't do it. Me, I think she did. But hey, they were living in Victorian days, so they missed a heck of a lot of evidence, and then, even if they'd had it, they didn't have the science we do today."

"In reality, she gave her *stepmother* nineteen whacks and her father ten or eleven. It was overkill either way, if, in fact, she was guilty. I tend to agree that she was," Vickie said, looking out the window as they drove.

Griffin smiled. Of course Vickie would know accurate details. She was a walking encyclopedia when it came to the state of Massachusetts.

"You also know about the murders in the 1970s, then, right?" he asked.

"Vickie is probably better than our files!" Devin said, turning to smile at Vickie.

"I know about them, yes—so tragic," she said. "There was a sudden rise in prostitution in the area. Teenagers, mostly. The first murdered girl was found with her head so beaten and bruised that it was difficult for authorities to make an identification. The second girl was found in the same condition. The third girl, Karen Marsden, had actually come in to the authorities—and then decided against testifying. Only her skull was ever found. At the trial, her 'ritual' beheading was graphically described. She had spoken against a man named Carl Drew, and his girlfriend, Robin Murphy, gave testimony against him and others in Marsden's murder. Anyway, I don't think it was really a case of Satanism as much as it was a method of manipulation, though the killings are known as Satanic cult murders. Robin Murphy might have been just seventeen, but she knew how to rule the ranks. She used all kinds of manipulation against people—including Satanic rituals out in the forest, and, of course, encouraging and helping in murders to carry out so-called rites."

She broke off and looked over at Griffin. "The words that people have been using in Boston, written on Alex and other victims, weren't linked to that group. In fact, what happened with the Drew/Murphy cult was so horrible and so terrifying that the other murder was barely noted. A single body was found by the river that didn't fit the other murders, and those words—*Hell's afire and Satan rules*, etc.—were found in the dirt by the river. The victim was a young woman named Sheena Petrie. The killing was accredited by many to the cult, but it was different. Her throat had been slit. She had recently left her husband, who had an alibi. It was never solved. Oh, and in the other case, both Drew and Murphy were convicted, but Murphy is eligible for patrol now and goes before the board every so often."

"That's terrifying," Devin said. "Though, honestly? The number of really chilling murderers who might be out on parole at any time is damned scary."

"True," Griffin murmured. "Today we're meeting with Robert Merton and Cole Magruder first—the detectives on our current missing-person case of Helena Matthews. Detective Merton is from Bristol, Rhode Island, and Detective Magruder has been working the case from the Fall River side of it. This afternoon, we're going to see one of the detectives on the 1970s case. Then tonight, we're meeting with a man named Syd Smith. He was almost drawn in years ago. But more important than that, he was also the one who came upon the writing in the ground—and the body of Sheena Petrie."

"So, we're definitely staying in Fall River tonight?" Vickie asked.

"Yep," Rocky said.

"Where are we staying?" Vickie asked.

"Where *are* we staying?" Griffin asked. Their sleeping arrangements had been set up by Angela Hawkins, a coagent and Jackson's wife, back in their Virginia headquarters.

Rocky laughed softly. "The Lizzie Borden Bed and Breakfast. Where else?"

Fall River was similar to many a New England town, a little bit sleepy now, riddled with church steeples and Victorian architecture, charming, of course, and, in areas, like most cities, a little worn out by history and poverty. Vickie knew that in the days when the Plymouth Colony had found birth upon the New World shore, the area had been inhabited by the Pokanoket Wampanoag tribe of Native Americans, with their actual center across from what was now Bristol County, Massachusetts, in the Mount Hope area of Bristol, Rhode Island. The name Fall River came from the tribal language—*Quequechan*—meaning, of course, "falling river."

Textile manufacturing was long gone. Tourism definitely helped. Beside the Lizzie Borden house, the Fall River Historical Society and Oak Grove Cemetery, there was Battleship Cove, a museum that offered the largest collection of naval vessels in the country. There was also an art center, marine museum and numerous other attractions. It helped, too, that Fall River wasn't terribly far from the fantastic mansions in Newport, Rhode Island, and for those who followed the H. P. Lovecraft trail, it was a close hop, skip and jump, as well.

Their foursome met with the detectives first. The men had already befriended one another on their quest to find Helena Matthews. Cole Magruder had suggested a restaurant on Pleasant Street that excelled in Portuguese food, a large part of the Fall River population being of Portuguese descent.

Everyone shook hands all way around, before finding chairs at a circular table in the far back corner of the restaurant. It was still early and the restaurant wasn't officially opened, but Magruder's wife was the owner's niece, and so it was open for them.

"From what we discussed on the phone," Magruder— a solid man in his late thirties, Vickie thought—said, "you believe that Helena Matthews is dead. Is it at all possible that she's still alive and being held somewhere?"

Griffin chose his words carefully. "We'd like to believe that she is alive. But according to our best medical and forensic people, the amount of blood that was thrown on Vickie indicates that Miss Matthews had to have lost a tremendous amount. So much so—"

"That she couldn't possibly be alive," Detective Robert Merton finished. He was older than Magruder, grizzled, wrinkled and weary looking, as if he'd seen the bad in humanity far too long. He glanced over at Merton. "We've been afraid that she's dead since she went missing," he added. "She wasn't the type to just disappear. She was a financial analyst for a large computer company in Bristol, Rhode Island. Beloved by her coworkers. She was originally from the Boston area, I believe, but she lost her parents when she was in grade school and grew up with an aunt, now deceased, as well."

"Did you know her?" Vickie asked him.

He shook his head. "I just feel that I knew her, I guess. I spent so much time finding out about her, trying to trace her footsteps. She had a boyfriend, but he wasn't all that much help because they'd only been seeing each other a few months when she disappeared."

"And you looked into him first, I imagine," Rocky said.

Merton nodded. "He had an ironclad alibi for the entire time from the evening she left work to the morning when she didn't show up."

"What was that?" Griffin asked.

"He's military. He was offshore on a training mission. His officers—and a hundred other US Navy men—were ready to swear to his whereabouts."

"Definitely sounds ironclad to me," Devin said.

"She must have been very nice, the way you speak about her," Vickie noted.

"So we think. I tried everything from my end," Merton said, "and I started working with Detective Magruder here when we traced her last credit card charge to a gas station right over the state border on the edge of Fall River."

"I spoke with all the friends she was to have met," Magruder said. "She wasn't a saint, but she leaned toward the angelic. She didn't just give to a number of causes, she worked them. Volunteered a day each weekend at her animal shelter."

"Coordinated fundraisers with her church, working to alleviate disasters anywhere in the world," Merton told them.

"So what do we know for sure about the day she disappeared? She was on her way here to dinner. She was seen leaving work, and she made it this far, we know, because she bought gas. But her credit cards haven't been used since. And there's been no sign of her whatsoever?" Griffin asked.

"You have the files," Merton told them, shaking his head. "You know what we know. We tried all the hospitals. The morgues. Every hotel and bed-and-breakfast, inn and hostel anywhere in the region. We've had our volunteer search teams through the woods. She just disappeared. We haven't found her car—it's probably in a lake somewhere." He leaned toward Griffin. "Obviously, though, she's somewhere."

"She didn't have any reason to want to leave her current life?" Griffin asked. "That you could discover, of course. It sounds as if she liked her job and her church and her life."

The two detectives looked at one another and shook their heads.

"I've been at this nearly forty years—I'm about to retire," Merton said. "Unless every single instinct I have is on the total blink, she was a happy and well-adjusted young woman. I realize that you have a connection—through her blood being thrown at Miss Preston—that there's a cult angle you're following. But I think I could swear that Helena Matthews was as far from being a cultist as one could get. She was a member of a very open, welcoming and laid-back Congregational church. She was into giving and working. She was also fun, so her friends assured me. She was excited about her new navy guy. No trouble in her past—a sterling record in school. Valued and recognized at her workplace. I just don't see it. She didn't run off—she was taken."

They talked awhile longer. The gas station attendants had told the police that they might or might not have really seen Helena Matthews; she had apparently used her card in one of the station's pumps. She might have been a pretty blonde who was chatting with an older man as she gassed up her car, but they couldn't be sure; it had been a busy day.

Both Merton and Magruder came across as extremely sincere and hardworking cops. It was good to meet with them.

While they talked, they also indulged in a great deal of delicious Portuguese food.

At last, they had discovered all that they could from the detectives.

"I hoped we've helped some. As I'm sure you surmised, we're both going to assist you in any way that we can," Magruder said.

"Thing is, of course, we caught a missing-person case," Merton said.

"And we've been hoping and praying that she was found alive—somehow," Magruder said.

"It's not impossible," Rocky told them. "Just not... not likely, unfortunately," he finished.

"I know you guys are good cops—and it's evident you care about this case, too. But I'd like to try that gas station and speak with the attendants. We might just get something," Griffin said.

"I'd send these lady agents, if I were you," Magruder suggested.

Griffin didn't tell him that Vickie wasn't an agent. He just asked, "Why's that?"

"Because you're looking at a pair of macho misfits, my friend. Chauvinists—but the kind who will respond to attractive women with far more enthusiasm than they will to a man," Merton said. "And hey! Trust me, please—my wife has made sure I don't have a chauvinistic bone in my body," he added dryly. "Thing is, I use whatever resources I've got when I'm looking for answers. And if that means exploiting other people's prejudices, I go with it."

"Not a problem," Devin Lyle said, smiling with only slightly suppressed amusement. "Vickie and I have no problem meeting Massachusetts rednecks at the gas station. We were all supposed to meet the retired detective where, Griffin? Maybe we can drop you off."

"Going to his home actually," Griffin said.

"Who you meeting up with?" Merton asked, easing back in his chair.

"A guy named Charlie Oakley," Griffin told him.

Merton smiled. "I know Charlie. Good cop. Well, he had been. He left the force soon after he caught the Sheena Petrie case. I guess he couldn't shake the fact that he was willing to pursue her murder—and everyone else wanted to believe that the cult kids were responsible for her death, as well. I'll take you by his place."

"You worked with him before?"

"I had just gotten my detective's badge late in the seventies," Merton said. "With everything going on back then there were task forces up the wazoo. There were things that were solved, and things that weren't solved. And the ones you never solve are the ones that haunt you." He stood up. "Ladies…sorry, agents—I don't mean to offend. You head off. I'll see to it that these fellows get to Charlie's place. You can pick them up there later. Oh—the brothers are Bruce and Bryan

Milner. Bryan has more teeth left. They're harmless in the end, but…well, hell. You'll figure it out."

"Actually, Devin is an agent, but I'm not," Vickie said, rising with the others at the table. "Feel free to call me a lady. And I don't think that Devin is all that hung up on titles," Vickie said, grinning at the man.

"Just don't call me 'sweetie' unless you're one of our friends' great-aunts from down in the Deep South. Anyway, we're out of here! Thank you both so much for your help. We'll see you gentlemen later," Devin promised.

Rocky handed her the keys.

Smiling and feeling hopeful, Vickie and Devin headed out.

Charlie Oakley was waiting for his visitors, standing down by his mailbox.

He lived in an old Victorian farmhouse on the outskirts of the town. He grinned with surprise, seeing that Robert Merton had brought them, shook hands with both Griffin and Rocky and asked them on in— offering them something to eat.

"Just ate, thanks. Excellent food," Griffin said.

"Coffee?" Charlie Oakley asked anxiously. "Robert, you can stay a few minutes?"

"Sure," Merton said.

"So, coffee?" Oakley pressed again.

"Hey, there's never too much coffee," Rocky said.

Oakley apparently wanted them to feel comfortable and at home. Maybe he wanted to feel comfortable himself.

He made their drinks. They sat around a big kitchen table with steaming mugs, but once they were seated, Oakley looked over at Detective Robert Merton as if he were gaining assurance that his words mattered. He had a headful of thick white hair and was a tall man, straight and dignified even when sitting. His awkward smile was endearing. When he started in, he was sincere, and his words were compelling.

"Everyone thought I was crazy. No, wait—I don't believe that. They wanted me to be crazy. They couldn't prove a lot—I mean, that's always part of it, right? There's what you know, and then there's what you can prove. But here's the thing. It was horrible. I mean, first, so damned sad. Beautiful teenagers, coming from all over. How the whole prostitution thing got going is just damned sad. But what it turned into, those killings…" He paused. "I saw the bodies, you see."

"Bad—I can only imagine," Griffin said.

Charlie Oakley nodded. "I guess I'm still waiting for this to be proved—somehow, some way! Thing is, you see, they knew the girls working the streets. Marsden had come to the police before she was killed. Foolish girl, what was done to her… Robin Murphy described the way Drew held her head back, severed her throat… decapitated her. It was so ugly. Only her skull was ever found. No teeth in it. Bad.

"So, you see, here's the thing. Sheena Petrie wasn't a prostitute. She was running away from a bad marriage. The guy liked to use her for a punching bag. He's long dead now, an alcoholic who died in the streets. So, she's here, and she takes up work as a chef in a restaurant.

Her coworkers said that she was all happy, seeing some kind of a mystery man, a guy who was a real gentleman. Only, none of them ever saw the guy. Now, to me, she's found dead in the river so don't you think the guy would have come forward? Nope. Never heard of him, and while the cult members denied anything to do with the murder of Sheena Petrie, there she was, dead in the river. And there, in the dirt, was written those words. 'Hell's afire and Satan rules, the witches, they were real. The time has come, the rites to read, the flesh, 'twas born to heal. Yes, Satan is coming!' Yeah, I've memorized the saying. It's been stuck in my head forever. Did all kinds of research—learned about Ezekiel Martin and his sick cult. Thing is, I just don't believe that Sheena died because of the cult. And where she was found, those words were left for her. Oh, and the teenagers and young adults involved in the cult murders? In my mind, nowhere near sophisticated enough to pull off the absolute disappearance of Sheena Petrie, or the writing in the ground. I believe, in my heart, that there is someone nice and sophisticated out there who did kill her. And, Agents, I don't think it would be so farfetched to think that person was just learning back then, and may still be out there—somewhere. Why not? 'Satan is coming!'"

Bryan Milner was the one who still had most of his teeth left!

So here he was, Vickie thought, watching the man who first came out of the station, wiping his fingers with an oil rag, when they parked and started to exit the car.

"Afternoon, ladies!" he greeted them. "What can I do for you? I am delighted to serve in any capacity whatsoever. Our gas is self-serve, but of course we're here. Oil change, engine trouble. Why, I promise you, I can oil anything at all into fine, purrrrr-ing condition!"

Vickie glanced at Devin. Since Bryan seemed to be staring at Vickie, Devin made a quick gagging motion with her fingers and mouth. Vickie tried not to smirk.

"Hello, and thank you," she said sweetly. "Actually, at the moment, everything is running just fine. But we could use your help."

"We're looking for a friend," Devin added. "And we would love help with that!"

The man gave them a shiny smile. "Sure!" he said helpfully.

"I know that the police already came by," Devin said. "Our friend's name is Helena Matthews. She's a very pretty woman, a tall slim blonde. She was here the day that she disappeared."

"That's what the cops said. Thing is, we were pretty damned busy that day."

"But surely you would have been out here to help such a lady—if you had seen her."

"Like I told the cops, I might have seen her. But she seemed to be with a man," he said.

"Did you know him?" Vickie asked.

Bryan Milner shook his head.

"No, Bruce and I were both in the station—bunch of people buying candy and drinks and what-not. And, you know, you gotta keep your eyes open in a place like this. People stealing right and left! But..."

"But?" Vickie pressed gently.

"But," he admitted, "we both noticed her." He hesitated again. He cleared his throat. "I hope you find your friend. To be honest, Bruce and me were kind of doing our business-argue over who should go out, and then we saw the man. Figured she was with someone. We weren't going to be able to get a few good words in or nothing. So we didn't go out."

"What about the man?" Devin asked.

"Never seen him before," Bryan Milner said.

"So, he wasn't from around here? I'm thinking you're pretty good at knowing who is and who isn't from around here, right?"

"Hey, this isn't a Podunk town!" he said indignantly. "What are you, from Boston? Think that's the only city in Massachusetts?"

Devin glanced at Vickie, amused. "Not me. I'm from Salem."

"One of those witches, huh?"

"Well, you just never do know, do you?" Devin said teasingly. "So, please, we do really appreciate everything that you're telling us. Can you describe the man for us? Was he young or old? How was he dressed?"

Milner shrugged. "Not too tall, not too big. Not short, neither."

"So about five-ten or so?" Vickie asked.

"Yeah, maybe, maybe a little taller."

"Young or old?" Devin asked.

"Like medium," Bryan said.

"Medium?" Vickie repeated, glancing at Devin. "Is that like middle-aged?"

"Fifty, maybe. Or late forties. Or sixty. That's medium!" Milner said.

"T-shirt, jeans, suit?"

Bryan thought about that a few minutes. "Think it was a suit or a jacket of some kind. I don't really remember."

"And you don't know if they were together or not? If they drove up together—or if they met at the pumps?" Vickie asked.

"No idea. No idea at all," Bryan said. "Hey, I told you. People steal things. You have to keep an eagle eye on folks in the store. Now, I appreciate a beauty, but I also appreciate making my living here, you know? It's Bruce and me. We're the workforce."

"That's understandable," Devin said. "But let me ask you just one more question."

Bryan suddenly pointed at her. "You're the law. You're some kind of cop."

"I'm really not a cop," Devin said, offering him a sweet smile. "Please, we understand. You were busy. You don't know if they came together or met at the pump. Did they leave together?"

Again he was thoughtful—puzzled, as if he was trying to pull up the images in his memory.

"I don't think so," he said at last.

They both thanked him and headed back for the car.

"Hey!" he called after them.

They turned back and waited.

"It was some kind of a gray jacket. Like a snooty

gray jacket. Yeah, and he had a scarf, too—it was a snooty scarf. You could just tell."

Vickie and Devin glanced at one another. They both shouted out their thanks; it was sincere.

Bryan gave them a smile—which had most of a mouthful of teeth. "Glad to help!"

Griffin was glad to see that Vickie and Devin seemed to have done well on their trek out to speak with the guys at the gas station.

When they arrived at Charlie Oakley's place, he insisted they come in for coffee, too.

Coffee seemed to be the retired detective's icebreaker. And both Vickie and Devin were very sweet and polite with the man. They obliged.

Griffin was glad. He was getting the sense that Charlie Oakley felt his memories and opinions were undervalued. Vickie and Devin—by not being determined to hurry off—seemed to validate the man, and he appeared to be happy and gratified. Griffin knew that a little extra time and attention now just might help them in the future.

It was also the right and decent way to treat the man.

So, as they all settled in, he asked, "How did it go?"

They summarized their conversation with Bryan, how he'd seen a man talking with Helena at the pumps, and how, just when they were leaving, he remembered what the man had been wearing.

Detective Merton grunted. "See? At least they remembered that she talked to a man when they spoke with you," he said.

"Yes, and we only spoke with Bryan. Seems they run a busy place. They have to be careful. People are mostly all thieves, you know? They have to watch all the time. It was very busy the day that Helena was there. But one of them would have taken the honor of flirting with her—if she hadn't been talking to a man already," Vickie said.

"Way more than they gave us!" Merton said.

"You know, of course," Rocky pointed out, "that this man could have been anyone, and he could have simply been saying, 'Hello, nice weather we're having.'"

"Yes, that's true. But now we know that he was 'medium' in age and size, dignified and a 'snooty' dresser. At least his scarf was snooty. But hey, sometimes those boys call it as they see it," Merton said.

"It's something," Griffin said. He stood, and the others rose, as well. They began the all-around goodbye handshakes, and then headed out.

"Of course, if you think of anything…" Griffin said as they were leaving.

"You'll get a call, absolutely," Charlie Oakley told them.

"You know that Magruder and I are also available in any capacity you need, at any time," Merton told Griffin. "By the way, where are you staying?"

"The Lizzie Borden Bed and Breakfast."

"Oh, yeah?" Merton asked, grinning. "Are you planning on a séance or something this evening?"

"No. I've stayed before, and love the place and the manager," Devin said. "Our director and his wife have stayed several times, too. No séances."

"I think they're usually trying to contact Lizzie— maybe get a confession out of her," Rocky said. "Or maybe Andrew or Abby Borden. We're looking for other answers."

"I've never stayed," Vickie said. "It will be interesting."

"Hey, it's a nice bed for the night. Sure, some people are into gruesome history, but the house is also just beautifully kept," Charlie Oakley told them.

"We're planning on meeting up with Syd Smith, who has been a guide there and worked at the history museum, too. He's popping in to join us tomorrow. You just never know," Griffin said.

"Nope, you never know just who may say what and when that may help," Charlie Oakley agreed. "I know Syd. He was the one who had to call it in when he found Sheena's body. Anyway, it may be late in the game, but I know that Sheena Petrie was the victim of a killer who was never caught. Even if it's been a lot of years, well, I'd love to see someone pay. That poor woman. At the very least, and no matter how late, she deserves justice."

Griffin nodded, meeting the older man's eyes.

"I agree, sir," he assured him. "It's never too late for justice."

7

"The home is a Greek Revival house, erected in 1845," Devin said to Vickie. "Lee Ann, the manager here, has done an incredible job of restoring the house to the appearance it had during the time of the murders."

They had just parked at the Lizzie Borden house; Griffin and Rocky were waiting in the small parking lot with the car while she and Devin checked in at the small building in back—a reproduction of the barn that had once stood at the same spot.

"So, have you ever encountered Lizzie here?" Vickie asked. She realized that it would be a crazy question for most people, but in their case, she wasn't teasing in the least.

But Devin shook her head. "No. And I don't believe I ever will. First, as we know, not everyone dead remains on earth as a spirit. Lizzie hated this house—she desperately wanted to live somewhere more in fitting with what she considered her position in life to be. I sincerely doubt she'd come back here. Of course, Abby and Andrew Borden died horribly, which might well mean that they would hang about. But no, when we've come, we've usually done so on a trip from Virginia to Salem, just as a nice stopover. I simply love Lee Ann, and I love the house."

"How on earth did you become so involved with this house?" Vickie asked, both amused and intrigued. She knew the story of the murders, of course. No child grew up in the state of Massachusetts without hearing the rhyme about Lizzie Borden taking up her ax. And she knew that the house where the crimes had occurred was a popular destination as a bed-and-breakfast and as a museum, as well.

She was just somewhat surprised that Devin—who had Auntie Mina, her own resident ghost—would be so drawn to a "haunted" house.

Devin laughed softly. "Actually, we have other friends from Salem who are agents now—Jenna Duffy and Sam Hall. Jenna was the one who brought me here first. She was with the Krewe before Sam, who was an attorney. Anyway, she and Sam both believe that studying the past helps us with the present. And, of course, unsolved cases usually captivate us the most. Think about it—everyone is fascinated by Jack the Ripper. Yet how many people have heard of Herman Mudgett, for instance? Mudgett killed dozens of people during the Chicago Exposition, but he was caught. The mysteries that remain are what compel us. Many wouldn't be mysteries these days, with the forensic science we've accrued. But we can't help but wonder what the truth is."

"Do you think the theories we've heard today could be the truth? That someone killed Sheena Petrie years ago—and that same someone has Helena Matthews now?" Vickie asked.

"Certainly possible," Devin said.

Lee Ann was in the office in the reproduction "barn" building in the back along with one of her clerks. She greeted Devin with a hug, and was pleased to meet Vickie. She joined them outside so that she could welcome Rocky back and meet Griffin, as well, apologizing that she didn't have the entire house for them, but Angela had called from Virginia to book rooms for them pretty much last minute.

"But my other guests are upstairs in the attic and in the Abby and Andrew Borden rooms," Lee Ann told them. "You have the girls' area to yourselves, front of the house." She smiled at Vickie and Griffin and explained. "The house is still in two sections, just as it was when the Borden family lived here. The front stairs lead to what we call the John V. Morse room—the guest room where Abby was murdered—and the Emma and Lizzie Borden rooms. The other rooms are accessed by the back stairs, which we'll go through now," she told them.

The house was both beautifully—and eerily—back to the way it had been when the murders of Abby and Andrew Borden had taken place in 1892. A period couch exactly like that on which Andrew Borden had lain sat exactly where the original had when Andrew Borden had died.

In the dining room, replicas of the couple's skulls were in a handsome cabinet.

The place was also squeaky clean, Vickie thought.

It was truly beautifully restored—besides being an intriguing destination for crime buffs and "ghost hunters."

Vickie and Griffin took the John V. Morse room and Devin and Rocky headed through the next doorway at the top of the stairs, the one that led to the connecting rooms that had once been Lizzie's and Emma's rooms. Emma had once had the larger, but Lizzie had wanted it for herself, Vickie learned. Emma was older; she was always taking care of Lizzie.

The John V. Morse room offered a crime scene photo of Abby Borden lying dead on the floor at the side of the bed.

"Nice," Griffin noted.

Vickie grinned. "Interesting," she said.

They had barely brought their bags in before Griffin's phone rang. He spoke briefly, and then hit the End button on his phone.

"Syd Smith, our next interview," he told her.

"And?"

"He's ready to meet us. Since tours are over and the other guests are out at dinner, we're going to talk down in the dining room."

"When?"

"Now."

Five minutes later they were gathered around the table in the dining room.

Mr. Smith was the epitome of an elder scholar; he was wearing a casual gray suit and had a full head of silver hair, blue eyes and a strong face, creased by time and—probably, Vickie thought—by his ability to smile quickly.

However, as they sat, and he talked, the story he told them was sad, and he still seemed touched by the death he described, even if it had occurred years and years before.

"I met Sheena Petrie when she came here," he said. "She'd managed to get away from her husband. He was an alcoholic, and when she first arrived, looking for work, she was using a lot of makeup to cover the bruises on her face. She'd already filed for divorce. She'd really just picked up and left."

"Did you know her husband?" Griffin asked. "We spoke with Charlie Oakley today, and he said that the guy was in the drunk tank the night Sheena was killed."

"Yep. Sure. I met him. He was in town. First, he came looking for her. Then, when her body was found, he was questioned. But the night she was killed, he did have that airtight alibi," Syd said. "He had been arrested for public indecency—he was falling over drunk and peeing into the back of a truck instead of the facilities at a gas station."

"But she had been seeing someone else?"

Syd hesitated. "I met Sheena when I was eating at Mac's Place on Main," he said. "The restaurant is long gone now—though I hear Mac is doing just fine out in Arizona or somewhere. He had hired Sheena on as one of his chefs. She was a wonderful cook—she knew just what spices and herbs were needed to elevate whatever she was making. I think her background was Irish, but she could do up some mean Italian dishes. Anyway, I complimented her lasagna one night. She came out of the kitchen to talk with me. She was interested in the history and lore of Fall River. Oh, and she was a huge fan of Lovecraft, and she—unlike many, many people," he said apologetically, "loved to hear me talk. We were really good friends."

"Good friends as in lovers?" Devin asked.

"My dear, I can honestly tell you now—which, of course, I wouldn't have done thirty years ago—that our being lovers was just not in the cards. I'm a gay man who had a wonderful partner for twenty-five years. I just lost him a few years back."

"It sounds like you were a good friend for Sheena to have," Vickie said.

He grinned. "We became close. I was working for a couple of different historical societies and museums back then. Total nerd, I suppose I would have been called." He turned to Vickie. "I understand you write history books," he said.

"Yes."

"You and I must talk! I mean…on other matters."

"So, she was seeing someone before she died, right?" Griffin asked.

Syd looked at him, nodding.

"But you don't know who?" Griffin persisted.

Syd sighed deeply. "That I didn't persist in meeting him is something that I've never forgiven myself for! She was so hesitant. She told me he was a gentleman. He was kind and soft-spoken. She was careful, of course, because, although she had signed the papers, her husband had come to town, trying to get her back. She had a restraining order out on him, but still… I think she was trying to keep that ugliness away from her new life. So she had promised that she and her 'new man' would go to dinner very soon with Hank and I—Hank Vidal, my longtime partner. She knew all about me, of course, and accepted everything long before it was politically correct to do so. But we never did get to dinner." He hesitated. "I found her when I was out with Ipswich—a little Jack Russell I had at the time. She'd been left on the riverbank. She was naked, and her throat had been slit. And on the embankment, right beside the place where her soaked body had been dragged up, were those words." He paused, shaking his head. "Words that were used by Ezekiel Martin—a crazy ex-Puritan from way back who made up his own pretty damned evil kind of religion. And words with a previous history right here, in Fall River."

"I've read a great deal about Ezekiel Martin," Vickie said. "He was basically rebuffed by Puritan society. They refused to allow him to become a minister. So, he started his own congregation, moved people westward and then twisted a totally rigid and repressive ethic into something else entirely. And, it sounds to me, as if the woman he became so obsessed with wanted nothing to do with him. He managed to kill her, as if she was some kind of sacrifice to the devil. The good thing, as I see it, is that Charles II was back on the throne of England and his men did come in and give Ezekiel his comeuppance."

"Yes, Ezekiel's reign of terror indeed came to an end. But here, years later—in 1804, to be exact—his words were used for murder once again. The place wasn't even called Fall River at the time—it had been named Troy. And the records on what happened were horribly sketchy because there was still a lot of wilderness around here and…well, I believe that it was one of those cases that horrified everyone, and they wanted to deny what they saw. Anyway, people began to hear strange noises coming from the woods. Like always, so it seems, the poor and the riffraff of society began to disappear. And then a body popped up on the riverbank. There were no arrests. Nothing was ever written down in official records. There were no newspaper reports of what happened. The locals wanted to pretend that it had *never* happened. Some undesirable parties had merely stopped by their woods, and surely had moved on. Bury the girl—that was what they had to do. The only way any of it is remembered is because of oral history—and what we've gleaned from a few personal diaries of the day. Massachusetts didn't want to admit to anything more that smacked of witchcraft, the persecution of witchcraft or—God forbid—of Satanism."

"Well," Griffin murmured, "at least we know that no one involved in 1804 is active in any way now."

"You're talking about the attacks in Boston?" Syd asked.

"Yes," Griffin said.

Syd nodded thoughtfully. "Been watching the news today. They've been doing a good job, showing pictures of women who are being sought by the police. A brunette, a redhead and a blonde." He hesitated, and then reached into a satchel he'd brought. He produced an old book—a very old book, Vickie noted, certainly a collector's item.

He glanced at her, as if reading her mind. "It's a

diary from 1820. Quite fine, bound in soft leather. I saved nearly a year to buy it!"

"Very nice," Vickie said.

"But here's what I want you to see."

Syd flipped open a page. Amid the faded writing, there was a sketch. It was of a blonde woman lying on the earth, posed almost as Botticelli's Venus, the way her long hair covered her nakedness.

But she was obviously dead.

A line across her neck indicated her throat had been slit.

It was a disturbing sketch, done with an effort at taste.

"Hmm," Devin murmured.

What was most disturbing were the similarities the woman in the sketch had to the picture of Helena Matthews that had gone out through media outlets that morning.

"Well, there is certainly a resemblance there," Griffin said flatly.

Vickie was quiet. Both pictures bore a strong likeness to the blonde woman she had seen watching her when she had gone to meet Alex at the coffee shop.

Had that woman been dead? Was she Helena Matthews? Or, like this woman in the sketch, did she just bear a tremendous resemblance to her—and to Sheena Petrie, who had been found dead here, also on the banks of a river?

"Yep," Syd said. "I've been watching the news. I couldn't help but note that this woman and Helena definitely share features. The heart-shaped face, the cheekbones, the long blond hair. Well, I guess lots of people have long blond hair, but seeing the picture of Helena on the news today and having this, and, of course, having known Sheena…"

"Sheena, I take it, had a heart-shaped face and long blond hair, as well?" Vickie asked.

"Her face was more of an oval, but…" He broke off and shrugged. "I remember the Ted Bundy case. The girls didn't look as if they were Xerox copies of one another, but they were a definite type—long dark hair, young…and usually sweet and kind, since he used the lure of needing help to kidnap them to murder them at his leisure."

They were all still for a moment.

"Well, there is no way that a killer from 1804 was around again in the 1970s," Griffin said flatly. "But our killer now—assuming that Helena is dead," he said softly, "could be the same man who attacked and killed Sheena in the 1970s."

"God help us, though, wouldn't he have been caught by now?" Syd asked. "I mean, I've read a lot, and you see all the TV shows with the forensics and all… Murderers like that either keep killing, or get locked up, or die."

"He may not be a serial killer—as we know serial killers," Griffin said.

"What does that mean?" Vickie asked, frowning.

"He may have a different motive that keeps his desire to kill in check. Or he may have kept killing through the years—and gotten away with it," Rocky explained.

There was an unhappy silence around the table.

"I hope I've helped," Syd said.

"Tremendously," Griffin said. "Thank you. We'd love

to believe that Helena Matthews is still alive—and it's possible that she is alive. But she remains missing, and her blood was in the hands of a young woman in a coma now. We keep hoping that she'll come to, that she'll give us some answers. As of now…well, we're lucky she's hanging on. We're determined to find out what is going on. One of Vickie's friends is missing, as well."

"Here's the thing," Syd said. "When the cult was active here, people kind of knew that there was something. I mean, it's not like this was a crime-free place, ever. We had the mills and some rough characters. You still have gangs, and you have alcohol and drugs. But the police were aware of the prostitution ring in the late 1970s, heading into 1980. I swear, I think that someone must know something. Cult members flock together, right? That's what makes them cult members. We don't seem to have anything like that going on now."

"They haven't found anything in Boston, either," Vickie said.

"Helena Matthews's trail ends here—at a gas station owned by a couple of small-minded brothers," Devin said. "Her blood was in Boston. But it doesn't mean that she is here or in Boston, not anymore, and she might not have been in Boston herself, ever."

"Just her blood!" Vickie said.

"Yes, just her blood," Griffin murmured.

Alex Maple jumped and swallowed hard.

Just as he did every time someone came to the door to the little windowless cell where they were keeping him.

It didn't help that the door had a god-awful screech to it every time it opened. As if it was screaming, crying out in agony.

It was a door.

An inanimate object.

This time, the figure that arrived in a red cloak and ridiculous cylindrical hat and mask was carrying a pile of books. Not books—tomes. They appeared to be ancient—very, very old leather-bound books. The kind Alex usually loved and appreciated.

They were placed reverently on the end of his cot.

"We're missing something," the figure said.

"Missing what?"

"A key word, a key phrase. Part of the rite, the ceremony. There's much I know, much I learned. Ezekiel knew, and I believe he did it. Satan did touch the earth. But Ezekiel wasn't strong enough. He let his belief slip when there was a threat about. Still, he knew the words. They are there. They are in the words of those who followed him. You will find them."

Alex started to laugh. It was just so ridiculous.

The figure leaned back. "Really. You find this humorous?"

"I just…"

Alex fell silent.

"Bright boy, yes. You've figured out that if you don't read every word in these books and decipher what it is that I need, I'll just kill you. You figured out that it's incredibly important that I find you necessary. Bright boy, bright, bright, boy. Except I do know, of course, that you think it's all impossible. That means that you'd really better work your ass off, right, bright boy?"

Alex looked at him and nodded fervently.

"And, by the way, I need to know exactly how and where to find Jehovah. The location is in those books somewhere, too."

He went out.

Closing the door behind him.

It shrieked and groaned in agony.

As if it echoed the terror in Alex's heart.

Devin and Rocky had taken the tour many times, so they sat it out, just waiting until the nighttime tour had passed through their rooms, then closing the door and calling it quits for the night.

Griffin and Vickie took the tour.

Vickie was surprised that her mind could focus on the things that had happened during the late nineteenth century—and those that had not. She saw Griffin shake his head slightly now and then—horrified by the restraints put on police officers of the time.

It had been a hot summer. Abby Borden was Lizzie's stepmother, not her birth mother. Andrew was actually very well off, but frugal with his money. There were theories that Andrew might have been a pedophile, abusing his young daughters—but their guide didn't believe that. He thought that Lizzie had just been so repressed that she had snapped and lost it—killed her stepmother, and then, in another burst of fury, killed her father, as well. But there were enough doubts that could be planted in the heads of the jury. The girls' uncle, John V. Morse, had stayed in the house the night before—in fact, it was where Abby had received the death blows, right where Griffin and Vickie were sleeping. He'd had a miraculous memory of his whereabouts when it came to an alibi, down to the numbers on the streetcar, names and precise times. Perhaps his memory had been too good.

And perhaps the biggest blow—other than the lack of forensic evidence—was the fact that other ax murders—unsolved—had taken place not far away.

Vickie thought that law enforcement and the people of Fall River at the time must have wanted to believe that someone else, other than a respectable young woman, had committed the murders.

Just as, it seemed, law enforcement and the people of Fall River had wanted to believe that, despite the differences in the modus operandi, Sheena Petrie had been killed by the occultists in town at the time, the same people who had chopped others to ribbons.

Smoke screens, she thought.

As they traveled the house, the guide pointed out the various period clothing on the several headless mannequins about the house. Some of the clothing was vintage. The dress on the mannequin in the John V. Morse room had been worn by the actress Elizabeth Montgomery in a dramatization of the murders.

Vickie found the clothing intriguing.

She found the headless mannequins eerie.

Eventually, the tour ended. A neighbor "medium" carried out a séance. Griffin wanted to observe; Vickie agreed, and sat with him across the room. They both watched and waited, glancing at each other now and then with a secret smile. Despite the medium's assertions, there were no ghosts about.

Out in the music room or front parlor, Vickie smiled as she noticed the music on the piano.

"You Can't Chop Your Poppa Up in Massachusetts" was actually a piece of sheet music.

Eventually, they went to bed for the night. As Griffin closed the door to their room, Vickie asked him, "Do you think we've gotten anywhere? It seems to me that the more we know, the farther away we get. Could the man who killed Sheena Petrie thirty-plus years ago somehow be responsible for the disappearance—and more than possible death—of Helena Matthews? And why take Alex Maple?"

"They're all pieces, Vickie. They're like pieces in a giant jigsaw, and they will start to come together," he told her. "Once we recognize the pattern."

"Griffin, there's something about the women all looking alike. Do you remember me telling you that a blonde woman was watching me the night we went to the café to meet Alex? Griffin, I think she was there looking for Alex, too. Or maybe she was looking for me because she knew that Alex had been taken. I think that she was dead. I think that she was one of these beautiful women with long blond hair, and that she is trying to reach us, trying to help."

"It's more than possible. Let's hope that she does find you," Griffin said. He stroked her hair. "Whatever is going on, Vickie, I honestly believe that Alex was taken because of his knowledge of history—and

I'm concerned that you're in danger because of yours. You need to be with one of us at all times until this case is solved."

"I wasn't physically attacked, Griffin. Our Jane Doe threw blood on me. She hasn't come to yet, has she?"

"No. Barnes said that they're hopeful. And, Vickie, they threw human blood on you—that may have been someone's sick idea of a warning."

"Yes, I know. I'll be careful. I'll be with you, Devin or Rocky at all times, promise." She shivered slightly. "Definitely."

"Great," Griffin murmured, pulling her closer. "So, here we are. Trying to catch a murderer—lying in a room where a tremendously brutal murder took place. And there could be a ghost—one we don't already know—trying to find you."

Vickie laughed softly. "Quit it! Or I'm going to have to get up, turn on every light I can find in the house and gather up the headless mannequins and start a bonfire."

"I think that would be considered really rude behavior by a guest!" Griffin teased.

Vickie lay in his arms, smiling, eyes open, wondering if she could sleep in that house. She lay just feet from where Abby Borden had been viciously murdered, where she had lain facedown in her own blood.

But it had been a long day that had come after other long days, and she found that she quickly drifted off.

If she'd been going to dream, she should have dreamed about one of the poor blonde women—victims of the cultist killers.

She did not.

She dreamed of the mannequins.

The mannequin in the Elizabeth Montgomery gown was standing before her. She was beckoning to her, with her arms, of course, since she had no head.

She was trying to get Vickie to rise, to follow her.

Vickie couldn't seem to help herself; she slipped out of bed. It was warm, but she reached for her light silk robe and followed the mannequin.

Out in the upstairs hall, other mannequins were waiting. They beckoned her downstairs. She walked through the girls' entry to the parlor where Andrew had been killed—and where he had lain through the night following his death, since the autopsies had taken place in the house.

Andrew lay there in her dream; Abby, she knew, was on the table in the dining room.

Andrew suddenly sat up. His head was a ruined mess, and he was missing one eye. "Misdirection." He shook his head sadly. "Misdirection. It works every time."

She turned away from him. From where she stood, she could see through to the dining room. Abby was on the table, but she wasn't moving.

Syd was sitting in a chair, just as he had been earlier. "The pictures are so alike," he said. "Ted Bundy had a type."

She felt a tap on her shoulder. She turned slowly, afraid that the headless mannequin was trying to summon her to move on.

It wasn't a mannequin. It was no one.

And suddenly, she wasn't in the bed-and-breakfast

at all anymore. She was standing in the forest. She could hear the rush of water.

And someone calling her name.

"Vickie, Vickie, please, please, please..."

She was following the path through the trees, dread filling her because she knew where it would take her.

She came to the clearing. She could still hear the whisper in her ear.

"Vickie, Vickie, Vickie, please."

Then the scream. The scream that seemed to rip through the air and the trees and even the water that rushed by, bloodred.

And there was the inverted cross, and the woman hanging upside down, her throat slit.

She'd never really recognized the woman as the blonde who had looked for her in the coffee shop because she hadn't been able to see...

That her hair had been blond. It was so drenched in blood that the color was impossible to ascertain.

And still...

She couldn't tell if the woman was Helena Matthews, or one of the poor victims who had died so many years ago.

Vickie didn't want to walk toward the cross; she knew that she had to. If she was ever going to see what she needed to see, she had to keep going.

She could feel the blood; it was all over her.

She walked closer and she saw the dirt of the clearing between her and the cross, with the water to their side. There was something etched in the dirt; it was difficult to read.

Then the blood began to fill the letters, and she could read them easily.

Hell's afire and Satan rules, the witches, they were real. The time has come, the rites to read, the flesh, 'twas born to heal. Yes, Satan is coming!

The blood filled the letters, and then they began to burn.

Light. Brightness.

Vickie woke with a start.

She blinked hard. Yes, light. Faint light peeked through the drapes.

At her side, Griffin stirred; he was always aware when she woke, so it seemed. But then, he slept in a way that seemed to allow him to waken at the slightest noise, even the least change in the light.

The mannequin...

The mannequin was right where it had been when they had gone to sleep.

Griffin rose, looking at her, a frown instantly furrowing his brow.

"She's in the woods, somewhere, Griffin. Helena Matthews is. Or she was killed in the woods, or she's going to be killed in the woods. I'm not sure if Helena is dead or not. But I know that I'm seeing one of the victims. I keep hearing her, or seeing her, or...oh, God, Griffin! Is there really a possibility that Helena Matthews is still alive?"

Griffin quickly sat up and took her into his arms, smoothing back her hair.

"You had the nightmare again?" he asked her.

She nodded.

"Tell me about it."

"The mannequins led me around the house," she said, waiting for him to crack a smile, to laugh at her.

He didn't.

"And then?"

She described the dream—the house, the woods, the cross and the blood.

"What else?" Griffin prompted again when she paused, still in the grip of the memory.

"This time, I saw a patch of earth. And it was dug out with letters, and I couldn't see them until the blood filled them…"

"Let me guess. 'Hell's afire and Satan rules…'"

"Amazing," Vickie said lightly. "You guessed it just right."

He was silent for a minute.

"And then?" he pressed.

"I woke up," she said, and added softly, "And you made me feel sane."

He cupped her head and pulled her against him. "You are sane. The dreams are telling us something. We need to find those woods. There are an awful lot of woods in Massachusetts. I'm not sure what it means, but I think it's all connected. And if we find the connection, we'll be closer to the truth and Alex—and Helena Matthews, alive or dead," he said softly. "We'll go pick up Charlie Oakley. We'll get him to take us to the place by the river where they found the words in the late 1970s, or actually 1980, I think it was. Maybe there's still something out there to be found."

He touched her cheeks gently. "We share the bath with the Lizzie and Emma rooms—I'm thinking we ought to hop in the shower before Rocky and Devin. Then we can all head down to the breakfast room for some johnnycakes. I'll call Barnes, find out if there were any results from the images of Audrey Benson and Helena Matthews and our red-haired Jane Doe in the media."

"It's a plan," Vickie said gravely. "Except…"

"Except?"

"Maybe I'll just have coffee."

"The breakfasts here are known to be pretty good."

"I'm sure they are. I just dream very vividly—quite graphically, you know."

"And?"

"Autopsy. Dining room table!" she said.

He grinned.

"Coffee, it is. And not to worry. We'll certainly find a Dunkin' Donuts close enough!"

Vickie smiled and hopped out of bed and dug through her little overnight bag for her clothing and toiletries.

She rose and headed into the bathroom just ahead of Griffin.

He followed. She smiled and quickly turned on the shower, stepping in ahead of him.

When she looked down, she saw that dirt was spilling down the drain.

This time, it was real.

And this time, it didn't seem to go away.

It had come from her feet. And it was real.

8

Devin and Rocky enjoyed the breakfast at the Lizzie Borden house along with the other overnight visitors who sat together in the dining room. Vickie just had a cup of coffee; she was seated in the corner of the room.

She'd spent a good twenty minutes on the phone with her parents. They had just gotten used to the fact that Vickie intended to move to Virginia with Griffin, and they were understandably upset that Vickie was again involved in everything going on.

She'd given Griffin a thumbs-up sign, however. She'd managed to say something to keep her parents in Europe.

Now, she was listening and engaging in the conversations that raged around the friendly crowd gathered in the dining room.

"Lizzie did do it!" a girl said.

"Don't be silly, it was a conspiracy. Her uncle was in on it," her boyfriend noted, nodding as if he'd completely solved the mystery.

Griffin grinned at Vickie and indicated that he was stepping outside.

"The phones have been ringing crazy off the hook here," Detective David Barnes told Griffin over the phone. "I can't tell you how many people called in with Audrey Benson sightings. I'd say at least a hundred of the coffee shop patrons have called in. They all saw her, naturally. The problem is that not a single call has led to anything. Not one caller knows where she lives or where she is now."

"She's run," Griffin said. "She's wherever they took Helena Matthews."

"You think she's still in Massachusetts?"

"I do. Where in Massachusetts, I don't know. But I do think that it goes back to the Puritan days, to Ezekiel Martin, and the words he originally wrote in the earth. I believe it's important that whatever is supposed to happen takes place in the original colony. Whether we have a crazy person or a manipulator, I think that all the history behind the 'Satan is coming' mantra of Ezekiel Martin is of tremendous importance," Griffin said. "I have a hard time accepting the fact that someone may really think that a few enchantments will bring Satan to earth, but we've seen a lot of strange concepts that rule men's minds. You have your copies of all the reports we acquired from Merton, Magruder and Oakley, right?"

"Came through clearly this morning, thank you. Oh, and we've had tech working around the clock on Alex Maple's cell phone. At first, they lost the trail right where he was taken. The phone had been turned off. But the cell provider was on notice and they called through this morning. Apparently, Alex had some kind of an alarm system set to remind him when he had scheduled consultations with his students. The phone was set to go on, even if he'd powered it off. It didn't last long, but they did get a ping."

"It wasn't over here, in this area, was it?" Griffin asked hopefully.

"No, sorry. Somewhere in western Massachusetts. I'll have something more for you on that soon," Barnes said.

"Jehovah," Griffin said.

"Jehovah doesn't exist anymore," Barnes said.

"Not as it once did, no. But the land is still there."

"The cell was probably tossed," Barnes said. "But when I have an exact location, I'll get it to you. Naturally, my guys are still working all the angles."

"Yeah, thanks. What about the picture of Helena? Did the calls generate anything on Helena?"

"Some, yes, of course, just not as many. None of them helpful—and not many of them real, either. Not in the opinion of our people working the lines. You know, someone saw her in this club or that club, and most of the sightings occurred after the blood was thrown at Vickie."

"What about our Jane Doe in the hospital?"

"Nothing yet. You know that I'll call you the minute we have a lead, or the minute she wakes up."

"Thanks," Griffin said.

"We're on it. We'll keep pressing."

They finished their conversation, and Griffin put

a call through to Jackson at headquarters; there was nothing new learned on that end.

"Pursue it until you find the truth," Jackson told him.

"Will do," Griffin said quietly.

He headed back inside. Conversations about Lizzie Borden's guilt or innocence were still going on, but breakfast was over.

They weren't going to stay another night; Griffin was pretty sure that they'd gotten what they could from Fall River. But they had an appointment with Charlie Oakley to go out to the site where Sheena Petrie's body had been found. They had records; they'd had their conversations with the people involved. And if Alex Maple's phone had been found in the west of the state, it was time to return to Boston and check out what leads had been generated by the pictures in the media, and then to head out to Jehovah—or, as best as had ever been fathomed, where Jehovah had been.

By ten o'clock, they were checking out and ready to head out, and they were due to pick up Charlie Oakley at eleven.

"We found out in conversation this morning that Sheena Petrie is buried in Oak Grove Cemetery. She's not far from the Borden graves. I thought we might stop by," Vickie said.

"Not a bad idea," Griffin determined. He was driving now; Rocky and Devin were pouring over files in the back seat. "Has anyone had a sense of anything?" Griffin asked pointedly.

"No," Devin said.

"No. Which isn't a bad thing, is it?" Vickie asked. "I mean, I'm sorry, it always seems so sad when someone is lingering years after a horrible event."

Griffin nodded, smiling at her. "But then," he reminded her, "you have those incredible souls like Dylan Ballantine. He's strong, he stays to help."

"He saved my life," Vickie agreed. "And he and Darlene...love after death. Very nice, I...guess?"

"The cemetery is quite pretty, anyway," Devin told them. "And, Vickie, I know you love the history in cemeteries. This one is lovely and intriguing."

The cemetery *was* beautiful. Griffin drove through gates that informed them they had reached Oak Grove.

Devin pointed out the building that once been the "ladies' comfort station" where Mr. and Mrs. Borden had received their second autopsies—and had their heads removed—prior to their burial.

"Death, and the investigation of it, has never been pretty," Griffin commented.

"Crazy, though, huh? They kept the bodies in the house all night and the first autopsies were done on them there—with Lizzie in the house!" Vickie said. "It seems...barbaric."

Griffin thought of many times he'd watched during an autopsy.

There was just no way to nicely rip up the human body.

"Maybe, years to come, there will be all new science—and they'll look back at us as barbaric," Griffin told her.

"Maybe we *are* barbaric," she murmured.

Devin knew exactly where the Borden family was

buried. They respectfully went to the graves; there, they talked about the fact that the wife of a Borden ancestor—years prior to the murders of Andrew and Abby—had gone into a terrible depression and tried to drown her children before killing herself. Two had drowned in the well; one had survived.

Naturally, the children were rumored to haunt the Borden house, next door to where their home had once been.

"So sad!" Vickie sad.

"The poor woman might have had help today. Those in the know seem to believe that she had postpartum depression. Medicine might have helped her."

"Maybe," Vickie murmured.

Griffin noticed the way that she looked out across the graveyard, as though she was expecting to see someone else there.

Vickie had discovered her own talent, curse, gift or ability when she had nearly been the victim of an escaped serial killer when she had been a teenager. The ghost of Dylan Ballantine, watching over his baby brother when Vickie was babysitting, had saved her life. And, in doing, opened a new world for her.

The world of the dead.

And now Vickie often saw the dead.

She had told him that the hundreds-of-years-old cemeteries of Boston weren't actually all that haunted, but sometimes she did come upon a lively discussion between spirits, or, now and then, an old-timer complaining about the way the world had gone.

He did, of course, know the dead himself. He'd learned to deal with it as a child.

And Devin and Rocky had their experiences, as well.

But that day, he didn't sense anything in the cemetery. He watched the others; Rocky noticed the way that he was looking at him and just shook his head.

Rocky had been a teenager, too, just about to graduate high school, when he'd heard a call in the night.

And found that a friend had been murdered, and that her cries had led him right to her.

Devin had grown up in what the neighbors had always considered to be a "witch" house, but she had actually been an adult when she had discovered what she was capable of seeing—who and what.

Vickie shielded her eyes from the sun looming above the cemetery.

She frowned and started walking.

"Vickie?" he murmured, starting after her.

Rocky caught his arm gently. He looked at his friend and fellow agent and nodded. He needed to let Vickie follow her own path.

They passed by an odd assortment of tombstones. Angels and cherubs.

The cemetery had been founded in the Victorian era; the art tended more toward the beautiful and ornate than the dire and horrible.

Vickie kept moving and they all followed at a distance, none of them seeing what she saw.

Then she stopped. She turned back to him, shaking her head.

"I don't understand. I saw…someone. Someone beautiful and blonde hurrying this way. She turned and looked at me. She was so sad! And then…she was gone. Just gone."

"Have you seen her before?" Devin asked.

"I think so. Yes. But…" Vickie said.

"But what?" Griffin asked her.

"This sounds crazy. I don't know. They all seem to be beautiful blondes with heart-shaped or oval faces. Am I seeing one woman, or more than one woman? I don't know!"

"Look where we're standing," Rocky said.

There was a beautiful marble angel in the center of the little hillock Vickie had come to, but the graves were all different, modern; none of them were ornate.

"Read the plaque," Devin said dryly.

And they did. The angel was watching over victims. She had been purchased by the law officers of Bristol Country, Massachusetts.

A very simple grave with nothing but a name and dates lay before them.

The name upon it was Sheena Petrie.

Griffin stood a slight distance away from the others, watching the river roll by. He kept thinking about Vickie's dreams.

Water seemed very important in the dreams. A large body of water.

The river was a large body of water, of course.

And Sheena Petrie had died here.

"A long time has gone by, but there are things you

never forget," Charlie Oakley told them. They were down on the bank of the river. The highway wasn't far off; they could see bridges in the background, hear the rush of traffic from every direction. "Sheena Petrie lay right there. You can still see some of the landmarks in the crime scene photos. But if you couldn't, well, I'd know where she was found. And the writing…they've widened the highway since she was killed, but we're walking now where the words were written."

Griffin held up the crime scene photos and compared them to the landscape that they saw. He could well imagine that Charlie Oakley had been haunted all his life by the scene he had encountered.

Devin, Rocky and Vickie looked over his shoulder, studying the photos, and then the landscape.

"Even now, with the highway widened, with cars here and there," Rocky said, hunkering down where the letters had once scarred the earth, "this isn't a bad place to leave a body. The trees along the embankment are still thick in places. We're at a slope, and I think we're about a mile out of town. By night, he could easily manage all this without being seen."

"And the report says no blood," Griffin noted, looking at Charlie Oakley.

He shook his head. "She was in the water at some point, and all the blood was washed away. Whether it all washed into the water or if it was taken for…some reason, we don't know. But it wasn't in her when she was found. She was white and cold and…so white. Drained of blood. Excuse me."

Charlie Oakley walked back to the car.

Griffin watched the water. He thought of the dead. He imagined Sheena Petrie, and Helena Matthews, and nothing came to him.

He walked back to the others.

"Does anyone get anything here?" Griffin asked quietly. "A sense of her spirit, anything?"

They all looked at one another.

And then at Vickie.

"Nothing," she said softly. "But we've all talked about this. If anything of Sheena Petrie does remain, it just doesn't seem likely that she'd be here, where her life ended."

"But you saw her today," Devin said. "You did see her at the cemetery. She is here…somewhere. She's trying to help. She's been dead years now, but I think she hates seeing this happen to anyone else."

Griffin considered Devin's words. "The dream that plagues Vickie over and over again is always about a woman on an inverted cross, her throat slit," he said. "It's certainly possible that Sheena Petrie died in such a manner, but not at the hands of those young adults playing at Satanism. I think we need to seriously consider that whoever killed Sheena was just getting started back then."

There seemed to be a lot of silence during the day.

Alex had received his breakfast—a tray with cornflakes, milk, a banana and coffee—and the tray had been picked up. He had received his lunch—ham and cheese on rye with an apple—in much the same way.

Breakfast and lunch had been dropped off by a red-cloaked figure.

Breakfast and lunch had been picked up by a red-cloaked figure.

He didn't know if the same person had brought the tray and picked it up; they had both looked pretty much the same.

He knew he was supposed to be reading. Perfecting the incantation that would bring forth the devil.

It wasn't that he hadn't looked at the massive and ancient tomes brought before him.

He had; he had admired every book, awed by the preservation.

He had to admit, too, that since he was a scholar, there was a certain thrill—almost euphoric, when forgetting to panic—to be reading books that had been handwritten by Ezekiel Martin himself.

The books declared that the devil was as real as God. As he had so nearly been a minister, Ezekiel knew about God. God, however, was destined to lose out to Satan. Worshiping Satan was much better than worshipping God; Satan enjoyed the pleasures of the flesh—through his priests, of course, except at such times when he came to earth himself, and his flock was then well-rewarded.

Alex did a lot of paraphrasing in his own mind, but basically, to Ezekiel Martin, it was ridiculously obvious that Satan would win the day. God was terrified of people turning to Satan. People were terrified of other people turning to Satan. Satan wasn't terrified at all. He was amused. He didn't care if people went to

God, because he knew that he would be the supreme ruler in the end.

God had sent down His Son.

That hadn't worked out terribly well.

It was Satan's turn. And he was ready. He had whispered in the night to Ezekiel, and he was ready and waiting for the signs to be right, the ceremony to be performed. Satan had high expectations from his servants on earth; Ezekiel meant to see that they were fulfilled.

Despite his fascination, Alex began to feel a creepy sensation, as if he was being watched. He wasn't, of course—he was in his cell. A cell once meant for someone criminally insane. There was a little slot—food trays or other such materials could be passed through it—and there was a little door, head-height. Of course, it could only be opened from the outside.

But it was open.

He left his book and hurried over to the door and looked out.

She was standing there. She was tall and slim and ethereal, beautiful and blonde.

She looked like an angel.

He thought at first that she was in the hall alone. But she wasn't. A red-clad figure was at her side.

She started to fall.

The figure quickly swept her up into his arms.

There was a sudden, hard bang against his door and he jumped back; he realized that someone was just outside the door.

Watching him.

The door opened, nearly sending him flying back. He caught his balance.

The red-cloaked figure walked in. He was alone. Alex wondered if he had imagined the woman—if she had been real.

If she had been an image from the past.

"Have you already found out everything that I need to know? You're supposed to be reading," the red-clad figure told him.

"I have been reading. I'm learning quite a bit."

He couldn't see the figure's face; it was the high priest, though. The guy calling the shots. Head honcho of Satan, or whatever. Strange thing, though. He wasn't always there. Or, at the least, he didn't always come to talk to Alex. When he did, Alex somehow knew. The others…they were lackeys. This guy was the main guy.

"Curiosity killed the cat, you know," red-cloak said. "You really should watch that."

"If I weren't curious, I wouldn't be such an amazing researcher," Alex said. He was scared, so scared, in fact, that it startled him that he wanted to try to hold his own.

Idiot! he told himself. *Right or wrong, cool or coward, none of it matters if you're dead.*

And he'd already seen one headless body!

Alex, of course, had no idea what reaction he had drawn from his masked jailor. At least it wasn't fury. It might have even been amusement.

"I like you, Alex," the man said. "Since I do like you, let me warn you. Don't think you can outsmart us. There is nothing that you can do. I actually like you so much that I'm considering the fact that maybe you'll come around to where you get to live. You *should* come around," he added huskily. He threw out an arm dramatically. "Satan is coming."

"Yeah, yeah," Alex said. "'Hell's afire and witches are real.'"

Okay, now he was really an idiot. What the hell was wrong with him?

"Hey!" Alex added quickly. "Maybe he is coming. The more I read, of course, the more sense that it makes. I mean, it is his turn, right? Satan's turn, that is."

"You don't believe."

"I haven't really believed in much of anything— other than man's inhumanity to man," he said. "As you know, I'm a historian. You can't help but get a lot of that."

"And most obviously," the man said, "you were not an English major."

There was something that suddenly struck Alex as odd; he couldn't place what.

Did he know the man?

"Don't play games with me, or you will die. I know when you're lying, and when you're telling the truth. And right now, you think this is all a bunch of bunk. Well, think of it this way, Alex. Satan is coming. And he will either arrive in a streak of brimstone—or he'll enter right into my flesh and blood and bone. Either way, he'll kill you, Alex. Unless, of course, he does decide to let you live. That's all going to be in the way that you come around, and the way that you behave.

So, I'll go back to where we started. Forget the woman. She's not going to be here for you." Alex sensed his smile. "I hope you did get some reading in. We need the place, Alex—the precise place where Ezekiel had his altar. And the precise words he used in his rite. You'll have more time tomorrow. I am patient. This evening, you're not going to feel so well."

"Why?" Alex asked, moving back nervously. "I'm feeling fine."

"Oh, you're not going to hurt or feel sick or anything, just a little weak," the man said. He moved back and two of his followers entered the room. Alex felt his mouth go dry.

They grabbed him by the arms. He was leaving his little cell. He was being dragged somewhere; they were going to do something to him.

He began to scream.

No one seemed to care.

They drove back to Boston for Griffin and Rocky to head to the station and study the endless pages of material they had received since the pictures of Audrey Benson, Helena Matthews and their red-haired Jane Doe had gone out in the press.

Devin accompanied Vickie to her apartment where they found Dylan Ballantine and Darlene—once again curled up on the sofa together, enjoying a season of *The Walking Dead*.

Dylan jumped up, clearly upset.

"You really need to leave a note or something. I didn't know where you were. No one knew where you were. I even had Noah ask our parents for me, and they were oblivious—they have no idea that you're involved in anything."

"You're a ghost," Vickie said. "Dylan, I'm sorry. I didn't think to leave a note."

"I'm dead, not stupid or illiterate," he informed her, talking to her as though she was a dumb little sister.

"Dylan!" Darlene warned, rising to squeeze his hand and smile at Vickie and Devin. "He was worried. I mean…we can't be everywhere, you know. And you guys were just…well, you were gone."

"It's okay," Vickie said. She looked at Dylan. "I'm sorry. We're going to be heading out again. I'm not sure exactly where we're going."

Devin's phone rang. She answered and they all looked at her as she listened to the person at the other end, replying here and there with monosyllables.

"What's going on?" Vickie asked her.

"Okay, so, I know where we're going."

"Where?" Vickie asked.

"Barre."

"Barre, Massachusetts?" Dylan asked.

"Yes. It seems that they finally pinpointed Alex Maple's phone," she said.

"And it's in Barre?" Vickie asked, trying to keep her voice steady. They'd found Alex's phone. It could mean they were coming closer to finding Alex.

Or it could mean that her friend was dead.

"Not exactly," Devin said. "It was actually at the bottom of the Quabbin. They had state police divers go down. Barre is the closest city to the area where it was discovered."

"Toward the west," Vickie said thoughtfully. "Four towns had to be destroyed to form the Quabbin. And, I believe, if it had been standing at the time the reservoir was formed, Jehovah might have barely made the cut."

"I still don't understand," Devin said. "Where exactly is this place? It doesn't sound to me as if there is an exact location that anyone can really pinpoint."

"There are theories," Vickie said.

"But if there isn't an exact, how come? Is there an almost exact? I'm thinking that there has to be an *educated guess* exact? I think we were so inundated with the stories of the witch hysteria, we never found out enough about Ezekiel Martin. He was a known rebel, and known to commit murder—without any kind of spectral evidence coming into the mix. Now, of course, everyone knows that the so-called Salem witches weren't witches at all—and if they'd confessed to being witches instead of risking their souls with a lie as they saw it, they wouldn't have been executed. But here's the thing. Ezekiel Martin *was* a murderer. He deserved the punishment for murder. And he claimed that he could summon Satan."

"Ezekiel Martin took his own life—slit his throat—when his people panicked and started to desert him." Vickie elaborated for her. "I believe when Charles II had his men come in, he was truly weary of the restrictive bull that had cost his father his head. Okay, so Charles I did believe in the divine right of kings and was kind of an arrogant bastard, but all in all, not really such a bad one. Still, while most historians say that Charles II showed admirable constraint against the enemies who had done in his father, he wasn't exactly any man's fool. And his commander in the field, Captain Magnus Grayson, knew what Charles II's opinion of a man like Martin would have been. No doubt about it, Ezekiel Martin would have been executed, so it's not a terrible surprise that he took his own life."

"Slashed his throat," Devin said. "That's meaningful, I think. He slashed his own throat."

"Well, there's definitely a pattern. We don't really know a lot about the crime in 1804, but we do know that the saying was used, and we could reasonably presume that whoever was killed also had their throat cut," Vickie murmured.

Devin looked at Vickie unhappily. "I don't want to believe that Helena Matthews is dead—no one does. But the amount of blood that was thrown at you was… was a lot. If she had her throat slit, too, I'm afraid that it's part of the ritual being carried out."

"Then why take Alex? It's so frustrating," Vickie said.

Devin nodded and smiled slightly. "It is frustrating work—but it can be rewarding, too."

"Oh, I know! It's just that Alex became my friend when he helped me with the Undertaker case. People did die, but some did live—including me!—so I care about him, and I owe him."

"We need to come with you," Dylan said.

"Out to Barre?" Vickie asked. "But, Dylan, your family is here, in Boston."

"I spent plenty of time down in New York City with you when you were in college," Dylan reminded Vickie.

"But when Noah and your parents were in danger, it was so important that you were here," Vickie said.

"They're not in danger—you're in danger," he told Vickie. "And besides, what? I could be in danger? I could die young?" He looked at the two of them determinedly. "You haven't come across anyone else ready to help you on this, right? I mean, to be specific, anyone dead?"

Vickie glanced at Devin, who was smiling. She shook her head.

"No," Vickie admitted.

"Shocking, really. These victims should be bitter and hateful and longing for justice somewhere along the line for someone!"

"There is someone out there. I see her, and then she disappears. I think that she may be a woman whose name was Sheena Petrie. She was killed in Fall River in 1980 and the truth regarding her death was never discovered."

"I know what it's like to be adrift, a remnant left behind, lost and unable to touch the world of the living," Darlene said quietly. "We just might be able to help."

"And we're going to need two cars, anyway," Devin said.

"I guess…" Vickie murmured.

"You guess?" Dylan asked.

"I guess you're coming with us," Vickie said.

9

"**S**he's awake!" Barnes said. He hadn't even hung up his phone before he conveyed the message to Griffin and Rocky.

They'd met in Barnes's office to go over the "sightings" that had been called in on the police tip. Most of what they had received had been about Audrey Benson, or the pretend Audrey Benson.

"Wonderful waitress—the police should not be hounding her," read one message.

"You'll find her at the coffee shop," read another.

Of course, a number of people had called in about Helena Matthews; they had met her somewhere at some time doing some good deed. She was a wonderful woman. She might have been at the bowling alley in Worcester; she might have been at a shoe store in Gloucester.

"The redhead…she might be a girl I dated in high school out in Orange, Massachusetts," was another message.

They had only found a few tips that might provide

any real leads; he did, indeed, intend to follow them through.

But for the moment, the announcement that Barnes had just made was of key importance.

"Our Jane Doe? She's awakened?" Rocky asked.

"Yes, that was the hospital. She's awake, and she's stable. The doctor warned me—there's no way to tell what kind of brain damage she may have suffered. She could have total recall, or remain a Jane Doe. So far, they've asked her what her name is, and she hasn't managed an answer. But her condition could change at any time."

"Let's go see her," Griffin said.

They were at the hospital in a matter of minutes. Their Jane Doe had been transferred from a critical care unit to a room.

She still had an IV bearing fluids into her body, but she was sitting up. Her hair had been brushed and smoothed from her face. She was, however, wearing a look of tremendous anxiety.

Griffin didn't ask before he took the lead. "I'm Griffin Pryce, miss. I'm with the FBI. My friend, Rocky—Craig Rockwell—is also with the FBI. And this gentleman here is Detective David Barnes. He's with the Boston Police Department."

"What did I do?" she asked him, her face crinkling with fear and worry.

"You don't remember?" he asked her.

She shook her head, looking as if she was about to cry. "I don't remember. I don't even know…well, they said that this was Boston. That I'm in Boston."

"Yes, you're in Boston," Griffin told her. "Do you know your name?"

Again, her face crumpled, and she looked terrified, and as if she was about to burst into tears.

He took her hand and squeezed it. "It's okay," he said quietly. "It may take you some time. Do you remember anything, anything at all? You don't know your name, and you were surprised to be in Boston."

She shook her head. "I remember…a park. There were guys playing music. I was listening to songs, and I heard it again, right before…before—oh, Lord! Right before I threw the blood. The same music."

"Do you think you were taken by someone—kidnapped?"

"I don't remember that… I'm not a bad person!" she whispered.

"It's okay—we believe you."

"I just remember the park… I went to the park. I think I met a man and then…then I don't remember. But I think…in the park, and then later, I kept hearing songs. Hearing music. I love music. I mean, I think I love music."

"Then you do love music," Griffin told her gently. He glanced up. The doctor had come into the room.

Naturally, he was watching out for his patient. The law was important, but his first priority was her physical well-being.

Griffin smiled at him, trying to assure him that they would go slowly. "Think about the music you love. A lot of songs have been written for young women, you know. Using names. Of course, that's true of men's names, too, but it does seem to me that more have been written for women. Let's see, there's Roxanne, Susie, Angie, Rhiannon—Rhiannon was written about a woman, but I actually think that it was the name of a Welsh prince first. There's Lola, of course, written for a drag queen."

He drew a smile from their Jane Doe at that. She was, he thought, very young. Not even twenty, if he was any judge. She was young and scared.

So how the hell had she come to have a cupful of a missing woman's blood—and go on a mission to throw it all over Vickie?

"And, of course, there's 'A Boy Named Sue'!" she reminded him.

"Exactly. 'Adia,' 'Along Comes Mary,' 'Peggy Sue,'" Griffin said.

"Eleanor—Eleanor Rigby, the Beatles!" she told him. And then, her smile and enthusiasm faded. "'Gloria,' Laura Branigan," she said. She looked at him. "That's it. That's my name. Gloria."

"There you go," Griffin said, smiling. "Do you know your last name?"

She shook her head. Her eyes suddenly seemed sunken and her entire posture seemed to deflate.

"Thank you," Griffin said. "Thank you. Rest. It will come back to you."

She nodded and her voice was ragged and husky when she said, "I'm…afraid. It's going to be bad. I don't think—God! I didn't think that I was a bad person, but… I'm afraid of my own memories."

Griffin squeezed her hand again. "I don't believe

you are bad. I think we just need to find out who you are and what happened, and we can get you going in the right direction. We'll be back," he told her.

He, Rocky and David Barnes left the room. Barnes was shaking his head. "This just about beats everything. She seems like the sweetest little angel who ever drew breath. What the hell?"

"I don't think she's faking it in any way," Rocky said.

"I don't think so, either," Griffin agreed.

The doctor stepped out into the hallway. "Detective, agents—thank you for stopping when you did. The patient is truly distressed. You can't fake blood pressure and pulse and physical reactions to stress."

"Of course, stress can be caused by fear—a righteous fear of the law," Barnes said.

"Detective," the doctor protested. "It's a miracle that young woman is alive. Just how much brain damage she might have suffered is still to be seen."

"Yes, of course, Doctor," Rocky said. "But—"

"What they're trying to say is that it is convenient that memory loss is the evident damage she's suffering at the moment—when she attacked a woman with a vial of blood from another woman who may well be dead," Griffin explained, lifting a hand quickly when it appeared the doctor would protest. "And, of course, she could be in seriously strained condition. We don't want to cause her further stress. I'd like to let her get some rest. But then I'd like to bring in Victoria Preston—the woman our Jane Doe attacked. Would you be against her seeing Vickie?"

The doctor stared at him a moment. "I realize that we're dealing with a serious situation here. And yes, seeing the young woman she attacked might be a trigger. However, right now, our Jane Doe is fragile. If she does show signs of distress, you will have to get Miss Preston out. At least until she's been stable for several days and is completely on the road to recovery."

The doctor looked hard at the three of them.

"When you wish to speak with my patient and bring in a new catalyst, please let me know."

"Of course," Griffin told him.

The doctor didn't appear to trust them in the hallway, but since they weren't moving, he finally strode away himself.

"Barnes, we were going to head out to Barre, but I really think that we have to bring Vickie in here first," Griffin said.

"Definitely," Rocky put in.

"Agreed," David Barnes said.

"I'll have her and Devin come in. They can meet us down in the cafeteria. Jane Doe will have a half hour or so to rest," Griffin said, and he pulled out his phone as the other two nodded.

Dylan had managed to access an on-demand program on the television that was considered to be an excellent documentary on the birth of the Massachusetts Bay Colony, the Age of Enlightenment and the growth of the city of Boston in particular.

Devin was at her computer.

Vickie was at her computer, as well.

She was flying from reference to reference on the possible whereabouts of Jehovah, since every scholar from the past seemed to place it a little bit differently. She researched the flooding of the Swift River Valley in order to create the Quabbin. At the very least, she thought, she was finding where Jehovah definitely *hadn't* been. The problem in such research now was that the natural landscape had been changed so drastically. In order to see what had been, she had to keep finding pictures, maps and images of the area before the Quabbin had been created.

What had once been hills and mountains were now tiny islands.

Her phone rang as she was working. She didn't recognize the number, but it had a Boston area code and she answered.

"Vickie?" asked an unfamiliar voice.

"Yes?"

"It's Professor Hanson. Milton Hanson."

She was definitely startled.

And wary.

"Hello, Professor. How are you?"

"As worried as you are, I imagine. No sign of Alex yet, right?"

"No sign of Alex," she agreed.

"Well, I probably can't help, but I'm trying all kinds of things from my end. But I needed to ask you for a favor."

"Oh?"

"Yes, I wanted to borrow one of your father's books," he said.

"My father is in Europe, working," she said.

"Yes, and I know after that he and your mom are taking a bit of vacation—though, to be honest, I've never seen your dad do anything that was really just vacation. I tried to reach him—seems he's out in the field on something today. There's something I'd like to look up rather urgently."

"Which book is it?" Vickie asked.

"I can't remember the title exactly. It's on the arrival of the first Puritans in the colony, up to the birth of Benjamin Franklin and how he, and others of his ilk, brought a repressed people into the Age of Enlightenment. It's by Nathaniel Alden, I believe."

"I can look for it for you, Professor Hanson," she said. "But I may not find it. My dad isn't the most organized man in the world. My mom tries to keep his books in some kind of order, but—"

"Maybe you could let me into their place and help me find it," he said.

"I'm leaving town today," she said.

"I'd just need five minutes. If you let me know when you're on your way out, I can meet you," he said hopefully.

Vickie glanced up to find that Devin was watching her; she also had her phone in her hand and was looking as if it was important that they speak.

"Excuse me a moment, please," Vickie said. She muted the call.

"Professor Hanson. He wants one of my dad's books," she said, pointing at the phone.

In turn, Devin pointed at her phone and said, "Griffin—he couldn't reach you so he called my number. They want us at the hospital. Jane Doe is awake and talking. But she doesn't remember anything. Griffin thinks that she should see you."

"Okay. Okay, so…what do I tell Professor Hanson? Devin, the man is kind of creepy. He was at the coffee shop when Roxanne and I were there the other night— waiting for Alex."

"We can meet him together, then. Just tell him that you'll call him and let him know what kind of timing will work."

"Okay."

Vickie did just as Devin had suggested. Devin was already up, reaching for her bag.

"Let's go. Maybe you can get some answers. There should be an officer waiting outside for us by now."

Once they were sitting together in the back of the cruiser, Vickie turned to Devin. "Amnesia. She doesn't remember anything, huh?"

"Some things, but not about the immediate past— or where she came from actually. She knows her first name—Gloria—but not her last."

"Do you think it's true? Or do you think it's some kind of fake?" Vickie asked.

"You mean, do I think she's faking amnesia?" Devin asked.

"Yeah, it just seems convenient. Bizarre. I feel as if we're being blocked all the time. I could be crazy, too," Vickie said. "The thing is, we were about to head out to Barre, but it's almost as if we're being stopped from getting out to where things are really taking place.

And, of course, we've been talking about Jehovah since this all began. Jehovah was out there somewhere between Barre and the Quabbin, or maybe half in what is the Quabbin now."

"I just don't think this girl could have known that we were heading to Barre today. And she just came to—so she doesn't know that we were in Fall River yesterday. Could she be a fraud? Sure. But we go through a lot of training. If she was playing us, I think that Griffin or Rocky would know, or Barnes would have a sense of it. You don't get to his position in a city like Boston without having a unique talent for reading people."

"Do you really think that her seeing me will help snap her out of it?"

"You never know," Devin said. "You just never know."

They arrived at the hospital and met up with Barnes, Rocky and Griffin in the cafeteria. The three men told them about their initial encounter with "Jane Doe."

"She's very young," Griffin said.

"You can be very young—and be an excellent performer," Devin pointed out.

"Don't forget, the person pulling all the strings during the Fall River Satanic murders in the late 1970s was a seventeen-year-old girl," Vickie pointed out.

"True," Griffin agreed.

Barnes cleared his throat. "Do you feel bitter about this girl because she targeted you? I don't blame you, but it might make it hard for you to go see her. She, of course, should be grateful to you. You and Devin saved her life."

"I'm not bitter. I guess I just wanted to get out west to Barre and get closer to finding Alex," Vickie said.

"We'll get out there," Griffin assured her. "And I'm not easily taken in. But I don't want to say anything else. I don't want to color what will happen, or what your feelings will be."

"And don't worry about heading west later than you had planned," Barnes said. "This in an interagency situation. State police have already been at the Quabbin. We've kept divers searching just in case…" He broke off with a shrug.

"In case Alex is dead, and weighted down somewhere in the Quabbin?" Vickie asked.

"We all know it's a possibility that he's dead, but I can't help but believe that he's been taken for his mind—his ability to search out the past," Griffin said. "Which, actually, should be something that we focus on now, too. I keep thinking that there is some person behind this—maybe the same guy who killed Sheena Petrie thirty-plus years ago—and that he's convinced that he needs to be in the same place Ezekiel Martin was during the 1600s. I don't think that's so farfetched. So, Vickie, that throws it into your corner. You're going to have to figure out exactly where Jehovah might have been."

"That is something we were both interested in since the night he was attacked," Vickie said. "I mean, I've been trying, but people have been searching for the exact location for well over three hundred years."

Griffin leaned toward her, smiling. "Those people

haven't been *you*—desperate to find a friend," he told her. He reached for her hand and squeezed it.

"Let's go talk to this young lady," Vickie said. "With any luck, she'll solve the whole thing for us!"

No one responded to that.

No one was expecting that much luck.

Upstairs, they waited while Griffin found the young redhead's doctor.

When he was present, they went into the room. The girl had been lying on her side, just staring at the wall. Her television was on; Griffin turned it off.

"Miss," he said quietly. She turned to look at him. And then she studied Devin and Vickie, and she began to frown, as if something stirred in her memory.

Huge tears suddenly filled her eyes.

"It was wrong. I'm so sorry. It was wrong!" she said.

Vickie perched on the side of her bed, looking into her troubled eyes.

"What was wrong?" she asked.

"I threw the blood on you! I condemned you!"

"You threw a cupful of blood at me," Vickie said softly. "But I'm fine."

"You're…you're trying to ruin us. You don't understand," the girl said.

Vickie was startled. "I'm trying to ruin you?" she asked. "But I don't even know who you are."

The girl was perplexed. "It was blood, yes. I know that it was blood. And you're…you're supposed to leave us alone. I wasn't going to hurt you. You just had to know that you're supposed to leave us alone. Your place is yet to be revealed. There will be no walking the line in the new world order. You are with us or against us. But he knows about you. He knows, and he is watching and deciding what your fate will be."

Despite herself, Vickie felt a tremor of fear. "Okay," she said flatly. "First off, who is 'us'? And who the hell is *'he'*?"

The girl's face seemed to be twisted into an anguished pucker. She was fighting hard within her own mind, trying to draw out some sense.

"He is all powerful," she said. But she said it strangely, as if it was a learned mantra, and not even something she really grasped herself.

"Satan? Who the hell, indeed!" Vickie murmured, looking at Griffin.

"Gloria, you're alive because of these two women," Griffin told her quietly. "You're glad to be alive, right?"

She nodded. "I am… I know that the award for obedience is eternal pleasure, but…the punishment for disobedience is eternal flame. I didn't obey. And… I failed. I'm supposed to be dead."

"Please keep trying," Vickie said. "Who am I going to ruin, and why are you supposed to be dead?"

The girl thought.

And thought.

And began to cry, tears coming down her cheeks as if her eyes had become waterfalls.

The doctor cleared his throat and started to move forward. Vickie didn't want him to stop her, not then.

She leaned forward and told the girl, "It's going to be all right now. You're not part of the cult anymore. You're safe. You're going to have a good life. But the blood came from another woman. It was a lot of blood. Please…is she dead, do you know? And what about Alex?"

Saying the name Alex seemed to trigger something.

"Audrey had Alex. I wasn't a part of that. Alex would watch the Dearborn brother and sister, and Audrey would take care of him. It's all right. Alex is a vessel—he is a messenger. He doesn't know it, but he will show the way," the girl said.

"So, they do have Alex," Vickie said. "Why? Because he is so smart?"

"Yes, our leader, the high priest, knows that Alex is very smart, especially when it comes to the Commonwealth of Massachusetts. That is why you may and may not live—you are a speaker for the past. You have been seen. You are watched."

"Is Vickie in danger?" Griffin asked, the sound of his voice like sandpaper.

"Vickie is like Alex. She may be a messenger," Gloria said. "Messengers are exalted. They must understand that they are messengers."

She started to weep again.

"We want to help you," Vickie assured her, "and we need you to help us."

"I am so…lost!" Gloria said.

"Gloria, do you think, if you tried for a while, you could remember your last name?" Griffin asked her.

Again, her face crinkled and puckered.

Vickie didn't think that anyone could feign that much pain.

"My last name," she repeated. "I am to forget my

first. I am to become Mary—we are all Mary. We will bring Satan's children in the flesh. We will all bear fruit. And we will be rewarded."

"Rewarded by who?" Griffin burst out, sounding frustrated.

The red-haired girl looked over at him and said solemnly, "Satan, of course. The devil. He will deliver us with his children, and the earth and his power will be ours."

They were all silent for a minute. Vickie asked quietly then, "Where do you live, Gloria? You aren't Mary, and you aren't going to have Satan's child."

"I live…"

She stared blankly at Vickie. She frowned, appearing painfully confused again. "I live somewhere in the woods."

"With other people?" Devin asked.

"Yes. There are others."

"Close to Boston? Far from Boston?" Griffin asked.

"We go in the van. We may travel far. We may stay in one place as we feel that we've traveled far," the girl said. Then she buried her face in her hands again. "I'm so sorry. These are the answers that come to me. I know that they're…crazy. And… I have been with Satan. I will have Satan's child. He came to me at the ceremony. I must have his child. If we don't embrace Satan, we are for sacrifice. If we don't please Satan, we will die. We must be chosen. We must…"

She stopped again, shaking her head.

"What about the blood that was thrown at me?" Vickie asked. "Do you know who it came from?"

"Mary. We are all Mary. But she hates him. She fights him," Gloria said. She began to cry softly again. "I don't know... I don't know what's wrong with me. I don't want to die. Thank you. And I'm still so afraid and... I don't know where I was. I don't remember... I don't remember anything before the woods, before... being Mary."

"Agents? Detective Barnes?" the doctor said, pressing them to leave.

Griffin nodded. He walked over and took Gloria's hand. "It's okay. Thank you. Thank you for trying to help us."

"I need to pay for what I did!" Gloria said.

"No. You were coerced into what you did. You were naive and foolish and they twisted and warped you. But you're away from them. You need help," Vickie told her. "Please keep trying to remember." She hesitated. "Alex, he *is* alive, right?"

The girl nodded solemnly. "Alex is the way. He is the messenger."

The doctor cleared his throat. "My patient is distressed," he said firmly.

"We'll be back!" Vickie promised cheerfully.

She smiled and squeezed the girl's hand, and then rose. She felt a fierce rise of anger and tension as they headed out of Gloria's hospital room.

It was very frightening. Gloria had said that *women*—plural—died. Those who did not please Satan—or the high priest, or whoever was playing Satan in the flesh.

They had to stop what was happening, stop anyone else from dying.

And they had to find Alex. He sure as hell wasn't going to bear Satan's child, but at any point, he might just rebel, refuse to help and refuse to believe...

And then, messenger or no, he might well find that he was a sacrifice himself.

"Where do we go from here?" she asked, turning to look at Griffin as he, Devin and Rocky and Detective Barnes joined her in the hallway.

"She might remember more and more," Griffin said. "And she might not."

"Alex is being kept somewhere. There's an entire group living and surviving somewhere—and we don't know where," Vickie said, frustrated. "It seems to me that we have to find them."

"And they could all be living in plain sight," Rocky said. "Like the woman who went by Audrey Benson. They could all just be living and working somewhere— and then meeting up at an unknown destination, or a destination that changes."

"But they have a prisoner. At least one prisoner. Alex. They have to be keeping him somewhere," Vickie argued. "We have to find Jehovah."

"And you think that you can?" Barnes asked, the tone of his voice dubious.

"I can try, and I can come darned close," she said.

"What about Professor Hanson?" Devin asked.

"What about him?" Griffin asked, frowning.

"He wants to borrow one of Vickie's dad's books," Devin explained.

"Really? What book?" Griffin demanded.

"He just wants to borrow a book," Vickie said. "He's an esteemed professor—there's no reason to suspect him of anything." She smiled at Griffin, though she had to admit she was feeling suspicious of everyone out there, as well.

Yeah, why the hell did the man suddenly want to borrow one of her father's books?

Vickie gave herself a mental shake.

"You think that Milton Hanson could be involved in any way?" Detective Barnes asked. "That's just crazy."

Vickie turned to look at Barnes. "It's all crazy—the very concept of everything going on is crazy. I'm sure you're right, but we can keep an eye on him. We'll start by checking out the book he wants."

"And," Griffin said, "since Gloria mentioned music, and since Audrey isn't really Audrey, we should know if Cathy and Ron Dearborn are really Cathy and Ron Dearborn. Cathy said that they're from Athol. Can we find out if they're who they say they are?"

"And I expect you want that checked out with Milton Hanson, too?" Barnes asked, his tone on the dry side.

"Actually, yes, we should do that," Griffin said. "Anyone could be a suspect. We don't even really know what we're looking at yet. Gloria said that *women* died. We don't know who—we don't know how many. We have to find out."

"And that means finding Jehovah," Vickie said determinedly.

10

"I think that I definitely need to find the book that Milton Hanson wants and look it over first!" Vickie told Griffin.

They'd gone to her parents' apartment. While the elder Preston pair were in Europe, Vickie felt as much at home in their place as she ever had, and completely welcome.

She adored her folks—and was really close to them. She was their only child.

But she was very grateful that her parents were away, that they weren't there to fret and worry about her when it simply made them crazy and wasn't helpful to anyone.

Griffin—for all of being a solid, talented, determined and striking agent—still was uneasy around her parents. He'd saved their daughter's life *twice*, but still worried about their approval, she supposed. But, she told herself, that was because he cared. And that was okay.

Even their apartment made him nervous, it seemed.

He appeared extremely uncomfortable, just standing near her father's desk, while she plowed through the bookcases, looking for anything that might have been written by a man named Nathaniel Alden.

"Griffin!"

"What?"

"Help me."

"Vickie, this is your father's very personal space."

"Dig in."

"You're his daughter."

"There is absolutely no reason to be afraid of my father."

"I'm not afraid of your father," he assured her.

"Good."

"I'm afraid of your mother."

"Griffin!"

"Okay, okay, I'm not really afraid of your mother," he said with a sigh. "Honestly, I just feel like I'm prying and—"

"These are his books, Griffin. Not his underwear."

"All right!

He moved over to one of the endless rows of books and began searching through the titles.

"Alden, you said?"

"Nathaniel Alden. I believe the book was written during the Civil War. It's out of print now. Hard to find, which is why Hanson needs our copy. It's a study of social norms in the Massachusetts Bay Colony from the founding through the Age of Enlightenment and onward, to the abolitionist movement in Massachusetts to the Civil War and beyond, to our treatment of veterans who returned from the war, of those who were crippled by it and those who apparently went insane because of it. Remember all the stuff we learned about Dr. Boylston and the crude method of inoculations he promoted? And how Cotton Mather—not my favorite historical person!—actually pressed for the science of it, as well? They were coming into what was then the modern world. But I'm thinking that, somewhere in that book, there's something that relates back to Jehovah."

"It was written right around the Civil War—before the Quabbin was engineered."

"Yes, but even though a number of the towns are gone, there will still be landmarks that are the same, or that compare to what is there now. There's a map in this book. I can get a good map of the landscape the way it is now, and go by some of the descriptions. There's a way."

"Well, if there is, and Milton Hanson can find Jehovah, shouldn't we let him?" Griffin asked her.

"He's…smarmy. That's what my dad says. But I agree that there's something off about him."

"You think that Milton Hanson could somehow be guilty in all this?" Griffin persisted. "Smarmy—there's a big difference in trying to pick up grad students from trying to bleed them and prepare them for a Satanic sacrifice," he pointed out.

"Of course! But we don't have any suspects. Except for Audrey Benson, who has disappeared. And in the hospital we have Gloria—no last name. No one knows anything, Griffin, and the people I noted the night after

Alex was last seen were Audrey Benson, Milton Hanson and Roy and Cathy Dearborn," she said.

Griffin moved over to her position and caught her by the shoulders, then lifted her chin so that he could look earnestly into her eyes. "I know it's the hardest thing in the world, but you can't let emotion get into your mind, Vickie. There's no reason to believe the man is evil because he was in a coffee shop, because he works with Alex."

"And is—according to my dad!—smarmy."

"Lots of smarmy people aren't murderers."

"Why does he want this book—now? I don't trust anyone right now, Griffin."

"He wants to find Alex."

"I don't believe he gives two figs about Alex."

"Then maybe he wants the *prestige* of finding him—or Jehovah," Griffin said.

His phone rang and he stepped away. She could hear that it was Rocky on the other end.

Rocky and Devin had gone into the police station with David Barnes; they were going to do some research on their own.

There would be a task force meeting later. It wasn't as if a known serial killer was loose in the city, but the circumstances were bizarre enough and foreboding enough that a task force of different law enforcement agencies throughout the city, county and state—with the help of the federal government—was being formed.

He listened for a few minutes. "All right. It works for me."

Griffin slipped his phone back into his pocket. He

was staring at her with a peculiar expression. He sighed suddenly.

"Okay, so there is no record of a sister and brother with the surname of Dearborn having been born in Athol in the last fifteen to thirty-five years."

"Oh!" Vickie gasped. "Then they aren't real, either! It *is* a conspiracy! Whoever is at the helm of this knew that Alex would go to see them. The not-real waitress, Audrey Benson, drugged him and somehow made away with him Saturday night."

"Just because we can't find a record of their births doesn't mean that they're in on a conspiracy," Griffin said. "They might have lied for many reasons. They might have come to Massachusetts from Arkansas or Alaska, for all we know."

He started scanning the bookshelves again.

"They were actual musicians. They have a website and a bunch of social media pages," Vickie said.

"Yes."

"And Rocky and Devin have been looking into the sites, right?" Vickie asked.

"Yep. Bingo."

"Bingo. Of course. They're very good at what they do. They'll find their tax returns or something. They'll—"

"No—bingo, I found your book. You want a book that was written by Nathaniel Alden, right?" Griffin asked, reaching for the book and turning to hand it to her.

"That's it, yes!" she said. She smiled at him radiantly and took the book from his hands. Nathaniel

Alden had been a professor at Harvard in his day. He had been one of the finest writers on social commentary that Vickie had read. She knew, of course, that her dad admired him, too.

As, apparently, did Milton Hanson.

But she surmised it was what he had written about Ezekiel Martin that Hanson wanted.

"I don't know what he's looking for," Vickie said. "But maybe he knows that he can find it in this book. I just know that I have to have a chance to read through it before I give it to him."

"Don't you think that when he can't find it, he'll know you have it?" Griffin asked her.

"Maybe. What's he going to do? Call me a liar? I don't have to loan him a book, anyway!" she said.

The doorbell rang.

"Did you want to get that?" Vickie asked Griffin.

"Oh, no, no. This is your deception. Right or wrong, I don't know."

"If there's any chance he's involved, it is right! Please let him in?" Vickie said.

He shrugged at that, pushing firmly past her on his way to the front door. He paused and turned back.

"I'd hide it, if I were you," he said.

"Yep!" she said. She ran into her parents' room to do so.

When she emerged, Griffin had opened the door to Milton Hanson. He had evidently introduced himself.

Hanson knew about him.

"Couldn't help but hear about you—and Vickie, of

course—after that entire Undertaker terror!" Hanson said. "Vickie!"

He lifted his arms to embrace her. She forced a smile and allowed the hug, then quickly moved away.

Hanson had never been accused of anything; he'd probably never been inappropriate with a student.

He just had a manner that seemed to exude some kind of sexuality—not a good kind, but an uncomfortable one.

Objectively, he was very distinguished with his iron-gray hair and strong facial structure. He was lean and muscled, as well. Vickie was sure many people probably found him attractive.

"Nice to see you, Professor," Vickie said.

"And you're on the hunt for Alex, right?"

"Yes, sir, we are," she said.

He looked at Griffin. "Of course, that's what you do. But, Vickie, don't you think you've already given your family enough of a scare? You should really join your folks in Europe. You'll be safe there. Leave Alex to the professionals."

"But aren't you looking for Alex, too?" Vickie asked.

"In an armchair kind of way," he agreed. "Anything I discover or think that I discover—well, I'd immediately bring to the law."

She smiled sweetly, leaning against Griffin. "Well, I'm already with the law," she said lightly.

She knew she should be polite; her dad would be horrified by her lack of manners, even if he wasn't fond of Hanson.

But she didn't want him to stay.

"Come into the office. You're welcome to look through the books. We have about, what, Griffin, a half hour or so?"

"About a half hour," Griffin agreed. "Press conference tonight," he told Hanson.

"Oh? And what can you conference on exactly? A missing professor?"

"And the very real possibility of a dangerous cult somewhere in the state—a cult who may already be responsible for several deaths. Anyway, let's head to the office. We'll see if we can find your book," Griffin said.

"You wanted something by Ashcroft?" Vickie asked innocently. "I don't think we have Ashcroft. We have John Millar—his work was more European, right? He was a Scotsman. And there's William Robertson, 1783, a history of America!"

"I said Alden, Nathaniel Alden," Hanson told her, smiling.

"That's right. Do you see it?" she asked.

"No. No, I could have sworn that he had it, but... hey, I could have been wrong."

"I don't see it, either, but really, there are a number of wonderful books here."

"It's a great collection."

"Okay, well, you do know how my father loves books. I know he'd be delighted to lend any to you, just so long as you return it, of course!"

"Collectible books—of course. I hear you have your own collection."

"I do!" Vickie said. "I love fiction, as well. I have a few very early printings of Daniel Defoe—and others. My library is nothing like my dad's, but we do all love books."

Griffin was quiet, just watching, his head slightly lowered as he tried not to betray a grin.

Vickie hoped that she really appeared to be helping Hanson.

"So many books!" she murmured.

"Well, I can't find the Alden, but I will borrow this," Hanson said, sliding a book from the shelves.

It wasn't a first printing, early printing or a collectible book in any way. It had been written by Ernst James, a Boston philosopher born in the late eighteenth century who went west after the Civil War and made it to the ripe old age of ninety. It was called *The World We Make*.

Vickie couldn't remember if there was a reference to witchcraft in the book; in her mind, James had been far more interested in science and in the fact that Boston was fulfilling her destiny as a port. But he did have the insight of having been born in one century and living far into the next.

But she couldn't hide every book her father owned. And, in truth, she wanted to lend him a book. It was good to have a reason to keep an eye on him. He was *smarmy*.

"I'll let you all get going. Give your parents my regards when you speak with them, Vickie," Hanson said.

"I will," she assured him.

And finally, he was out the door.

Griffin looked at her, shaking his head, amused.

"I think he knows you have that book."

"Maybe."

"He warned you to be careful."

"And I warned him to be careful," she said.

"Let's go. We need to get to the police station."

The task force meeting went smoothly. The city and state police had been on guard since the attacks had begun. Griffin, Rocky and Barnes explained various facets of the case.

It was the pills, of course, that Darryl Hillford and Gloria last-name-as-yet-unknown had taken that were the definite tie to put it all together.

A few of the officers asked how they could be certain that the words left on the victims referring to Satan's arrival definitely connected the cases with those that had come before.

"Nothing is definite. Someone is, however, using the past as inspiration."

Police divers had been in the Quabbin. They had recovered Alex Maple's phone.

They now intended to concentrate on areas surrounding the Quabbin. They would be looking for Jehovah.

They would be looking for a hidden sanctuary where they believed Alex, and perhaps others, were being held.

Cult members might be living and working in other nearby towns. It would be a place where others might come and go.When the task force meeting was over, they met outside with reporters.

They shared much of the same information; however, they left out the fact that they were looking for Jehovah.

They warned people to watch for suspicious activity.

And then the press meeting was over, too.

"Quick Italian food?" Rocky asked. "I know of a pizza place just down the block."

They'd only planned on being a foursome, but Barnes seemed to need a diversion, and so he was quickly invited, as well.

Soon, they were down the block, promptly ordering and dining quickly on Boston's best pizza.

"I can't help but think…" Vickie said.

"What?" Griffin asked her.

She shook her head. "I keep feeling that we're being held here—that even Fall River was some kind of a distraction."

"We'll head west tomorrow," Rocky told her.

"And I'll be here," Barnes said. "So much has happened. What about Fall River? What was your feeling?"

He looked from Griffin to Rocky. Devin smiled slightly, looking down. She was a full-fledged agent. She'd gone through the academy. She and Rocky had even worked a case in Ireland on what was supposed to have been their honeymoon. But Barnes had some old-fashioned ways about him, even if he had some fine women officers on his force.

"One of the detectives working the new case is

friends with the detective who worked the old case," Griffin said.

"Oakley. Charlie Oakley. The murder shook him up so badly he left the force. Worked private security," Rocky said.

"And Helena Matthews was seen with someone at a gas station?" Barnes asked.

"Yes. By a not particularly reliable duo of brothers," Devin said.

"I was thinking... Fall River has a department, but I wonder if they'd mind if we sent an artist out to do up a likeness of the man who appeared to be with Helena. Officer Tracy was very good, I thought," Vickie said.

"I'm sure we can make it happen. But you said that they're unreliable," Barnes said, nodding toward Devin.

Devin smiled. "I say, better than nothing. We're not going into court. We're just trying to get an image, an idea."

"Even if we recognize a man—or have an image— it doesn't mean that it's the person who kidnapped her or...or worse," Barnes said.

"Still, won't hurt," Griffin said.

"So we'll make it happen," Barnes agreed.

Alex wondered at first if he was dead.

He couldn't move. He was lying down, but he wasn't on a gurney; he wasn't in the horrible room where he had first awakened—where the headless body had been huddled in the corner.

There was a bandage on his arm. He was weak, so weak...

He tried again to move. He could barely open his eyes. When he managed to do so, he realized that he was in darkness…but not complete darkness. There were shadows, and he was not alone.

He'd been drugged again.

He could remember struggling, wondering where he was being taken. Then he realized that there were too many of them…six, seven, eight people in the red robes. He'd gone limp. Then he'd been on this bed…

And then the world had faded.

He heard someone speaking to him suddenly, someone who spoke softly with a gentle, female voice.

"Rest, it's important. Please just lie there…you'll be okay. But you have to be careful. Don't rip out the bandage on your arm. Rest, lie there, be careful…"

There was someone near him. He wondered if he was having a hallucination. She was beautiful and blonde, dressed in something flowy, and she seemed to hover near him in extreme sorrow.

"Lie still, rest."

She looked up, and he realized that he could hear noise from outside.

Chanting, in Latin.

He heard a scream.

Then more and more screams…

Laughter, cries of exultation.

No more screaming.

"Lie still, rest, please. You'll be okay, but you must be careful."

Then she slipped away. The blonde woman was gone.

And he had no idea if she had been real, if she had

been the beautiful young woman he had seen at the rite he had attended...

Or if she was a result of his mind.

The mind he seemed to be losing.

He was alive! He was still alive. That was something that he had to cling to.

Rest, she had told him. Whether she was real, or a creature he created to combat his fear, she had told him to rest, to be careful.

There was a bandage on his arm. As he tried to sit up and found that he was ridiculously dizzy, he thought he knew what they had done.

They had taken his blood! He was alive...but they had taken his blood!

They really could have headed out that night; they were only talking about a drive of about an hour and a half, including traffic.

But they decided they would leave bright and early the following morning. The state police had continued to search the Quabbin, but as yet found nothing. Officers would meet up with them by the water the next morning at ten at the landing that would allow them closest access.

Rocky and Devin had taken Vickie home, but Griffin had stayed with Barnes and returned to the station, going over what they knew—and what they didn't.

Barnes had finally shaken his head in frustration and left; Griffin was about to do the same, but he hesitated, just going over it all one more time.

It had to be a matter of time before they found out

what was going on. Whoever was running this operation had to be crazy—and crazy eventually would make a mistake.

Soon enough, they had to be found out. Because there had to be a place where they were congregating, where they were carrying out their rites. And somewhere along the line, they had to find that place, especially since they were all searching for the same thing.

Jehovah.

The brutal beating attacks had started a month ago, Alex the first victim. He'd been in the hospital for over a week; his name had been on TV screens, in newspapers and magazines and constantly online. Everything had been known about Alex Maple. Most importantly, the fact that few people alive, even his superiors at his college, knew more about Massachusetts history, from colony days to commonwealth.

Then the other attacks had occurred: on the young woman in Beacon Hill, a man in Brookline and, finally, the other night, the woman in Hyde Park.

Apparently, the next step had been the kidnapping of Alex Maple, and the next night, the fourth brutal attack—and the suicide by Darryl Hillford when Griffin caught up with him. Then the blood had been thrown on Vickie, and they had found out that the blood had belonged to Helena Matthews, who had gone missing just about six weeks earlier.

Was Helena dead or alive?

Who was the woman Vickie kept seeing? Could it be poor Missy Prior, murdered centuries ago? Or a victim of the 1800s or the 1970s? Was she Sheena Petrie, found on the bank with the Satanist words written in the earth, or was she Helena?

And what the hell did Audrey Benson have to do with it? Or the singing duo who weren't really from Athol?

Was Vickie right? Could an esteemed professor have gone so deeply into history that he had traded his soul and sanity for a vision of Dante Alighieri's hell?

He had no answers.

Griffin stood in the conference room at the police station and stared at the wall that was covered with a timeline chart of the crimes associated with the attacks. Finally, he shook his head and headed back to Vickie's apartment.

Devin and Rocky had not left Vickie alone. They were in the kitchen, chatting quietly.

Vickie was in the shower. She spent as much time bathing as possible, or so it seemed to Griffin, since the "blood" attack.

He understood.

"Anything?" he asked Rocky and Devin, helping himself to the coffee someone had brewed.

It had been years since coffee had kept him awake in any way.

"We've been thinking about Vickie's dreams," Rocky said.

"And?"

"Getting nowhere, really," Devin said. "We're wondering if Helena Matthews can still be alive—with the amount of blood she apparently lost." She hesitated. "I talked to Vickie about getting a better sense of who she is seeing. It could be Missy Prior. It could be a victim from the 1800s. It could be Sheena Petrie. Or..."

"Helena," Griffin finished.

"I know it's hard, but I suggested that she kind of embrace her nightmare, since something seems to be trying to communicate through it," Devin said. "Though, actually, I wasn't sleeping when I first heard the dead."

"Nor I," Rocky said.

"So Vickie's skill is a little different."

"All right, we're out of here," Rocky said. "We'll line up to drive out about eight-thirty, right?"

"We're taking two cars?"

Devin grinned. "Your resident ghosts, Dylan and Darlene, are coming. They think we need help, and they're right. They figured they could slip in anywhere—with or without our knowing, I guess, but it's much more comfortable for them when the living aren't sitting on top of them."

"Great, see you then," Griffin said.

He saw them out, and carefully locked up.

He headed into her room and stripped down, calling out to her to let her know he was there before he headed into the shower to join her.

She was just standing there, head bowed, eyes closed, steam rising around, water sluicing over her.

She opened her eyes and looked up and smiled as he joined her.

"Hey."

"Didn't want to scare you," he said huskily.

She nodded. "Are we alone?"

"It's just us."

"Ah." She curled her arms around his neck. "So, this is cool. This really hot hard-bodied guy just walking naked into my shower."

"I haven't a thing in the world against flattery," he told her.

She shrugged, grinning, pressing against him, and bringing about instant arousal. Her hands slid down his back. "Nice buns, too."

He returned the touch. She was sleek and wet and her flesh was so hot from the water.

"Your buns aren't bad at all, either," he said.

"Oh, stop, that will go to my head," she teased.

Then he kissed her, and she kissed him, and they touched in the water while the heat of it and the steam seemed to grow all around them. They were laughing because she was a fairly tall woman and he was very tall and they weren't fitting at all in the shower.

Stepping out they paused again, drying each other. And then they looked at one another and smiled, and making love began in earnest as they made their way to the bed.

Finally, spent, they lay together. For the longest time, they didn't talk. Then Vickie rolled to him and said, "Devin suggested I try to embrace my nightmare. I'm not sure how. I mean, it's a dream, and we don't really have a lot of control over dreams."

"No, we don't."

"So, how do I embrace it?"

"You just don't fight it."

She shook her head, looking determined. "I haven't

been fighting it. Really, I can be quite tough. I think I could be as tough as Devin."

He eased back slightly, staring at her. "You mean… you'd like to apply to the academy—and the Krewe of Hunters."

She grinned. "Or just be a consultant!" she said with a laugh. "Hold me, my love," she said, easing down as close as she could to him. "Let me embrace all my inner demons."

He lay awake, stroking a finger gently along her arm.

There was nothing like trying to go to sleep; it usually meant that you never would.

But in a while he felt her ease against him. And her breathing became even and relaxed.

He didn't sleep.

He felt it when she suddenly grew tighter. Her eyes flew open.

But she didn't see him.

"Where are you, Vickie?" he asked softly.

"The woods."

"Do you know where?"

"No, but it's rich and overgrown and…there's water. And…she's there ahead of me."

"Who is there?" he asked.

"The blonde woman. She's so lovely. I'm walking with her and she's trying to warn me that the time is getting closer and closer."

"The time for what?"

"For Satan's time on earth. The high priest feels that

they are close. They are waiting for just a few more details. But...oh, God!"

"What?"

"She's...gone. It's ahead of me. The inverted cross... and there's a woman. She's hanging upside down— and...the blood. The blood is coming from her throat. There's so much of it. It's running into the river and the lake and..."

Vickie sat up abruptly. She was shaking.

Griffin quickly pulled her into his arms.

"What?" he asked softly. "What was ahead? Why is it that you stop every time you come to this point? There can't be that much blood, Vickie."

She looked at him, her eyes wide.

"I think," Vickie said softly, "I think that I stop be- cause...because it's me. I'm the woman on the inverted cross, and the blood that is flowing everywhere... Grif- fin! It's *my* blood."

11

The town of Barre was charming, Vickie thought. It was along the Mohawk Trail, part of a meandering journey that went through some of the most beautiful countryside to be found anywhere.

The town common was certainly one of the loveliest she'd ever seen and the picturesque bed-and-breakfast they had chosen—an early Victorian manor that bordered the common—was a stunning display of architecture, as well.

They were just sixty-one miles west of Boston, which, of course, made it a growing "bedroom" community. It was just about twenty miles from the city of Worcester, and part of Worcester County, making it even more of a bedroom community.

Once, it had been part of the northern area of Rutland, another area known for exceptional geography.

"Imagine this place when all the leaves change color!" Devin said, echoing thoughts Vickie hadn't voiced. "I've never been out here in the fall—actually, I've barely been out here ever."

"I'll bet it is beautiful," Vickie said, smiling. "I haven't been out here in that season, either. Then again, most of New England is seriously beautiful in fall. And nice in summer, too."

Devin laughed softly. "And hell in winter."

But it was a beautiful summer's day. They stood outside, just waiting for Griffin and Rocky to come out; they were bringing in the luggage and chatting with the sweet, elderly woman who was their hostess at the bed-and-breakfast, a place she had dubbed Common Court.

Dylan and Darlene had already taken off on foot, determined to understand the town and listen for whatever gossip they could come across.

Darlene had died by drowning, the first victim of the Undertaker. There was no way she wanted to visit the Quabbin, the Massachusetts man-made giant lake and reservoir.

Quite understandable.

The rest of them were ready to head out to meet up with the police divers.

For the general public, diving in the Quabbin was not permitted. In fact, doing so could get one arrested, facing serious charges.

The men appeared at the front door, still speaking with Mrs. McFall, their octogenarian hostess.

Vickie and Devin waved; she smiled and waved in return, and went into the house. Rocky and Griffin came down the stairs.

"Flirting, were you?" Devin teased Rocky.

"She's a fascinating woman," Griffin said. "*I* was

flirting—at least a little. She gave us something very important."

"Oh? What was that?"

"About a year or so ago, she had a guest, a young woman. She was just with her for a night, signed in as Nell Patton," Rocky said.

"When she checked out," Griffin continued, "she forgot one of her bags. It was just a little toiletries bag, but our Mrs. McFall is a good woman. She tried to reach Nell so that she could return the bag. She was never able to get in touch. Apparently, the phone number Nell gave her was written hastily—and it was missing a number. And—she has a real sign-in book, the kind with which you actually use a pen!—the address she wrote is illegible. She's going to find the old book and show it to us."

"But did she hear anything that might suggest something bad had happened to Nell?" Vickie asked.

"She spoke to Wendell Harper—Detective Barnes's friend out here with the state police," Griffin said. "He made an inquiry, but there wasn't really much he could do. There was no sign of foul play, no one knew how to find Nell…and it all just dropped."

"But you think that something bad happened to her?" Devin asked.

"I think that we're possibly looking at a number of people who are a) dead, or b) part of the cult. We know that there are followers—Darryl Hillford and our girl Gloria were definitely part of the cult. So, yes, I think this woman was part of the cult or possibly came to harm at the hands of the cult. Which, I don't know.

But Wendell Harper is one of the men who is going to meet us by the Quabbin. We'll have a chance to talk to him," Griffin said.

"Then we should go."

"This is actually an intriguing place when you're talking about people coming and going," Rocky said, once they had all slid into the car.

This time, he and Devin were in the back.

Griffin was driving; Vickie was staring ahead at the scenery.

She turned to look at Rocky. "Because tourists come through for the natural beauty, the Mohawk Trail and the Quabbin itself?"

Rocky nodded. "There's a lot of space up here."

"And an interesting situation," Vickie said. She half turned in her seat to address them all. "When they determined through whatever legal machination one actually uses that they would flood the valley and create the Quabbin, they immediately set about clearing the ground, and leveling the towns that had to be destroyed to create the reservoir," she said.

"Creepy!" Devin said.

"I thought so when I was a kid and first learned about it," Vickie said. "It was built between 1930 and 1939 and four towns were basically destroyed for it— Dana, Prescott, Greenwich and Enfield."

"She knows that," Devin said, shaking her head. "She just knows that!"

Vickie laughed. "I am good with dates and all that, but I also just looked up a lot of this stuff when I first started reading about Ezekiel Martin. Anyway, when I was a kid, I thought that they just flooded whole towns with all the buildings standing—that wasn't the case. They were torn down. You can maybe find roads and some foundations under the water, but Massachusetts did a pretty good job of tearing everything down, doing some burning…ridding it of the vestiges of dry life!" she said. "It is fascinating. There's a bunch of videos on it—one that's really good is called 'Under the Quabbin' by PBS. They can find shards of pottery, steps, bits of daily life, as in old prescription or liquor bottles or the like, but not much else."

"What did they do with the dead people?" Devin asked.

"The dead people!" Rocky said.

"Yes! Old Massachusetts towns. There had to have been a lot of dead people!" Devin said.

"Quabbin Park Cemetery," Vickie said. "It's actually very cool. Okay, I don't remember exact numbers on this, but over seventy-five hundred graves were moved from I *think* thirty-four cemeteries for eight towns—sometimes, you might not lose the town, but you might lose the cemetery! So, all those graves were moved. You can get to the entrance by Route 9, in Ware. Not far at all—we can go!" she said.

"And I do want to go there," Devin said.

"Me, too," Vickie agreed. "Of course, even if everything hadn't been disturbed—torn down and dug up—for the Quabbin, nature takes a toll, the same way progress and populations do. There are many areas where you'll see a cemetery and people basically respecting the cemetery when—in a city—it originally extended over the road, as well, and people are walking or driving over graves all the time. But I do believe that they tried very hard to see that when graveyards were going to be flooded, the known dead were reburied or reinterred."

"Connecticut has Candlewood Lake," Devin noted. "When populations need water, I suppose that we, as human beings, are incredibly lucky that engineers have long figured out how to change even the landscape around us."

"Pretty incredible. Now, if we can only figure out how to stop earthquakes and tornadoes," Rocky said, shaking his head.

"Maybe they will, eventually," Vickie murmured.

"We're coming up on the water," Griffin commented. "The water we need here, now, in Massachusetts," he added, glancing at them dryly.

Vickie could see a number of police vehicles and a large equipment van drawn up at the end of the road ahead of them. Two divers were seated at the tail end of the van; the doors were open and they sat—half in and half out—of their suits, sipping coffee as they waited.

Griffin pulled the car off the road and parked it. They all got out. As they did so, a man hailed them. "Agents! And Miss Preston, of course. I'm Wendell Harper. Nice to meet you. David Barnes spoke highly of you all. I'm hoping we solve whatever this is together!"

Wendell Harper was a big man—a very big man. He was about six foot four, and while not in the least fat, he was solidly built. With his shirtsleeves rolled up, it was easy to see that his arms were composed of a weight lifter's muscle. He was probably in his early forties with buzz-cut hair and a friendly, no-nonsense manner.

Introductions went around.

"They're going to go down in a few minutes, though I'm not expecting to find anything. We've been in the last few days, searching the area where the phone was found," Harper told them.

"But you've been expanding, right?" Vickie asked.

"Yes, we've been expanding, Miss Preston," Harper said. "Thing is, a lot of people—when they hear that towns were flooded—think that there are whole watery cities down here. Sure, things were missed here and there. We find a lot of foundations. But it's not as if there are fully standing houses—though I do understand that there is one in Candlewood Lake, not forgotten, but dropped while moving! But trees were cleared, bushes were cleared, areas were burned…not to mention that this area was as it is now almost ninety years. Water takes a toll in that kind of time."

"We're looking for…for a body that might have been there a short amount of time," Vickie said.

He nodded. "Any of you dive? I mean, you have to know what you're doing—we're not instructors. But if you do know what you're doing, we can always use more sets of eyes. May be your one and only opportunity, you know, out here on a sanctioned police dive. Of course, we have gone in before—research with professors out from Worcester and Boston. But you never know when the powers that be will sanction another such situation."

Vickie was stunned to see that Griffin, Rocky and Devin piped up immediately, all saying that they were divers.

"How?" Vickie demanded, looking at the three of them. "This is Massachusetts. You're supposed to be skiers!"

"Well, I can't ice skate to save my life," Devin told her, "but I learned to dive in Salem in high school—lobstering is a big deal for us."

"And you, too?" Vickie asked Griffin.

"Nope. I never caught a lobster," Griffin said, glancing over at Rocky.

"We had an opportunity to become certified through work," Rocky said.

"Oh, not fair!" Vickie said.

"Well, then, if this makes it any better," Harper told her, "the water is very cold—very, very cold. These guys have some major dry suits. You can use the van for your changing room, those who are coming."

"I guess I'll just be up here," Vickie said. She looked at Harper hopefully. "Unless…this isn't like Florida or a cruise, or anything? Some dive, some snorkel…"

"Why not?" Harper said. "You're going to need dive suits. Like I said, it's cold—cold as a witch's teat. Hey, it is Massachusetts, huh?"

"You just happen to be prepared for us to dive?" Griffin asked.

"Nope. Talked to Barnes for a while yesterday. You'd mentioned to him on the last case you were working together that you and a number of your associates had your dive certificates." He grinned. Proud of himself.

Kyle Perry—the diver who had found the phone—was the one to take their group in hand, handing out equipment. He introduced them to Belinda Carvel, his partner. They both appeared to be in their midthirties, helpful and determined, *and* not at all averse to having fellow divers search the water.

"It's hard as hell searching the reservoir. There's ninety-plus years of tremendous natural growth down there now. But you'll see."

Vickie fervently wished that she knew how to dive. She was grateful, however, for the suit she was given.

Especially after they got into the water.

It might be summer, but that did little to combat the initial shock of the water. Even in the suit, she could feel the brutal cold.

They'd received a bit more information on the area of the water they were searching as they headed out in the police boat.

While diving wasn't allowed, fishing was. The thing that mattered most was that the Quabbin supplied drinking water for well over two million people. That meant that it was important that it not be contaminated. Fishing was allowed from the shore, and a limited number of fishing boats were allowed out on the water, but they had to have an intact Quabbin boat seal and it had to pass inspection at the boat launch area. For those who loved nature, it was a fantasyland.

The bird-watching was fantastic, and if they were lucky, sometime while they were in the area, they would see moose, foxes, deer, porcupine, weasels, coyotes, black bear—and maybe even a wildcat. Even as he talked, Harper, who wasn't a diver and wasn't going in—*What me? I'm an old land-loving cop. I don't go freezing my ass off with the youngsters*—pointed out a loon, and then a bald eagle.

The deepest part of the Quabbin was about one hundred and fifty feet—the median about fifty. There were shallower areas—the water was about forty feet deep where they would be that day.

Not that deep, Vickie thought. She wasn't a diver, but she was a really good swimmer.

Kyle had chosen their dive location. Using a GPS system, he had them right over the spot where Alex Maple's phone had been found. Before he went over—followed by Griffin, Rocky and Devin—he told them that they'd already been over the area, and that they were now searching a bit south of where the phone had actually been found.

Belinda had stayed behind to follow Vickie into the water; apparently, they seemed to feel that she was most likely to need help.

That was okay.

She might be!

But once she had adjusted to the temperature, she was fine, though she wasn't sure at all if there was anything any of them could find, or if their time was being spent in any useful way.

Time and nature had taken their toll; the water was filled with various plants, some growing nearly to the surface.

She could see far below her, but not well, and so caught a big breath and dived down low. She noticed, just vaguely—and perhaps because she did have some distance—where a road had once been, leading to what appeared to be the remnants of a foundation.

She surfaced for air, and went back down, shooting for the depth.

She saw Griffin, Rocky and Devin ahead; they were basically walking along the bottom, led along by Kyle...searching.

She turned and kicked and went the other way. There seemed to be a long string of some kind of algae ahead of her. She surfaced for air, and went back down on the other side of the algae.

And that was went she saw it; or saw *something.*

Something that seemed to catch just a ray of the sun...and glint.

Vickie desperately wished that she knew how to dive. She surfaced for a huge gulp of air and went back down.

The others had just been in this area, she thought.

They had moved through it; they had touched the old bricks that might have once been part of a stone wall around an old farmstead.

Some seemed to have fallen. And beneath one...

Something was glinting. She made it down to the bottom... She touched it. Tugged and pulled at it. And then...it and something else came free.

Stunned, she sucked in water. Her lungs burned; she was going to die.

She shot for the surface, and came up, ripping away

her mask and snorkel, treading water furiously as she coughed and sputtered.

Belinda came up right by her.

"Hey! We'll get you on the boat—"

"No! Down. Get the others. Down there—just below." She had to stop to cough again. "Please get down there. Please! Now."

"Because—"

"There's a rotting body down there. They dislodged the bricks when they went by. Now you can see... there's a body!"

"I believe that we'd have eventually found her," Wendell Harper said, his voice a monotone. "Maybe not. Whoever—whoever put her down there did a good job. What you saw...what glinted first," he told Vickie, "was a very old and heavy anvil—probably lost by a blacksmith way back when. Nothing that can be traced to anyone today, certainly. The boat was over an area that had been a farm." He paused and cleared his throat. "She was beginning to disarticulate, so body pieces might have floated up."

They were still out by the water. Many officials had come and gone.

Most notably, of course, the medical examiner.

It had been a very long day.

The remnants of the body had been brought up. The search area had been expanded, and the immediate area searched more thoroughly.

Nothing else had been found, and the body was now with the medical examiner.

One thing that Vickie couldn't shake was the fact that—although little had been left of the flesh on the face—the skull had still been topped with a headful of long, blond hair.

Was she the woman that Vickie had been seeing?

Was she Helena Matthews?

There had been no apparition in the water; no one to take her hand and lead her to the remains.

"The skull seems to be intact. Hopefully, we'll find something from her DNA or dental records." Harper cleared his throat again. "There's no possibility of fingerprints at this point."

Of course not. There were too many creatures who lived in the water. And water itself...

"The ME reckoned that she'd been down there about two weeks," Griffin said. "Have you heard of any disappearances in the area in the last two weeks? Have you seen or heard anything?" Vickie noted that Griffin sounded frustrated.

"The Quabbin area is just short of 120,000 acres," Harper said. "Water, forests—and there's even more land surrounding the area that is privately held. We will get the state police out in force now. But...here's the thing. You had a man attacking people in Boston. The Quabbin supplies water for Boston—but this isn't Boston. You were out at Fall River. Miss Preston was attacked with blood from a woman who actually disappeared in Fall River. Professor Alex Maple disappeared from Boston. This is all over the place—there's no reason to believe that whatever is going on is actually going on here."

"Sir, we just found a body," Griffin pointed out.

"Yes, and we're looking. And now you agents are here," Harper murmured. He sighed, drumming his fingers on the table. "We're looking," he said, sounding helpless—and defensive.

"This Quabbin area is so huge, so much could go on with no one knowing," she said. "And, of course, it's possible that someone is in a nice normal house somewhere, creating a mantra of hate, causing all these things to happen, and just living in plain sight. The thing is, people are missing. And people are…dead."

"You think this woman might be Helena Matthews?" Harper asked them.

"She has the blond hair, but at this moment, it's impossible for us to know. Obviously," Griffin said.

"Well, I'm letting my people go," Harper told them. "I'm calling it a night myself. I'll get a fresh dive team out in the morning. We'll see what else…*who* else might be down there."

They bid him good-night and headed back to their car.

They all, naturally, wanted to shower.

They were quiet on the way in, all wondering if they had found Helena Matthews.

"There was no suggestion that…Alex is down there," Griffin noted softly.

"And no suggestion that he isn't," Vickie said.

"Do you think that he's dead? Or do you think that maybe, just maybe, he's working with some kind of ESP? That he is calling out to you? You don't see Alex in your dreams—you see...a blonde woman," Devin pointed out.

"Maybe," Vickie said, trying to sound hopeful.

When they reached their bed-and-breakfast, Mrs. McFall was on the porch with her other guests: a young couple from Georgia, an older man from Arizona and a fortysomething executive on break from his stressful job in New York City.

Mrs. McFall had teatime for her guests each evening, offering them tea, of course, coffee, sodas, beer or wine and little appetizers.

Mrs. McFall jumped up, and the group on the porch fell silent and waited for Vickie, Griffin, Rocky and Devin when they saw them approaching.

"They've heard something," Griffin murmured.

"It's all over the news!" Mrs. McFall called to them. "The body in the Quabbin. Of course, that's all that they're saying. They don't seem to know much. There was an interview with a police liaison, but that's all that anyone said. Oh—and that it was a woman!"

"That's all we know, too," Griffin said, coming up the steps.

"You look cold and tired, and your hair is damp," Mrs. McFall noted. She gasped. "You were in there. You were in the Quabbin. Oh! They let you in the Quabbin. It wasn't my Nell, was it? The young lady I told you about? The one who disappeared—and no one would believe had really disappeared?"

"Mrs. McFall," Griffin said gently. "We have no idea. No one knows anything yet. I'm sure there will be more information out tomorrow."

"Tea!" Vickie said, walking ahead of him. "I would love tea!"

In the next few minutes, Rocky and Devin escaped to shower. Vickie and Griffin stayed long enough to field the same questions, and to have tea and some miniscones.

Vickie was starving, she realized.

Sandwiches had been brought out to the Quabbin in the afternoon, but she hadn't been able to eat any of them.

At that time, she still couldn't get the ravaged face she had seen out of her mind.

She tried to change the subject, asking the young couple about Georgia, the younger man about Arizona and the executive about his life in New York City.

Then she and Griffin managed to get away, as well.

They showered quickly; they were both anxious to find a place for dinner. Mrs. McFall recommended a family-run place on West Street.

"It's an inn and restaurant!" she told them cheerfully. "The food is very good, but don't you all go deserting me for the inn!"

"We never would," Griffin promised her solemnly.

The restaurant was charming and friendly. They all started with lobster bisque, which was creamy, rich and delicious.

They had just finished with the meal—and were still quietly discussing the day themselves—when Griffin said, "Hey. That's our executive from the B and B over there at the end of the counter. He's watching us."

"So he is," Rocky agreed. "I noticed that he was still

on the porch, in one of the rockers, when Mrs. McFall was telling us about the local restaurants."

"You think that he's following us?" Vickie asked. She smiled; she was at the edge of the booth and she quickly slid out and stood, determined to walk over and find out.

She opted not to ask permission from the agents; if she was ever going to really be of value among them, she needed to become proactive.

She tried to remember his name; Mrs. McFall had introduced all her guests. This man's name was something unusual…

Isaac. Isaac Sherman.

"Mr. Sherman!" she said. "Nice to see you here. Frankly, it's interesting to see, as well, that you're watching us. Did you follow us here? Did you want to speak with us?"

He was, very much so, the authoritative NYC type. He might have been on vacation, but he was still wearing a button-down shirt and a blazer. He was tall and lean, with brown hair just beginning to recede.

He looked at her with surprise. She thought he was going to ask her to take him to someone with authority—someone who mattered.

He didn't. He smiled at her.

"Yes. I followed you here. I…wanted to talk to you and your friends. I mean, it's not like you came in secret. You spent the day with the police. You're FBI, right?"

"Well, they're federal agents," Vickie said. "Come over. Talk to us."

"I'd rather talk when we're out of here," he said softly.

"Back at Mrs. McFall's?"

"Over at the common," he said. "If you don't mind."

"Sure," Vickie said.

She walked back to the table and took her seat again. The other three were staring at her.

"Isaac wants to talk to us," she said.

"He does?" Griffin asked. They all watched as Isaac Sherman walked past their table and out of the restaurant.

"Over at the common. I think he wants us to be subtle," Vickie said.

Devin laughed softly. "All right. I wonder what Isaac knows?"

Griffin paid the bill and they all wandered out. They began a casual stroll back to the bed-and-breakfast.

Except that they strolled into the common instead of around it.

"There," Vickie murmured to the others.

Isaac Sherman was standing by a nineteenth-century horse trough and hay scales. The town common here had been laid out around 1795 and had, Vickie knew, through the years, seen militia practice, speeches, games, bands and more.

Thankfully, that night, all was quiet.

"Mr. Sherman!" Griffin said, heading over to him. He didn't perform any introductions; Mrs. McFall had done that earlier.

"You are FBI, right?" he asked them.

"Agents in a specialized unit, yes," Griffin told him.

"If we're meeting in secret, I believe we can still be seen from any number of structures around the common."

Isaac Sherman ran a finger beneath his collar and shook his head. "It's not that we're meeting in secret. None of what I'm about to say is secret. I just don't think that the cop knows that I'm in town right now, and I'd just as soon avoid him."

"The cop?" Rocky asked. "You mean Harper?"

"Yeah. Harper. He's not a bad guy—he just has no patience for me right now." Isaac Sherman hesitated another minute, and then let out a long sigh. "I came out here with my fiancée, Brenda Noonan, about a year ago. Brenda actually grew up in the city of Auburn, but her family was from out this way and she loved to come here, loved the whole Mohawk Trail, and just old New England. We had an argument—a public argument. She disappeared right after it. I was staying right where we are now—with Mrs. McFall. Thank God for Mrs. McFall! I was upset, and she stayed up with me through the night while we waited for Brenda to come back. But she didn't come back. I filled out a police form. I stayed here—for weeks. Then I was on the verge of being fired, so I had to go back to work. The police promised to keep looking for Brenda. They did. Eventually, they found her. She wasn't in Barre, but around north by the Quabbin. They didn't know it was her at first—what they found was mostly bones. They were never able to determine a cause of death. She might have gotten lost, she might have cut herself and bled out—they didn't have anything definitive.

Her official cause of death was something like 'accidental, nature unknown,' but there had been a few bear attacks reported by hikers in the area, and because all they really had was bones."

He paused for a minute. "Brenda and I fought, yes. We were both passionate. Anyway, to do the best that I can with a long story, there was never anything done about her death. But I know Brenda. I knew Brenda, I should say. She didn't just disappear. She didn't just wander off. And I don't care what they could or couldn't find on her body or around her body—she was murdered. And now…now, they've found a body in the Quabbin. Agents, this has been going on for a while! That's two dead women that I know about now. And, of course, you spoke with Mrs. McFall! That other guest of hers disappeared, too. And on that one, I don't think there was much of an inquiry at all."

"Mr. Sherman, I'm so sorry!" Vickie said, touching his arm.

"I think that, when she was found, I would have been suspected of the murder, if it hadn't been for Mrs. McFall. She told the police how we'd stayed up, waiting and hoping that Brenda would come back. And, thankfully, this is a good town. Other people reported that I'd asked about her endlessly and a lot of the cops—local and state—helped me, but…in the end, Brenda was dead."

"And you come back here frequently?" Griffin asked him.

"I'm not returning to the site of the crime, if that's what you're suggesting," Sherman said. "We're almost at the anniversary of her death, so I felt I needed to be here."

"Where is Brenda buried now?" Devin asked.

Sherman looked over at her. "She's in the Quabbin Park Cemetery. Her family hailed from Enfield, and her great-great-grandparents were moved there when the Quabbin was constructed and the local remains were moved. You need to be a descendant to buy a plot. I saw that Brenda was able to join her parents there. Why?"

Griffin didn't hesitate. "We may have to disinter her, Mr. Sherman."

He nodded.

"Does she have other family?"

"Dozens of second or third cousins, but...no one who will protest," he said, wincing. "There's no one out there who wouldn't want the truth." He kicked the ground in a sudden bitter movement. "I'm just glad they never found the damned bear they were blaming— I just don't believe it. No bear killed Brenda. You believe me? You know that I'm right?"

"Mr. Sherman," Griffin told him. "We don't know anything—as yet. But we will look into it."

Sherman nodded. "I know who you are—I knew who you were before Mrs. McFall introduced us. And I know that you're looking for people who have disappeared. I hope you don't find more of them like you did today, in the Quabbin. Or like Brenda."

"We hope not, too," Vickie said. "Mr. Sherman—"

"Hey," he said, interrupting her. "We're all at the

B and B. I'm Mr. Sherman on Wall Street. I sure wish you'd just call me Isaac."

"Isaac," Vickie said. "Have you heard about any occult activity? If you've heard about the fact that the FBI is looking for missing people in conjunction with the attacks in Boston, you know what was written on the people who were attacked."

"That crap about Satan?" he asked.

She nodded.

"Brenda was from out here," he said.

"Yes?" Vickie murmured.

"I'm from New York. A Satan cult in the Big Apple would most probably be an entrepreneur trying to come up with a new motif for a nightclub. I haven't heard anything. I mean…"

His voice trailed suddenly.

"What?" Griffin asked.

"Carly. Carly Sanderson. Her dad, Frank, filled out a missing-person report on her. I know, because it was when I first came back after they found Brenda's body. I spoke to him."

"I've seen the report," Griffin said. "Carly Sanderson, twenty-three, a college student. She was going to school in Worcester, right? She was at Clark?"

"Her mother lives in Oregon. She remarried and has a whole host of kids. But Carly was her father's only child. And he's here. Thing is, the cops aren't considering it as a missing person anymore. Frank Sanderson got a call from her. She told him that she was happy, she didn't want to go back to school and she just wanted to be left alone."

"Is Frank still here, in Barre?" Griffin asked.

"I believe so. He's a retired guy. He was in construction but now he hangs around and helps out Mrs. McFall sometimes," Isaac said.

"All right. Let's get back, get some sleep," Griffin said. "A few of us will be attending the autopsy tomorrow. We'll see what they come up with on that. She was weighted down with an anvil, so I don't think that anyone is going to suspect a bear. We will look into this, Isaac. I promise."

"Thank you!" the man said. He looked at them all. "They—as in the police—may tell you that I'm a kook who may have been guilty myself, and if not, I'm paranoid, I won't move on…whatever. But she was murdered. And other people have been murdered because her killer wasn't caught."

"We'll do everything humanly possible," Griffin promised him.

Isaac seemed to believe them.

"Thank you," he said again.

He turned and walked ahead of them.

They looked at one another and headed back to the bed-and-breakfast.

It was quiet. The others had gone to bed; Isaac, just ahead of them, had left the front door open. They locked it when they were in, and then headed up to their rooms on the second floor of the old Victorian.

"Eight," Griffin said to Rocky.

"Eight," he agreed.

They parted ways, Griffin and Vickie stepping into

their own room. "Eight o'clock—the autopsy?" she asked.

He nodded. "I mean, you can come, but…"

"That's all right. I'm assuming that our ghosts will be around in the morning, and I'm assuming, as well, that they will have heard a lot of gossip. Devin and I can hang around town, see what else is going on."

Griffin took off his jacket and reached behind his back for his Glock and its little holster. As always, he set the gun on the bedside table.

"There is definitely something going on. If not here, per se, then nearby. And it's worse than we knew. The problem is connecting all the dots. A woman was found dead in the woods. We didn't have that information, because it was chalked up to a bear or other accident. Another woman is missing—but she was leaving town, so she wasn't noted as missing. And now…"

"The body," Vickie said softly.

"The body," he agreed.

He slipped his arms around her. "I still believe Alex is alive."

"I do, too," she said. "I just wonder how long he can stay alive. Griffin, I so hope we're getting somewhere with this! It seems it has been going on a long time… and no one knew! Well, of course, someone knew. The people involved with it had to know. What about Gloria? Is there anything they can do to force her to remember?"

Griffin had his phone out; he was tapping at it with an aggravated expression. "I'm going to step outside. I don't know what this old house has for insulation or what might be in its construction, but I can't get any service. I'll be right back—I'll see if Barnes has discovered anything new."

"Excellent," Vickie murmured.

She crawled into bed to wait for him. She was afraid to sleep. If she fell asleep here…after being in the Quabbin, after seeing all the forest that surrounded it, she was bound to have nightmares.

But just maybe, eventually, they would be helpful instead of terrifying.

Griffin closed the door to their room quietly as he left. Vickie closed her eyes.

She could see the water again, in her mind's eye.

The water of the Quabbin. And then she could see, caught in a rare glint of light, a bit of a shimmer. The sun making it through the water—just barely!—to land on the anvil.

She saw the anvil…

And then, what remained of the woman's face.

Then suddenly, she was out of the water. Her hair was wet and dripping; she was still wearing the dive suit. She walked a forest path. She'd shed the flippers she'd been wearing, and her feet were bare.

For a moment, it felt like she'd entered a cartoon. Little forest creatures were all around her. She could hear State Police Officer Harper as he spoke to them. The area around the reservoir was filled with animals—moose, foxes, deer, raccoons, panthers, bears…

A mountain lion walked next to her. He was a sandy color, large and sleek, and he looked up at her as he padded along by her side.

"It wasn't the bear," the panther said.

She spoke aloud in her dream.

"I am going crazy," she told herself.

Syd Smith from Fall River was in her dream. He was seated on a log in front of her. Retired detective Charlie Oakley was on his one side while Detective Cole Magruder and Detective Robert Merton were on his other side.

"It could all be a distraction, misdirection," Syd said.

"People take the easy way out," Oakley agreed.

"If you've got a Satanist, what the hell, use him!" Syd said.

They didn't see Vickie. She kept walking. She could hear her name being called; it had been called so many times before.

Then she saw the inverted cross in front of her.

A woman had been hung, upside down, upon the cross.

Vickie couldn't see her face, or the color of her hair. Because of the blood.

"Vickie, please, I'm calling you! Look at me, look at me, please. You can't change the past. You have to focus."

She couldn't see him! But she knew the voice! It was Alex...

Alex was alive.

The blonde woman was standing before her again. She was tiny, Vickie realized. Tiny and very pretty, and there was something about her...

"Vickie, help me."

She could hear Alex's voice.

"Vickie, Vickie, Vickie..."

The blonde stood before her; but there was still a body on the cross.

Blood was rising, as if the rivers and lakes everywhere were rising...

"No! Vickie, run. Stay away, run!"

12

"Nothing!" Barnes said, sounding disgusted. "I got nothing!"

Griffin had filled him in about their time at the Quabbin, Vickie's discovery of the body and their conversation with Isaac Sherman. Barnes had promised to keep up with all the help he could give from Boston, but that what they needed to do was keep it open with Harper—who was state police.

"Sounds like you're moving toward something out there at least. We're sitting on a plateau here, so it seems. 'Gloria' is doing well enough as far as her health goes, though the doc says she might have done some damage to her organs that will kick back on her when she's older. But as far as her memory...still nothing. I've asked him about bringing in a hypnotist, and he's agreed, so probably tomorrow, we'll do something in that direction. Oh, and as you asked, we've sent Officer Jim Tracy to Fall River." He hesitated. "He asked Vickie's friend, Roxanne, to accompany him. He believes she does an amazing job with portraits. She agreed to accompany him as a police consultant."

"Okay," Griffin said. "Well, let's hope that they can put something together!"

"Let's hope," Barnes said. "If we get anything at all, we'll let you know."

"Thanks. We'll attend the autopsy tomorrow. I believe we'll discover that our victim's throat was slit. I'm going to speak with your friend, Harper, about getting Brenda Noonan's remains disinterred. They thought they were looking at a bear attack. Maybe a fresh look will help. Also, I'll find Frank Sanderson. His daughter disappeared—and then called him and told him to leave her alone."

"She over twenty-one?" Barnes asked.

"Twenty-three. She was a student at Clark when she came out here to see her dad—and then just didn't make it back to school," Griffin said.

"You think she's dead, too?" Barnes asked.

"No."

"No?"

"I think she's in on it. I think that her calling her father helps prove that some people are missing because they choose to be missing. I don't know what our mastermind behind the whole Satanist thing is doing, but he has a group somewhere out in the woods. And we're going to find them."

"Careful—you could have a whole suicide-pact thing going on out there," Barnes said glumly.

"I know," Griffin said.

But he was determined to save who he could.

"We'll talk tomorrow," he said, and Barnes bid him good-night.

Griffin went back in the house, carefully locking the main door as he did so. He started for the stairs, and then he was aware that someone was standing in the shadows near the passageway between the dining room and the kitchen.

It was their hostess, Mrs. McFall.

"Are you all right, Mrs. McFall?" he asked her, heading her way.

The kitchen light was on behind her; he could see that she was holding a cup of tea, leaning against the doorframe—watching him.

"I'm fine. I was wondering if Isaac had gotten it together to speak with you," she said.

"Yes, he spoke with us," Griffin told her.

"I'm so glad you're here! I've had the oddest feeling for the longest time now…"

"What do you mean?"

"Well, for one, I see strangers on the street sometimes. They're here for a day, and then they're gone. And I don't know why they're here, except that I think they're looking for something."

"And do you know what they're looking for?" Griffin asked her.

"Call me crazy, Special Agent Pryce," she said softly, "but I am eighty, and I have lived here a long time, and seen a great deal. I think that they're looking for people."

"People?"

"People like Brenda Noonan, Nell Patton or Carly Sanderson."

"They believe that Carly Sanderson is alive."

"And she may well be. She may be one of them now."

"One of them—who?"

"The murderers, Special Agent Pryce, the murderers. You really do need to believe me. I'm not a crazy old lady. I've heard about what's going on in Boston—and I've seen what's going on out here. I'm very grateful that you're here. You stop these monsters, sir! Somebody is pulling puppet strings. I just don't believe that they're bringing fire and brimstone and Satan in the flesh to the forest—but I do believe that there is a flesh-and-blood monster out there, and he's going to kill until he is stopped." She paused, setting her cup on the table. "Well, thank you for listening. Good night, Special Agent Pryce!"

She started to walk by him.

"Mrs. McFall?"

"Yes?"

"Please, call me Griffin. It's a lot shorter."

She laughed softly. "Okay." Then she hesitated. "Mona. You may call me Mona. No, never mind. I like being Mrs. McFall!"

He laughed. "Good night, Mrs. McFall!"

She went on up. Griffin followed.

He opened the door to his room, wondering if Vickie had waited up for him, but expecting that she crashed out, was sound asleep and lying curled up on her side of the bed.

To his surprise, she was not.

She was standing beside the bed, facing the windows. Her eyes were open, but she didn't see him; she didn't turn as he came in.

"Vickie?" he said softly.

She didn't respond.

"Vickie!"

He walked over to her. He gently turned her to look at him, and then took her into his arms.

"Vickie!"

She started suddenly, and blinked. For a long moment, she was completely disoriented, staring at him, and then she murmured, "Griffin!"

"Yes, it's me, Vickie. It's okay, you were…"

"Dreaming. Griffin, it was so weird! Tonight, the animals in the woods talked. They wanted me to know that the bear didn't do it."

"The bear told you that, right?"

"No, a mountain lion. I guess he was speaking for the bear. But there is a connection, I know it—but we can't become too fixated on the connection. Griffin, they were all in my dream—the beautiful blonde, who I don't think is the same woman we found in the Quabbin today. She was very tiny. Although, I don't know. I didn't actually see that much… Anyway, the men from Fall River were all in the dream. Charlie Oakley, Syd Smith, Robert Merton and Cole Magruder. They were on a log when I walked through, and Syd was talking about misdirection again. We can't lose focus—we have to concentrate on finding Alex."

He held her tightly and gently, looking into her eyes.

He understood.

None of them could help the emotion that came with

the job—and it was actually important that they never did. There was something horrible that tore at the heart to see what man was capable of doing to man.

And yet, for both justice and a chance to help the living, they had to see the dead.

For them, in more ways than one.

"We're going to find Alex," he assured her, gently smoothing back her hair.

She still seemed worried as he held her. He eased back, studying her again. "Are you okay?" he asked her. "I've been thinking that you are just too close to this. First, there is the point that Alex is your friend. And then, whoever is doing this wanted you warned away, or something. That's why Gloria knew your name—why blood was thrown at you. I should call your dad—"

She started to laugh suddenly. "Oh, Griffin, really— you're going to call my dad on me?"

He laughed, too. "I meant that it might be a lot safer for you right now, joining your parents."

She shook her head. "You need me, and I'm staying. You're right. I have a feeling I know what it's all about, too."

"You do?"

"At first, I think whoever it is wanted me to stop. To be terrified—and just stop. What was happening in Boston, I think, was to keep people from noticing what was going on elsewhere. If this guy really thinks that he can kill and kill and be ignored, he's crazy. I don't think that I need to be frightened, Griffin. I wasn't physically attacked, not really, not in the sense to hurt me.

The blood washed off. If I'm in any danger, it's because this person may think that if Alex fails, I might find something that he didn't. We're back to Jehovah, Griffin. I've got to figure out where it was—not vaguely that it was out here somewhere. We have to find out where it really was, and then ruin any possibility of this creature using it for whatever his plan may be!"

She was fierce when she spoke to him, and he nodded slowly. "Okay, but you have to stay close. One of us will always be with you."

They went to bed. For a long time, he just held her. They both started to drift off to sleep, but then a brush became a touch, and they made love.

Quietly, slowly...

The moon made its way in through the window, and it was beautiful.

"Vickie!"

The phone rang bright and early—or at least it felt bright and early when Vickie groped for her cell on the bedside table.

Griffin, however, was up and gone; a note lay on his pillow.

"Vickie! Are you there?"

The caller was Roxanne. Her voice was exuberant. Annoyingly so, since Vickie was barely awake.

"Yes, yes, I'm here. Roxanne. Hey. How are you?"

"I'm great—I mean, really great. Vickie, I know I make a lot of mistakes, and you're always warning me, and yes, I need to be careful. But—and thank you, because this is all you!—I'm in love!"

"What?"

"I'm in love!"

"That's truly wonderful. Who are you in love with?"

"The cop, Vickie! The incredible artist cop. Jim Tracy. James Bradford Tracy. He's so wonderful, Vickie. And shy, even. First, he asked me out for coffee so we could compare our sketches. Then he asked me to dinner. Then he asked me to come with him on this trip," Roxanne said.

"That's—um, great."

"We're in Fall River. In an hour, we're heading over to the gas station to get the brothers to describe the man they saw with the missing woman. Vickie, he is so cute. I mean, Jim Tracy is so cute. Not the creepy brothers. Honestly, I haven't even met them yet, but everyone says that they're creepy. And I am so crazy about him. Jim, I mean, obviously! He likes art. He loves art."

"Roxanne, I'm… I guess I'm happy for you both. But should I be worried about you? You told me you were a chicken."

"I was a chicken. Well, I'm still a chicken. But coming out here with Jim…it isn't doing anything dangerous. Hey, he knows how to use a gun *and* he's taken all kinds of martial arts classes. I don't think I could be in safer company. Besides, we're not after anyone. We're just here to listen to a description and try to do up a likeness. I thought it was so amazing of Jim to ask me. I mean, he had permission. Your guy, your Griffin, thinks he's really good. So, we were sent out from Boston. I think he's really good, and he thinks I'm really good. I am in love!"

"Aren't you...rushing things?"

"No...don't be silly. I haven't told him that I'm in love with him or anything! But we're at a bed-and-breakfast." Roxanne paused to giggle. "You'll never guess where. Yes, you will."

"The Lizzie Borden Bed and Breakfast," Vickie said.

"Yes—I love it. The tour was great. And Jim and I both sat up and drew last night, and we did fun pictures for people.

"He has a room, and I have a room. We didn't sleep together. We were both up in the attic. I slept really soundly. No ghosts."

"Great."

"Oh! I know that you wanted to fix me up with Alex, but under the circumstances, I mean, he might be... uh, I mean, under the circumstances...actually, like I said, in a weird, roundabout way, you did set me up!"

"Well, then I'm superhappy for you," Vickie said. "Just don't forget to send us the likeness you guys come up with as soon as possible, okay?"

"Of course!" Roxanne said, slightly indignant. "This is a work expedition!"

Vickie smiled. "Go forth and draw well."

"I will, I promise!" Roxanne told her. "I had to call you. I'm so happy."

"And I am so glad. And, by the way, Alex isn't dead."

"You found him?"

"No. I just know that he isn't dead. Gotta go—and so do you! Talk soon!"

Vickie hung up before Roxanne could continue

speaking. She reached over for the note on Griffin's pillow.

At autopsy—Devin waiting downstairs for you.

Vickie quickly got ready, and headed down to breakfast where she found that Devin, Mrs. McFall and Isaac Sherman were still at the table.

"Good morning," she told them all, heading to the sideboard to pour herself coffee from the urn there.

"Good morning" came back from all three, as if in an echo.

"I'd offer you something, dear, even though you're late, if you weren't going out," Mrs. McFall told her.

"Oh, well, thank you," Vickie said, looking at Devin.

"Isaac has told me that Carly Sanderson's dad, Frank, usually has breakfast at a place down the road a bit before heading out for whatever he's up to during the day. He's retired, so sometimes he works construction side jobs, and sometimes…he hikes," Devin said.

"Oh, well, great. I look forward to meeting him," Vickie said.

Devin and Isaac rose. "Okay, then, we're off. We'll see you a bit later," Devin told Mrs. McFall.

"Have a good day," Mrs. McFall said.

Vickie hoped they had a good day.

One in which they found the living, rather than the dead.

Mrs. McFall rose and followed them to the door. "I always keep it locked, as you know," she told them.

They waved goodbye to her as they headed down the steps to the driveway.

Griffin and Rocky had apparently taken Griffin's car, but Devin tossed the keys to Vickie and asked, "Do you mind doing the driving? Isaac, want to sit next to Vickie up front? You know the way."

"Sure."

And so Vickie drove, following the roads as Isaac directed. They didn't even go five miles before he pointed to a building ahead on the left. It was Aunt Priscilla's House of Pancakes.

She drove into the lot. Isaac walked ahead and Devin caught up with Vickie.

"Isaac seems to be the real deal—we had him checked out last night. But still…you drive, he's next to you—and I watch him. Keeps us safe," Devin said.

"You're the trained agent—I follow your advice!" Vickie assured her. She paused, however, outside of the restaurant.

"What is it?" Devin asked.

"Dylan and Darlene. They're here somewhere. I didn't see them last night, or this morning. They took off once we reached town, and I haven't seen them since."

"Well, maybe they're on to something," Devin said. "And…"

"What?"

"Well, they have to be all right." She paused just a second. "I mean, they're already dead. They're really the best help we have."

"Hey!"

They both looked over to Isaac at the door to the restaurant. "Are you coming in?" he called to them.

They hurried after him.

Isaac saw Frank Sanderson right away and lifted a hand in greeting. He encouraged Vickie and Devin to follow him to the booth where Frank was waiting.

Isaac had evidently told him that they were coming; the booth had four water glasses and four sets of silver.

Frank stood as they approached. He appeared to be in his early sixties; he was about five foot eleven and still had the body of a man who kept busy and fit. His hair was salt-and-pepper and thinning and his eyes were a pale blue that seemed to mirror a great deal of sadness—even when he smiled and greeted them.

"You're a government agent," he said to Devin.

"I am, sir."

"There's something wrong. I'm told that no one can tell an adult that they have to keep up a relationship with their parents, but…it's not my girl. It's not Carly. There's something wrong. I know that… I know that my girl doesn't hate me."

"Did the police even try to talk to her?" Vickie asked him.

"She sent a postcard—from Boston. When she called, it was from one of those pay-as-you-go things. When I tried the number, there was no answer. And then it was disconnected or whatever. I think that my Carly is out there somewhere. But I swear, something is wrong and she can't come back to me. She would— I know that she would if she could."

"Just like I know that Brenda wasn't attacked by any bear," Isaac said.

"Tell me about Carly," Devin said. "When she did disappear—did anything out of the ordinary happen?"

He shook his head. "I was just seeing her every other weekend—she had an apartment in Worcester. Everything was fine. In fact, she was talking about meeting a guy. Someone smart—someone into studying, like she was. My girl…she loved school. Sounds strange, but I was glad. She was a late bloomer, didn't date during high school. She never knew, but I paid a neighbor kid to bring her to her prom. Oh, it was all fine. I don't believe she ever found out. Sounds bad for a father, huh?"

"Sounds like you love your daughter," Vickie said.

"Then she called and said she wouldn't be home for a while. And when I didn't hear from her, I went to Worcester. She hadn't been in her classes. She'd told her landlady she was leaving, and she was gone—lock, stock and barrel. I reported her missing to the police. But they never put much credence in my story. After all, she left on her own accord—told her professors and her landlady she was leaving. Then I heard from her, but it…it was strange. I can't tell you how strange. It didn't sound like her. Sounded like she was…distant. Distant and dopey. So, I figured maybe she was on some kind of dope or something like that. That someone out there was holding her—and keeping her doped up."

"What about Carly's mother, sir?" Devin asked.

He waved a hand in the air. "Linda and me, we just

weren't meant to be. She was seventeen when Carly was born. We were divorced by the time Carly was five. Linda met a surfer—she headed off with him to California. She has three boys now. She sends Carly birthday cards and Christmas cards, but that's it."

"Could she have gone out to see your wife?" Vickie asked.

"Ex-wife. And no. Carly wrote her once, wanting to come out and meet her brothers. Linda told her it wasn't a good time. Hurt the kid badly. I tried to make up for it. Carly... Carly was my life. Carly *is* my life. She's got to be alive out there somewhere."

He seemed like a devoted single father to Vickie. He wasn't giving up on his daughter.

He went on to talk about her. Carly was sweet and impressionable. Terribly bright when it came to books, pathetically naive when it had to do with street smarts.

As Vickie listened, she couldn't help but notice an older man who was at the counter, paying his check. There was something familiar about him.

At last, he turned to face her.

She was startled to see that it was Charlie Oakley.

What was he doing now, out here by the Quabbin?

"We're not going to get anything from soft tissue—other than DNA, which might help, at least in identifying her," the ME said.

They were at the county morgue.

Griffin and Rocky were staying for the autopsy.

Wendell Harper had been in only long enough to ask

that the report be emailed to him as soon as possible. He was heading back out to the Quabbin.

Dive teams were going to go over the area once again, just in case.

The good thing that morning was that the morgue wasn't busy, and there was no question that their lady from the lake would be getting first priority.

There were only two others awaiting autopsy at the moment; one was an eighty-year-old who had suffered from cancer and died in her home, and a ninety-year-old who had simply died in his sleep.

Death, for the most part, had been gentle in the area the last day or so.

Except for the poor woman on the gurney before them.

"Even pinning down a date and time for when she was killed is almost impossible—the damage to the body is so great," the ME said.

He was a young man, ironically named Dr. Graves, Dr. Evan Graves. But he was as serious and seemed to be as thorough as a doctor could possibly be.

The body had been cleaned by Graves's dernier, or assistant. It lay naked—and heavily, heavily decomposed.

Graves pointed out every factor that he could. "I'm going on a lot of scientific research," he said. "Bodies found in the water—especially cold water—in the first week are usually in decent condition. After eight days—according to research done for a paper called *Legal Medicine*—decay begins to set in. They looked at bodies off the coast of Portugal—those found in the first week were easily identified. After twenty days—DNA was their only method of identification."

Griffin held silent, letting him talk. The young doctor was still a newbie; in a few years, he'd get to where he'd tell law enforcement just what they needed to know. He'd come to realize that most of them had been through enough autopsies to have a decent rudimentary grasp of what happened to a body after death.

Then again, there was always something that could be learned.

"About ten years ago," Graves continued, "studies were done on plane crash victims—one off the coast of Sicily and off the coast of Namibia. At three weeks, the body found was partially skeletonized. At thirty-four days, in that kind of water, the second body found was completely skeletonized. I've read a great deal about such studies," he assured them. "So, looking at our body today, considering the cold water, I'd estimate three to four weeks. Decomposition—in the water *or* on land—begins immediately at the point of death. The water allows for other creatures, but kept insects away. Fish eat each other often enough—and they have no problem nibbling on a decaying human being. Crabs are brutal on a body—crabs are probably responsible for the fact that there's really no face left.

"And the water was cold," Graves told them, "so that creates a different timeline. Had she been down there for months, we'd have had nothing but bone, and maybe a bit of something here and there."

"So, you believe, three to four weeks."

"I'm going to say, because of the water temperature, possibly almost four weeks." He sighed. "From what I can thus far fathom from the bones, she was young—twenty to twenty-five years of age." He hesitated. "We'll probably strip her down to bone, and get our best answers that way at this point."

"Thank you," Griffin said. "The main question here is, can you tell us how she died?"

Graves looked up at him. "I most certainly can." He indicated the neck. "Her throat was slit, gentlemen. Slit hard and far back—if she had received much more of a blow from the knife, the head would have been decapitated. Actually, it's a miracle that it was still attached when you found the body."

Vickie didn't mean to slam Devin in the ribs with the force that she did. She was just so startled to see Charlie Oakley she had reacted without thought.

Devin yelped, then smiled at Frank Sanderson across the table from her. "Cramp!" she said. "I'm so sorry."

"Excuse me!" Vickie said. "A friend just walked in." She slid out of the booth, catching Devin's eyes and indicating the man who was about to leave. Devin quickly appraised the situation.

"Vickie," Devin said, "ask retired detective Oakley to join us."

Vickie nodded and hurried over to catch up with Oakley. She tapped him on the back, startling him.

He turned around and stared at her. "Vickie!" he said. "Miss Preston."

"Charlie. Hi. What are you doing out here?" she asked.

He lowered his head and eyes, squirming uncomfortably. "I couldn't stay away," he told her, looking up at her at last. "It was on the news, Vickie. That a body was found. In the Quabbin. I had to come out here. I have to know what's going on."

"Charlie, Sheena died long ago."

"And I'm still around, right?" he asked.

She nodded. "Charlie, where are you staying?"

He hesitated again, she thought.

"With a friend," he told her.

"In Barre?"

"In Ware," he told her.

She nodded, looking at him. The restaurant was on Route 32, almost in between Barre and Ware. Ware itself was something like fourteen miles, about a twenty- or twenty-five-minute drive, due to the winding roads in the area.

"We're sitting with a couple of new friends who are also involved with this situation," Vickie told him. "Won't you join us? I'll tell you quickly first—Isaac Sherman's fiancée disappeared about a year ago. Her body was found in the woods near the Quabbin. A bear attack was blamed. Frank Sanderson's daughter, Carly, is missing. The police believe that she's alive. Sanderson thinks that she's being held somewhere against her will. Because she's an adult, there isn't a great deal that the police can do."

"I'm happy to come meet them," Charlie Oakley told her.

She brought him over to their table.

Frank Sanderson and Isaac Sherman rose to meet him. Charlie sat with them. He told them about the case in Fall River.

And about the murder of Sheena Petrie, and how he never believed that it was connected—or that the prostitution ring had been real Satanists in any way, shape or form. It was his sincere belief that someone else had carved the Satanic words into the earth near the place that Sheena Petrie's body had been found, and that the "cult" had been purposely set up to take the fall, since they were already going up on murder charges and no one was believing a word they said, anyway.

"They're out there!" Isaac Sherman announced suddenly. "Can't you feel it? They're out there in the woods, and they're planning for something very, very bad."

Vickie glanced over at Devin. Goose bumps had risen on her arms.

Because she believed it was true.

They were out there.

But they were hiding in acre upon acre of forest, and her group had no idea where!

"I wish we were just at headquarters with this one—with Angela Hawkins and all her wonderful boards," Rocky said.

They had left the morgue, and were traveling back to Barre.

"We have dead people. We have missing people," he said. "We have massive acreage where someone could be hiding. Why are they hiding? Cults are usually out in the open. They have great big compounds."

"And then, they sent people into Boston to attack others," Griffin noted.

"Think that was to keep us away from this area?"

"If that's the case, it wasn't really a bright move—not if you consider the fact that most historians know the quotation links to Ezekiel Martin, and that Jehovah was out here somewhere."

"Say that our killer—and I use that term whether he or she wielded the knife themselves or not—is a bright person. Extremely bright. Sometimes, those who are superintelligent don't really have a lot of street smarts," Rocky pointed out.

"Theory?" Griffin said.

"Sure, let's hear your theory."

"Our killer may or may not really believe that he can bring Satan in the flesh to the world. But he's been working this cult for a long time—authorities didn't notice at first, because there were day-to-day problems in Massachusetts and, of course, the Undertaker case. Our killer liked it that way. He didn't want people realizing what was going on out here in the more westerly area of the state—so send people on suicide missions to keep authorities thinking that if something was going on, it was going on in the big city of Boston. But, as you pointed out, he might not have been quite as bright as he thinks. Using the saying from old Ezekiel Martin sent us out here," Griffin said.

"Okay, why was the blood of Helena Matthews thrown at Vickie?" Rocky asked.

"The killer knows about Vickie. He knows she's friends with Alex Maple. He has taken Alex because Alex is so very knowledgeable, *and* if you didn't have Alex, you might well want to have Vickie."

"And what about Helena Matthews?" Rocky asked. "And, for that matter, Sheena Petrie."

"Sheena Petrie is the hardest to connect, I think. But it is possible that she was our killer's first victim."

"And Helena Matthews?"

"Well," Griffin said, "we don't yet know if we might have just found her or not."

"And Carly Sanderson," Rocky said.

"I think that Carly is one of the number of followers," Griffin said. "Just like Darryl Hillford and Gloria. In fact, I haven't heard from Barnes in a while. I'll call in and see if they've gotten anything more from Gloria."

"How would you do that, Griffin?" Rocky asked, shaking his head. "How would you get people so caught up in something so ridiculous that they'd kill themselves? Young people, with everything to live for?"

Griffin was quiet for a minute. "Where do you find terrorists? Among the poor and the disenfranchised—those who have nothing and feel powerless. Our killer staked out his converts—he chose young people who were searching for something to believe in."

"But Carly Sanderson has a father who loves her," Rocky pointed out.

"She was socially awkward. She was lured somehow. Then I believe that our killer is working with a number of drugs—drugs known to have an effect on memory, drugs that can cause hallucinations, as well."

"Where would you get all those drugs?" Rocky mused, and then he looked at Griffin and answered himself. "What's the matter with me—after all these years, I should know that just about anything is available on the street anywhere."

"True," Griffin agreed. "But I think there's something else we should look into that might help. Okay, so we don't know this for fact yet, but I do believe that our killer is keeping his little cult under control by ensuring they are obedient and docile. I mean, give someone a hallucinogenic, and you can make them panicked enough to kill themselves. I'm willing to bet that a few pharmacies have been held up—that they've been cleaned out so that certain prescription drugs can be mixed with street drugs. You don't have to be a chemist to discover what properties can destroy memory and stability, or make someone susceptible to suggestion."

"There are many—and far too available on the street and in a store," Rocky noted.

Griffin started to put through a call to David Barnes.

His timing was pretty amazing; he never made the call. Barnes was calling him.

"Hey, Barnes," Griffin said, answering the phone and glancing over at Rocky with a nod. "We were just about to call you."

"Did you get something out there?" Barnes asked.

"This morning? No. Not yet. We've been at the morgue. Our only chance on an ID is going to be DNA, and if we don't have DNA to compare it to, well…we'll have a Jane Doe. Anything there?"

"Gloria seems to be doing well. I've gone by to see her each afternoon, of course. She hasn't remembered anything else as yet—not for certain. It might not be a bad idea to drive back in for a morning or an afternoon. The drive, even with traffic, shouldn't take you more than a few hours. I keep thinking that it doesn't hurt for Vickie to talk to her. She was supposed to attack Vickie, so that means she had to know something about her. If we could just jar that somewhat, you never know."

"You're right. I'll see about driving back in for a bit and let you know. I'm not with Vickie right now. She and Devin were going to have breakfast with a fellow here—Frank Sanderson. His daughter is missing. I remembered seeing her name in some of the reports I'd pulled."

"Ah, well! I do have something for you—hot off the press—or email, I should say. I believe it's coming straight from Officer Tracy."

"We have a likeness? A sketch?" Griffin asked.

"Yes, Officer Tracy and Vickie's friend, the artist Roxanne Greeley, just finished with the two characters from the gas station in Fall River. They had something, though how good it is, we don't know, of course. But better than nothing."

"Roxanne went with him to Fall River?"

"You asked for him, and he asked for her. She's apparently a really talented artist—with a nice ability to draw a face from memory or someone's description.

She could have a nice career with the BPD, if she were interested. Anyway, we've got the sketch."

"Great. I'll find it on my phone," Griffin said. "Anyone you know?"

"No. But that doesn't mean it isn't someone that one of you might recognize. We can also distribute it widely, which has been not perfect, but helpful for us thus far. Check it out and see what you think. And let me know when you're coming in. Gloria's doctor has been slacking off. He doesn't believe she's ever going to get back all of her memory, and he isn't sure how much longer she should be in a hospital."

"Will do. We might be able to drive in this afternoon. Though…"

Though he felt that they needed to stay out where they were.

Why?

Because Jehovah was out here somewhere.

"Whatever you need done, we'll be out here," Rocky told him quietly.

Griffin nodded. "Thanks. I'd like Brenda Noonan disinterred."

"I'll get going on the paperwork, and I'll stay out at the Quabbin waterfront with Wendell and his officers," Rocky promised him. "We need to move in every direction," he added.

Yes, they did!

"Okay, Barnes, I'll let you know about timing this afternoon. Other than that, we'd like you to do what you can to find out if drugstores—pharmacies of any kind—have been robbed in this area. We're pretty sure this guy has to be dealing with a lot of drugs. Cyanide is one thing—getting people to take it rather than face the law is another."

"I'll get on it right away."

Griffin rang off from Barnes and went to his email, finding the message that had been sent to him from Officer Jim Tracy.

He opened the attachment and stared at the picture.

And he was stunned.

He knew the man.

Yes, it was a good likeness.

An uncanny likeness.

He definitely knew the man.

And so did Vickie.

13

"Lie there. Just lie there. Let it go. Even if you feel that you have strength, that you know what you're doing, just lie there."

Alex Maple blinked.

It was the blonde woman. An angel? Was she angel? Or was she a ghost?

Or maybe a real live woman, just trying to help him!

"What did they do to me?" he asked her. "Why do I feel this way?"

"They took your blood."

"They took my blood? Why?"

"They will use some in the ceremony tonight. They will drink it, to gain your knowledge, to gain your strength. Don't worry, they don't expect you at this ceremony. They expect us both to be in and out of consciousness."

In and out of consciousness—that meant that the blonde woman was not a ghost or an angel. She was alive. She was real; she was flesh and blood.

He wasn't on a table; he was on a bed. The bandage

was still on his arm, but there were no needles or anything else attached to him. He was in a ward of some kind, he thought. Maybe, when it had been a mental institute, this had been where the sick patients had been brought. It had been the infirmary.

Sick patients!

Sicker than usual…

"They took blood from you?" he asked her.

"Yes."

"To drink?"

"I'm not that kind of worthy," she said, a bitter amusement in her voice. "I don't even know. But he's done it before. He'll do it again. You can't fight…you're very pliable when you have no blood."

"But we need to fight!"

"Those who fight, die."

Alex was quiet for a minute, afraid.

"Do they die just because they fight?" he asked.

"They die at the full moon. The full moon is closest, you see. Go figure—it makes the darkness lighter, but it's when the power of hell is supposed to be the strongest. He wants to bring Satan to earth—or, perhaps, make all his followers believe that he is Satan."

"Why?"

"Power? Money? All the good things."

Alex was thoughtful. Blood! They'd bled him. Yes, that would make him weak. He wouldn't be able to fight. But the person who had attacked him and the others in Boston had not been weak.

She must have been reading his mind.

"Hallucinogenics and other drugs. He makes people

forget where they came from. He shows them what will happen to them if they don't obey. Death is not evil, you see, not in his world. Those who die in the service of the master are rewarded."

"How…how do you know all this?" he asked her.

"Because I pretend all the time," she said, and again she laughed softly, and it was a bitter and pained laugh. "Because I have been here…waiting my turn. I'm the sacrifice for what he sees as his high holy day—as soon as he's exactly in Jehovah."

"He can't do that…he doesn't know where it is. I don't know where it is!"

"Make him think that you do—or he will kill you. He already doubts you. He has talked about taking your friend. Victoria Preston. She is, you must see, in his mind, perfect. Because she could be the messenger—and the sacrifice!"

"But…" Alex was stunned. He thought about Vickie constantly. He was holding on to the irrational belief that he could communicate with her, that she could somehow hear him when he shouted with his mind. He'd wanted her to find him—and he'd wanted her to stay far away. Both. And now…

"She's not a virgin!" he said triumphantly. "Not meaning to be rude here or anything, but she sure as hell isn't a virgin, so she wouldn't be a good sacrifice!"

"While I don't know your friend, I doubt it matters if she's a virgin. That really doesn't mean anything anymore. He creates his religion as he goes along. He is like any fanatic—he can twist anything into his way of seeing it."

"We have to escape. That's all there is to it. Somehow, we have to escape."

"When you've figured out how," she told him softly, "you let me know. Shush! Someone is coming."

Someone *was* coming.

Hooded figures.

"Come along, come along now!" one of them told the woman.

"Yes, yes, of course," she said, leaning heavily upon the one who spoke.

"Are you okay?" he asked her.

"Yes, of course. I am always okay. I am so honored! It is my time to see the master."

Then they were all gone. And Alex tried to rise and he fell back; he didn't have the strength.

He began to weep.

He wanted to fight so badly.

He could only fight with his mind.

But then again, throughout his life, his greatest strength had been his mind.

Now, he just needed to figure out how to wage the battle.

Vickie was still sitting at the table with Devin, Isaac Sherman, Charlie Oakley and Frank Sanderson when the email came through from Roxanne.

She stared at the picture.

It could only be one man, and that one man was someone she knew—and someone Roxanne had met, as well.

Professor Milton Hanson.

Barnes, she reckoned, hadn't recognized the man in the picture because he really had no reason to know the professor.

And, Vickie reckoned, Roxanne hadn't said anything, because of course she and Officer Jim Tracy had worked together to create the likeness.

She must have just been staring at her phone in shock because, this time, Devin kicked her beneath the table. She managed not to cry out, startled.

She was sure that Devin had the same email and just hadn't seen it yet.

"I think," she murmured, looking around the table, "that Devin and I have to get back. I'm not sure what our plan is for the day."

"I hope it's to find Brenda's killer," Isaac said.

"And maybe, in that, Sheena Petrie's killer, too," Charlie added.

Frank waved a hand in the air. "Inch by inch—every last acre in the forest by the Quabbin must be searched. My Carly might still be alive."

They all rose, leaving the table.

Charlie asked, "You're going to keep me apprised of what's going on? I may be retired for a long time, but I worked security. I know my way around trouble."

"Of course!" Devin assured him.

She was looking at her phone, frowning.

Devin had never met Milton Hanson.

Vickie wasn't going to speak to her until they were alone.

She realized she didn't trust anyone.

Not even Charlie Oakley.

"Oh, my God!" Vickie said when they were in the car. "The picture—the likeness!"

"Who is it?"

"Milton Hanson. Brilliant professor. Political science, theology and history. He works with Alex, Devin. And the night I was supposed to meet up with Alex at the coffee shop, he was there!"

"Okay...if he was there, how did he have Alex?"

"Because he kidnapped him the night before, and spirited him away somewhere. Smarmy! That's what my dad always called him. And he wanted to borrow a book. A book I took and hid. I have to get into that book, Devin—"

She broke off.

Her phone was ringing.

And it was Griffin.

"The sketch!" she said.

"Yes, it's Milton Hanson. I'm trying to stay sane here. Is it possible that Roxanne got the description from the brothers, and twisted it to look like Hanson because she knows him?"

"No. Roxanne is an artist. She would have listened to every word said. She was with Jim, too, and Jim doesn't know Hanson. Griffin! It's him. I told you— he's a smarmy bastard!"

"Smarmy still doesn't mean murderer."

"But it could!" Vickie insisted.

"Anyway, we've got to head back to Boston," Griffin said.

"But we just got here. We just found a body in the Quabbin. And, Griffin, when we were at breakfast, we ran into Charlie Oakley—he's out here."

"We're just going so you can talk to Gloria again, to try to stir something. We'll drive in and drive back. Rocky and Devin will stay here. They can start searching the area. And Wendell Harper is on everything. Plus the state police will still be working while we're gone."

"All right. Why do you think that Charlie Oakley is out here, Griffin?" she asked.

"Because the death of Sheena Petrie ruined his life," Griffin suggested.

"You think…"

"What?"

"You think that there's any possibility he killed her himself?"

"We have no reason to suspect that," Griffin said.

"But you don't think that it's suspicious that he's here?"

"Sure. It's suspicious. Rocky and I are going to meet up with Wendell Harper, then we'll come back to the bed-and-breakfast for you."

Vickie hung up and told Devin about her conversation.

"Something has to crack somewhere," Devin said. "Maybe Gloria will remember something. She's really the only lead we've got—the only *living* person we now have in custody who might know what's going on, somewhere in the far reaches of her mind."

Barnes had brought in a police hypnotist, but that had availed them little.

Gloria had certainly had a family at some time, and she was sure that she'd had a puppy. The puppy had seemed to have been the best thing in her life. He'd gotten big, he'd become a great dog and his name had been Wolfen. Then, Barnes told them, Gloria had begun to cry, and they'd had to end the session.

They were at the hospital, outside Gloria's room. Vickie still seemed baffled—willing to help, but baffled.

"A hypnotist got nowhere, but you think that I can do something?" Vickie asked Barnes.

"I think she reacts to you," Barnes said. "Vickie, this case just seems to grow and grow. Gloria's a connector. She could remember things today. She could remember them in five years, according to both the doctor and the hypnotist. Unless something jars her memory."

"And I'm that something," Vickie said.

Barnes shrugged.

"Okay. But here's a suggestion. Get me a puppy."

"What?"

"She reacted to having had a puppy. Did she mention what kind?"

"A yellow Lab."

"Find me a yellow Lab," Vickie said.

"I can do that," Barnes said. "You want to go in with her now?"

"Where's her doctor?"

"Her primary physician is off today," Barnes told her. "The on-call doctor is seriously busy with a patient down the hall."

Griffin shook his head, wondering how Barnes had managed to get another patient to keep the doctor occupied.

"I'll go in with Vickie," Griffin said. "Barnes, find that puppy, please. Oh! And what about Milton Hanson?" He'd told Barnes that the man who had apparently been with Helena Matthews when she had last been seen was a dead ringer for the professor.

"I have men looking for him. He didn't respond at his residence. But don't worry—we'll find him."

Vickie looked at Griffin. "Smarmy," she reminded him beneath her breath.

Gloria looked better than she had the last time they had seen her—even though it hadn't been long at all. Her color was better—she didn't seem as pinched and strung out as she had, either.

She blinked, and then almost smiled when Vickie walked in ahead of Griffin.

And then she said her name.

"Vickie."

Vickie nodded, smiling. "You remember me."

"You saved my life. You and…" She paused, looking around and seeing Griffin, but no one else. "The other agent," she said. "Oh, nothing against you, sir!" she told Griffin. "But I was told that Vickie and her agent friend saved my life."

"And that's true," Griffin assured her.

"We still need to know why you wanted to take your life, Gloria," Vickie said.

"I don't want to take my life!" Gloria said fervently. "I don't know why I did what I did, except that they're out there. And I know that if we don't do what we're supposed to do, it's worse. He'll find us."

"Who will find you?" Griffin asked.

Gloria thought about that. "Satan himself, I think."

"Satan," Griffin murmured.

"He told us that we believe in God, and if there is God, then there is Satan," she said. "And…if we carry out his tasks, we sit with the great and those who are rewarded. If we don't… I've seen what they do. It was better…" She stopped speaking, perplexed again. "And I'm so sorry. I know I should remember things, but I don't. There are snatches of things that come back, but…" She broke off, shaking her head.

"I think you're already doing better," Vickie said pleasantly.

"Yes?" Gloria asked hopefully.

"Yeah. Well, you were living somewhere before you came here. I don't think that you were staying in Boston. I think you were out by the Quabbin somewhere," Vickie said.

"The Quabbin," Gloria said softly. "Yes, the reservoir. We used to do nature walks there."

"When you were a child?" Vickie asked her.

"No. No…not long ago. We would walk and look for things. For landmarks."

"By the Quabbin," Vickie said.

"And do you know what you were looking for?" Griffin asked her.

"There was a hill, a very pleasant hill, with a beautiful valley. And it was all surrounded by rich forests. There was an area where granite struck out of the earth, and it formed a natural podium, and it was where the high priests could speak to their flocks. And it was where…"

"Where what?" Griffin persisted.

Gloria turned to look at him. "It was where they gave to him that which was his. It was where they were before, years before... It's where he will come now."

Griffin glanced at Vickie.

"He had you looking for Jehovah?"

"Yes. Jehovah is out there, so near. Jehovah is key. He must find Jehovah. When he is there, he will find the granite high altar. The place where the words were written is there, by the granite. And when he finds it, we will bring Satan to earth, and be richly rewarded," Gloria said. She blinked and shook her head. "I don't want a reward. I just remember that there would be a reward. I—I don't know what I wanted," she said. "They...they all liked me. It was like...having a home."

"You were with a group of people. There was someone who was a high priest, and you all flocked around him, right?" Vickie asked.

"Yes, I think so."

"And you remember walking around the Quabbin?" Griffin asked.

"Yes, we had to find the hill and the granite shelf that made a podium. And there was a patch of land before it. Ezekiel Martin wrote into the earth. He knew that Satan was coming."

"Satan was coming," Vickie murmured, "but Captain Magnus Grayson, under the authority of King Charles II, made it first."

"I didn't even want Satan to come!" Gloria whispered. She frowned. "But... Martin. I thought that maybe we were related. I think that it was one of my names. That's what he told me."

"That's what who told you?" Griffin asked.

"The high priest. He serves as Satan's voice and body on earth, while we await the coming."

"Do you remember where you met the high priest?" Vickie asked.

Gloria stared at her blankly. Then it seemed that her face brightened and new energy filled the whole of her body. "Music! I was at a concert. A concert in the park. It was…a big park. It wasn't far from that big building that used to be a museum. It was full of all kinds of arms and armor, but now…they moved the stuff to an art museum. But the park isn't far. There were a number of acts. A really great Beatles group. Some guys who did… Dylan! They did a bunch of Dylan."

"Guys? Or a brother-and-sister act?" Vickie asked.

Gloria nearly jumped out of the bed. "Yes! A brother-and-sister act. They were very good!"

The duo. Cathy and Ron Dearborn.

She went on to name several of the cover songs the sister and brother did, songs that Vickie had seen them perform.

"So, you met the high priest at a music concert. What did he look like?" Griffin asked her.

"Oh, he…"

Gloria went dead blank again. "I… I remember his voice. I remember him saying that I should join with him, that it was wonderful, that it was sweet music all the time. He had such a way about him, such a smile, such a tone of voice…"

"But you don't remember what he looked like?"

"Red. He wore red. Like a sheet over his face. No... like a cloak and then a weird headdress kind of a thing, and then—I think it hung from the hood he was wearing."

"He wasn't wearing anything like that at a concert, was he?" Vickie asked.

"No..."

"Will you help a sketch artist lay out what you do remember?" Griffin asked her.

"Of course—but it's just a mask. Or a scarf, or a little sheet. His eyes...they gleam. I think that they gleam all the time. As if hell's fires are really alive in him."

Griffin and Vickie looked at one another.

She had started to shake; Vickie quickly changed the subject.

"What about your puppy?" Vickie asked. She smiled at Gloria. "We're trying to get you a puppy now—or, I should say, Detective Barnes is trying to find a puppy. You can't keep it at the hospital, and I'm not sure how we're going to get you situated once you're out, but my parents are friends with a really great vet, and he'll keep him until you're ready."

"I'm not going to be charged with...with something horrible?" Gloria asked her.

"I don't believe so. Not unless you remember you did something?" Vickie asked her.

"We had our calling. We were sent out for our calling," Gloria said. She seemed excited again. "I had other names, but I could swear... Martin. Gloria Martin!"

"We'll tell Detective Barnes. He can try to find you

in the system now that we have a name that may be the right one," Vickie told her.

Barnes had great timing; he chose that moment to come in with a puppy.

He was something of a miracle worker, Griffin thought, because he had, in less than twenty minutes, come up with the cutest little ball of yellow fluff imaginable.

Gloria cried out with delight; Barnes put the puppy into her arms. It began to lick her face, its little tail going a million miles an hour.

"Just like Wolfen! He can be Wolfen II!" Gloria said. "He's beautiful, he's… But really? How do I keep him? I don't have a home, I…"

"You do have help," Vickie told her.

Of course, within a matter of minutes, someone on the hospital staff had called out the administrators; the dog had to go. It wasn't a service dog of any kind.

"We'll watch out for him, I promise," Vickie told her.

Gloria was staring at the puppy. "Martin. I wasn't born with that name. But it is my legal name now. My mother married him." She looked at the three of them, one by one. "My friend gave me the dog. It was okay for a long time. But he drank. He started to beat my mother. Then he started to beat me. And then they took me away, and they took the dog away. I think that I was about ten."

Vickie looked over at Griffin. He saw the expression on her face. She felt so much for kids who had it hard.

Gloria had been easy prey.

They left the hospital, assuring Gloria that things would be figured out soon enough, and the puppy would be fine, waiting for her, when she was ready.

"You two are something!" Barnes said. "How did you know I didn't borrow that dog? He could be a prize pooch, worth thousands."

Griffin laughed. "He's not. You sent someone to the local animal shelter."

"All right, I did. So what are you going to do now?"

"Exactly what I said. Thankfully, between them, my parents have friends everywhere!" Vickie told him.

"So we'll stop by the vet. And you'll try to find out where our girl, Gloria, came from?" Griffin asked.

"I'm on it," Barnes assured them. "No sign of Milton Hanson as of yet. And he isn't answering his cell phone, work phone or home phone."

"Gloria mentioned the couple again—the sister-and-brother act who sang at the coffee shop. I think we need to find them. They said they were going to be in Worcester."

"I'll call Wendell on that—get the state police looking for them. And if you can, use all the federal help we can get on the two, as well," Barnes said.

"I'll call my office," Griffin said. "They'll check New England, and keep going if they need to."

"Living in plain sight," Vickie said. She shook her head. "If they're part of it…well, it has to be on their own terms. They're working…they were staying in Boston. But still, Gloria definitely described a band that sounded tremendously like them, playing when she met the high priest. And they lied about coming from Athol."

"And who the hell lies about coming from Athol?" Barnes said. "We'll be on it. She didn't happen to have a good recollection of what the high priest looked like, did she?"

"His face was like a red sheet—that's what she said. She couldn't think of anything else," Vickie told him. "It worried her. I'm sure he played one of his memory mind games on her—with the right combination of drugs once he gathered her into his fold."

"We'll be back out in Barre," Griffin told him.

They parted ways, Vickie holding the little Lab puppy.

"I'm praying that you really do know this great vet!" Griffin said. "I don't think that Mrs. McFall allows pets at the bed-and-breakfast."

She laughed. "Yep. You can turn right, next corner. He's just a few blocks away. And after that, we need to stop by my parents' place."

"Oh?"

"I hid that book from Milton Hanson. Now, I have to find it and read it myself."

Vickie read for the two-hour trip back to Barre.

They arrived just as the sun was setting over the array of hills and mountain peaks that could be seen in the distance, and it was beautiful. She remembered that the creation of the Quabbin had taken mountains and turned them into islands, but she still couldn't find a reference to a place where there was a hill or mountain with a great granite slab.

But she had found really interesting information as regarded Ezekiel Martin.

"You looked perplexed," Griffin told Vickie as they drove into the driveway at Mrs. McFall's.

"It is perplexing. Okay, Ezekiel Martin was born in England. He came to the New World with his family when he was still fairly young. While his parents had been hard-line Puritans—lovers of all things Cromwell and far beyond—they weren't that far from a more prosperous form of life."

"You lost me," Griffin told her.

She smiled. "His family had been wealthy in England. Remember, Puritans didn't believe in any of the trappings of the traditional church. Gold chalices and all that. Anyway, Ezekiel's father was a fanatic, but his grandfather had been a lord. Supposedly, the Martin family of his village—in England—had been ridiculously wealthy. They'd been responsible for tearing down a number of churches. All kinds of gold and jewel-encrusted implements that had once belonged to the church supposedly disappeared—among the Martin family."

"So, our devil-rouser—Ezekiel Martin—wound up pissed off at everybody," Griffin said. "The Church of England, the Puritan church, his family—and everyone else."

"He was a bitter man, certainly. I still don't get it—I just don't understand how people can play others in such a way. I mean, convince them of ridiculous things."

Griffin was thoughtful for a moment, and then he shrugged and turned to her with a self-deprecating grin. "Ridiculous is different to different people. Remember, it was ridiculous to think that the earth was round. Many people find the entire Judeo-Christian concept of God—with or without Christ being the son of God—as ridiculous. I happen to have my faith, and you have yours. But that's what faith is. Easy to think back about how people in the Middle Ages fell victim to their beliefs—especially here, in Massachusetts!—when they first came over. Imagine! The world was dark and frightening. The indigenous people weren't always friendly. Sicknesses raged—it was probably easy for Ezekiel Martin to convince others that God had totally forgotten them, but raising Satan could provide them with lives that were good and rich and safe."

"I understand how we're all willing to believe what we want to believe, but it's disturbing that young people can be talked into something so dark."

"Hey. Children and teenagers are talked into becoming suicide bombers. What's in our minds is usually far more important than what is truth."

"Well," Vickie said, aggravated. "I don't believe that the real killer here—the man behind it all, head Satanist or whatever—believes in his cause. He's a horrible human being, evil—for real! But there's something else he wants that has nothing to do with Satan. Griffin, call Barnes again, please," Vickie said. "We really need to know if he's found Milton Hanson yet."

Griffin pulled out his phone, although he looked

as if he wanted to tell her that he would have let them know immediately if they'd found the man.

He spoke briefly with Barnes. "No Hanson," he told Vickie. "But he said that it's important that we get out to the Quabbin as quickly as possible."

"Something has happened there?" Vickie asked.

He nodded.

"Another body has been found."

Griffin was glad that young doctor Evan Graves was the medical examiner they met when they reached the end of the road—literally, the end of the road, as it continued, but did so right into the water. Graves was knowledgeable and serious, and he was with the remains—which had been removed to the back of an ambulance—when they reached the spot.

"Remember what I was telling you about our other victim?" he asked Griffin. "This girl is down to bone. And, of course, the bone is why I know that we're looking at a young woman. Probably about the same age as the last victim we found."

"But this girl was killed earlier, right?" Griffin asked.

"I'd say she was killed a month before the other girl. You have two victims here...and I'm afraid that a year ago we also found another body. I wasn't working here at the time, and they had it down as a bear attack."

"The divers will have to keep looking for...more bodies," Griffin said.

"Yes," Dr. Graves told him. "Look. Look here."

He paused and pointed to what should have been the victim's neck. There was barely anything there anymore—and whether what was there was muscle or sinew, Griffin didn't know.

"Right where I'm pointing," Graves said.

For a moment, Griffin couldn't see anything. Then he saw what appeared to be a slight scratch on the bone.

It was easy enough to see, once it had been pointed out to him.

The flesh was all but gone.

"Her throat was slit," Griffin said.

Graves nodded. "Her throat was slit. I have a feeling that, if we disinter the young lady supposedly killed by a bear attack, we'll find similar marks. Here's the thing. I'm taking nothing away from the previous coroner. The victim—Brenda Noonan—was found in a terrible state, completely decomposed, just about. We have had a few bear attacks in the area. Lost in the woods, wandering… Even if the bear hadn't killed her, it was more than possible that a bear had mauled her remains, or that other creatures had set in on her."

"We were already looking to disinter Brenda," Griffin told him. "My colleague was working on paperwork to make it happen earlier today," he assured him.

Graves looked unhappy. "There's talk, you know. There's always talk around here. Wild parties out in the forest! Usually they tend to be frat parties—kids who come out here from Amherst, or one of the colleges in Worcester or elsewhere around the state. Most of the time, when we hear about something illegal going on, it's because of a bunch of drunk frat boys. But…"

"But?"

"There's talk. There's always talk. A tourist heard

something crashing through the woods. Bigfoot, usually—and, if bigfoot were to exist, hell, why not in the midst of deep woods like these. They've reported hearing music. Oh, of course people hear all kinds of things, late at night, in the woods. Ghosts. A lot of people enjoy creating drama. There are stories that there were old farmers who didn't want to leave the Swift River Valley—they died, flooded out. There are stories that all the graves weren't moved when the valley was flooded—the ghosts of those who were ignored rise above the water at night, calling out for help."

"Dr. Graves, we believe that there is a Satanist cult alive and well and working in the area somewhere."

"And I believe they're killing a girl once a month," Dr. Graves said.

Griffin hadn't realized that Vickie had come to stand beside him at the back of the ambulance. She was staring in at the corpse—at what remained of the corpse.

"I think that Dr. Graves is right," she said. "Maybe Brenda Noonan was his first victim—and he hadn't learned how to dispose of the bodies. Or maybe he was just learning with her. But I do think that he's killing once a month. Once a month—possibly when the moon is full. Referencing many religions and cults, there's power in a full moon."

"Just two days to go until the next full moon," Dr. Graves pointed out.

"Just two days," Griffin murmured.

He looked around. Night was falling on the Quabbin. The water glistened, bizarrely serene and peaceful. In the half-light, it was all exceptionally beautiful.

Endlessly big, or so it seemed. Old mountaintops now perching here and there in the water, having become little islands.

The forests grew darker, cloaked in mystery as the day came to an end.

"Forty-eight hours," Vickie said. "Griffin, two days. If that's true, we have just two days to save a woman who is being held out there somewhere. And Alex… Alex is out here."

"There's a slim chance. Vickie, we all want to catch this guy—just as quickly as possible."

"Of course. But this guy has something special planned. He wants to know where Jehovah is. And he's killing a woman a month now, at every full moon! I am so afraid."

Griffin realized that he didn't know if the woman was or wasn't alive; he didn't know if Alex Maple was still living.

He was very afraid that someone else was going to die.

And, looking at Vickie, he was suddenly very frightened that the killer intended for it to be her.

14

"I know you're going to argue with me, but I really believe that it's absolutely too dangerous for you to stay here," Griffin told Vickie.

She stared back at him, frustrated. That afternoon—between Gloria's words and reading the book by Nathaniel Alden—she felt as if she was coming closer than she'd ever come before to figuring out just what was going on.

She shook her head.

With all the officers from various departments milling about, and Griffin by her side, she couldn't feel safer, really.

"Griffin, that's just being ridiculous," she said. Though she was uneasy. She hadn't mentioned anything to him about the part in her nightmare where it had been indicated that she might be in danger. She didn't understand why he had suddenly decided that she shouldn't be involved.

"Ridiculous? You're a civilian," he reminded her.

"I was a civilian when you came and asked for my

help during the Undertaker case!" she reminded him. "Griffin, you need me. And where are you going to send me? Helena Matthews from Rhode Island was apparently abducted in Fall River. We don't know where the other victims came from—*because we don't know who they are.* Seriously, just where would you send me?" she demanded.

"Virginia," he said flatly.

"What?"

"Virginia. Let me finish—if they know you're out of the picture, it may be a catalyst," Griffin told her. "Someone might make a mistake. It could help us."

"Or get someone else killed," Vickie snapped.

"Okay, sorry, stepping in here!" Devin said, glancing at Rocky and then taking a deep breath and literally standing between Vickie and Griffin. "Vickie, we can keep in contact with you daily. Or they can. I can go with you. We—as in the Krewe of Hunters—have a safe house in Virginia with all kinds of alarms and bells and a half dozen agents on call at any time. You can be in constant contact, but there, you're also safe. If this killer has a thing for you, as we suspect from the things Gloria said, it doesn't have anything to do with being a civilian, or less capable, or anything of the like. Sometimes we have to step back. If we're being targeted, we just have to step back."

Vickie looked at her. Devin had spoken earnestly. She was speaking the truth.

But it wasn't right.

Vickie let out a breath. "Let's sleep on this, please?" she asked Griffin. "You've been teaching me to shoot—

I'm not bad. I'll be with you. Rocky and Devin are with us. Please, let's just sleep on it!" she begged.

Griffin looked at Rocky, who looked at Devin, who looked at her.

"You can't make me go," she said flatly.

"Try me," Griffin told her.

She smiled. "Hmm. Lots of cops around here. And not all of them like *special* agents."

"Oh, really?" he inquired. His tone was cold and distant.

Angry.

"I'm not saying that you're wrong. I'm saying that we need to sleep on it," Vickie begged.

"It's late. It's been a really long day," Devin said. She was trying very hard to sound bright and cheerful.

Griffin nodded. "All right," he said, glancing at his watch. "Dinner? Is anything still open around here?" he asked.

"The place we went this morning. It's open until midnight—I saw it on one of the signs," Devin told them.

A half hour later, they had gathered there.

Once again, Charlie Oakley was there, as well. Griffin excused himself the minute they got into the restaurant and saw him, speaking with Charlie where he sat.

He looked to be just finishing up.

"Why isn't he asking him to join us?" Vickie asked, irritated.

"Maybe he thinks we need to talk as agents, and doesn't want a retired cop around," Rocky said.

Vickie watched. Griffin just spoke with the man, and then excused himself because his phone was ringing.

She watched Griffin's expression. He gave little away.

He hung up, said something else to Charlie and then came over to join Rocky, Devin and Vickie.

"We could have all spoken with him," Vickie said. "We could have found out what he's been doing all day."

"He's heading home now. I did ask him to join us. He said thanks, but he's worn out—he's been walking in the forest," Griffin said.

"Walking where? The area is huge," Rocky said.

"He wasn't specific," Griffin told them. "He was with Isaac Sherman for part of it. Charlie still seems pretty tough. I just hope that Isaac Sherman can hold his own if…"

"If a mob of Satan-worshippers comes after them?"

"Whatever is happening, the main person has tremendous control over the others. And he considers them all to be expendable. In a fight, he'd sacrifice everyone he has. He wouldn't think twice," Griffin said. He hesitated. "That's where this is most frightening. He has the power to make people commit suicide. I'm very afraid of how many young people he has with him, listening to his rhetoric—*besides* those he intends to use as 'Mary' receptacles for his own entertainment or to create his own tribe. I have a feeling it's more for his entertainment. But he managed to get people to attack others in Boston—and when Darryl Hillford was caught, he killed himself. Gloria Martin nearly killed herself. In fact, I'm worried about people just enjoying the wildlife and the trails in the Quabbin area."

He paused, looking at Vickie. "You might have been on to something else, too."

"What's that?" Vickie asked.

"Angela Hawkins just called from our main office. Our best people have been on it all day—and they still haven't found out where Cathy and Ron Dearborn are really from. They were scheduled to play a number of parks in Worcester—they canceled. Just out of the clear blue. They are now entirely in the wind, too."

"They're gathering!" Vickie said.

"Maybe," Griffin said. "Which makes it all the more important that you—"

"That I find Jehovah by tomorrow, and figure out exactly what it is that this person really wants!" Vickie said.

"You don't think that…that he wants Satan to come to earth?" Devin asked.

"I think that Ezekiel Martin was a spoiled rich kid who didn't get his way. He lived in a repressed society. He couldn't get what he wanted one way. He was going to get it in another. Listen! He left behind the main congregation and the larger cities or towns. He wanted to live as a lord—he became a *high priest*, rather than a minister. He eventually wanted to create a world where he lived in splendor, I believe."

"And what would that have to do with now?"

"This ass isn't trying to bring Satan to earth—he's trying to find the treasure that Ezekiel Martin *left* here on earth," Vickie said.

"How close are you to finding Jehovah?" Griffin asked her.

Vickie made a tiny measurement with her fingers. "This close. I need to finish the book—the Alden book on Ezekiel—and then drive the circumference of the

Quabbin. I'm pretty sure I can find the landscape that Alden talks about."

"What are we looking for?" Rocky asked.

"First, dinner—waitress!" Devin warned.

They ordered. Before Vickie could start describing what they were looking for, she noted that their co-guest at the bed-and-breakfast—Isaac Sherman—had come in.

He appeared to be looking for them, and she wondered how he would have known that they were here—unless, of course, he was aware that they ate late and there weren't many places open that late in the vicinity.

He waved, and hurried over to join them.

"May I?" he asked.

"Of course," Vickie said.

Griffin skooched over in the booth and she did the same and Isaac sat by her side.

"I heard another body was found," he said. "Brenda... Brenda was a year ago. It made me think there may be a lot more," he told them grimly.

"Yes, they found another body," Griffin said. "And we have to hope that there aren't any more. We just saw Charlie Oakley. He said that you were walking with him today."

Isaac nodded. "Yes, I was out with him. Someone out there—those murderers are keeping up some kind of a... I don't know! A campground. Or they've made houses deep in the woods. But I know it—they're out there somewhere."

"Did you find anything?" Vickie asked.

"Charlie picked up some cigarette butts and beer cans. Probably from kids fooling around in the woods, but…hey, do Satanists smoke? Cigarettes, I mean. And do they drink beer?"

"None of us is an expert, I'm afraid. And I don't think there are hard and fast rules. I imagine that someone is making a lot of it up as they go along," Griffin told him.

"Well, anyway, can't hurt to look, right?"

"Just so long as you and Charlie are careful," Rocky said.

"We're careful. He still has a license to carry a gun, so we're good," Isaac said.

Griffin glanced at Rocky, and Vickie was pretty sure they were worried about the others who might be out there. Charlie seemed to be a little too involved, although it was certainly possible to understand his emotion over the case that haunted him still.

"How long do you have out here, Isaac, before you have to be back at work?" Devin asked.

"I work for myself nowadays. I'll go back when I'm ready. Which won't be until after you dig up Brenda," he said, running a finger along the sugar container.

Their food arrived.

"Did you want something to eat?" Griffin invited Isaac. "Coffee, anything?"

Isaac smiled at the waitress and then them, a slightly apologetic smile. "I'm going to leave you to your dinner, late as it is. I just wanted… I just want her killer caught. And," he added, his voice growing husky, "I want them to stop saying that she was killed by a bear."

"We'll tell you what we uncover, Isaac," Griffin said.

"Legally, I can be there, right?" Isaac asked.

No one answered for a minute.

"Legally, you can be at the cemetery, yes," Griffin said. "But...not at the morgue. The ME we have working with us is Dr. Graves. He's excellent."

"You're kidding," Isaac said.

"Dr. Evan Graves," Rocky said, "and he is really good at his job. He'll get answers for us."

"I don't want to see her, but... I feel I should be there when you...when you dig her up."

"Maybe tomorrow," Griffin said. "We're waiting on paperwork."

"You will let me know."

"Yes, we will," Griffin assured him.

Isaac Sherman stood up to leave. "Okay, then. Enjoy dinner. I'll be seeing you."

He gave them a wave and headed out of the restaurant.

"That's scary," Rocky said. "Him and Charlie Oakley, running around the Quabbin with a gun."

"A little scary. Charlie does have training—and when he left the police force, he worked security. I'm sure they're... Okay, I *hope* they're fine. If he's licensed, there's nothing we can do. He has the right to walk in the woods."

"I need to drive around the Quabbin. See the access roads. And," Vickie added, "I need to use the printer at the police station. I want to scan a map from the Nathaniel Alden book and a map from the present site of the Quabbin. I can make an overlay, and see how they work together."

"You don't need to do that," Devin said. "I can take

pictures with my phone and get them to the main office. They can mock up what you want."

"Can we do that tonight?" Vickie asked.

"Yes, of course. You'll have anything you want by the morning."

"So, let's eat up," Vickie said, "and get back!"

"Fine, but you're never anywhere without one of us!" Griffin said.

She nodded, lowering her head slightly. "Hey. I do remember being buried alive by the Undertakers! I plan on being careful—so careful it will make you crazy!" she promised.

The bed-and-breakfast was quiet when they made it back for the night.

Vickie showed Devin the Nathaniel Alden book in the empty dining room, and Devin took pictures of the map that was in the book.

"I really think that this map is the key," Vickie said. "I think it's the reason that Professor Hanson wanted the book."

"Maybe," Devin told Vickie. "But you have to be careful and not see people as guilty because you don't like them."

"I do know that. Honestly. But he's missing—that means he could be out here. He would have been around twenty or twenty-two back when Sheena Petrie was killed. His image is that which two of the best artists I know came up with from descriptions linking him to Helena Matthews before she disappeared."

"There is an APB out on him," Devin assured her.

"They'll arrest him?"

"They'll bring him in for questioning when they find him. The fact that he was with her—and that he's old enough to have killed Sheena Petrie—isn't enough for an indictment."

"But what about a lineup? Those gas station attendants might recognize him!"

"Even if the brothers were to identify him, it's still an eyewitness account, and we'd need a lot more to take to court."

"People are dying."

"That's why they'll bring him in, get search warrants going…all that," Devin assured her. "But you have to remember, it may not be him."

"I'll try. He's looking very suspicious to me. Why else would he want that book?"

"Maybe we need to be grateful he was just after the book, and didn't kidnap you to interpret it, the way they took Alex," Devin said quietly.

Vickie shook her head. "That's really crazy. To think that Alex or I could actually pinpoint a place after well over three centuries—on landscape that has been drastically changed."

"You don't think the whole thing is crazy?" Devin asked her.

"Okay, yes."

"Well, I've mailed in these pics. Angela will do an overlay. She'll get us what we need. But…even if we find it, we're going to have to be really careful. We need to find Jehovah—without anyone knowing that we've found Jehovah."

"Because...that will ruin it for this guy? Wouldn't that be good?" Vickie asked.

"Not if we don't want a slew of corpses," Devin said. She hesitated. "I'm afraid that this guy will kill everyone with him—if he thinks we've really got him, or whatever it is that he really wants."

"Good point," Vickie murmured. "Let's get to bed."

"Rocky made sure that the front door is locked," Devin said. "But of course, make sure you lock your room door. Well, never mind. I know Griffin. He'll check it a few times over."

"Yes, he checks every door and window—all of the time."

"Habit of the trade!" Devin said. "Well, good night!"

They'd come up the stairs together and stood on the second-floor landing. Vickie smiled as she watched Devin go into her room.

She turned to her own.

"Vickie!"

She spun around, her heart nearly in her throat, as she heard her name whispered.

It was Dylan. Darlene was at his side, her hand in his, hanging just a bit behind him.

"Dylan! You nearly scared me to death. Why are you whispering to me on the landing?"

"Well, we're not walking into the bedroom!" Dylan said.

"That would be creepy—and very rude!" Darlene assured her.

"Well, Griffin is in there," Vickie said.

"Kind of the point," Dylan said.

She sighed. "Okay, so…what's up?"

"Not that much," Dylan said. "I mean, if it were long or complicated, I'd have you go in and make sure that he was dressed, so we could talk to him, too."

"But it's not that much," Darlene said.

"What do you have to tell me?"

"We've been following them around all day," Dylan said.

"Who?" Vickie asked.

"Isaac Sherman and Charlie Oakley, of course," Dylan told her, shaking his head as if his words had been so obvious he was at a loss as to her failure to understand. "Charlie Oakley first."

"And then Isaac Sherman," Darlene added.

"And?" Vickie asked.

"Well, first, they were being watched from the woods!" Dylan said.

"By who?" Vickie asked.

"We don't really know. We saw the movement in the trees and naturally ran up—they were walking along a trail between a couple of hills," Dylan explained. "We didn't catch anyone, but, Vickie, I swear—they were being watched."

"Okay, thank you!" Vickie said. "Keep following them—that's great."

"Oh, we did keep following them," Dylan assured her.

"I followed Isaac," Darlene said. "And…nothing."

"I followed Charlie Oakley," Dylan said. "And guess what? He was on the phone with the dude who is his friend—and still a cop," Dylan said. "The old dude, not the young one."

Vickie shook her head slightly. "You mean Robert Merton? The detective from Rhode Island?"

"Exactly!" Dylan said.

"That's not really shocking—they've known each other for years."

"Aha! But here's the thing," Dylan told her proudly. "He's coming here. Well, he's coming to where Charlie Oakley is staying. Which is Ware. I mean W-a-r-e, not w-h-e-r-e. Well, Ware is where, if that makes sense. I mean, it does, but—"

"He is coming here?" Vickie asked. "On business? But he's not state police. He's a detective. Hmm. That *is* interesting."

"See!"

"If you want to just come in, you can…"

"Oh, no. We're going back to the sofa in the parlor!" Darlene said.

"Long day," Dylan said. "But there's more."

"Okay?"

"I think we saw…someone you're seeing."

"The blonde woman? A…dead woman?" Vickie asked. She looked at Dylan, not Darlene.

Vickie had seen Darlene's dead body, had found her, during the Undertaker case.

"She's shy," Darlene said.

"Very. She disappeared, as if she was afraid, really," Dylan said.

"We saw her up on the hill—when we were trying

to figure out who was stalking Isaac Sherman and Charlie Oakley."

"I think she's been dead a very long time—with no one!" Dylan told Vickie.

"Thank you. I'll keep watching for her. You two… maybe you can help her."

"We'll certainly try," Darlene said.

"But I think she's trying to reach you. I think she's *been* trying to reach you," Dylan said.

"Thank you. Well, good night, then." She turned to open her own door.

"Vickie?" Dylan said.

"Yes?" she asked him, pausing.

"I don't know about all this. I mean, where you're concerned. You're not carrying a gun, are you?"

"No. I've only been to the range about five times. I don't have a license. But I do know how to use Griffin's Glock, and the agents are all armed," Vickie said.

Darlene and Dylan looked at one another worriedly.

"Can't help but think that they want you, too," Dylan said.

"They have Alex. He truly is brilliant," Vickie said. "I think he'd made some kind of a super research find the night…the night he disappeared, when he didn't meet with me and Roxanne."

"But maybe having Alex wasn't enough," Dylan said.

They looked at each other again. "We were, uh, kind of hanging around eavesdropping," Dylan said to her.

"We heard Griffin say that you needed to…well, to get away from all this," Darlene said.

"Just saying!" Dylan put in quickly, apparently seeing the set in her expression. "Yup, heading down to the sofa now," Dylan said.

"Yes, sadly, no television there, but..." Darlene said.

"We do have each other!" Dylan said.

"I really do wish I could just get the two of you a room!" Vickie said. "Good night, then. I'll tell Griffin what you've told me."

She waved to the two of them as they made their ghostly way—disappearing as they raced down the stairs, hand in hand.

She walked into her room.

Griffin wasn't exactly dressed, but he was down to boxers. The minute she came in, he walked over to the door, closed it, locked it and even slid a chair before it.

"You can never be too safe," he told her. Then he smiled. "I heard you with Dylan and Darlene. What's going on? Oh, by the way, Robert Merton is coming out here tomorrow. He called Barnes and told him that he actually took some personal time. He wanted to help Charlie Oakley. Barnes doesn't know Oakley, but Merton thought that it was important that we all know what's going on and who is where."

"Well. That's the big news I was just about to tell you. Dylan and Darlene have been following Charlie and Isaac Sherman around all day."

"And they knew about Merton coming?"

"Dylan followed Charlie Oakley. Oakley had a conversation with Merton on the phone," Vickie said.

"So that's why he's coming out here," Griffin said. He hesitated. "This has to be... Whatever the plan between them, I imagine, it has to be really careful. They have to have their actions synced and coordinated. Whoever is involved in all this."

"So you do believe that Hanson might have something to do with it?" Vickie asked him.

"I'm not saying that he didn't. Vickie, we don't know."

She hesitated and then told him, "They saw the blonde woman—a dead one."

"And who was she?"

"They don't know. Griffin, she's the woman I see in my dreams. I'm certain."

He took her into his arms. "Tomorrow," he said softly. "It's late. Let's take tonight."

He pulled her close. She quickly smiled, feeling his arousal grow as he helped strip her of her clothing.

"The walls are paper-thin," she murmured.

"Nah, not that thin."

"Pretty thin."

"So we'll be kind of quiet!" he said.

And of course they were. Quiet.

Kind of…

But with or without sound, it was certainly a wonderful night.

"I had to come," Robert Merton said, standing by Griffin as the machinery worked to extract Brenda Noonan's coffin from the ground. His voice was quiet and his gaze was sad as he focused on the work being done.

Griffin looked around the cemetery. It appeared as

any other; the situation of graves might have been a natural one. But graves had been moved here from eight cemeteries affected by the flooding. There was really nothing at all haphazard about the place.

Or the group of people milling about as the morning faded to noon, and the machinations of getting the buried out of the ground went on.

Griffin couldn't help but wonder how many stones were actually over the remains of those they commemorated. They ranged from slate to marble; cherubs, angels and other funerary art manifested here and there. The cemetery was an homage to lives that had been led in places that had become nonexistent.

Brenda Noonan was in a section where a number of graves—dated from the early 1800s into the early 1900s—bore her family name.

The coffin was out of the ground; there was shouting among the workers as it was first set down and then hiked onto the vehicle that would carry it back to the morgue. Comparisons would be made to the wounds on the bodies that had been found in the Quabbin.

Griffin looked across the cemetery. Vickie and Devin had wandered off; they were reading old stones and pointing at epitaphs here and there.

Isaac Sherman was standing a few feet away, his arms crossed over his chest as he watched the action. Charlie Oakley was just a few feet away from him, watching alongside Rocky.

And now, Robert Merton. Here. Along with Charlie Oakley.

Why?

"I had to be here," Merton repeated, and Griffin wasn't sure if he was speaking to him—or to himself. But Merton looked over at him then. "I remember her, too, you know. I remember Sheena Petrie. I remember what the case did to Charlie. And now…now Helena," he said.

"They're doing DNA testing, but they've made comparisons," Griffin said. "Neither of the bodies found in the Quabbin has been identified as Helena. There is still the remote possibility that she's alive."

Dr. Evan Graves, who had stood like the grand conductor of the action, came over to Griffin. "We're heading to the morgue now, if you want to make your way there."

Griffin found himself looking around the Quabbin cemetery again.

There seemed to be something infinitely sad about it. All these graves brought here…and yet, so many lost, so many stones and monuments moved…

Ashes to ashes, dust to dust. Nothing of the mortal coil lasted forever.

And looking across the slopes of the landscape, Griffin wondered if he wouldn't see something, *someone*, a whisper of the past, of those who had come before. But there was nothing—no one.

Vickie and Devin were walking back toward them.

The empty hole of Brenda Noonan's grave seemed to gape like a mouth that screamed a silent protest.

"You're going into the morgue?" Vickie asked him.

It was as if they were all trying not to look at the gaping hole.

He nodded to her. "I know what they're going to find. That's part of the process, though. It will only take a few hours."

"Devin and I are going to drive around the Quabbin, heading out on Route 9. Angela got my map from the book and a more current map superimposed," Vickie told him. She paused, looking around the cemetery, as well, speaking softly as she added, "We're not getting anywhere here."

Charlie Oakley, Robert Merton and Isaac Sherman were now standing together, watching as the ambulance drivers closed up the doors on the vehicle that would bear Brenda's remains to the morgue, second time around.

"I know that Devin will be with you, but stay in the car, please? If you find the landmark that you're looking for, call me. Rocky and I will run out of the autopsy—out of anything—to be with you, okay?" he asked her.

She smiled and nodded.

"Don't get out of the car, even if you see your blonde woman," he said. "Promise me. I still think that you should be heading out of town today, going as far as you can go."

"I will not get out of the car. I promise—pinkie promise, promise on the lives of all I love and so on. Okay?"

"Okay," Griffin agreed.

Merton came striding over to them. "We'll be out here. Call us if…anything," he said. He lowered his voice, looking at Griffin, and then Rocky, who was moving their way, as well. "Isaac Sherman, Charlie and me. We'll be searching the Quabbin. I hear that Wendell Harper has his boys—whoops, sorry, Miss Preston—his men and *women* out searching for whatever can be found also."

Griffin looked at him unhappily. "Be careful," he said.

"I'm an old warhorse, Special Agent Pryce. I'll be fine," Merton told him. "I'm out of my district, but I am a cop."

"With Charlie and Isaac," Vickie said.

"Charlie is solid—and Isaac seems to be steady enough," Merton said.

"It's not just you all. We do have a noose here, and we are pulling it in. On a fellow who likes handing out cyanide pills," Griffin reminded him.

"We're just two old geezers and a young'un, walking around the Quabbin. Hey, the bike tours are still out in full bloom and it remains one of the greatest tourist attraction areas here. We blend in. Honest. Not so sure the rest of you law-keeper types do, though!"

He grinned over at them, turned and headed toward the others.

Charlie and Isaac waved at them. They spoke among themselves for a minute, and then all of them got into a large blue sedan.

"And they're off," Rocky murmured, joining them.

"Two of them in the state and involved with or aware of what had happened from the time Sheena Petrie was killed," Devin noted.

"But they didn't find her."

"No, Syd Smith found her. But Syd isn't here," Vickie pointed out.

"He isn't," Griffin agreed. He shrugged. "Syd was her friend. He watched out for her when she was alive. If he's not at peace with what happened to her, he is, at least, at peace with the fact that he was there for her in life. Maybe these guys don't feel that they did the right thing back then."

"Or maybe they were involved," Vickie said. "What about Milton Hanson?" she asked. "Has there been any word of him at all? Have they found anything on him?"

"No, not yet," Griffin said.

"Suspicious," Vickie said.

"Yes, suspicious," Griffin agreed.

"All right," Griffin said. He hesitated, looking at Devin and Vickie. "I talked to Barnes this morning. He found reports on fifteen robberies of pharmacies around the state. Three of those were armed and, thank God, two out of three the alarms went off, but the perps were gone when cops got there. The others were all robberies in which the stores were really burglarized—cameras knocked out, supplies stolen—but no one threatened, hurt or killed. This is a really organized group. Vickie, you stay out of harm's way."

"We've got it, promise," Vickie said. "We're just going to find the landmarks using the overlay, and by evening we'll be back with you."

"Promise," Devin agreed.

"Okay," Griffin agreed. He wasn't happy.

Vickie spoke softly to him. "Griffin. I've had the dreams. I have the Nathaniel Alden book. I have the information that Gloria Martin gave to us. And, before Alex disappeared, there was something that he wanted to tell me. There are two situations that combine as one, and there is a lot we have to be afraid of happening very, very soon. One, Alex is being held somewhere, along with a blonde woman—whether she's Helena Matthews or not. They could both die by tomorrow night. We have to find the truth quickly. Because, if I'm right, a killer is using the past. He wants everyone to think that there is a crazy suicide cult out here, ready to bring back Satan. But he's holding Alex to find Jehovah, because, somehow, the Martin treasure that the Puritans denied him is buried in Jehovah."

"Maybe," he told her.

"Maybe!"

"And maybe there's a crazy-ass suicide Satan cult out there. But you're right about one thing—time matters. So, go be brilliant. But don't get out of the car. Wait for us, please."

"Until the ends of the earth!" she promised him, smiling.

"I don't intend to be nearly that long," he assured her.

"Come on," Rocky said to him. "The sooner we get in on this, the sooner we'll be meeting up with these two!" He smiled at Devin, paused, kissed her quickly and headed for Griffin's rental.

Devin was already heading toward the car they had taken, a Jeep. Vickie grinned and waved at Griffin, hurrying to run after Devin.

15

"Did you notice which way our friends went?" Devin asked Vickie.

She was doing the driving; that allowed Vickie to hold the map.

"You're referring to Charlie Oakley, Robert Merton and Isaac Sherman, right?" Vickie asked in return. "They seem a strange trio, don't they?"

"I guess. Robert and Charlie have known each other for years. I'm sure Robert is here because he's worried about Charlie, who seems to believe that he has to pay for what happened all those years ago. And Isaac... well, he's latched onto them. He wants justice. Not so sure they're a trio—other than that happenstance has thrown them together."

"They went to a blue car," Vickie said. "Of course, that was hours ago. Who knows where they are now."

"Right. When they got into the car, did they go north or south, east or west?"

"I didn't notice," she told Devin. "I think that Griffin wishes that they weren't out exploring, though. I believe he and Rocky are seriously worried about people running around without anything like a real plan."

"And they don't even know that we expect another murder in about twenty-four hours, either," Devin murmured.

"It is scary," Vickie said. "Hey. Some of these peaks—that look like little hilly islands now!—appeared to have been pretty high once, long ago," she murmured. "Devin, see that little road ahead? Take that."

"It's a dirt road. It isn't real anymore, Vickie. It's one of those roads that will end up in the water," Devin said.

They'd been driving a long time; they'd stopped several times, surveying the landscape, going over what they had heard, what they knew and what they could theorize.

"I know—I think it goes to the water and ends there, or maybe becomes a path, though I don't see any of the paths for bikers or hikers around there. In fact…" She paused, frowning, and looked over at Devin. "That area has warnings—heavy forests and danger from bears and other wildlife."

"You want me to go to where there is no path?"

"I think there will be a path."

"We're not supposed to get out of the car."

"We're not going to get out of the car. But look. There's a little crossroad there, and then the dirt road continues, goes into something like a forest path." She paused. She wasn't sure why, but when she looked ahead—through the depth of the forest around them—

she could have sworn she was seeing the same path she had seen before, over and over again, in a dream.

"Devin, I just want to get up there. I think, from the end of that path, if we look to the right, there's... something!"

"Something like what?"

"I'm not sure, but Alex was excited. He had been eager to see me the night he didn't show up. He said he had something cool to tell me. Devin, I think that there's a building here. A building on the old map and...wow." Vickie paused and looked at Devin. "The current map we used is an 'Earth' map, showing true landmarks. The 'true landmark' sits right over an old landmark. A building of some kind. Buildings were supposedly torn down in this area!"

She fumbled in her bag to find the larger tablet she carried with her, swearing softly when she couldn't get any internet service.

"What are you doing?"

"Trying to look up the old mental institution. Oh, it may be in the Nathaniel Alden book. I have that here, too."

"We are in the middle of the woods! I can't even get my phone to work. How are you expecting internet service?" Devin asked her.

"Hey! Satellites are way up above everything!"

To Vickie's amazement, one of those satellites picked up their location.

She keyed in her coordinates and discovered with amazement and elation that she could connect to the internet.

Her fingers went still.

"Devin!"

"What?"

"There's an abandoned building on the Earth-view map!" She set aside the tablet, picked up the old book and quickly flipped to a page she had marked. "It was supposedly torn down. Apparently, it never was. That's what we're seeing. It was recorded as destroyed on the day it was supposed to have been demolished, but there's mention in this record that…doctors were still placing patients! Oh, whoa! Alex did make a discovery, but I think someone made that discovery before him." She looked back at the map on the tablet. "The dirt road ends, but there's a smaller path, which disappears as you get to the water. But the building…it was an insane asylum! The Mariana Institute for the Mentally Unfit. That's what Alex wanted to tell me about—that's why he'd been so silly and secretive."

"It's where he's being held!" Devin said.

Devin had slowed to a stop as they reached the crossroad; she was looking over Vickie's shoulder at the tablet, and the map that had been created as a combination of past and present.

Neither of them saw the truck coming.

They just started to look up, aware of the sound of wheels moving over the rough terrain…

And then Vickie saw the vehicle—and the face of the man in the passenger's seat.

Then it broadsided them with tremendous speed and force, and sent their Jeep flying and flipping into the woods.

* * *

It was a different smell, one all its own, that clung to the long dead—better, of course, than the horror smell of certain stages of decay that curled even the strongest stomach.

And still...

That smell was all around the corpse of Brenda Noonan.

What had been left of her had been embalmed, but she'd been so ripped and torn by the time that she'd been found that she resembled a creature from a zombie flick.

Dr. Graves barely noticed.

He was looking for one thing.

"It's possible, it's possible," he murmured, "but so unlikely... This tear, or these tears, the loss of tissue and flesh... Yes, that would have been forest creatures. Yes, and yes, but they happened after death, not before it. Some of them...vultures, crows, insects, other birds, some land creatures...they're all waiting, all of the time. It can be difficult to tell..."

Griffin stood still, watching, not commenting.

Dr. Graves didn't really want conversation right then. He was comparing the body to the chart in his hand, which was from the previous autopsy completed by the last medical examiner.

"Not that he was bad at his work!" Graves said, pausing to look at Griffin and Rocky. "He wasn't looking for a wound on the throat, on the small bones, the way that I am!"

He turned his attention back to this work.

Griffin was glad that he did so.

Because he was suddenly aware of someone in the room with them.

Someone dead.

Rocky let out a small sound at his side; he tensed.

Yes, he saw her, too.

But he didn't think that it was the spirit of the woman lying so horribly mutilated on the stainless-steel gurney before him.

There was just something too different about her.

She was tiny, for one. And her hair was long and blond, but there were delicate curls that just edged her face, reminiscent of a style from a period long, long ago.

Was she the woman Vickie saw? He didn't know.

A tragic frown marred her beautiful face.

She definitely wanted his attention. He nodded to her, trying to let her know that he had to finish listening to Dr. Graves.

The medical examiner was still speaking, pointing out various aspects of the havoc created upon the body, and then he let out a guttural sound of both disgust and victory.

He'd found the telltale mark upon a piece of cervical spine.

Brenda Noonan's throat had been slashed. Soft tissue was gone; the proof remained upon a tiny part of bone.

Griffin's phone rang and he excused himself and answered it quickly.

It was Jackson Crow from headquarters.

"We've just gotten a call from the remote security and diagnostic car service the rental car agency uses. Vickie's SUV was in an accident and they're sending people out. The car was struck hard enough to flip and roll. We can't reach Vickie or Devin," Jackson said. "You need to get out to—"

Griffin wasn't listening anymore; he could see that Rocky had also gotten a message and was already heading out the door.

Griffin barely explained to Dr. Graves.

"We have coordinates," Rocky said. "I've got the directions on my phone."

"How the hell do you go fast enough, or make the kind of mistake on roads like this, to flip and then roll?" Griffin asked.

He and Rocky looked at one another.

"You don't!" they said at once.

Vickie never blacked out, not for a single moment. The air bags, however, were blinding at first, and she was so shocked that she was momentarily paralyzed, trying desperately to comprehend what had happened.

"Devin!" she murmured, struggling to reach for something sharp—anything to extract herself.

Then, just as suddenly as it had inflated, the air bag deflated.

So did Devin's.

Her friend, however, was unconscious.

"Devin, Devin!" she called.

She realized that they were still upside down. She extricated herself from her seat belt carefully, and then reached for Devin's wrist. There was no blood on her anywhere, and she had a pulse.

She had to get her out of the car.

That was the plan! They had been hit on purpose; someone was coming to get them!

The gun.

Devin carried a gun. She needed to find it.

She tried to find the hook on Devin's seat belt. Even as Vickie grabbed for the buckle, Devin's eyes opened. She blinked, then focused on Vickie. "Get out of here!" she told her. "Get away—fast! Rocky and Griffin will be on their way. Find them. Get out of here now. I can hear someone coming!"

People were coming.

Vickie could hear voices. And movement. The people who had caused the crash were coming through the woods.

"I'll get myself out—you go!" Devin told her. "Go, hide. The car has a GPS system thing on it that notifies the rental office of a crash—our people will come. Hide, now!"

"I can't leave you—"

"Yes, you can! Go! I'll be all right. You won't be! Move! Go now! I'm stuck. My belt is stuck. I'll get out, and then I'll be running like crazy, somewhere behind you. But now…go!"

"You're bleeding!" Vickie told Devin.

"Just flesh wounds, honestly. I swear. I'm begging you—go!"

Agonized and torn, Vickie finally realized that

Devin would be better off alone—she'd only have herself to worry about, not an unarmed civilian, as well.

She unclipped her own belt and let herself fall. The voices were coming closer and closer.

Shimmying through the crushed window, she made it out of the car.

"Go! I'll be close behind you. Get away from the car!" Devin urged her.

Away from the car, yes! Those who had hit them would be there within seconds. Help would not be so nearly close behind.

Vickie ran, hard.

Deep, deep into the trees, into the forest, into a maze of green darkness.

Griffin could see the wreck from a distance as they approached a crossroad.

One vehicle—a truck with its front end crushed in—was off on the side of the narrow road. It must have slammed into the Jeep.

The Jeep was far ahead down the road; it had been struck with such force that it had flipped and flown and landed a good distance away. Griffin had no intention of stopping by the truck; he didn't look. He didn't have to.

Rocky verified what Griffin expected.

"Empty."

Griffin slammed the gas pedal, maneuvering around the truck. There was another car on the road ahead of them.

The blue sedan that had been driven by Robert Merton and carried Isaac Sherman and Charlie Oakley was stopped just behind the nearly crushed, upside-down Jeep.

He pulled alongside the vacant vehicle, aware that as he did so someone was moving off into the woods.

He'd barely put the car in Park before he and Rocky were out of their vehicle, racing for the Jeep.

By then, he heard a siren in the distance, as well.

He quickly saw that there was no one in the passenger's seat; Devin Lyle, covered with blood and glass, was emerging from the hole left by the broken windshield, which was flush with the road.

Rocky was on his knees, screaming Devin's name as he helped her out.

"I'm fine!" she cried. "Superficial…these are superficial. The crash was on purpose—they came at the car. They would have… I don't know…"

Rocky was holding her.

"Where's Vickie?" Griffin demanded. His voice was thick; his head was ringing. "They have her…oh, God! They have her—"

"No!" Devin told him. "No, she ran. A while ago. I was stuck in my seat belt. She's in the woods. But she found it—she found something at least, their hideout—right before we were hit. We have to find it. She's going to go there, Griffin—I know she will. She's going to try to figure out a way to free Alex. I know it."

Griffin spun around, his gaze desperately searching through the trees for any sign of movement, a clue to which direction Vickie might have gone. He pulled his phone out. Wendell Harper answered on the first ring.

"Vickie is out in the woods—running. Devin has a possible location on the cult hideout. Get me every officer you have. Whatever is going down, it's happening now. We have to find Vickie. Please. We have to find her."

"I know where you are. We're on our way. We'll tear the forest to shreds."

Griffin hung up. He closed his eyes. He could hear Rocky talking to Devin; she'd seen Robert Merton and Isaac Sherman arrive. They had followed the horrible sound of the crash that had echoed all over the forest. But whoever had been driving the truck was already gone; the men had chased them into the trees.

He had to concentrate. Concentrate on Vickie.

And he saw…he thought he saw…

The blonde woman was there again, the very beautiful blonde. She was leading him along the path, the path that Vickie had followed in her dreams. He recognized the path because she had described it so vividly.

He heard a scream.

He saw an inverted cross ahead in a clearing; the woman had been hung upon the cross, and blood streamed from her down to the earth—it was everywhere.

But there was more. There was something behind the inverted cross. It seemed to grow, find substance, as he stared at it…

There were suddenly words. Words that had been written into the earth.

Satan is coming!

Was Satan coming?

Or was Satan already there?

"Griffin!"

Devin was in front of him; she had her hands on either side of his face. Her eyes were on his. "Griffin, listen. Vickie found a building with the maps. It shouldn't be there—it was supposedly torn down. It's at the end of the path that leads from this road once it peters out. It was an old insane asylum. She's—"

"Gone there!" He grabbed Devin by the cheeks and pulled her close, planting a kiss on her forehead.

"Wait!" Devin cried. "Griffin, I think we saw… *Hanson.* He was in the passenger's side of the truck as it came at us.

"So she was right. It *is* him!" Griffin said. "I'll find him. So help me, I'll find him. If he was in the passenger's seat, who was driving?"

"I don't know what I saw," Devin said.

"What do you mean? Who was driving?"

"Satan," she told him. "Someone with a giant ram's head and a red hood."

Griffin looked at her and nodded.

And then he began to run.

They would be right behind him—he trusted Rocky to have his back.

"Griffin!" Rocky cried. "When we reach it—"

"We figure out how to go from there!" Griffin said.

Vickie wished that she'd been a Girl Scout.

She hadn't been.

It wasn't that she'd never been hiking or never been in the woods, but she was from Boston.

She was a city girl.

The forest was ridiculously thick. When she looked up, she realized that, to make matters much worse, it seemed that the afternoon was waning. The morning had disappeared while they had been digging up Brenda Noonan.

And then they had driven and searched, and…

She prayed that Devin was all right, and she kept running.

It was strange; when she had been in the car, she had known where she was—according to the map at least.

And she had known where she was going, and why. Now, out of the car, having run so hard and so fast, she wasn't at all sure of where she was. She stopped, breathing desperately, not even sure of which direction she had come from. The good thing was that she had evaded whoever had been coming to the car; she was far ahead of them.

That made her worry about Devin again.

But Devin was trained. Devin was smart.

And how long had it been? Surely help had come. Devin would be fine.

If the cult members hadn't gotten to her first.

She stopped suddenly, her heart beating at what seemed like a million miles an hour, as she heard voices.

Two voices… They belonged to two women. The women were walking along what seemed to be a path, and it was near her.

Vickie ducked low into the bushes next to a heavy oak with thick branches.

"He'll kill us. We haven't got her," said the first. She had a soft voice. Straining to see, Vickie caught a glimpse of her. She couldn't have been more than eighteen or nineteen. She was pretty, with sandy hair in a ponytail.

The girl at her side was a brunette of just about the same age.

"He won't kill us, he'll understand," the brunette said.

"He wants her. It's time. Victoria Preston. He said that the time is here, and he must have her. And he said that the first messenger failed. He needs her now. What will happen to us? Maybe…"

"Maybe what?" the brunette asked.

"Maybe we shouldn't go back! I remember…"

"What? What?"

"I remember what it was like. Before. I mean… I had a life."

"No, don't forget, there is no going back," the young brunette said worriedly. "We've turned our backs on God. We have given ourselves over to Satan. We can't walk away. Carly, remember the things that we've… that we've seen?"

"Yes—things we've seen! I didn't do any of it!" the girl named Carly said. "I was just…there. I was… scared. I'm scared now. We've failed! Darryl went to Boston and he…he failed. He didn't come back. And Gloria went to Boston, and they said that she's dead, too, that they killed her. They shot her down in the streets. Because she failed. Sarah, he'll wonder why we didn't punish ourselves. We failed. We are…done."

"That's not true at all! And we didn't fail alone. The others are going to be back already. They'll have explained what happened. Hey! We weren't driving the truck. *He* was driving the truck, remember?"

He was driving the truck. The high priest? The man behind it all?

"We didn't bring back the woman he wanted—we'll be made to pay!" Carly said.

"Hey, we weren't alone," Sarah said. "We didn't fail alone."

"We've got to get back quickly. He's going to drag out the messenger. He's going to find Jehovah so that we may call upon the great master, Satan. We must—"

"You go back! I'm not going," Carly said.

The two had stopped walking; they weren't twenty feet away from Vickie.

"Carly, we're almost there!" Sarah whispered. "Others could be watching us already."

Almost there—almost where? Vickie tried to gauge where she was.

She was looking for a building that shouldn't exist. The old insane asylum that wasn't razed—because those who were supposed to have razed it had to wait, and it was written down as done.

The two stared at one another nervously, neither speaking for a minute. And then, suddenly, another voice, male and deep, broke through the forest.

"Help me!"

It was him—surely, it was him, Vickie thought.

Milton Hanson.

She'd seen his face so briefly—seen him sitting in

the passenger's side of the truck just a split second before the truck had broadsided the Jeep, sending her and Devin on a deadly roll.

He staggered toward the girls; blood was pouring from his forehead.

"Help me!" he cried again.

"No, no, oh, God, oh, no!" Sarah cried.

"Bitches! I'll kill you!" Hanson roared.

Carly screamed; Sarah screamed. And the two were gone, racing away.

Milton Hanson came staggering on through the trees. And then Vickie realized that he saw her. He seemed to gain strength. There was a massive branch in his hand and he held it with a death grip. He was coming toward her, and he was going to bash her head in.

"There you are! You—there you are. God help me, I will make you pay!" he exclaimed.

She held no weapon; she wasn't sure if she looked just as bloodied and torn apart herself.

She let out a cry; every bit of adrenaline in her came to the fore.

And she rushed toward him, using all her strength to shove him down. She was like a catapult, and when she hit him, it might have been comical. He staggered back and lost his grip of the branch. He went down as hard as a pile of bricks, his head cracking on a tree trunk as he fell.

He was out, she thought, looking at him. Out cold, like a prizefighter taken down with a surprise right hook to the jaw.

She gasped in a slew of air, stood over him a second and then looked for where the girls had gone.

Close, she was so close. She stepped over Milton. And there was a path. She went in the direction that the girls, Carly and Sarah, had gone.

It would lead, she was certain, to the old insane asylum. And once she was there, she would find Alex, and she would learn if Helena was, by any prayer, still alive.

She started to move. It wasn't much of a path, but she could begin to make out the fact that it had been used often enough lately. It meandered through the rich growth of trees and seemed to elevate as she kept moving. At one time, she thought, she would have been leaving the valley below; she would have been heading up a slope.

Then suddenly, there was a break in the trees; an expanse appeared before her. Bushes and brush had grown about haphazardly, but she had reached what had once been a yard...some kind of a garden or a patio.

What had probably once been a garden table had been draped in black fabric and adorned with black candles. Around it, the trees, as well, had been dressed with skulls—from rams, or goats, she believed.

Real skulls.

Torches were stuck into the ground; fires burned already.

And on the stone garden table, shimmering in the torch light, was a knife. A large, curved knife.

A sacrificial knife!

Vickie held fast where she was, trying to judge where people were.

She was here! She had found it. And she was, of course, an idiot if she tried to go into any of the decaying buildings to find Alex or Helena on her own. She had to get back. If she could just find the road she had come from, Griffin and Rocky and a score of officers would be there.

She barely stopped herself from crying out as a door to the building opened, and people emerged.

They were wearing long red robes, and conical hats, and had red scarf-like face masks that fell from the hats, leaving nothing but their eyes visible. She couldn't help but think that they resembled a flock of blood-drenched KKK members, the apparel was so similar—other than the color.

Two emerged from the building…

And then two more, dragging someone along behind them. Someone barely able to walk…

Alex!

For a moment she stood there, wishing that she'd gotten a branch and made sure that she'd bashed in Milton Hanson's head. He was the leader here. And whatever he had planned was for tonight—not tomorrow night!

Hanson! He'd been coming out here…for how long? Years—thirty years? Would they find that they had been blind for too long, and that Hanson had been killing and killing and killing?

Well, she'd hit him pretty good. But his followers were all here, without him, getting ready…

Two more of the figures came out of the building. They were also in the crazy red costumes. And they were half leading, half carrying a woman. A blonde woman…

But not the woman from Vickie's dreams.

Vickie didn't know her, but she had seen her picture often enough.

It was Helena Matthews.

Vickie forced herself to remain still. The two were led out to the garden table.

The sacrificial table!

They were being forced down upon it.

Vickie's breath caught in her throat. It wasn't so much a matter of force. The two were so weak they obeyed. They needed help, even, to obey. They appeared to be half dead already.

Drugged? What was it?

Helena lay, faceup, in one direction. Alex lay, faceup, in the other. One of the red-cloaked thugs picked up the sacrificial knife.

Vickie's heart seemed to stand still. She tried to tell herself that they were just being prepared for the rite.

The rite that couldn't take place now, because Milton Hanson had gotten hurt. He wasn't there to conduct the rite. They would just be prepping…

One of them was behind the altar. He had the knife, the giant knife.

Vickie had to do something. There wasn't time to wait. She backed against the tree, trying to think, trying to breathe. And then one of the girls she had seen earlier stepped by her. She was making her own way through the trees, trying not to be seen.

It was the very scared one named Carly.

Vickie crept up behind her, praying that she had what it took to make her plan work.

She caught the girl from behind, forcefully grabbing her, a hand over her mouth.

"You failed your master, but you can live. Help is coming. The law is coming. You can survive. You have to get the hell out of here, do you hear me?"

The girl nodded, swallowing hard.

"They'll come with guns, so you need to be far away. Take this trail, until you're out—far, far from here. Do you understand me?"

"Yes."

"First, I need one of those." And Vickie pointed.

The girl nodded strenuously. Vickie eased her hold and Carly turned to her. "My…my cloak is in the building. You're…you're her. You're the true messenger. You know where Jehovah is."

"Yes, actually, I think I do," Vickie said.

"You can't go in. Everyone has seen pictures of you. I'll… I'll get a cloak."

The girl was shaking.

Vickie knew that it could go either way.

The girl could bring her out a cloak.

Or she could bring all the cultists down upon her.

But she couldn't wait. Alex and Helena already lay on a table.

"Get me a cloak. Please."

She prayed that she knew what she was doing.

16

Griffin cursed, wondering how the day had gone so quickly.

It wasn't dark; darkness was still more than an hour away.

But here, around the Quabbin, the towering trees created shadowed canopies that seemed to rule even the light of day.

It was easy enough to find the road, and then the crossroad, where Devin and Vickie had been headed.

Griffin was in front, running, leaving Rocky to organize, to meet up with the others, to follow as silently as they could, lest they be seen, lest their arrival cause the high priest to demand instant sacrifice from those who served him.

It was a terrible, anguishing dilemma. They had to be so careful.

He followed what remained of the road; it disappeared into the trees.

He could hear a rush of water, and the thought that they were very near the reservoir, or one of the little streams leading to it.

The road was gone, but it seemed that a path remained. He hurried—as quietly as he could—along the path. And then he nearly tripped over a body.

He dropped down on his knees.

Yes, a body, lying prone on the pine needles. Griffin hunkered down, quickly trying to ascertain if the person was dead or alive.

It was a man. He quickly realized that it was Isaac Sherman.

Griffin felt for a pulse. The others were behind him, but Isaac seemed to need help—now. He'd been bashed hard on the head.

Blood dripped down his forehead.

He pulled out his phone, praying it worked out here. A signal! He spoke rapidly.

"Rocky, we need an ambulance, now. Someone has bashed Isaac Sherman on the head. He's here on the trail. I'm going to keep moving forward."

"Got it," Rocky said. "Go."

Griffin hesitated, moving away. "Are you close?"

"Yes."

"Stay ahead of the med techs and others. I don't know what's going on. I believe that there might be someone following behind me. Keep close."

"Gotcha."

Griffin checked Isaac's airway; the man was breathing on his own. He stayed hunkered down, trying to figure out how the hell he'd wound up where he was, beaten down on the path. The forest created such a strange darkness.

And finally, against the brush and the rocks and the shadows, Griffin saw a shape.

He drew his gun, and pointed it. "Get up, now. Show yourself."

The shape began to rise. Slowly. And then he saw that it did, indeed, have human form.

"It's not what you think. I didn't do that," the shape said. "I've been hiding. They used me. They knew that...that I wanted Jehovah so badly. I didn't do it... I didn't hurt that man. I didn't want to be in the truck."

It was Milton Hanson walking toward him. He was carrying a massive branch; Griffin couldn't tell if it did or didn't have blood on it.

"Drop it!" he told the man.

Hanson did. And, as he did, someone rushed through the trees, moving with strength and fury, coming straight at Griffin.

Vickie was so relieved that she began shaking.

She couldn't let the girl see her shake. But Carly came back to where Vickie waited, wearing her red cloak and conical hat and mask.

Once in the trees, she began to divest herself of it as quickly as she could.

"Never, oh, God, never, never do I want to have this on me again! I don't know why I believed. It was the stuff he gave us. It was so good and I was so happy here, for a while."

"It doesn't matter now. Go—just go. Quickly. Help is coming, really. They can't be more than fifteen or twenty minutes behind me. Head out, head toward Route 9. Do you understand me?" Vickie asked her.

The girl nodded vigorously.

She impulsively hugged Vickie.

Then she turned and ran.

Vickie struggled quickly into the red outfit, making sure that her conical hat was on properly and that it allowed for the scarf-like face mask to fall well and conceal her face.

A mirror would have helped! she thought.

Then again, a nice big gun would have helped more!

She straightened herself and her clothing.

Then she walked out from her hiding place in the trees, straight toward the sacrificial table.

Griffin didn't want to shoot; the sound would alert anyone nearby that someone with firepower was in the woods.

So he stepped aside, and the blurry figure coming at him pitched headfirst into one of the trees behind him before falling prone, jumping up, trying for Griffin again.

Easily enough, Griffin caught him by the shoulders, dragged him up and nearly belted him in the jaw.

"You!" Charlie Oakley gasped.

There was a rush of sound behind them.

Milton Hanson was trying to escape. Griffin rushed after him, tackled him and brought him down to the ground.

"That bastard! He was in the woods ahead of us! He attacked Isaac," Charlie said.

"No!"

Milton Hanson was beneath Griffin then, protesting. "No, no, you don't understand. They kidnapped me. They seized me when I was hiking through the woods. They threw me in a cell. Oh, Lord! It's still there. The Mariana Institute is there—the asylum! From the 1800s! That's how no one knows…because no one goes there. The woods here, so dense…" He broke off. "I swear to you, I swear to you. I was kidnapped! I was taken. He's going for anyone—anyone at all who might be able to figure out Ezekiel Martin's rite or message or whatever…to find Jehovah!"

Griffin looked back. Charlie Oakley leaned against a tree, panting.

Griffin reached into his pocket for a set of plastic zip-tie cuffs; he put them on Milton Hanson.

He pulled out his phone, but this time he couldn't get a signal.

Rocky would figure out where he was.

"Where is it?" he demanded, the rage and urgency in his voice enough to make Hanson flinch.

"That way. Keep following. It winds… They used me! They put me in the car on purpose. You were supposed to see me, I think, and kill me. Satan…he's Satan. You have to see him. I don't know who, I just know that…"

Griffin left Hanson cuffed and lying on the path. He turned around, but Charlie Oakley was already gone.

Griffin kept moving forward, dodging here and there, trying to ascertain just what was part of the path and what winding trail took him farther away.

Then he nearly tripped over another body.

He bent down.

It was a man. Another man. He felt for a pulse... yes. Slight.

He rose. He had to leave the man. No choice. He had to pray that Rocky and Devin and EMT help would reach him in time, as well.

He knew the killer.

And he knew he had to hurry.

The first thing she had to do, Vickie reckoned, was get Helena and Alex off the table.

They were both so weak...

She wasn't at all sure how she was going to manage such a task. But, of course, Milton Hanson was back on the ground somewhere. Nothing could happen until he showed up. Their grand master, high priest or head man—whatever!

And still, she felt the frantic urge to get them out of there.

She thought desperately, and then she raised her arms high and started walking straight out into the middle of the clearing, toward the table.

She thought of all the Latin she had learned in church when she'd been young—and she thought of the spattering of languages she'd learned during her years of study.

She wasn't really sure what she said.

She tried to make it sound as if she was preparing the two people for a grand offering.

She was pretty sure that what she was really saying had to do with buying chicken soup and bread in the market.

Nevertheless…

She'd gambled well. People, clad in their similar red robes, were milling about, preparing to come out for the rite. Three…four…seven. She counted about eight young men and women, and she was quite certain that more were in the building.

Help was coming; she held on to the idea that help was coming.

She made her way around the table. She stood behind it. She kept up with her flow of Latin, staring at the man who was behind the table, the one who had the knife.

She reached for the knife.

To her tremendous relief, he handed it to her.

She raised it over Helena and Alex. She kept up with a dramatic flow of babble.

She was pretty sure she was asking where to find the train for Rome at that point.

She saw that Alex was staring up at her. His expression was troubled and bewildered at first; then it was incredulous.

Alex had figured it out. Alex knew it was her.

She nodded slightly. *"Si deve andare!"* she said, using contemporary Italian to tell him that he must go.

But with his eyes, Alex indicated Helena. He wasn't going anywhere without her.

Vickie nodded again.

Once more, she raised her voice. She made a massive display, waving the knife around over the two of them, and then she began to chant.

"Arise! Arise! Arise!"

She knew that it took every ounce of strength in Alex, but he rose. And, as he did so, he caught Helena's arms, so that they seemed to rise together.

"Arise and go before us. Go into the forest. Go! And as he commands, see to the pleasures of the flesh, open the way for these, his faithful!" She had no idea what she was saying then, but it seemed she needed something for them to be doing.

The way the two stumbled, she thought, hot Satanic sex was probably out of the question, but she was pretty sure that wanton fornicating was probably part of the rich rewards promised, and sending the two of them off as if they were an evil Adam and Eve might just be the ticket.

She kept talking. She watched them go.

They staggered away.

"The time is coming! Take this time! Find what you will! Find who you will!"

Griffin's phone was on vibrate; he caught it the minute it started to buzz in his pocket, looking up and silently thanking God that, somehow, the satellites in the sky were being kind—and they had phone service.

He answered in a whisper.

"We've caught a few men," Rocky told him. "They were sent back to make sure that the men who were attacked along the way were dead."

"You still close?"

"On your tail. Wendell Harper is just behind with his men. Those who need it are getting medical attention."

"I'm almost there. I'm moving fast."

"I've got your back."

Griffin hung up.

He was ready…

Griffin looked to the sky again.

He prayed he was in time. He turned his focus before him, wishing that the forest wasn't so thick—that there weren't different ways to go.

Then he saw her again.

The beautiful blonde woman who seemed so sad.

She beckoned to him.

Griffin began to move through the trails again, following her as quickly as he could.

Vickie tried to figure out how to make her own getaway. She kept talking, switching from Latin—*My, what a beautiful cat you have!*—to English. "Follow in his ways, do what thou will! Follow, frolic, taste the pleasures of this earth!"

She stopped talking. One of the figures was coming toward her, head bowed.

He was followed by three others. Two went to Vickie's left side. One went to her right.

She gripped the knife hilt tight in her hands.

The one red-clad figure was just across the garden table altar from her; he raised his head.

Satan!

He wore a mask. A ram's head mask.

As if he were, indeed, a fallen angel, the embodiment of all evil.

Milton Hanson had been in the passenger's seat of the truck that had hit them; this man—or at least a man wearing this mask!—had been driving.

She couldn't see behind the mask—it hid all, except his eyes, and in the weird glow of the torches and the dying green-tinted light of the evening, she thought that his eyes burned like red fire.

"Well, well, well. Thank you, brave, sweet Vickie! You've cleared the table for me. Your friends are gone, and here you are."

He stared at her; she felt her knees tremble. And she tried to place the voice, because it was, of course, a voice that she knew.

"Where's Jehovah?" he asked.

"You don't really give a damn about these people or Satan. You've sacrificed a number of women, and had people commit suicide, for pure greed," Vickie said. She hoped that Alex and Helena had made it away. Far away.

She couldn't see, but she felt sure that the face behind the mask was lit up with a wicked smile.

"More can die. All I do is say the word, and they slip little pills into their mouths, every last one of them."

"I don't know where Jehovah is."

"Yes, you do. Alex was close. Hanson was close. You, looking for the both of them, hearing what was out here… I'm certain you know where Jehovah is!"

She smiled. "You don't really give a damn about finding Jehovah in order to raise Satan. You're looking for Ezekiel Martin's family treasure. You think that if you find Jehovah, you'll know where it's buried."

"It hasn't been a bad gig, being high priest, Satan's rep in the flesh. I do really enjoy sex, and I guess I've always had a thing for young blonde women. Of course, your hair is as black as sin, but I'll live with that. I mean, at this point, there's no time. You'll do just fine as a sacrifice."

Vickie realized that the figures close to her—his right-hand men or women?—were slowly creeping closer, hemming her in on both sides.

But others were milling around, watching. They all seemed to waver, as if they were uncertain.

Vickie raised her voice. "Did you hear that? He doesn't give a damn. Satan is definitely not coming. None of this is real. It's all a sham. There's no reward here on earth for you for listening to this man—for watching him kill!"

"Um, actually, there is a reward," the figure nearest Vickie said.

And Vickie turned. She studied the figure—a woman.

"Oh, Vickie, Vickie, Vickie!" she said. "Of course there's a reward."

"Audrey Benson!" Vickie said. "I wondered when we'd find you. But it had to do with the café—you were one of the first followers in this 'Satanic' cult. You were sent to get Alex—and to watch out for Hanson and me. The leader got to you first—whoever he is."

"Doesn't matter. You can just call me rich when we're done!"

To her other side, one of the figures was laughing

softly. Again, Vickie was sure that she recognized the voice, even in laughter.

"Cathy and Ron Dearborn! You two are good—how did you get sucked into this? You could have... done well."

"Well?" Cathy Dearborn said. "Playing two-bit coffeehouses and parks where the kids spill grape juice on us and the babies poop and vomit in the middle of our numbers? Please."

"Vickie," Ron Dearborn urged, "you don't have to die. If you just show us the way to Jehovah, we'll drag someone else to the table."

"Sacrifice another woman? For your treasure hunt?" Vickie asked.

"Lie down on the table, Vickie. Lie down," the ram's head mask, red-clad, would-be Satan said. "If you tell me where to find Jehovah, I may let you live. But hey, my faithful are gathering. You've lost me Alex and Helena. What I have is you. I suggest you start telling me everything you can about Jehovah. That way, you may live."

She shook her head. "You were crazy before—now you're as crazy as can be. The law is right behind you."

"The law has been right behind me for years. They can't find this place. No one knows it exists. Get on the table. Do what I say."

"Why would I do that?" Vickie asked. "I've got the knife."

"For now," he said menacingly, as he and the Dearborns moved even closer.

"How the hell have you gotten away with this so

long?" Vickie demanded. "Charlie Oakley! You killed her, didn't you? You killed Sheena Petrie over thirty years ago. You let Syd Smith find her. You let the cult in Fall River take the blame—and then you used what you learned about the cult to start up your own. Why did you kill her, Charlie? Because she turned you down? You were a cop—you were supposed to protect her!"

"Sheena Petrie was a bitch. A frigid bitch. I know why her husband left her."

"Did you kill her by accident?" Vickie asked.

"You need to hurry," Ron Dearborn, sounding nervous, warned Charlie. "Cops are coming. They're about to find this place. Come on, we're in this for the money. Kill her or leave her, and let's get out of here. We can keep looking—we can find Jehovah ourselves."

"She's going to give me Jehovah! Milton Hanson is dead. I just saw your precious Griffin Pryce, Vickie, and he thinks he saved Milton and I'm sure he's going to think that he's saved Isaac Sherman and Robert Merton, but my people were going back. They're all going to be dead when the cops get to them. We're always a step ahead!" Charlie said, waving his gun in the air.

He looked at Vickie and spoke again, fury filling his voice. "So, you want the story now? Sure! No, I didn't kill Sheena Petrie *by accident*. I slit her throat—and I liked it. I liked seeing her blood flow out. Guess what? I get a kick out of drinking blood. And if you take blood from people and keep them on drugs, you can really do whatever the hell you want with them. And you can make them believe anything—anything at all. So, yes…when Brenda was found last year, people started snooping around out here. I started with the Boston attacks so people would look at Boston. Then I saw all the hype about Alex Maple in the news, after he was attacked. Figured if anyone could find the Martin family treasure, it would be Alex. But I was wrong. Then what about Hanson? But they're both academic asses. And you've got about sixty seconds to tell me what you know."

"You'll be caught. Federal charges. You could face death," Vickie said.

"I won't be caught. A dozen kids will be found in these robes. I'll be long gone—with my true faithful, these friends right here. Oh, not to worry—anyone who might have suspected me is dead along the trail. If they haven't expired yet, they will, soon enough."

"You know what? I do know where Jehovah is, Charlie," Vickie told him quietly. "And I will never, ever tell you!"

Charlie Oakley let out a bellow of rage. "Get her down!" he commanded the Dearborn brother and sister. "Get her on the table."

They reached for her.

Vickie wasn't going down without a fight. She turned with the knife in her hand and she stabbed out at the man and the two women trying to force her onto the table. She stabbed at them blindly, shouting all the while, screaming that there was no great power coming that day, only the downfall of everyone involved.

Audrey and Cathy were yelling, shouting, screaming and bleeding, as well—she'd gotten them good.

There was blood everywhere...

Hard to see against the red robes.

And then one of them had her arm, her wrist, wrenching the knife away from her, and she was pushed onto the table. Charlie—in his ram's head mask—was over her; Audrey, Cathy and Ron were holding her down.

Charlie had the knife.

He held it over her.

"Where is Jehovah?" he demanded.

"Fuck you!" she told him.

He started to lower the knife. She saw it, saw it coming toward her...

And then, in a flash, the knife was gone.

Charlie was gone.

She kicked out with all her might; Ron Dearborn went flying back. Audrey was shoved aside.

Audrey, letting out a scream of fury, came at her again.

But then the sound of bullets firing into the air filled the night.

Vickie punched Audrey, hard. She staggered back.

Suddenly, there were cops and agents everywhere; chaos reigned. Vickie slipped to the ground in front of the altar, trembling. And then she saw Griffin.

Someone was walking away with Charlie Oakley, his hands cuffed behind his back. She saw that Devin was taking Cathy Dearborn into custody.

Rocky was there, cuffing Ron.

None too gently.

Griffin was coming toward her. She smiled.

He took her into his arms.

"Vickie, my God, Vickie. I've been so scared. My God..."

She hugged him. She cupped his face between her hands. "I love you! Griffin, I did it! I found them. I stopped them! I was actually pretty darned good. If I'd just been armed. Griffin, I want to go through the academy. I'm going to meet your bosses and I'm going to beg them and—"

"Hey!" He rose, drawing her to her feet, holding her tight.

"Let's just get through tonight, huh?" he asked.

She smiled.

"Sure. I can tell you where to find Jehovah tomorrow!"

Even as she spoke, it seemed that the darkness of the night fell for real. For a moment, they were together in a field of black velvet.

Then the moon broke through the clouds. It was a day away from full, but it was huge and red-rimmed in the night sky, casting down a glow that seemed to light up everything around them.

"Okay, okay, so...maybe tonight. As soon as the chaos dies down a little!"

"Well, everything helps," Vickie said. "That's what research is. I mean, you go to all the sources there are, and you seize whatever little piece it is from each source that goes into solving your puzzle."

The compound was down to almost empty—all that

remained were Rocky, Devin, Griffin and Vickie, Wendell Harper and a number of his men.

Vickie had ditched the red robe she'd had on over her clothing. She'd worried that she'd been injured in all the tussling.

She had not, thank God. Tomorrow, she'd be sore, and she might have a few bruises, but she hadn't suffered any serious injuries.

The cultists had been taken away. The group was grateful not to have lost a single soul—not that night. Not one of the remaining red-clad figures had taken the suicide pills they'd carried.

Many had seemed relieved to be arrested.

Isaac Sherman, Robert Merton and Milton Hanson were in the hospital—as were Helena Matthews and Alex Maple, who clung to one another like a pair of long-lost lovers. Vickie was happy to have seen them, if only for a minute.

All this…

And it was just midnight.

"Okay, okay!" Devin said, and laughed. "We all appreciate your mad research skills. Come out with it. Where is Jehovah?"

"It's all in the words," Vickie said.

"'Hell's afire and Satan rules, the witches, they were real. The time has come, the rites to read, the flesh, 'twas born to heal. Yes, Satan is coming!'" Griffin quoted.

Vickie nodded. "And, luckily, the moon is high enough for you to see. In fact, if you turn, the rise of granite right behind us looks red. 'Hell's afire,'" she said.

"Okay, so then?" Rocky asked.

"There's where it gets tricky," Vickie admitted. "The 'rites' weren't rites. They were *rights*, as in the direction. If you look at the old maps, there were three natural twists in the roads, the earth and the rivers, just below that giant 'red' slab of granite. One was a hillock, one a river and one a natural path between. The water has been diverted, but we're standing about where the three would most closely converge." She hesitated. "This place was chosen for the insane asylum for a reason. It sat on a barren plateau—barren, compared to all else around here!—that was referred to as—"

"The flesh!" Devin exclaimed.

"Exactly," Vickie agreed.

"So, he was here all along? Charlie Oakley was hiding out at Jehovah—*looking for Jehovah*?" Rocky demanded.

"So I believe," Vickie said. "I don't know where to go digging, but if they get out here with metal detectors, I'd say that way…just by the clearing before you wind up back into the thick growth of trees. I think that's where you'll find the treasure."

"Not only that," Griffin said quietly, "but it's where Missy Prior was killed. It's where Ezekiel Martin had her 'sacrificed' when she despised him so much that he wanted her dead." He smiled at them all. "We've wondered which blonde has been haunting Vickie's dreams. Rocky, we saw her at the morgue today. It's been Missy Prior. She was murdered here, and I think she's been trying to stop the killing ever since."

"Hopefully," Vickie said, "we may have brought her peace at last."

She looked up at the moon again. It was strange; it was beautiful.

Not quite full...one more night.

"Look!" Griffin urged. The sky brightened suddenly as a gorgeous glitter of gold and red seemed to light up the night.

For a moment, the blonde appeared to be standing before them.

She smiled.

She was surrounded by a small group of others who were like her, and not quite like her.

One of them might have been Brenda Noonan.

Another...Sheena Petrie.

The sky seemed alive with the beauty of the shimmering light.

And then they were gone.

Griffin pulled Vickie close.

"Peace!" he said softly. "Maybe we managed that much. We gave them peace."

Vickie smiled, resting her head on his chest.

"And, for Helena, life!" she said.

"For Helena, life!"

Back at the bed-and-breakfast, they had to spend at least an hour calming down Mrs. McFall.

She was grateful, of course, to know that Isaac Sherman was going to be fine.

And that it was over.

The ghosts of Dylan Ballantine and Darlene Dutton were there for all the explanations, so Vickie didn't have to repeat herself.

Eventually, Vickie and Griffin were alone together in their bedroom. Griffin stood before Vickie, his eyes enigmatic as he looked at her. She stood on tiptoe and kissed his lips and said, "Griffin, I know what you said. I mean, what you said about staying in the car..."

"Yeah, I noticed. Getting out of the car and hiding after the crash—yes, that made sense. Let me see... putting on a red robe, taking over the altar in the middle of a group of cultists—not so sure about that one."

"I had to," she said softly. "I had to. They might have died, Griffin. Helena and Alex, not to mention others."

"I know."

"Please understand. I mean, I'm sure I have to pass some tests, but I am young, healthy, fairly bright—"

"Some of the time."

"Amusing! Griffin, I need to go to the academy."

"You're damned right."

"What?"

"Well, let's face it. I've figured out that it is truly a thankless job, trying to keep you out of trouble. If you're going to keep on getting into trouble, it's going to make a hell of a lot of sense for you to go through the academy and work with other agents, especially other Krewe agents."

She laughed and kissed him.

And kissed him...

And they began to work at each other's clothing.

"Quiet..." Vickie murmured.

"Thin walls..."

Clothing fell away. It had seldom seemed quite as incredible just to feel her naked flesh against the heat and vitality of Griffin's body, Vickie thought.

Making love...

Such an affirmation of life!

A sound of sheer pleasure escaped her.

She gasped and admonished herself. "Quiet!"

And he came to her and whispered softly, "Whatever!"

They laughed, and the night went on.

They found the treasure—Ezekiel Martin's family trove—the following day. The amount of jewels, jeweled crosses, bracelets, necklaces and more that were found in a chest couldn't even be given an approximate value until they were studied.

A number of the plundered relics were clearly from Catholic churches.

So much for Satan.

Riches had been worshipped, and nothing more.

A week later, they talked about it—back at the coffee shop where Audrey was no longer working, and where the Dearborn duo would no longer play.

It was a charming group—they'd met there before heading to dinner.

Rocky and Devin were there, of course. And Alex—with Helena. They were now a couple, one with an exceptional bond that probably would never be broken.

And Roxanne was there—with Officer Jim Tracy. She and Alex thought that it was tremendously funny that Vickie had never intended to fix up the two of them.

"What really happened?" Alex asked Vickie. "I mean…you heard me calling to you, didn't you? You knew right away I was in trouble."

"I heard something, yes," Vickie said. "Some of it was intuition. And logic. You're just not rude enough to stand a girl up."

Alex laughed. "Thank you for that." He looked over at Helena. "I thought I was seeing a ghost."

"And it was me!" Helena said. She shivered. "And I was so close to being a ghost!"

"But one thing is still confusing. You were seen with Milton Hanson," Devin said. "The Milner brothers saw you with him."

"It was Hanson, right?" Roxanne said. "Our sketches are good!" She squeezed Jim Tracy's hand.

"I never knew his name. We were both just pumping gas. He was making conversation. He said he was there looking into the cult murders. I didn't even really know about them. I think that Milton Hanson is a jerk—a bit of a lecher—but I do believe now he was trying to find Alex, and maybe have the prestige of finding Jehovah, too. But he was no killer."

Griffin glanced at Vickie. She shrugged and smiled.

"Well, it's over," she said. "Oh! Except who took you, Helena? You were kidnapped by the cult, right? I mean, we'd all assumed that, but who, when, how?"

"She was indeed kidnapped," Griffin said, answering for Helena, who didn't look ready to talk about it. "By Cathy Dearborn—who is, naturally, swearing that

Helena came with her willingly after the Dearborns had been playing at the park." Turning his attention to Helena, he continued. "None of law enforcement believes that—you are truly an amazing and solid citizen. We firmly believe that, from the beginning, you were drugged, and kept on drugs. The good thing is that you are alive—and with some good friends who are here to help, you have a full life ahead of you."

"For sure!" Vickie said.

Helena smiled hopefully and leaned into Alex.

"Definitely. Barnes is dealing with the press, and we'll be heading out soon," Griffin said.

"You're really going to Virginia?" Alex asked Vickie.

"It's not that far. We can all Skype—stay friends!" Vickie said.

"To staying friends!"

They all raised their cups and toasted friendship.

Vickie saw that, just a table away, Dylan and Darlene had taken up pretend cups, as well.

"To friendship!" her ghost told her.

She smiled back at him, and nodded.

"We really are amazing creatures," Alex said. He looked at Vickie. "We are capable of so much that is horrible, and so much that is so good. I am alive because of you."

"Well, no, really, because—"

Devin broke in, laughing. "Hey! To the Krewe of Hunters!" she said, lifting her cup again. "And to Vickie! May she soon be among our number!"

Vickie smiled at that.

It was a good night. A very good night.

And when it was over, they went home. For a moment, she paused in the parlor she would soon be leaving. They were going to keep Griffin's apartment in Boston, but not hers. They just didn't need two places, especially since her parents still had a room for her, as well.

Griffin came up behind her; his arms went around her waist. "Goodbye to this place," he said softly. He turned her to face him. "We really should give it a fitting farewell!"

She laughed and kissed him.

"Yes, and loudly…" she said.

Leaving the apartment didn't really matter.

She was leaving with him, and that did.

* * * * *

Acknowledgments

I've always loved New England. I married into a large and incredible Italian family, all of whom first found New England to be their home. I thank them so much for the love I have for the region, and much of what I came to know about it as well. So, of course, anything that has to do with New England goes out to everyone in the now massive Pozzessere/Mero clans. (Including Derek, Zhenia and Korbin in New Haven!)

But this book especially goes out to a few other places and people in the region.

For Camp Necon, an amazing writing conference that takes place at Roger Williams University, Rhode Island. In memory of Papa—Bob Booth—and for his amazing family (specifically Mary, Sara, Dan and Jillian Booth). Of course, at Camp Necon, we all become family.

With special thanks to F. Paul Wilson and Tom Monteleone—great friends and writers who also happened to be the first to introduce me to Camp Necon.

Thanks to Lisa Mannetti and Corrinne de Winter, N.E.

friends with whom I have shared much that is bizarre and wonderful—and with whom I've laughed and cried and learned so much. To so many more members of the Necon family—Lynne Hanson, Jeff Strand, Brian Keene, Christopher Golden, John McIlveen, Mary SanGiovanni, Matt Bechtel, Linda Addison, Elizabeth Massie, Rio Youers, Sephera Giron, Yvonne Navarro, Weston Ochse, James A. Moore, Jack Ketchum, Matt Schwartz, John and Diane Buja, Paul Dobish, Barbara Gardner and Craig Shaw Gardner, Dot and John Godin, Jack Haringa, Laura Hickman, Nicholas Kaufmann, Mike Myers, Patti Riendeau, Rick Sardinha, Carole Whitney, Jill Bauman, Hal Bodner, Ginjer Buchanan, Alex Corona, David Price, David Silverman, Jennine Agnew, Alyson Benoit, Jan Kozlowski and so many, many more!

For Lee-Ann Wilbur, who runs the Lizzie Borden House, one of the most wonderful and unusual bed-and-breakfast establishments in the country. Somehow, she keeps the house pristine and historic and yet very livable for guests. It's historic—it's haunted! It's an amazing experience. If you believe in ghosts, you just might find them. If you don't, you'll still love the history and the detail. Real life is always more bizarre than anything we can invent.

In memory of Michael Palmer, and for his son, Daniel, a brilliant and wonderful musician and—with his dad and on his own—an equally talented writer.

For all things New England, the hardships and cruelty of history—and all the wonder and growth and beauty, too!

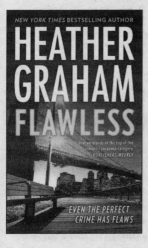

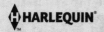

Get 2 Free Books,
<u>Plus</u> 2 Free Gifts –
just for trying the *Reader Service!*

HEATHER GRAHAM